ANSHAN SAGA

LIZZY FORD

KIERA'S MOON

ONE

KIERA SETTLED AT AN UNCOMFORTABLE ANGLE. The sandpapery red roofing beneath her snagged her polyester disco clothing and prevented her from sliding over the nearby edge of the three-story row house. A warm, late spring breeze held just a dash of chill, which was kept at bay by the internal warmth of the three margaritas she'd downed less than an hour before. Evelyn, her best friend and landlord, shifted beside her before waving a manicured hand at the clear night above them and asking,

"Ever wonder what's out there?"

"Sure. I think everyone does," Kiera answered.

"Do you think people *reeeeeeally* want to know?"

"That's pretty philosophical for a blonde."

"You're so wrooooong!"

Kiera giggled. The dinner party Evelyn threw to celebrate Kiera's first commissioned piece of art had been a success, as was expected. The bombshell blonde always threw good dinner parties with fun themes; this theme had been Disco Night, complete with lava lamps, disco ball, tacky '70s music that still jammed out the open windows, and costumes for those who chose to wear them.

They'd gone shopping at the local Goodwill for their polyester outfits.

"Well, do you?" Evelyn whispered.

Kiera's thoughts, warm and fuzzy after too much of Evelyn's special punch, drifted as she gazed into the quiet night sky.

"Do I what?" she asked.

"Think people really want to know what's out there?"

"Probably not. People don't know what they want, Evelyn, or life wouldn't suck."

"It doesn't really suck," Evelyn sang in such a happy voice that Kiera rolled her eyes.

"Not for you! You haven't been home in, like, three months, and when you're here, it's all Rum-ass this, Rum-ass that," she complained.

"Romas!" Evelyn corrected with another giggle. "Stop calling him that!"

"Whatever."

"You're so bitter!" Evelyn's giggle turned into outright laughter.

"Don't laugh at me!" Kiera managed a hurt tone and rolled on her side to frown at her blurry best friend of fifteen years. "Why are you laughing at me?"

Evelyn didn't stop for a full minute. She wiped her eyes and drew a shuddering breath.

"You're so cute, and so funny, Kiera," she sighed, and giggled again.

"Puppies are cute. I'm fierce!"

"Yeah!" Evelyn snorted. "Romas says you're as fierce as a kitten."

"A kitten?" Kiera's tone grew more hurt. "I'm not afraid of him, just because he's twelve feet tall and can bench press me with his toes. It's not nice of him to say that."

"It's nicer than your nickname for him," Evelyn pointed out. "He wants to hook you up with his brother, by the way."

"No!"

"You've never met him!"

"If he's half as alpha-male as Rum-ass, hell no!" Kiera snapped.

"And why did you dump Brian?"

Kiera was quiet and flopped onto her back.

"Didn't you say he was an indecisive sissy?" Evelyn prodded. "He wasn't a lightweight either. I saw him box."

"I'm not interested," Kiera said. "Men are heartache and more trouble than they're worth. Either they're huge babies you have to take care of, or they want to lock you in their palace with eunuchs."

"Well, you could at least meet them. He has seven brothers. Maybe one of them will fall somewhere in the middle of your man-scale."

"Omigod. No!"

"What do you think?" Evelyn prodded again.

"I'm not going on blind dates or being hooked up with hairy alpha males."

"No, about the aliens."

"What aliens?" Kiera asked.

"You know, the ones out there." Evelyn tossed a hand toward the dark night sky again.

"I don't know," Kiera answered. "I imagine if there are aliens, they've been discreet for a reason. I don't see any reason to change that."

"You don't want to see other worlds?"

"Other worlds?" she echoed. "I want to explore mine first! I've never been to Europe, or Africa, or anywhere yet. I paint what I *think* they look like, but I want to see them. I like the sun and sky and ocean —what is there to say other worlds have those?"

"I guess." Evelyn sounded unusually pensive. "But if it were a world like ours, I imagine it would be okay, right?"

"You mean a kind of other dimension thing, where it's really earth just in a different way?"

"No, a different world completely, but similar in that it has a sun, moon, oceans, grass, and stuff."

"Oh," Kiera murmured. The conversation was almost too serious for her muddled thoughts to follow. She sensed Evelyn's sudden melancholy and tried to focus. "You want to go to another world? Like, with aliens and stuff?"

"It would be neat, don't you think? Hypothetically speaking ..."

"Could you come home when you wanted?" she asked.

"I don't know."

"Could you take your cat?"

"Probably not," Evelyn replied.

"Would there be lots of people there with four arms or something freakish?"

Evelyn giggled, then said, "No."

"There'd have to be some sort of difference, wouldn't there?" Kiera's brow furrowed. "If no two people are alike on our planet, how could we be like anything from somewhere else?"

"I don't know," Evelyn admitted.

"I bet they'd be ruled by spiders the size of your car," Kiera said with a shudder. "Could you imagine?"

"They don't have spiders," Evelyn said firmly. "And the people are pretty normal. I imagine I'd want to know if I could come home to visit you."

"Yes, that'd be cool. I'll take care of your house while you're gone," Kiera offered. Drowsiness was beginning to take hold of her. She closed her eyes, content.

"And the cat," Evelyn added.

"Okay."

"But wouldn't you want to go, too?"

"I'm not sure," Kiera murmured, hovering at the edge of sleep.

"Would you be afraid?"

"Probably."

"Maybe you should stay."

"Probably," she said. "I guess I could visit for a week, if it means so much to you."

Evelyn's happy response was lost as she faded into sleep.

Kiera dreamt of a planet filled with spiders and dinosaurs and awoke in her bed a couple of hours later to the soft sound of her alarm clock going off. She blinked her bleary eyes, unwilling to move for fear of the distant headache intensifying. The lingering images of recliner-size tarantulas from her dream made her shudder and look around self-consciously to make sure none were in her room. The scent of bacon reached her from the kitchen.

Romas was there. Evelyn only cooked when he spent the night, which would also explain how she ended up in her bed. She recalled falling asleep on the roof and knew Evelyn to be too tipsy to carry or drag her down to her room. Romas had tossed her in bed more than once over the past three months, though he had stopped lecturing her on how unbecoming a lush was to a man looking for a wife.

He had some unworldly views on things, Kiera mused. She rolled onto her back and stared at the ceiling, where she had pinned one of her inspiration posters above the bed. This one showed a determined kitty hanging from a tree branch and always made her smile, even when she was hung-over.

"K-K!" Evelyn sang, her voice muffled through the door. "I'm sending in Romas!"

Kiera scowled at the closed door. Romas had no qualms about invading her bedroom to drag her out of bed if Evelyn directed him to. He had no qualms about ordering dinner for her when she went out with them or telling her what to do with her life. He despised her video game playing and art, instead saying she needed a man capable of keeping her feet on the ground long enough for her to focus on doing something real with her life.

"I'm up!" she shouted.

The fact that he worshiped the ground Evelyn walked on and took care of her made Kiera jealous. She'd never dated a man half as handsome, annoying, or caring as Romas, and she expected there were very few men like him to go around.

She stumbled up and crossed to her bathroom to brush her teeth before going out to breakfast. One look at her disheveled '70s garb, and she decided to change into pajamas.

When she walked into the kitchen, Evelyn was gazing with adoration up at the huge man, leaning against him in a purely anti-feministic way. Romas was a towering example of male perfection: blond with golden skin and bright blue eyes, a chiseled face and buff body, and *tall*. Evelyn was six feet tall and Romas a full head taller than her. They made a perfect couple, and Kiera was disgusted at the perfection before her that represented everything she had no hopes of ever attaining.

"Hel-*lo*, I'm here!" she called. Evelyn gave a brilliant smile, and Romas eyed her. She eyed him back. "You again."

"Hello, kitten," he said in his thick accent. She sometimes thought his accent sounded Russian, sometimes Irish.

"Everyone sit!" Evelyn ordered.

Kiera took her usual chair, and Romas ruffled her hair as he passed her. Evelyn brought the last of three trays to the table.

"You didn't come to the party last night," Kiera said as she helped herself to eggs before Romas could fill her plate. Serving them was another of his annoying habits. She couldn't yet determine if the action were pure chauvinism or old-fashioned civility.

"I had business," Romas said, serving a glowing Evelyn.

"Tell her what kind," Evelyn urged, squirming in her chair. They exchanged a heated look so intense Kiera blushed. She focused on her food and banged her fork against her plate.

"Romas proposed!" Evelyn exclaimed.

Kiera's eyes flew up.

"We're getting married!"

"Wh ... bu... ah ..." Kiera stuttered. "But ... you've only known each other for three months! It takes you longer to plan a dinner party, Evey!"

Evelyn laughed. Stunned, Kiera tried to figure out what to say as they both looked expectantly at her.

"Well, what do you think?" Evelyn prodded.

Evelyn had been so happy the past few months, and having

Romas around was not *that* bad. After all, he could fix things around the house that she and Evelyn ignored.

"I think it's really neat," she said. "When are you getting hitched?"

"Saturday."

"Saturday when?"

"*This* Saturday."

"In two days?" she asked. "Wow. That's ... wow! Well, congrats!"

Evelyn looked ready to burst. Kiera found she truly was happy for her, though her own happiness was clouded by a sense of sadness and yearning. She'd known Evelyn since they were in elementary school, and she'd been renting a room from her for the past two years since graduating high school. She didn't want to lose the friend she regarded as a sister.

"Oh, but wait!" she exclaimed. "You won't kick me out?"

"Not if you behave," Romas said.

"Of course not! We're a package deal, right, Romas?" Evelyn grinned. He said nothing. Kiera frowned, concerned by his silence.

"You really don't like me, Romas?" she asked.

"You're tolerable," was the response. Kiera stared at him. He winked with a faint smile, and she relaxed.

"Because I know how alpha males like you work," she retorted. "You'll have everything of Evelyn's put in your name and lock her in her bathroom or something."

"The bathroom is big enough for both of you," Romas said.

"Well, congrats anyway," she said with a sigh. And she smiled, happy for her friend and not too unhappy with her choice of husband-to-be. The couple gave each other another heated look, and she wolfed down her food before leaving them in peace.

An hour later, she dismounted her bike and leaned it against the brick front of the art gallery where her work was displayed. The quaint streets of Pacific Grove were quiet during the weekday, with a small group of women lingering in the midmorning sun at the café on the corner.

"Kevin!" she called as she entered the quiet art gallery. From the outside, it looked like the other small mom-and-pop stores lining the street. Inside, the first and second levels had been combined to create a large, tall space whose walls and ceilings were lined with paintings. She maneuvered through sculptures and other exhibits on the floor to the small office in the back.

Kevin, a small man with a quick smile and trendy glasses, smiled as she opened the door.

"Good to see you, Kiera!" he said, rising to kiss her cheek. "I guess you got my message."

"Made my day! How many did you sell?" she asked.

"Two of the three you left me. And the best part—one of my best customers wants you to paint Cannery Row. This is your second commissioned art project in two weeks!"

"Awesome, awesome, awesome!" she exclaimed, and clapped her hands. "I can start whenever!"

"I did the paperwork for the sales. Just need your signature," he said, pulling a file out of one of the drawers in his desk. "Sign away, and I'll get your cash."

Thrilled, Kiera looked over the paperwork outlining her first sales. Kevin's cut was hefty, but she didn't care: she was a real artist! Kevin crossed his office to the small safe and drew out a small pile of cash.

"I'll have him come in next week to sit down with you and discuss the project."

"The same guy bought the paintings?" she asked.

"No. The guy who bought your paintings I'd never seen before. His name is on the paperwork, if you're curious. It took me some time to convince Mr. Hardy you were the best painter in the area for his Cannery Row project."

She looked more closely at the paper she'd just signed and flipped the page to the receipt he'd stapled there.

Romas Qatwal.

"Oh, damn you," she muttered, irritated her first sale was a pity sale and yet thinking even better of Romas for supporting his fiancée's hopeless friend. "I hope you charged him full price."

"He didn't even flinch. Here's your cut—two thousand and forty three dollars," Kevin said, and counted out the money on the desk.

She looked at the money, unable to remember when she'd last seen that much in one place before. Her bank account was rarely over two hundred. Her first thought went to Evelyn's wedding, and another thrill went through her as she realized she could actually afford something nice for her friend.

"Congrats, Kiera!" Kevin said.

"I know, right? Took long enough. You want me to bring you a couple more paintings? I've got three more completed."

"Definitely. The Cannery Row project will make you a hot commodity around here. Then maybe, just maybe, you'll go out with me."

She laughed at his latest attempt to hit on her. With his small frame and bright eyes, he'd always reminded her of an elf of some sort. She'd even included him—in his elf-like form—in one of her paintings depicting a fantastical scene of sea creatures frolicking on a beach.

"Sorry, Kevin," she said. "You should know better than to date moody artists by now. You've been burned by enough of us."

"I wouldn't own an art gallery if I didn't love artists. The art is a bonus," he said with a wink.

"Keep trying," she replied with a flirtatious smile. "And thank you for talking me up to Mr. Hardy."

Kevin shrugged. She leaned forward to give him a quick hug, gathered her money, and left. Rather than return home right away, she explored several small jewelry stores, looking for the perfect gift for Evelyn before she took her daily trip to the gym.

By the time she returned to the large row house, she was looking forward to an addition to their home who may not fear killing spiders and other bugs. She walked into the living room, puzzled to see Evelyn boxing up her bookshelf.

"Making room for Rum-ass's stuff?" she asked, flinging herself on the couch nearby to watch.

"Um, not really. You might have the house to yourself," Evelyn said. She pushed blonde hair from her face. "We're thinking about returning to his place to live."

"Really?" Kiera frowned. "He's from San Francisco, right?"

"No, his *real* home." Evelyn watched her digest the information.

"You're leaving me," Kiera said.

"You can come," Evelyn offered. "I'd like for you to come."

"To where?"

"You know how you said you'd like to explore other places?"

"I did?" Kiera asked, thinking hard.

"Last night, on the roof."

"Vaguely," she said. "You mean he lives really, really far away?"

"Yeah. Pretty far," Evelyn replied.

"You're okay with just leaving?"

"I want to be with him, and we think it'll be better for us both in his home."

"You're okay with just leaving *me*?" Kiera asked with a frown.

"I don't want to leave you! You're my sister, as far as I'm concerned. I'd like for you to come with us. You said last night you'd go for a week, but you can stay with us for as long as you want."

"That's not really normal though," Kiera said. "You show up on your in-laws' doorstep with your friend in tow? I mean, this is supposed to be you starting your lives together, not hauling around your poor spinster of a friend who's about to be abandoned."

"You're guilt tripping me already?" Evelyn grinned and tossed a paperback at Kiera.

"*Abused* spinster of a friend!"

"As Romas pointed out, you have no real life and nothing really to tie you down," Evelyn said. "You can play video games and paint or draw from anywhere. They might appreciate artists more where he's from."

"I know very well what Rum-ass thinks of my life!" she retorted.

"I take it this is his way of hooking me up with a man to keep me in line?"

"He's got seven brothers," Evelyn said. "I've seen pictures. Damn sexy bunch."

"You seriously want me to go?"

"Of course, K. You like adventures, right?"

"Yes, but I'm happy here with my video games and painting," Kiera reminded her.

"Well, you can do those things there. I'll be there. And Romas. He'll protect you from the bad people and spiders."

"I don't know," Kiera said after a pause. "It seems weird, and I'd totally feel like the loser I pretend not to be if you have to take me with you. Can I just stay here and guard your house and cat for you?"

"I know it's far, Kiera," Evelyn said, frowning in disappointment. "Please just think about it some more? We'll leave after the wedding, so you have a couple of days. At the very least, you'll still come for a week?"

Kiera doubted she would change her mind but decided to humor her happy friend.

"Yes, I'll go for a week. The rest is a lot to think about. I just got my first commission ever, and I think my displays at Kevin's gallery are picking up interest. He said someone else is interested in commissioning a piece. I feel like I'm in a good place with all that," Kiera said. "Where is Romas from exactly?"

"You've never heard of it."

"One of those little Eastern European, pocket-sized countries?"

"Pretty much," Evelyn said vaguely.

"Wow. Are you really ready to use outhouses and haul your own water?"

"It's actually a wealthy, highly advanced society," Evelyn said with a chuckle. "We'll have servants to haul our water for us."

Kiera had suspected Romas to be independently wealthy by his complete lack of concern for being anywhere but with Evelyn for the last three months. He'd never mentioned working or making or

missing appointments, and Evelyn had never mentioned his employ-
ment either. Confirmation of the fact was comforting; Evelyn would
never have to worry about money again. And, hopefully, Evelyn
never raised her rent, either.

"I'll miss you," Kiera said.

"Think about it! I've gotta go get ready. We're going out in a
little bit."

Kiera rolled her eyes. There was a soft knock at the door. Evelyn
bolted for the stairwell, unwilling to allow anyone but Kiera to see her
without make-up, while Kiera went to the door. She let Romas in
with a glare.

"Where are you taking Evelyn?" she demanded as the large man
folded himself to sit on the couch. Romas's gaze flickered over her in
what she now knew to be amusement. The emotions were almost
imperceptible, and it had taken her a long time of studying him to
read him.

"Another day at home with your invisible friends?" he teased.

She crossed her arms and sat on the arm of the couch, pinning
him with a withering look. She'd planned on spending her Thursday
evening in a raid for *World of Warcraft*, which Romas never approved
of. He didn't believe she was interacting with real people and instead
called the other online players *invisible friends*. She'd given up trying
to convince him they were real.

"I'm taking her far, far away," he said. "And you're welcome—
encouraged—to come."

She softened at the inclusion. It was expected from Evelyn but
not from the man himself.

"Why are you leaving so soon?" she asked.

"We'd like to start afresh, preferably in the place we intend to
raise half a dozen unruly kids," he said.

"You're really okay with me going for a week? I won't interfere
with any honeymoon plans?"

"Of course we want you there. I think you'd be happy in my ...
country."

"So you can find me a man?" she challenged, raising an eyebrow.

"I've got several in mind."

"It's very nice of you," she said with an unladylike snort that made him grimace. "But I don't think ... it doesn't make sense for me to go. I'd feel like a third wheel."

"Third wheel?"

Kiera sought an explanation, recalling he was not familiar with most slang despite his mastery of English.

"Out of place," she explained. "As in, there are the two of you being lovey-dovey and happy, and me hanging out by the bushes."

This drew a smile.

"You are not a third wheel by the bushes," Romas assured her. "You would be treated like a queen at my home. You're a guest, and if you happened to be hooked onto a good man, so be it."

"Hooked *up* with a good man," she corrected. "Thank you, but I don't need to be hooked up."

"You'll come," he said. "And I'll find you a man. My oldest brother Kisolm needs a woman. He might object to you, but I can convince him to take you."

He hadn't uttered anything so stupid in a long time, after she yelled at him for talking like that. She couldn't help wondering if Evelyn really understood that going to his home country would mean she'd hear this kind of nonsense all the time. She marched out of the room.

"Evelyn! *That man* is here!" she shouted up the stairwell, and disappeared into her studio. She flipped on her computer and tossed her shoes next to the couch. Her latest painting—another seaside depiction of Fisherman's Wharf—leaned against one wall, ready to be delivered to Kevin's shop. Several minutes later, Evelyn's footsteps sounded on the wooden stairs.

Kiera shook her head, perplexed by their odd invitation to stay with them. Evelyn made it sound permanent, as though Kiera would just pick up and leave for another country. Her gaze went to her desk, and she realized she didn't even have a passport. She might have to wait a few weeks just to visit.

She relaxed into the comfortable black desk chair in front of her computer, wondering if Romas had told Evelyn of the half a dozen kids he expected.

TWO

A'RAN L'ANSHANTUWEI, the exiled *dhjan*—king—of the planet Anshan, looked over the three women before him. Each was a specimen of perfection to her people. He turned away from them, his gaze going upward and peering through the skylight in his spacious battle command center.

No one but the *dhjan* could understand that choosing a lifemate wasn't so simple. The *dhjan nishani*—king's lifemate—would complete the circle of Anshan's life force. Her presence would make the rivers run with water again and bring new life to the dying planet that was his domain. If he were allowed to pick his mate, he'd have chosen long ago and saved his planet. But the planet chose for him, according to what his father told him long ago.

He met the gaze of his only ally, Jetr, a man from a distant galaxy who had been an ally of Anshan for three generations. The small man waited next to A'Ran's trusted second-in-command, Ne'Rin, whose sister was one of the three before him. Ne'Rin was a man whose forefathers had been chief advisors to the *dhjan* dynasty since Anshan's inception and had served A'Ran's family for a millennium.

Jetr and Ne'Rin were both patient and hopeful, and A'Ran steeled himself to tell them what he must.

None of the three beauties was the woman chosen by his planet, or he'd *know*. His own mother had been far from beautiful, and his father had told him the signs he'd found the right woman were unmistakable. The earth would drop from beneath his feet and the sun pierce his soul. He felt nothing like this when he looked at the three women.

Like his sisters and advisors, he was losing faith that his *nishani* existed. He was thirty-two sun-cycles, beyond the age when his forefathers had found their lifemates. Half the population of his planet had been decimated by famine and war. For all he knew, his intended was among them. The Planetary Council, his second-in-command, even his sister, had paraded women through his home every time he returned from a battle. His lifemate simply wasn't there.

"None of them," A'Ran said. Ne'Rin frowned but escorted the women out.

The *dhjan* had known nothing but war for over half his life, since exiled with his sisters to the tiny moon across the galaxy from his home of Anshan. It was the smallest moon in the Five Galaxies, the section of space under the influence of the meddling Planetary Council. He'd continue the war until he won back his planet and birthright by force, then find another way to heal his planet, since it didn't seem likely that he had a lifemate.

"I think you prefer war, my friend," Jetr said with his gentle humor.

"You know well the bond between the lifemate and the planet. Without her, the rivers are dry, the women are barren, and the mines produce no ore," A'Ran replied, then added pointedly, "And the Planetary Council interferes with everything you try to do to reclaim what's rightfully yours."

"You've refused women from every Council member's family. It's no wonder they don't favor you."

"It has nothing to do with that, Jetr, as you know," he said. "They want the ore only Anshan can produce but don't understand why there will be none until I claim my lifemate."

"In the meantime, you've driven up a debt to them," Jetr reminded him.

"The Council has a selective memory," A'Ran said in irritation. "Every ship, every weapon they own, came from Anshan ore."

"True," Jetr said. "But until they choose to remember that, they ask another favor of you, their last."

"I've heard this before, Jetr," A'Ran said.

"I brokered this one."

A'Ran waited, observing the tiny man with white eyes. Jetr, the only Council member he trusted, had been an ally for three generations of his family without appearing to age. He wore heavy clothing, as if easily chilled, and moved with the smoothness of a warrior. There was a time when A'Ran would've scoffed at Jetr's mention of a favor. That time eroded fast when he was faced with the suffering of his people and the ability of the Council to coerce all his allies but one to leave his side.

He had to repay the odious debt to the Council. Only then would he be free of their interference and maybe even gain the support of some of its members.

"The Council wants an end to the millennia-old blood war between Anshan and Qatwal," Jetr said. "You have the dominant armies in this galaxy, and the other civilizations in your solar system are sick of the war. The ruler of Tri'trij has vacated his planet and lives on colonies outside the solar system. Too much of the on-again, off-again war has impacted your neighbors."

"So it is up to me to broker a peace deal with Qatwal," A'Ran said. "I have no planet, half an army, no food or water for my people, and I must broker a peace deal."

"I'm not saying I agree, just that it must be done," Jetr said. "If you do this, the Council will leave you alone."

"A peace deal depends on two parties, not one," A'Ran reminded him.

"If they refuse, they refuse. But we will work with them to come to some sort of terms. Peace will benefit the solar system, and your neighbors will be happy."

"My neighbors will be fortunate if I don't destroy them next. They stood aside while my planet was overrun by the Council-sanctioned vagrant Yirkin forces!"

"Not sanctioned, just not prevented," Jetr corrected. "The Yirkin are wanderers. The Council wants nothing to do with them and views the presence of your father's betrayer and your people on the planet as a sign the Yirkin are willing to share your planet rather than take it over."

There is no negotiating with the Yirkin scum or my father's killer, A'Ran thought but held his tongue, aware his only ally believed himself right in this.

He thought for a long moment, knowing no peace treaty could be reached with Qatwal. Their war was passive-aggressive rather than open, consisting of Qatwal making his ore ships disappear and then reappear without the ore. Or his affront at the last Council meeting, where A'Ran had Kisolm, the man who would be *dhjan*, imprisoned in his quarters and miss the Council's final vote on who would maintain distribution rights to the ore only Anshan possessed. A'Ran won the vote by one.

He'd done his part to agitate Kisolm and received every bit as much as he'd given. They'd trained together on one of the Council's neutral planets and ended up rivals in everything.

"I'll do it, Jetr, for you, not the Council. You swear the Council will consider my debt to them repaid?" he asked.

"I swear it. Peace cannot be underestimated, A'Ran. Several members, including Qatwal, may be willing to aid you in regaining your planet after you've reached a peace treaty."

"If they do, it will be to steal my ore. I'll do this and go back to war. I've given up on finding a *nishani* for my planet."

"This system is truly unique. I didn't believe the planets died without the *dhjan* and his lifemate until I saw what happened to Anshan."

A'Ran desperately needed allies, food, and water for his people. He clenched his jaw, his pain deep and hidden as he thought of his people and his planet. He fought hard to build alliances. The Council then destroyed them, and bartered, cheated, and stole for the weaponry needed to defeat the invaders, the Yirkin, a sophisticated race whose goal was to claim as many planets as they could in their empire-building. It was the Yirkins' first venture into their system. They chose Anshan for its ore then wooed traitors within his father's government with the promise of ruling their own planet.

"A'Ran, there is something else I must tell you." Jetr's voice grew quieter, and he drew near. "My warriors intercepted information from Anshan. Your father's betrayer planted a traitor among those closest to you. I don't know who, but I suspect Ne'Rin."

"Ne'Rin?" A'Ran said, crossing his arms. "His father may have betrayed mine, but he has been loyal for all these years we've been exiled. He saved my sisters from his own father. If he could've saved my father and mother, he would've."

"You must consider this a possibility. The whereabouts of this moon on which you claim exile have been leaked off-planet. My men intercepted it before it went to Anshan, just as they've intercepted other messages from Anshan directed to someone here."

"There are hundreds of thousands of my warriors here," A'Ran said. "Why do you think it's Ne'Rin?"

"He has direct access to you and the most to gain. You forget: I am not a warrior bound by honor but a diplomat accustomed to undermining others," Jetr replied. "Ne'Rin does his part to prevent you from suspecting him. As an observer, I can tell you there's a great deal of motivation for someone in his position to betray you."

The words stung. If they came from someone other than the man who'd supported his father and grandfather, he'd disregard the warning and have the messenger killed. But this was Jetr warning him. Jetr was stacking a new problem on a pile of other problems he couldn't deal with.

"Brother?"

They both turned at the soft voice. His youngest sister, Talal, stood in the doorway to his war quarters, her gaze hopeful.

"Not yet," he said, aware of what misery he was bringing his sisters. They'd been praying that the last three women would yield his *nishani*.

His people's hope had turned to desperation in the hands of the Yirkin when every sun-cycle passed and there was no *nishani*. From the *dhjan* came strength and stability; from the *nishani*, restoration and healing. His planet was dying without either, and many had begun to accept this was the planet's fate. He was helpless to find her. He had to wait for the fates to bring his *nishani* to him.

Talal's face fell, and he had no words to offer. He'd already broken promises of finding his lifemate by his thirtieth, his thirty-first, his thirty-second birthdays.

"I'll think on what you've told me," he said, turning to Jetr. "Promise you'll barter my freedom if Qatwali imprisons me on this peace mission."

"I'll do my best. If that doesn't work, I'll take your sisters to my planet," Jetr answered. "It's all I can offer."

A'Ran nodded in agreement, knowing it was the best he could do. He had a feeling Kisolm, the crown prince of Qatwal, would not even hear him out but would view his attempt to barter peace as a sign of weakness and keep him as a trophy.

"Talal, send Ne'Rin to the practice fields."

His sister hurried away. Jetr bowed his head, sensing the dismissal. A'Ran left the command center for the practice fields, the area where his men trained. He stepped into the bright sunlight and withdrew one of hundreds of grey swords housed in small racks along the back side of the dwelling that was his temporary home, until he reclaimed his planet. The field was empty, his men preparing for another space battle.

He hefted the curved sword and marveled at the grey metal. Only the ore on Anshan could produce the metal that was not only unbreakable but easily molded. All the spaceships, computers, and weapons within the Five Galaxies were made from ore from Anshan mines—even the swords, the only weapons sanctioned by the Planetary Council as fair and appropriate for man-to-man combat. The Council disallowed lasers or other advanced weapons, instead opting for the traditional weapons of their ancestors, and the only weapons used by some planets with their less developed civilizations.

Swiping at the air, A'Ran couldn't help but feel furious that the Council would protect such civilizations from those that were more advanced out of some sense of fairness while sitting by doing nothing as his planet was overrun and his parents murdered. Despite his hatred for the politics, he knew he needed the Council's help. His people were starving as the planet died, and soon, the Council would realize the planet produced no ore without its rightful ruler.

Anshan—a chunk of rock in space—was smarter than the entire Council combined, even Jetr, who was content to mediate between him and the Council without truly choosing sides. Jetr had been loyal to his family for generations. A'Ran respected him for his service. The odd-looking man was the only reason the Council hadn't ceded to the Yirkins' petitions to claim the planet officially.

And yet, he couldn't help feeling as if he alone bore the weight of his planet on his back as he struggled to pay for food, water, and weapons. He was running out of ore and other means to barter; he'd need the Council's mercy soon.

"I am sorry my sister did not please you, A'Ran," Ne'Rin said as he stepped into the field.

"She pleased me, Ne'Rin, but she is not meant to be my *nishani*," he replied.

"What do you wait for?"

A'Ran was quiet. He didn't know how to explain it and wondered if he should even try with Jetr's suspicions fresh in his mind. His father said Anshan would tell him, and the feeling would be unmistakable. He hadn't been on his own planet since his parents were killed, and he wasn't sure how the planet would choose someone for him when he wasn't there.

"I'll know," he said with more confidence than he felt. "Are the warriors ready for the next campaign?"

"They are."

"You and I have a different mission. A very unpleasant one."

"Jetr told me."

"Ready my personal ship for the flight to Qatwal."

"Yes, *dhjan.*"

A'Ran watched him go, sensing the same disappointment and doubt he'd seen in his sister earlier. He wondered if years of disappointment had driven his most trusted friend away as greed did Ne'Rin's father.

He could do nothing but continue to fight. He swiped at the air again, unable to shake his anger.

THREE

THE NEXT TWO days passed quickly as Kiera helped Evelyn set up her sudden wedding. Evelyn handled it all with cheerfulness while Kiera stressed over the shade of flowers clashing with the décor, and the cake containing nuts, which Romas was allergic to. Evelyn's wedding was for a hundred invitees in a small chapel by the ocean, followed by a reception for over twice that many guests. Most of the guests were Evelyn's friends and family; Romas's small party consisted of only a handful of men—cousins, according to Evelyn—that resembled an NFL team dressed uncomfortably in their tuxes.

The newlyweds spent the night at a local luxury hotel—also an arrangement made by Kiera—and she was left alone in the row house full of boxes.

Given her first chance to rest in over two days, she sighed, exhausted and irritated at having to dig her own clothing out of a box. The movers had gone crazy and even packed her stuff. Her make-up was smeared from walking through the Monterey mists, her maid-of-honor dress wrinkled from constant sitting and standing. She wove her way to her bathroom through the maze of boxes and took a long shower to ease her tired body. The day had gone beautifully, and the sight of Evelyn's beaming, glowing face stuck in her head.

Kiera had never seen anyone so happy. Hot water ran over her head and down her body, soothing her. Would *she* ever be so happy?

Not if it has to do with a man.

She smiled, finished washing, and emerged from the shower. The new necklace she wore that matched the one she bought for Evelyn glimmered in the mirror. Disappointed her friend was leaving for somewhere across the world, she'd bought them matching necklaces featuring whimsical half moons in rose gold with a single, small, sparkling diamond of a star embedded in the moon.

She left the bathroom, pulling on an oversized, soft T-shirt Evelyn had shanghaied from Romas and Kiera had shanghaied from Evelyn.

The boxes were gone. Startled, she looked around twice. She listened but heard no one downstairs to indicate the movers had been through and glanced at the clock on her nightstand. It was nearly one thirty.

Perplexed as to what kind of movers worked at such an hour, she roamed through the row house from top to bottom. All the boxes were gone. No strangers were in the house, and the doors were bolted. She briefly considered calling Evelyn to ask about her moving arrangements. Evelyn might love her but would probably not welcome a call on her wedding night.

Kiera glanced around again, shook her head, and crawled into bed. Evelyn had a way of ensuring things were done, even if she didn't seem to have time to do them. She probably had a mover scheduled and forgot to mention it.

In the morning, Kiera planned to clean up the house. After, she'd start working on another painting, the portrait of Evelyn and Romas she wanted to give the two of them as their joint wedding present. Mentally, she started on the portrait.

Although tired, sleep didn't come. Kiera rose and trotted down to her studio, happy to see the movers had left her studio alone. She flooded the studio with light, then pulled another blank canvas from the closet and perched it on her easel. She sat at her desk and started to sketch the visage of Evelyn in her long wedding dress and Romas in his dark tux on a piece of paper, glancing up occasionally at the blank canvas as she thought of proportions.

Comfortable in the plush office chair, she propped her feet up on her desk and continued to sketch until the picture began to look as she wanted it to. She dozed as she drew, caught herself twice, then dropped into sleep, unaware that those who removed the boxes were coming next for her.

Soon after confirming she was asleep, the two large men who had emptied the house of boxes returned for her. They ignored her studio and its contents. One placed a sleep patch on her ear to prevent her from waking and scooped her up while the other grabbed the last suitcase out of her bedroom. They left the row house for the park across the street, where a small spacecraft awaited them.

Settling Kiera on a grey slab bench, the first man straightened and motioned the other over.

"Not like our women," he said as the other warrior joined him. "Very small."

"Like a doll," the second agreed. "Pretty for so small a creature."

"You have no mate. Ask for her band."

The second snorted and strode into the cockpit, followed by the first.

"She will mate with no one like us. Her sister is mated to the second son of our ruler. This one is too exquisite. She must be intended for Kisolm," he replied.

"You brought all her belongings?"

"Everything, as Romas said, except the pictures. Not a noble pastime for one who will wed our next ruler," the second said with a frown. "Only Anshan barbarians would use their hands to create pictures."

"I think the pictures are too advanced for Anshan-kind," the first said with a chuckle. "If they didn't own the ore mines, they'd be using rocks to fight."

The second chuckled as he ordered the computer to rendezvous with the massive grey spaceship awaiting them outside the planet's atmosphere. The small woman's soft snores filled the transport ship.

EVELYN STOOD in the dark grey room of the spaceship with its cozy, dim lighting and the soft purr of hidden machines. She didn't really care what the dark grey walls, floors, and ceilings were made of or why the floor felt like carpet and looked like gun metal. The room was vacant except for a metal slab that served as a bed and the six-legged, cat-like creature sitting on the edge of the bed watching its sleeping occupant.

She leaned against the wall, pensive. Her plan, while brilliant when plotted the past month, didn't seem quite so wonderful right now. Kiera hadn't wanted to come, even for the proposed week. Evelyn knew—and Romas assured her—Kiera would be fine. She could paint anywhere, and her life was otherwise so unfulfilling, Evelyn didn't know how she could stand it. She wanted her friend to be happy, and Romas thought this was the best way. She had few instincts, unlike Kiera's hyperactive intuition, but she felt a definite tingling. She had to bring Kiera with her. It was meant to be.

And then she ran into several of the cat-like creatures roaming the ship. They were furry and about knee-height full grown with similar triangular ears and a tail. The rest of their bodies were unlike cats. They had six legs with little pads for feet instead of toes and claws, a delicate snout not quite the length of an anteater's, lined with fine hairs and tiny teeth used to vacuum up mold, dust, and dirt that was its main food source, and an odd habit of climbing walls with hidden suckers in its padded feet. From what Romas said, every household on his planet had at least one or two of the critters to keep things clean.

One sat perched on Kiera's bed, watching her sleep. Its legs were jointed outwards like a spider's, and its ability to climb walls resembled that of a spider. It didn't spin webs and looked more to Evelyn like a mutated cat, but the moment she recalled Kiera's fear, she also realized that the cat-like creature would easily pass as a large spider.

That's gonna be a problem, Evelyn contemplated. Kiera would freak when she saw the cats.

She grabbed the sitting creature. It twisted its odd little face to look at her and sniffed at her arm with its small trunk. It didn't purr like a cat but growled. Turning away, she missed the movement behind her as another of the creatures appeared from beneath the bed. She tucked the creature in her hands under one arm and left the small room for a long corridor in similar dark grey which glowed more brightly from indistinguishable light sources. She trailed her fingers down a wall, smiling when she saw soft glimmers light up beneath her touch, trail her fingers a short distance, and blink out.

The cat-like creature squirmed. She set it down.

"You leave Kiera alone," she ordered sternly.

The creature loped ahead, darting out of sight down another hall. Evelyn followed leisurely, unconcerned with being lost on the massive ship. If she became turned around, all she needed to do was touch the wall and tell it where she wanted to go. The glimmers would guide her there. Or Romas would come searching for her.

Evelyn hugged herself before looking down at the massive diamond on her ring finger. Bubbling with happiness, she hummed as she strode through the corridors in search of Romas.

He was in their quarters and stood as she entered. He was naked, as if awaiting her. She smiled and flung herself into his arms. They made love for the umpteenth time since their wedding. Afterwards, she snuggled into his arms, content with the sound of his heartbeat and the feel of his arms around her. Just as she drifted into sleep, the spaceship's internal communication system awoke her.

"Your woman's sister needs attending to."

The male voice came from nowhere and everywhere and

disturbed the two naked forms on the dark grey bed. Evelyn raised her head lazily, unable to quell the urge to seek out the source of the voice even knowing she wouldn't find it.

Your woman. There had been several dozen mistranslations from the small translator attached to her ear lobe. This one was oft repeated and irritated her whenever she heard it. She started to sit.

"She'll be well," Romas said. He nuzzled her and pulled her back into his body. She relaxed, his warmth and presence lulling her into comfort she didn't want to leave.

"Your woman's sister needs attending to."

This time, the calm male voice was accompanied by a distinctly feminine wail in the background. She shot up and scrambled for her clothes. Romas followed. If she looked, she feared she might find him amused. After Kiera's three months of tormenting him, he would find turning the tables satisfying.

"You have to be understanding," she reminded him again. "You know Kiera well enough. She's really emotional. You have to be less … you know. You just have to be understanding."

Romas snorted in response. She hurried from the room without her shoes and tucked in the alien clothing: soft, silky tunic into soft, silky pants that adjusted in size to fit her form. She stepped into the hallway, unwilling to await a purposely slower-moving Romas, and touched the wall.

"Take me to Kiera," she said. Glimmers lit up along one wall, guiding her through the maze of the ship. She'd been contemplating how to break the news to Kiera.

How did you tell your best friend that aliens were real and oh, by the way, I married one and am taking you with me to his planet, for your own good? She was doing what she thought was best for her friend, and Kiera would *hate* that.

She mulled it over again as she trotted down the corridors. There was no choice now; she had some explaining to do. What would she say? That there was a better chance of her selling art if she painted something no one else on earth could imagine? That Kiera would have her ocean, sky, and grass on the new planet? That they were going to some other planet millions of light years from earth because Romas knew a few good men they'd like to hook her up with?

Her pace slowed as she thought until she was walking, troubled. Romas caught up to her and swept her into his arms for a quick kiss.

"I've completely forgotten what I should tell her," she said.

"I'll explain things."

"She's not going to like hearing it from you."

Romas said nothing.

"You have to be gentle, Romas."

They heard her before turning the corner. Kiera was cursing and shouting. The softened expression on Romas's face—only present for her—hardened as he prepared himself to deal with whichever of his warriors had happened upon Kiera. Romas was all business by the time they rounded the corner; he even released Evelyn's hand and quickened his step into one that befitted a warrior prince.

Evelyn loved his game face. It was sexy as hell, like everything about him. Having spent enough time on the ship to understand the odd society, she knew better than to charge in and handle what he would consider his duty. She hung back when she reached the other three warriors in the hall watching the scene in the room. Romas strode in unasked, and she cursed quietly as she saw the cat-like critter chasing Kiera.

Kiera was yelling at it, her blue eyes large and wild. She clung to one of the warriors, attempting to climb him as the cat-like critter—convinced it was a game—wagged its tail and chased her around the large man in the center of the room.

Evelyn would've laughed had Kiera not appeared so terrified and bewildered. The warriors made no move to corner the critter or even calm Kiera down. They watched instead with curiosity.

Romas snatched the critter with one hand and tossed it to one of the warriors at the door. He grabbed Kiera with the other arm and flung her over his shoulder. She stilled and grew silent, then pushed away from him.

"Evelyn!" she shouted, panicked. "What are you doing here? God, this is a horrible dream! There are monsters and big men with funny ..."

At that point her talking became too quick for the translator hooked on Evelyn's ear to keep up. She removed it, irritated. The warrior Kiera had been attempting to scale addressed Romas. Romas's response was abrupt and sharp enough to be hostile. Evelyn glanced between them, uneasy at the exchange. The warrior stepped away.

"Kiera, it's okay, just calm—"

"Evelyn!"

Kiera was near tears and began to squirm when the six-legged creature came into sight again. Romas strode out of the room and down the hall. Evelyn scrambled after him, jogging to keep pace with his long legs. He didn't slow until they reached their quarters.

Kiera babbled the entire time, convinced it was a dream. Evelyn listened and cringed, not sure how she would explain everything. They reached their quarters and closed the door.

Romas set Kiera down gently. Kiera bounded away from him and flung her arms around Evelyn, who gave a startled laugh and hugged her back. She met Romas's eyes over her friend's head. Romas crossed his arms and raised an eyebrow in silent inquiry. Evelyn shook her head.

"K-K!" she cooed, trying to pry Kiera's grip off her and break through her babbling. "Calm down, Kiera."

Neither worked, so Evelyn let her talk and hugged her hard. Romas shook his head and stepped forward.

"No, I can—" she objected.

Romas ignored her and grabbed Kiera, pulled her away to face him, and gave her a stiff shake. She fell silent and stared at him, her striking eyes even larger.

"Do you understand me?" Romas demanded.

Kiera blinked.

"Yes or no?"

She nodded.

"Be calm. Do you understand?"

Another nod. Evelyn sighed. She elbowed Romas away to stand before Kiera. The smaller woman was still, as if afraid to move.

"Kiera, I need to explain something to you," she started. "It's not going to be easy for you to take, but hear me out, okay?"

Another stiff nod.

"Are you holding your breath?" she asked. Kiera released it. She blinked a few times as tears lined her eyes.

"Romas, can you give us a minute?"

He grunted and left. Kiera's eyes strayed from Evelyn's, and she twisted all the way around, taking in everything, before she started to cry. Evelyn was silent, debating what to say. Finally, she asked lamely, "Are you okay?"

Kiera wiped her eyes and gazed at her with a deep frown, then said, "I had a dream once about being sent into outer space."

"So it's not as much of a shock?" Evelyn asked hopefully. Kiera's face skewed again as she started crying once more.

"In my dream ... the aliens ... took me ... to a planet ruled by spiders!"

Evelyn sighed. Kiera was bound to be traumatized until she saw for herself there were no monster-sized spiders on Romas's home planet. Hopefully, *hopefully*, that would be the largest obstacle Evelyn faced in explaining the situation to her.

"Come on. I'll tell you about Romas and where we're going."

KIERA'S TEARS stopped sometime during the hours of explanation and history lessons Evelyn gave. She heard very little of any of them but somehow managed to nod when required and even respond with words her shocked mind did not hear or understand. She sat very still on the dark grey bed, her legs folded and hands in her lap, and stared at Evelyn.

She wondered if she had died, for she seemed able to see the conversation occurring from a dozen feet away, as if she were watching television instead of involved in it. She nodded and accepted Evelyn's far-fetched explanations just as she might nod and temporarily accept the equally unreal world of *Star Wars*. When the movie was over, she would smile, get up, and go home.

But this movie had no end. The world around her was real. And it was uglier than she imagined a spaceship to be. There was dark grey and sterility in the absence of anything remotely friendly, homey, or welcoming. A yellowish glow emitted from some unseen light source in the grey walls reminded her of a late winter afternoon that never ended.

Kiera wasn't watching *Star Wars* but living it. The only thing that seemed to click was Evelyn's insistence that there were no spiders. Yet she'd seen the most incredibly huge spider dangling over her head when she awoke. It even slapped her with one of its long legs. She shuddered and asked again, "Are there more spiders on the planet?"

Evelyn looked defeated, and Kiera expected she had already covered the subject exhaustively.

"That was a cat, not a spider."

"It had eight legs," Kiera insisted.

"It has six legs."

"It's still more than four. Cats have four legs."

"Kiera!" Evelyn snapped. "It's their version of a cat!"

"Does their version of a dog have eight legs?"

"No! They don't have dogs, and it only has six legs!"

"What does? The dog?"

"The cat!"

"What else has more than four legs?" Kiera pressed.

"My God, Kiera!" Evelyn sighed and rubbed her face. "You want Romas to come in here and explain things?"

"I want to go home," Kiera replied.

"This will be better than home," Evelyn promised. "I'll be with you. So will Romas. You needn't worry about anything. Besides, you said you'd stay at least a week, right?"

"And the cats?"

"The cats ... they're domesticated and really very nice."

"Are there other creatures with more than four legs?"

"I really, *really* don't know." Evelyn shook her head. "Can you think of anything else but spiders?"

"Is there air on your planet?" Before Evelyn could answer, another thought occurred to Kiera. "Are *you* an alien, too?"

"No, no, no! I was born in Mississippi. I swear it to you, Kiera. I wouldn't lie to you about anything like that."

"Just keep it from me until I awaken on a spaceship?" she retorted.

"I asked you if you wanted to come," Evelyn reminded her.

"I said no!"

"You said you'd think about it."

"You didn't tell me where we were going!" she said, incredulous.

"It's far away, like I said!" Evelyn said somewhat defensively.

"Omigod! It's so *not* just far away!" Kiera replied. "And women don't have any rights where Romas is from. He said as much! So I'm going to be stuck on a planet far away without a bus ticket home surrounded by spiders the size of basketballs and being bossed around by Neanderthal barbarians who forbid me to talk and lock me in the bathroom!"

"You're adorable even when you're so upset!" Evelyn grinned. Kiera's chest clenched as she began crying again. Evelyn threw her arms around her and hugged her, chuckling. "You'll be okay, K-K. You'll see."

Kiera squeezed her back, feeling very, very lost. She forced herself to withdraw from the surreal world and let herself go numb. After all, when she finally awoke from this nightmare, all would be back to normal, and she would have new inspiration for her paintings. She kept telling herself she'd wake up from this wacky dream soon.

Six days passed on the ship. She awoke six more times willing the nightmare to be over. On the seventh morning—if there were such a thing in space—she lay in bed and stared at the dark grey ceiling. The world was becoming more real as the days passed. She'd avoided the galley Evelyn had tried for three days to drag her to and said it would prove they were on a ship after she challenged Evelyn to prove it wasn't a dream.

She sat and crossed her legs, thoughtful. She didn't feel quite as traumatized today. In fact, she felt angry, and she wanted to see the galley to confirm this all wasn't an elaborate hallucination. She tucked in her shirt in the way Evelyn had told her was customary. She liked the space clothing. It was comfortable, like wearing pajamas all day long. All she had to do was choose the color she wanted to wear—black for the past several days in silent objection to her presence aboard the ship—and the ship's computer wove it for her.

At least, that was her version. Romas had attempted once to explain the clothing was not *woven* aboard the ship but created on his home planet, molecularly broken into invisible pieces and stored somewhere aboard the ship.

She didn't understand. It was safer for her to imagine someone sitting just behind her wall weaving clothing and sending it to her or anyone else as they requested. It made the clothing unit much less intimidating than Romas's lecture on matter and antimatter and how to store the two successfully without blowing up something.

The parts of the room were well hidden. It had taken her two days to work up the courage to walk alone into what appeared to be the rear wall but was really a mirage disguising a grey bathroom with a clothing unit in the corner. She closed her eyes as she stepped into and through the wall and opened them after two steps. A waist-high bathtub and a round disc serving as an alien toilet, also waist-high, were on one wall. If she asked, a mirror would appear on the opposite wall.

"Teal," she said to the clothing unit.

There was no other purr aside from the constant, low hum similar to the hum surrounding electric wires. A flicker of light, and the clothing appeared on a slate grey slab serving as a bench near the door.

She changed into the comfortable clothing. She stood spread-eagle until it shrank to fit her, shuddered at the creepy sensation of life-like silk caressing her skin, and hurried out of the bathroom.

She held her forearm out to the door as she approached, glancing again at the gold band around her wrist that Romas had emphasized she needed to wear *at all the times*. For once, she hadn't corrected his English, only nodded once more and held out her arm for the bracelet. What had appeared to be a thick, gold, hard band of about three inches in width had molded around her arm and felt no heavier than the clothing she wore. It was flexible and moved with her when she tested it by flexing or releasing her forearm muscles.

Romas had felt no need to explain his insistence of her wearing it, but Evelyn had explained it acted as a visual identifying piece and also happened to open all the doors on the ship.

All the doors.

It made her mind leap until she recalled she was supposedly on a spaceship. She couldn't order the exit door open and walk home. If there were more of those monstrous spiders on board, she probably did not *want* to wander around opening doors at random.

Except for today. Today she wanted to see the window to space in the galley Evelyn wanted her to see.

Kiera placed a dark grey device the size of a small button on her earlobe like an earring. It stuck, but she forced herself not to ask why. It was allegedly her translator and emitted a low-level hum similar to the walls. Without it, the ship wouldn't understand her outside of her room. She exited and touched the wall of one corridor.

"Main galley," she said.

A trickle of lights lit up on the wall to her right. She followed. Several of what Evelyn had called warriors passed her in the hall. She thought she recognized one or two from the men who had accompanied Romas to the wedding.

Evelyn's many history lessons had covered the strange kin of Romas's, explaining they weren't the cousins Romas claimed them to be at the wedding. They weren't relatives at all, but members of Romas's army. Kiera had nodded as was expected while wondering what the hell Evelyn drank to make all this seem reasonable.

Romas's clan was very large and his father's influence the greatest on the planet of Qatwal. The race of warriors was ancient, dating back a hundred millennia. Their planet had been a barbarian planet, until the Five Galaxies zone, in which Qatwal sat in the middle, was discovered by a master race of super-genius aliens Evelyn referred to as *the Brains*. The Brains set up the Planetary Council—the alien version of the United Nations—several generations before to mediate between the warring planets within the Five Galaxies. The Brains also brought technological advancement that—

A massive man passed her in the hall, and she stopped mid-thought to stare at him as he walked away. All the men on Romas's planet were larger than those on hers. She believed Evelyn's tale of a race of people bred for war. The man she just passed was a foot taller than Romas and one and a half times as wide. She felt dwarfed whenever she crossed one of the men aboard the ship.

When he disappeared around the corner, she returned to her thoughts and following the lights. There were still wars, Evelyn had confided, even though it was frowned upon by the Council.

Another giant of a man passed her, and she shook her head, amazed. The warriors never spoke or even gave her more than a passing glance. She continued down the hall, watching the lights. They stopped a short time later and surrounded a metal door. She waved her arm band, and the door opened. The room she stepped into was triangular shaped, consisting of a wall of angled windows, small tables against the other wall, and round seats facing the windows. The galley was occupied by three hulking men at a table.

She gazed out the windows, unease making her stomach churn. She couldn't help feeling disappointed; space looked no different than it had when she was lying on the roof of Evelyn's house. She expected *real* space to look closer if nothing else.

Which way was home? She didn't see any glowing blue planets. She sat in one of the chairs and slid down in it until her head rested against the back. They seemed to be moving very slowly for being on a spaceship, she mused.

"I thought you would come here eventually." Evelyn's voice was soft. Kiera grunted without turning. Evelyn slid into the chair beside her. "You okay?"

"I don't know. I can't make sense of things," Kiera said.

"You overanalyze things. Don't try, just accept," Evelyn advised.

"Is that what you did?" Kiera glanced at her.

"Don't give this blonde the credit for thinking too deeply."

The three warriors at the table relocated several chairs down.

"Take off your earpiece," Evelyn whispered. Kiera did so and set it carefully on her knee. It would blend in with everything around her if she dropped it.

"Neat little things," Evelyn said with some excitement as she placed hers on the chair's slender arm. "I see you're not wearing black today."

"Too depressed," Kiera said. "Needed some color."

"Don't think they like not knowing what we're saying," she said with some satisfaction. "Romas isn't bad, but I can imagine most of these guys have a bit too much testosterone."

"Romas has too much testosterone," Kiera retorted. "I bet this was his idea, wasn't it? Dragging me away from home?"

"No, it was mostly mine," she said. "He agreed you needed a real life, though."

"That's bad enough."

"You'll be fascinating to his people," Evelyn continued. "You're what they might call petite."

"Petite?" Kiera echoed with a raised eyebrow. "I've never been called petite in my life! I'm of above average height by an inch and above average weight by ten pounds."

"The women there are grown bigger, too," Evelyn explained. "Like me."

"Omigod. So I'm going to a planet of models and body builders," Kiera said. "I'll be the rotund brunette no one wants to talk to!"

"Stop! Romas said you're being a five-year-old, and I agree! They *like* you Kiera," Evelyn said, and raised her chin toward the warriors near them. "The one who saved you from the cat asked Romas on the spot to marry you."

Kiera gave an unladylike snort. "I'm sure Romas told him he wouldn't want to deal with my fiery tongue. That's absurd, Evelyn."

"Well, they're different, hon," Evelyn said with some frustration. "I have the feeling we'll both stick out."

Kiera glanced at her, hearing the nervousness for the first time.

"Are you worried about ... things?" she queried. "Other than being on a spaceship with aliens and super-tarantulas?"

"Yeah. The usual, I guess. Meeting his parents, them accepting me, fitting in with the new place, you know."

"You'll do great, Evelyn," Kiera said. "You're perfect, brilliant, and beautiful. Rum-ass thinks so, and so do I. There's no way they won't be bowled over by you."

"That's sweet, K-K," Evelyn answered.

"If not, we can steal a spaceship and go home," Kiera added under her breath.

Evelyn giggled. "Not if Romas hooks you up with one of his brothers." She grinned. "You'll get to meet them all when we land tomorrow."

"Tomorrow?" Kiera echoed.

"Their traditions are a little different." Evelyn gave her a sidelong look. "You may not have much control over some things."

"I think I'm already experiencing that."

"Yeah ... " Evelyn said, and hesitated before continuing. "You might not have a choice in what man decides ... to like you or propose or something."

"What?"

"You know. Think of it as a tribal warrior society that's kinda backwards or antiquated in its customs."

"I'm not following."

"You're a guest of Romas right now, but if he decides to put you on the market, so to speak, pretty much anyone can ... um ... claim you as a ... you know, a bride."

"But I'm going home," Kiera said blankly.

"Well, I'll talk to him," Evelyn said, and rushed into a new subject. "Isn't this an awesome view?"

Kiera looked at her, attempting to decipher her warning. It sounded very much like Evelyn was trying to tell her Romas could marry her off at his will when he pleased. The idea was absurd, even for someone as chauvinistic as Romas. Her instincts didn't like Evelyn's nonchalance on the subject.

"Yeah, nice view," she murmured. "Do they have anything unusual, like four moons?"

"There are two moons and two suns, but the suns are so close together, you can't tell," Evelyn said. "The standard day is longer than ours, about thirty hours instead of twenty-four, with that divided evenly between day and night."

"Have you been there before?" Kiera asked.

"No. I've been interrogating Romas for about two months now," Evelyn admitted with a smile. "They have green grass, oceans, and blue sky just like us."

"Is the sun yellow?"

"Yes, Kiera!"

"So the only difference is their animals and the size of their people," Kiera said.

"Pretty much."

She shifted in her chair. She had many more questions, but the more she asked, the less she could deny the world around her was real. Tomorrow she would meet Romas's alien-brothers and parents. Or maybe, just maybe, tomorrow morning she would finally wake up.

They sat for a while before she felt a familiar sense of anxiety at the reality of her situation. She wandered back to the safety of her room, wanting paper and pencils, her favorite jeans ... anything familiar to comfort her. She lay on the bed as she had for several days already, sick of the jerky-like food Evelyn brought her.

She couldn't sleep, even when the computer turned her lights out in the only sign it was bedtime. She spent the night waiting for the nightmare world to end and dressed the next morning with an undertaker's solemnity. Soon after, a warrior came to her door and led her down several halls and into a tiny box resembling an elevator. Unlike an elevator, it didn't appear to move. She felt silly standing in it with the three warrior strangers around her, waiting for something to happen that never did. When the doors opened, she realized everything had changed. For one, she was no longer faced with dark grey. For two, it was not just Romas and Evelyn before her.

There were hundreds, maybe *thousands,* of cheerfully clothed giants and models lining a petal-strewn pathway. Brilliant sunlight blinded her after days of grey, and she blinked at the bright, *familiar* blue sky.

It was morning. She smelled dew. A light, warm breeze brushed her cheek. The sensations made her want to cry. Relieved, she focused on the blue skies, yellow suns, and thick emerald grass that reminded her of pictures from a tour book of Ireland. She felt more grounded as she stepped out of the horrible grey elevator onto a thick carpet of green. She was no longer confined in purgatory, afloat in space. She avoided turning around to see what must have been a hulking grey mass of metal spaceship.

One of the warriors flanking her nudged her forward. Romas and Evelyn were already several dozen feet down the flowered path. Evelyn appeared serene and perfect, as usual. Romas was detached and unreadable, the supreme warrior prince.

Kiera stepped forward, eager to reach Evelyn. Her friend hadn't been joking about her being considered petite and unique. She didn't see one woman under six feet tall or any man who didn't tower over six feet. Romas's people were fair skinned with light hair in varying shades of blond and red. She saw a full range of eye colors, though she noticed with some interest that blue or green eyes were unnaturally clear—unlike her Mediterranean, green-blue-grey gaze.

She took in their bright clothing, glad she thought to wear light blue today. Any darker color, and she would stand out even more.

She reached Evelyn and Romas and forced herself not to crowd them. She kept her eyes on the couple instead of the crowd. People stare at her with varying looks of curiosity and intensity. Her face warmed and reddened beneath the scrutiny. Evelyn was the queen of handling crowds, but Kiera could think of nothing more than ducking into a safe corner and staying there with her back to the wall.

The warriors with her closed around her, blocking some of the crowd from sight.

The couple before her stopped, and she brought her gaze back to them. They stood in front of an airy, light tent resembling a silk sheet suspended in midair over a table. A man and a woman in their prime stood before them, and the light murmuring of the crowd hushed. They were a handsome couple, the elegant woman's hair so fine and blonde it resembled white silk. The man beside her had dark blond hair, serious brown eyes in a chiseled face, and a form as fit as his son's.

Evelyn's in-laws. Kiera held her breath for her friend as Evelyn stepped forward. Her friend was sure-footed and confident, but Kiera knew she was nervous. Evelyn's words were too quiet for Kiera to hear.

The scent of real food wafted towards her. Her mouth watered, and her eyes dropped to the source. It was not the chewy ship food. It looked like real food packed on the low tables with meat, gravies, and tons of dishes of what might have been casseroles of varying colors. Pillows passed as chairs, and bowls as cups.

She leaned to see past Romas and saw that the tent before her was only the head tent. Tables and pillows stretched as far as she could see to create a massive circle she assumed was large enough to seat the crowd. Her eyes caught movement at the edge of the crowd.

Three massive warriors escorted a fourth whose hands were bound. They moved out of sight at her blink, and she wondered how criminals were treated on such a planet.

Evelyn turned, motioning her forward. Kiera went.

"My friend, Kiera." Evelyn's voice was quiet and respectful.

Kiera felt she should have curtseyed or saluted or something. Uncertainly, she remained where she was and gazed at the man and woman before her. They looked her over curiously. The woman appeared bright-eyed and pleasant, the warrior-husband unreadable.

"Kiera, this is Romas's mother, Lishana, and his father, Mison," Evelyn said.

A slight smile drew up one side of Lishana's mouth, and Kiera felt the urge to smile as well. There was a gentle air around the woman, and her large brown eyes lacked the rigid stoniness of her husband's. At first glance, Lishana did not seem the kind of mother-in-law that might cause Evelyn problems.

"You are welcome, Kiera." Lishana's voice was as soft as her features. "May the suns long grace you."

"Thank you," Kiera responded.

"Will you join us?" The invitation was addressed to all three of them. As if on cue, the crowd began to break up, with cheerful groups moving to various positions around the circle. Kiera watched them, somewhat relieved not to be the center of attention any longer. She trailed the two couples up shallow stairs and took the seat beside Evelyn not occupied by Romas. Her gaze dropped to the feast before them.

Did any of the animals on the table look like spiders while alive?

She stared at a tray of meat for a long moment. Several giants with Romas's shade of blond hair and similar blue eyes seated themselves across from them. She knew by their similar facial features they were brothers, and Romas's threat of hooking her up with one made her more self-conscious.

Mison motioned for those at his table to eat, and she reached for the plate of meat before her before Romas or any of his brothers could assist her. She tapped the earpiece as the conversation around picked up but the words faded in and out of translation. Even an elite, advanced society like Romas's had technical difficulties. She removed the earpiece and replaced it. The translator hummed once more.

"Romas had all the cats corralled and kept elsewhere for this feast, just for you," Evelyn leaned over to whisper. "Isn't he just awesome?"

"He's awesome if he keeps them corralled for my entire visit, which hopefully won't be long," Kiera replied. Evelyn frowned and shifted away. Kiera almost apologized, but the approach and introduction of two pre-teen boys with white-blond hair and bright blue eyes distracted her.

"My brothers, Lilan and Hilan," Romas announced.

The grinning boys were between ten and twelve, already tall and lanky. The two scuffled for a seat next to one of their older brothers across from Kiera before a look from Mison quieted them. They sat dutifully, sharing the pillow, and were calm for several moments before a discreet elbow match broke out between them. She was grateful to see even alien kids behaved like typical kids.

She took her first bite of what looked like beef. It certainly tasted like beef, though the tangy spices were unfamiliar. Evelyn poured clear, steaming broth into a bowl beside her plate.

"This is good. You can dip anything in this," she said.

Kiera tried it. The clear broth held a tangy, rich flavor, like spiced butter. As a fan of good food, Kiera found Evelyn's words to be quite true. She dipped everything she tried—from meat to casseroles with odd textures—in the clear broth. They even had a version of bread; it was unleavened and came in large, round, flat ears.

She ate until full, then pushed her plate from the edge of the table. The two boys across from her had managed to make messes of themselves and the table in what might have been a competition. They cast several glances her way and appeared as interested in her as they were in looking past her. Romas's eldest brother, who sat across and down the table from her, rose, a look of anger on his face. She watched him circle the table and twisted to see where he went.

Behind the tent and its low, shallow steps was a small group of blond warriors surrounding a fifth man with darker skin and hair. Romas's brother spoke to the group. The boys across from Kiera began giggling. Uninterested in watching people talk, she glanced again at the boys and nudged Evelyn.

"Evelyn, I need to use the little girls' room," she said.

Evelyn leaned to whisper to Romas, whose response was a tad too long for Kiera's impatient bladder.

"He says to enter the main house by the first entrance you find. Your bracelet—"

The translator cut out on her, and Evelyn's next foreign words were incomprehensible. Kiera removed the translator from her ear. Evelyn did the same.

"Enter the main house using the nearest entrance. Your bracelet acts as a sort of master key, so you can go anywhere in the whole house. There should be a servant or someone posted near the entrance who can guide you to the restroom. If not, it's along the same hallway as the door. Just go four or five doors, and it'll be on your right."

Something splashed Kiera, and she pushed the droplets from her face, concentrating on Evelyn.

"Is it four or five?" she asked. "If it's four and I go five and interrupt someone's conference or walk into a room full of tarantulas, I'm going to go crazy."

"No, no. I think he said four," Evelyn said. "I'm sure there will be someone—oh, hell, don't look down!"

Something furry dropped into Kiera's lap. The two pre-teen boys laughed.

Kiera's eyes dropped to her lap, and she stared at the mass of furry legs, freezing in place for a long moment. The cats' fur was matted from a bath in her dipping soup. She gave a startled cry, shot up from her seat, and swiped the creatures from her lap in one movement. Two of the cats, young and small enough to be kittens or perfectly sized adult tarantulas, detangled and darted from her pillow to the table.

Kiera took two steps back, shuddering in disgust and fear. God, she hated spiders. Hated them, hated them, *hated them*! A sharp word from Romas, and the two boys looked suddenly abashed. One of the kittens dashed toward Kiera, moving sideways like a spider on its flexible legs, and she skittered farther away.

Romas leaned back and snatched the kitten trotting toward her, and Evelyn rose to her knees, looking both surprised and dismayed. Suddenly, Kiera really, *really* wanted to go home.

"I'm going ... to the restroom," she said, heart thudding in her ears.

"I'm so sorry, K. I'll go with you," Evelyn offered.

"No. I'm okay. I'll go and we can talk about going home when I get back!"

Romas tossed the kitten, which darted for her again. She took another hasty step back as he grabbed it once more. Her left foot found the first shallow step, and she took another step back, her eyes pinned on the second kitten running along the table. She'd just made a complete fool of herself and Evelyn ... how would she react if someone were as terrified of kittens on earth?

Embarrassed, she didn't notice her right foot reaching nothing but air until she toppled backwards. She gasped, waiting to feel the impact of the hard ground. Two hands caught her. An unexpected heat jarred her to her core, and the earth beneath her feet shook violently enough to rattle her teeth. The strange spell left her breathing hard and confused as to whether she'd had a heart attack or worse. The strange fever remained, making her feel as if she'd been sitting in a sauna for hours. Her head hurt and her body ached from the inside out, like she had the flu.

Unable to understand or control the strange sensations, she tried to help right herself as the hands gripping her ribcage steadied her. The hot energy circulating through her body came from the large, olive-hued hands touching her. She looked up, wondering who she now owed an apology for her embarrassing scene.

Her gaze was immediately riveted to that of an alien unlike those of Romas's clan. His skin was darker, the color of honey as opposed to alabaster, his eyes a rich, dark brown, and his features lacking the delicate, chiseled beauty of Romas's family. This man's features were scarred and masculine with a crooked nose that had been broken more than once. Long, dark hair was held in place at the base of his neck by a thick band of rose gold.

His gaze was so direct it seemed to sear through her. The heat of his large hands made her feel as if she wore no clothing. He held her against him, his dark, spicy-sweet scent seizing her senses. Inexplicable scenes tore through her mind too fast for her to focus on any one of them.

A blue planet, two thrones, a hacienda-style dwelling, an older man and woman, fire in the sky, a red planet, war. The emotions behind the scenes were hot and angry before one more scene emerged—this one lingering for what felt like minutes.

She held the hand of the man before her, walking on a dead planet of nothing but rocky hills, dried streams, and cracked earth. The planet's energy warmed her, ran through her and into him, and grass grew beneath her feet. She smiled up at him, content to be with her mate.

Another hand clamped around her arm and snatched her away. She blinked out of the spell and saw Romas's oldest brother, his eyes glittering with anger. Her gaze fell to the bound hands of the man who'd caught her. Given his guard of four warriors and his unfriendly gaze, maybe she should be grateful someone wrenched her arm off to get her away from him. And yet, she still felt his hands on her body, smelled his scent, saw the vision from their touch.

Fate. The sense was fleeting and overwhelming. She didn't know the honey-hued man before her, but she couldn't help but feel their paths were entwined.

The idea scared her. She was going home, not staying on some dead planet with some hunky stranger!

The hunky stranger spoke to Romas's oldest brother. The translator was dead and picked up none of the men's terse discussion. She tried not to stare at the man staring at her. He was the most stunning man she'd ever seen despite his crooked nose. Whatever they discussed, Romas's brother was getting more pissed; his grip on her tightened until she gave a verbal, "Let me go!"

Whether or not it translated or whether her voice was enough to alert him, all eyes fell to her before the conversation resumed. It was Romas—the man responsible for dragging her across the universe—who rescued her. He took her free arm and drew her away from his brother. Kiera went more than willingly, near the emergency point for reaching the bathroom. He pushed her past him and joined in the conversation. Evelyn smiled tightly from her position a couple of feet away, her attention riveted to the situation before her. Kiera looked at her arm, where a bruise was already forming from Kisolm's grip.

Whatever the men were squabbling about, it wasn't worth hurting her. Kiera looked at them all, her gaze settling on the prisoner. The thrum of warm energy coursed through her again, and she felt again her destiny was tied with his.

He still watched her. He was shorter than the seven-foot giants around him, standing right at Romas's height. His clothing was styled differently, with a dark V-neck tunic, dark pants, and a thick belt around his lower abdomen. He wore a rose gold bracelet very similar to Romas's in all but color, and soft, dark boots. He was, without a doubt, a warrior. His frame was thick beneath the snug clothing, with a tucked waist and flared upper body extending from the tucked waist to his wide, broad shoulders. His brow was low and his eyebrows dark, making his unwavering gaze even more intense.

Heat flared within her body, and her imagination painted an image of the warrior before her without the clothing. Kiera rubbed her arm with a small wince and forced herself to turn away. She wanted nothing to do with this world or its inhabitants, despite that unexpected, intimate connection with the most beautiful man she'd ever seen. She hadn't felt instant attraction to a man since high school.

She was going home, sexy alien be damned. She turned to face Evelyn but still felt him watch her. Evelyn was upset at what was being said, emotions crossing her face quickly. Her look turned to anger, then softened into concern. By the end of the conversation, she appeared relieved.

The prisoner was led away. Kiera relaxed, no longer feeling his gaze on her. Evelyn spoke to her, her words foreign. Kiera tapped her translator and shook her head. Evelyn removed hers.

"You didn't understand anything?" Evelyn asked.

"I have to pee, *now*," Kiera answered.

"Oh. Sorry. I'll go, too."

Evelyn made a motion to Romas, who looked grimmer than usual. He nodded and returned to the tent. Kiera followed as Evelyn turned toward the main house, a sprawling, single-story compound made of brilliant white stone and dotted with hundreds of glass-less windows. It was open and airy, bright and cheerful. They walked across the open field before it, the bright sun and solid ground beneath her easing some of her anxiety about the day.

"You didn't understand anything?" Evelyn asked again.

"Nope. Evelyn, I'm so sorry I've totally embarrassed you today," Kiera said. "I wanted it to be special for you and managed to mortify both of us."

"Oh, no, K-K!" Evelyn said. "They know we're from another place. His family has been very understanding."

"Except those boys," Kiera muttered. "Stupid kids."

"Just kids, though, K-K. I'm sorry they upset you."

Kiera shrugged.

"Are you really ready to go home so soon?" Evelyn asked.

"Yeah, I think so."

Evelyn sighed in disappointment. Kiera looked at her friend, guilty for hurting her feelings despite her need to return to her own world. Her thoughts went to the prisoner, and she wondered if she'd see him again if she stayed a little longer.

"If you want, I'll stay for a few more days," she offered half-heartedly. "As your wedding present. I'm not overly anxious to get back on that depressing ship."

"Thanks, Kiera," Evelyn said. "It really would mean a lot to me. The next few days will be nothing but feasts and parties in celebration of our marriage!"

"So then you'll be very happy."

"Even happier because I didn't have to plan them," Evelyn said. "And you'll have fun, too, Kiera. I promise."

Kiera shook tension from her shoulders. Evelyn did have a way of making even the most gruesome day of spring cleaning fun. Perhaps, if Romas kept the spiders away and Evelyn could make the days pass quickly, she might survive her visit. She may go so far as to not be disappointed with it if she saw the handsome man again.

"What did that guy do to be arrested?" she asked. "Steal something? Kill someone?"

"He's more of a prisoner of war," Evelyn said. "A lippy one at that. We need to get you a new translator."

"I thought there weren't any wars right now."

"I guess he's not a war prisoner in the traditional sense," Evelyn replied. "I'm not always sure about things here either. I think there's no openly declared war, but there's lots of unrest and skirmishes among the clans. From what I understood, that guy and Romas's eldest brother have personal issues with each other and are constantly hazing each other. I guess the other guy just got caught this time."

"Typical male ego," Kiera said. "Probably fighting over who stole whose cat when they were five."

"Something like that."

"You looked really upset for a while though."

"Just stupid traditions and stuff," Evelyn said a little too casually.

"They're fighting over a woman, and I really don't take to the way they do things here in that regard."

Satisfied to find the sexy man wasn't a serial killer or worse, Kiera's attention shifted to the main house as they approached. The house was as brilliant white on the inside as it was outside. There were no traditional decorations such as pictures or mirrors on the walls, but colorful cords and streams of what might have been silk edging the corners and dangling from high ceilings. The wide hallways were lit by skylights and lined with inset doors whose access pads glowed to the right of each door.

The women counted four doors, and Kiera held out her bracelet to the access pad. The door slid open. Evelyn waited outside while Kiera entered the massive bathroom. She removed the translator and replaced it, satisfied at the faint hum indicating it was working once more.

She went about her business and was about to leave when the door opened and two beautiful, tall women entered. One looked her over with disdain, and the other whispered to the first, "She could not possibly ally to the *dhjan* family, sister. She is too small and *khorj* to bear warriors."

Kiera offered a smile and hurried past them, heart pounding and face red with embarrassment. The translator was not always good at picking up every word, but she didn't need the translation of the unknown word. The two women had just called her short and fat.

"What's wrong?" Evelyn asked, eyes on her face as she exited quickly.

"Oh, nothing," Kiera lied. "Just not used to their bathrooms yet."

She didn't want to stay even a few days, not if it meant she was viewed as nothing more than a short-and-fat foreigner! That reputation could not possibly help Evelyn's standing in the clan either; the sooner the clan forgot the blemish of a friend, the sooner they'd accept Evelyn. No sexy warrior—even a prisoner—would want anything to do with her at all.

"I'm feeling tired, Evelyn. Could I lie down for a while?" she asked. She hated the disappointed look on Evelyn's face.

"Sure, Kiera. I'm sorry for stressing you. Can you wait here for a minute, so I can ask Romas where your room is?"

Kiera nodded, content to hide from the crowd. Of all the things to think about, she couldn't get the prisoner out of her thoughts, even when Evelyn returned with sweet bread she normally would've pounced on. She took it absent-mindedly and followed her friend through the mansion.

FOUR

EVELYN LEFT Kiera's room with a frown, uncertain how to make everything up to her friend. Kiera would figure things out soon, especially once Evelyn got her into this new world and its customs. The party tonight would be a perfect way to start. There would be no pressure on Kiera, and Evelyn would be there to support her.

Kiera had no clue how curious Romas's brothers were about her. To them, she was an exotic little doll with her huge, gem-hued eyes, black hair, and toned hour-glass shape. *Everyone* was fascinated by something so exotic compared to their standards. Even Romas's mother had inquired about Kiera.

None of your savage brothers would properly complement such a beautiful little treasure, Romas, the woman had said with gentle humor. *Though one of them must try. Kisolm has already spoken to your father.*

Romas had then been given the painful job of explaining to Kisolm that Kiera would most likely not meld well with their traditions, and Kisolm would have to be disappointed. Evelyn had almost laughed when Lishana's eyebrows shot up in response gave but loved

Romas so much more for understanding Kiera well enough to defend her.

"Is she well?" Romas's voice distracted her from her thoughts. She turned to wait for him to join her and smiled.

"I think so. Shocked, upset. Can't blame her," she said. "She thinks everyone here views her as short and fat."

"My brothers are lining up to make her their mate," he said with a shake of his head. "If only she understood our culture better."

"She doesn't," she said with a warning look. "We dragged her here, but that's as far as I can go."

"I know, love," he said, and kissed her on the forehead. "I told them all so."

They hugged for a long moment, her heart singing. How she loved his scent and strong arms! She looked at the band on her arm, then down the hall toward Kiera before propping her chin on his chest to gaze at him.

"You're sure your brother won't try anything after what that guy said? They were fighting over her. That A'Ran guy sounded pretty convincing about kidnapping her."

Romas was thoughtful before responding. "A'Ran and Kisolm have been competing against each other for years. They taunt each other whenever they have the chance and oftentimes want to anger the other but don't intend to follow through. A'Ran comes from the barbarian planet, but he won't disrespect our family. I have warned all my brothers, and Kisolm will respect my wishes."

"A'Ran looked pretty savage," she said with a shiver. "He's locked up, right?"

"He is."

"And someone other than Kisolm has the key?"

"We don't use keys," he answered. "We use honor. He is placed in a room where he must stay, unless someone frees him. He won't leave."

"You *trust* him?" she asked skeptically.

"It has always been this way. Before we had spaceships, we still had war. The only way to protect innocent people from the blood feud that runs between my family and A'Ran's was to use honor." He took her hand as they started to walk down the hall.

Evelyn glanced over her shoulder again, feeling uneasy. If only Kiera had stayed seated or didn't have such a hyperactive bladder or just *waited* five minutes! Romas could have convinced his brother to leave Kiera be, but now, with a blatant challenge from the prisoner, who had *dared* Kisolm to claim Kiera before *he* did ... Romas trusted his brother, but Evelyn had seen the look on Kisolm's face when he looked at Kiera.

"Do not worry, love," Romas said, looking at her.

"I feel like I should've warned her about the arm band," she said. "She doesn't know that giving it to any man she comes across basically makes her his wife."

"Kiera is an honored guest. I've told my family she is your sister. They will not dishonor you or me by doing anything without coming to me first."

Dear God, I hope not!

Evelyn smiled at him but wasn't so sure. She'd keep an eye on her friend to make sure nothing else happened.

KIERA LAY on the bed an hour after Evelyn left, staring at the white ceiling with its brightly corded edges. A midmorning breeze drifted through the windows to her right, and she closed her eyes.

She needed to leave. What had started out as a favor to her friend was turning into something else. Her gaze fell again to the closet in which boxes were stacked. They didn't contain Evelyn's things; they contained *her* things, down to her dirty socks. She'd found them when trying to find the invisible bathroom door.

Evelyn—or Romas—never intended for her to leave. There was no way she was staying! Yet home was a very long way away, which meant she needed to go home on a spaceship. Who piloted them? How did she go about getting one discreetly?

She pondered the spaceship dilemma and how to commission one to take her home without Evelyn, Romas, or anyone else finding out. Given that she had no money or belongings that might possibly be of interest to the people of this planet, how could she bribe or pay someone to take her home? As much as she loved her friend, she couldn't help feeling betrayed.

She hid in the room most of the day to prevent any more run-ins with cats or models and to think. It wasn't until dusk, when Evelyn had said she'd come back, that she forced herself up. She sat on the bed and watched the sunset through the window. It was just as spectacular as those on earth, a brilliant mix of pinks, oranges, burnt yellows, reds, and purples. She raised her bracelet to the light, watching the colors reflect off of it and turning it pinkish-gold, like the prisoner's bracelet.

And then it hit her. She needed someone who could sneak her out of Romas's reach and to a spaceship.

Prisoner... personal issues ... hazing ... just got caught this time.

He wasn't a criminal, a thief, or murderer but someone who happened to have a bone to pick with Romas's brother and managed to get caught. Freeing a man should put him in her debt, and he was the last person in the house who would rat her out to Romas's family!

Maybe this was how their fates were tied?

Kiera tossed the thoughts around in her head, guilty at the thought of ditching Evelyn yet offended that Evey thought to keep her here without telling her. She'd lost complete control of her life overnight!

She bristled, angry again. What did it matter if she decided to leave and went about doing it her own way? Why was she worried about upsetting her friend when her friend hadn't given her the same consideration?

She felt more guilty about thinking badly about Evelyn. She could not—would not—hold Evelyn responsible for everything. If not for Romas, there would be no distant planet, spaceships, or tarantula-like cats!

Her thoughts drifted to the prisoner, the memory of his touch and the strange energy making her blood quicken. There was something about him ... she didn't know what. Another memory crossed her mind, and her face grew warm for a different reason.

Short and fat. As if she needed another reason to want to escape!

"K-K?"

Evelyn's voice preceded her entrance by only a second. Kiera jerked out of her thoughts and twisted on the bed to face her. Evelyn was splendidly dressed in blues and greens, her elegant shape clad in a very earthly, off the shoulder dress.

"You're not ready!"

Her eyes strayed to the closet, as if wondering if Kiera found the boxes. Kiera pretended not to notice and rose.

"I've been sleeping," she said. "You look great!"

"Thanks." Evelyn smiled. "You'll have to go in their clothing since you're not ready yet." She strode to the clothing unit in the corner and ordered her a set.

"Evelyn, I was thinking about the prisoner," Kiera started, debating how to get the information she wanted without alarming Evelyn.

To her surprise, Evelyn stiffened and gave an oh-so-casual, "Oh?"

Kiera felt again that she was missing something but didn't know what. She ignored the instinct and said, "I want to roam around the main house, but I'm really afraid of opening doors to random rooms and finding, you know, hordes of tarantulas that attack me or angry prisoners of war."

"Oh! The *cats* were moved out of the main house, so you don't have to worry about them. I'm pretty sure the prisoners are kept on the same floor as the warriors. You probably shouldn't go down that way anyway."

"Okay," Kiera said. "Which hall is that in case I start wandering in the morning?"

"It's the first corridor leading out of the main house into what I think is the eastern wing. It's actually where I'm staying with Romas."

"Really? Why don't they have a dungeon or something?"

"I think they believe themselves to be more civilized than that. Up! Change!"

Kiera groaned, dreading the idea of a party with so many strangers who were bound to think of her as the women in the bathroom had earlier.

"It'll be fun!" Evelyn said cheerfully. "All kinds of people to meet, great food."

"I think they already know I don't fit in. I don't expect anyone to talk to me," Kiera muttered as she changed.

"Of course they will! Is your translator working?"

"For now. It fades in and out."

"Tomorrow we'll get you a new one," Evelyn promised. "And I won't leave your side tonight. I want you to have a good time."

"Thanks," Kiera said, doubting her outgoing friend would sit in a corner like she planned on doing. "I'm ready."

"You're adorable, K-K." Evelyn beamed. "I chose a color that brings out your eyes."

"Thanks."

She wore a rich tanzanite blue-purple that was darker than the colors worn by the people of this planet. She sighed, resigned to the fact that she would stick out no matter what she wore. Kiera braced herself and exited behind Evelyn, whose quick step led them back to the main house and outside, where the floating tents were still in place.

She stepped into the crowd with Evelyn, who was soon spirited away by Lishana. Being shorter than everyone else would be a boon this night; she waited until the two were out of sight before fading back toward the house. She passed through the throng without making eye contact for fear of leers or judging looks and reached the entrance foyer. Several people loitered there, and she passed them all with a glance.

First corridor out of the main house.

Kiera almost missed it as she thought of where the cats had been placed. She turned right into the first corridor, urging her courage not to falter just yet. She scoured each side of the hall for signs labeling what doors might lead to what.

One of the doors opened as she passed, and a couple emerged. Kiera's heart jumped, but they ignored her and walked toward the main foyer. She continued faster, and followed the corridor as it curved to the left. The doors lining the halls were unmarked, and she began to suspect her plan would fail fast if she had to open every door in the hallway.

It was as she neared a dead end that she saw the single door with two access pads, the only door with additional security in the wing. She stopped in front of it, adrenaline making her heart quicken. Was she *really* going to free some prisoner in exchange for a trip home?

Faced with the reality of the situation, she paced in front of the door, arguing with herself. Romas's world wasn't *that* bad, and Evelyn might help her get home in due time.

Due time was too far away and too uncertain; she wanted to leave *now!*

She stopped and stared at the door, then began pacing again. She had never been one to take risks such as this. What better place to be a bit more daring in life than on another planet? She was about to walk away in defeat and take her place in a dark corner watching the partygoers when she heard the sounds of approaching footsteps.

Romas. The thought made her panic. On his planet, he'd have no qualms about following through with his threat to lock her in the bathroom if he found out what she was doing.

Her decision made itself. Kiera approached the door in two quick steps, waved her bracelet in front of one then the second access pad, and pushed the door to hurry it. She ducked into the room and whirled to push it closed just as quickly. She pressed her ear to the door. The sound of footsteps grew closer. Just when she was about to dart away from the door and hide behind any piece of furniture she could find, the footsteps stopped. Kiera held her breath. The footsteps started again, this time in retreat.

She rested against the door, jarred when the flash of a grey knife crossed inches before her eyes, followed by a muted *thunk* as the weapon buried itself in the door. After a surprised pause, she waved her bracelet in front of the internal access pad. Before the door could open more than an inch, a large honey-hued hand planted on it and pushed it closed.

She knew before she turned who stood behind her. She *felt* him with an instinct she didn't understand. She sucked in a deep breath and turned to face the music.

The music was every bit as masculine and warrior as she remembered him. He towered before her with one hand planted just above her head. The intensity of his look pinned her to the door behind her.

He felt close, too close. She pushed her heels against the door and gazed up at him, her courage gone in the face of such a man. The odd energy flowing between them held them both in silence for a long moment before he spoke.

"I do no favors for any this night."

"I don't know what that means," she managed.

He stared at her, considering and wary, in a way that made her uncomfortably fevered. For a long moment, she thought her translator had died again. The warrior looked her over from head to toe. Kiera felt her ire rise at the blatant appraisal. Anger awoke her from the odd spell he seemed to cast over her.

"I will consider a favor to you," he recanted.

"I don't want a favor, unless that means you're willing to help me escape," she replied. "I've come to offer you the chance to escape, so long as you take me to a ... to a spaceship."

"You speak of escape?" he asked with a frown.

"Escape for you and for me."

"Escape for you?"

"Yes. I don't want to stay here. I want to go home. I need you to take me to a spaceship so I can arrange to go home," she said with exaggerated slowness to make sure he understood despite her faulty translator.

His gaze turned curious. He dropped his arm and stepped away. Kiera drew a breath as the intensity of his presence left. The massive warrior paced to the window. He looked out for a long moment, pensive, before returning his attention to her.

"You want me to help you leave."

She nodded in response.

"It might onset a war."

"Onset a war?" she repeated. "No, you just have to take me to a ship."

He looked her over once more. She crossed her arms. There was something more than interest in his gaze. If she hadn't thought it impossible for an alleged warrior to feel such a thing, she might have thought him troubled.

"Would you stop that? Where I'm from, that's rude."

He said nothing but let his eyes do as they pleased. She recalled what Evelyn had said about him goading Kisolm.

"It would really upset Kisolm," she added. "If you escaped. You could get back at him for whatever it is you're fighting about."

"No," he said, though his eyes fell to the band around her forearm in consideration.

Surprised, she fell speechless. Even a prisoner on this planet was unwilling to associate with her! Yet another embarrassing event to add to her day's tally! Face flaming, Kiera turned to go. She waved her wrist before the access pad, but once more, the warrior prevented the door from opening. She tensed and waited for him, too, to insult her or boss her around like Romas did before she walked away.

"No, I will not do this to bait Kisolm, as much as I enjoy it," he clarified. "I will help you on three conditions."

"Isn't your freedom enough?" she asked.

"Not for onset of war," he responded, and waved his own wrist in front of the access pad. To her surprise, the door nudged her back. He closed it again. She turned to face him.

"Why would you stay if you don't have to?"

"You are not from here," he observed. "I am honor bound to stay."

He was too close again. She pressed herself against the door, almost wishing Romas *would* discover them. The warrior before her had an intensity that made her breath catch, and the energy between them made her insides tingle. His movements were smooth and controlled, his emotions hidden, his dark, dark eyes alone enough to keep her immobile.

"What are your conditions?" she asked. Her body was doing funny things, like growing warm in places it should not and scattering her thoughts like confetti in a stiff breeze.

"One, your arm band."

She glanced down at it and nodded without a second thought. She hadn't thought to use it as a bribe; if it were gold, it might be worth something. She held up her arm, uncertain how to release it.

"You give it willingly?" he asked.

She searched his gaze and responded with irritation, "If coercion is willing, then yes."

He stared at her with his head cocked, and she judged the words had not translated.

"Yes, I do," she clarified.

He dropped his arm from the door and took her forearm. At his touch, the band loosened enough to slide over her hand. Kiera watched as he slid the band over his right hand to settle it at his wrist before stripping his own band off his left arm. He slid it over her opposite hand, and she looked up at him.

"It's okay. You can keep both," she said, confused. "I won't need it where I'm going."

"Two, a kiss."

"That's ridiculous!" Kiera retorted even as her heart leapt at the prospect.

"You want to leave."

"Yes, but—"

One moment she was protesting, the next his warm, soft lips covered hers. She froze, surprised by his action as well as the warm shock running through her. He plied her lips gently, testing and encouraging, and she felt herself respond despite her indignation. The kiss grew deep. She yielded to his prodding and parted her lips for him. His tongue slid between them. He licked and nipped her lips, explored her mouth, and pulled her deeper and deeper into a state of compliance. She groaned at tasting him; he was as sweetly spicy as he smelled.

Suddenly, he withdrew. Disoriented, she kept her eyes closed as she savored the kiss. Her breathing was erratic, her pulse flying, her lower belly ablaze with warmth. She leaned against him to steady her balance.

"Do you concur with my three conditions?" the warrior asked in a husky voice.

"Yes," she murmured.

"Good. We go."

He moved away from her, nearly throwing off her balance. Her eyes snapped open. He was playing with her. Had the thought been able to gather support among her disjointed faculties, she would have walked away from him. The warrior opened the door and strode into the corridor without waiting. Kiera watched him go, startled. She'd expected him to go out the window to avoid detection.

"Do you have a plan for leaving?" she asked, trotting to reach him. The hum of the translator was gone. She tapped it and repeated the question.

"Yes."

"What is it?"

He said nothing but continued at a quick pace. She tapped her translator again despite the hum and determined he was ignoring her. As he neared the main house, she slowed.

The warrior had no intention of *avoiding* the people he meant to escape. She stopped in the doorway of the main house leading onto the crowded lawn, aghast. She rose on her tiptoes to follow him with her eyes but soon found she didn't need to. The raised tent where she had feasted earlier was still occupied by Romas's immediate family. The moment the prisoner crossed the third step, she saw him.

Disbelief made her look twice to ensure her eyes hadn't gone as crazy as her thoughts. The prisoner went straight to Romas's family, which meant she just made her mess bigger. He would tell Romas of her involvement in the plot to free an enemy and escape, and she would be locked in her bathroom for all of eternity. She felt faint and stepped back into the main house, near tears.

It wasn't fair! Not only had she been dragged to another planet by her best friend, but now she was about to be betrayed by a prisoner she tried to free. She pushed herself away from the doorframe and retreated to her room, only to find the prisoner's bracelet didn't work. She sat with her back to her door, defeated. She was meant to stay here, to marry one of Romas's brothers, and to be miserable the rest of her life. She blinked back tears, emotionally exhausted. Dwelling in her misery, she was surprised when his shadow fell across her.

"We go." The familiar voice made her frown.

"You've already ruined it!" she exclaimed. She looked up at the prisoner. "You told Romas I was trying to leave, and now he's going to—"

"I told him a member of his family freed me. He can do nothing. We go."

"He knows I helped you?" She rested her head against the door, not understanding.

"He knows a member of his family helped me," was the response. "He knows not *who*."

"But they know you're leaving. They won't let you, will they?"

"You freed me," he repeated. She rose, confused but hopeful once more.

"You'll still help me?"

He responded with a curt nod. She wiped her eyes. He was studying her closely, as if awaiting something.

"I'm ready," she said uncertainly. "Is something wrong?"

"No." Still he stared until her face grew warm again. A startled cry drew her attention, and she leaned to see past him.

Evelyn.

She paled. Evelyn stared at the prisoner, then at her, then back. Her gaze settled on Kiera, a wounded look of betrayal there. Kiera was about to grovel to her friend and apologize when the prisoner snatched her, wrapped a thick arm around her neck, and dragged her against his body. Surprised, she froze when she felt the knife against her cheek.

"Do not call out for your man, woman," the prisoner growled at Evelyn.

Evelyn's eyes widened, and she looked at Kiera again, this time in anger and concern. Kiera squirmed. The prisoner gripped her more tightly, and she stilled.

Evelyn took two steps back and let loose a bellowing, "ROMAS!" She turned and ran down the hall.

"What are you doing?" Kiera asked, and tried to pull away.

"Quiet, woman, if you want to leave."

"As long as you hold to your end of the bargain," she hissed.

"And you."

"I will."

He released her and snatched her arm, starting down the hall. They made it several doors before three of Romas's clan charged around the corner of a nearby intersection. The prisoner tucked her behind him with one hand and met the first attacker's blow, blocked it, and flung him down the hall.

Astonished, she watched the rapid battle. She'd never seen men that big move so quickly, even when watching professional wrestling. The prisoner disabled without killing and without using his knife, which was tucked in his boot. His punch had the impact of a bag of bricks, his kick of a sledgehammer. The giants battled, and she couldn't help feeling awed by the prisoner's abilities as he met the blows of all three foes and remained standing. He dispatched the last challenger and strode toward her, eyes roving for more opponents. Unsettled by the display of power, she started to skirt away. He snagged her arm and pulled her down the hall.

They broke free of the house into the dark night on a side of the house far from the light and merriment of the party. The prisoner ducked down just outside the doorway, dragging her with him. She caught herself with her hands before she did a face-plant on the ground and tried to catch her breath. The prisoner squatted below a window and appeared to be listening for signs of pursuit. She rested on her knees, looking around.

The night was clear and cool, the sky a beautiful pageant of dark blue silk and brilliant stars, of streaking meteors and two glowing orbs. Her attention was caught on the falling stars of the meteor shower. She'd never seen one on earth. Imagine coming so far to see something she might've seen there!

A bug crawled across her leg, and she swiped it away. It persisted, and she looked down, jumping to see one of several curious cats nudging her leg. She leapt up, knocking the prisoner off balance in her haste to escape.

"Omigod those things are—"

The prisoner righted himself, then grabbed her and dragged her down to her knees once more. He wrapped a thick arm around her and pulled her against him until her back was pressed against his chest. She squirmed, unwilling to be defenseless with the tarantulas so close and uneasy with the warm energy flowing again between them.

"Woman," the prisoner growled.

Her movement upset his balance again, and he shifted twice before finally allowing his knees to drop beside hers. His chin rested at her temple. He nudged her head aside, out of his view. Forced to be still, she glanced down. His thighs rested against hers and extended well beyond hers. They were twice as thick. She looked truly tiny compared to him.

His body was warm against hers, his breathing and heartbeat

deep and slow. His thick arms were around her, his muscular chest at her back. He was calm and quiet, waiting.

It had been a very, very long time since any man had held her. His incredible strength, heat, and scent calmed her fear as much as they excited the woman within her. On her walks at Lover's Lane near Evelyn's row house, she'd often seen couples entranced by the rhythmic movement of waves stand at a railing, the man's arms wrapped around the woman in front of him, his chin on her head. They had looked so peaceful, so comfortable, and she never understood the appeal until this moment.

She forgot about the tarantula-cats and watched the meteor shower again, protected from the chill of evening by his body heat and the odd energy running between them. The moment dragged out for quite a few minutes, and still no one gave chase. His grip loosened, but she made no attempt to move. They waited a short time longer before the prisoner shifted to rise.

Kiera roused herself, climbed to her feet, and stretched before the prisoner snagged her arm once more and began the quick pace again. Irritated at the sudden break of warmth and intimacy, she sighed as she trotted to keep up.

They didn't go far, and she was surprised to see the grassy slopes end at an abrupt cliff. The dual moons seemed to hover somewhere in the middle of the air of a massive chasm, just like the dozen or so hulking spaceships, whose dark grey skins reflected like skins of massive grey whales in the moonlight. Many were distant enough to be the size of her fist, while those closer were the size of football stadiums.

She neared the edge and started to panic again. How did she hire a ship?

Her ill-planned idea was unraveling again, this time at a much more alarming pace. How did she find the one to take her home without telling Romas? There *must* be a way! She blinked and turned, remembering the prisoner. He stood a short distance from her, watching her intently.

"Thank you," she told him uncertainly. "You've fulfilled your end of the bargain. I've reached the ships."

If a warrior could be amused, he was. The emotion was fleeting, more in a subtle shift of his eyebrows than in a smile or sudden change. He waited.

"You can go," she said.

A small, round object twice the size of a dinner plate appeared from the chasm and skimmed over several feet of grass to reach them. She stepped back. It settled into the grass near the prisoner's feet. He motioned her to it.

She shook her head, not understanding what it was. The prisoner took her arm and pulled her forward.

"Noooo," she said, and tugged away. "Our bargain is over. You're free. I'm going my own way; you go yours."

He looked at her hard, then slung her over his shoulder in one smooth movement. She was about to object when the disc beneath his feet levitated and launched them into the air. Kiera grabbed the prisoner's tunic, staring in horror as the ground dropped from beneath them. She squeezed her eyes closed, praying.

They hovered through the air, at last reaching one of the ships, where a doorway yawned open to reveal the damp yellow light and grey corridors beyond. The prisoner stepped into it, the disc soaring away once more. She sucked in deep breaths, on the verge of hysterics after the freaky trip from cliff to spaceship. Her head spun from the journey.

When he did not immediately set her down, she began to wiggle. The prisoner's arm was locked around her. He paid no attention and continued to stride down the corridor.

He was kidnapping her, taking her far away to a place Evelyn would never find her. She'd never see home or Evelyn or earth again! Even *Romas*! She would gladly put up with the man if he rescued her!

Where would the prisoner take her? He could be from some other planet, one far enough away that Romas would never find her!

A door opened, and the prisoner entered, setting her down. Her head spun as her blood dropped from her head to her body, and she sat heavily.

"Wait!" she shouted at him as his blurry form moved away. "Where are you taking me? We had a deal!"

He ignored her. The door closed behind him. Kiera made out a bed beneath her and gripped her head with a grimace. She was a fool, the greatest of them all!

With a groan, she dropped back onto the bed, her head pounding. She was doomed. He would take her to a planet with larger tarantula-cats, where she would be trapped in some room like this for the rest of her miserable life! All because she was too stubborn to ask Evelyn to leave. No ... all because Evelyn fell in love with an alien ... no, all because Romas *was* an alien!

A'RAN, *dhjan* of Anshan, strode from the room in which he'd left her into the secondary control deck, a small room lit up with scenes of space, the planet, their destination, and the internal corridors of the craft. Ne'Rin stood staring at one screen with interest. Wondering how much he should say, A'Ran's gaze went to another screen first, the one listing the details of their unsuccessful peace mission. He'd known it would fail, but the elders of the Planetary Council had called in their last favor. He was relieved it was over with in so short a time; he had more battles to plan and more potential allies to recruit, now that the Council was done with its stranglehold on him. He owed them nothing after his mission, which cleared a path for him to do what he must to regain his throne. He'd contact Jetr when they were clear of Qatwal to let him know everything had gone as he predicted.

Except he hadn't planned on stoking the fire with Kisolm for what would certainly end in another war. He never did anything without planning it carefully ahead of time, and he'd never broken his honor code, even with Qatwalis.

"What is this?" Ne'Rin asked.

His gaze slid to the screen Ne'Rin faced. The woman—his woman—was curled on her bed, her back to him.

This wasn't planned, and her appearance was almost too late. His people were decimated, his planet virtually dead. But she was here, and she was his.

His gaze lingered on her, satisfied after years of rejecting life-mates chosen by his advisors and the Council, and even Ne'Rin's sister. He'd spent ten sun-cycles looking for her. For fifteen sun-cycles, Anshan women had borne no male children, and drought and dwindling supplies of the ore that made his *dhjan* wealthy and respected had driven his planet into abject poverty. Now he had the key: his lifemate.

He knew her on sight, felt the connection pierce his tanned hide and rattle his bones. It was as his father had told him, as if the suns burned a hole straight through his head and the ground beneath him shook. While he never believed he'd overlooked her among the throngs of women he'd met, he had heard even his sisters speak of the missing lifemate and how he had refused every woman on the planet and perhaps somehow overlooked her. Now he knew he was right.

A potential war with Qatwal wasn't planned, but he'd seal the fate of his people if he walked away from her. She was worth his honor and his life.

His lifemate was tiny, standing a full head shorter than the average woman and a head and shoulders shorter than him. She was delicate, with long hair as dark as the night sky and large eyes that turned from blue to green to grey. Her shape was firm but lush and had fit in his arms with her shoulders settling between his when he'd held her outside of the house.

She reminded him of the little dolls his youngest sister had rejected several sun-cycles before. Her skin was golden from the sun, which brought out the enigmatic eyes, and made them glow with the otherworldly beauty displayed by her and the one called Evelyn.

Ne'Rin turned to him, and he realized he hadn't answered his advisor's question.

"That is *nishani*."

"I thought so," Ne'Rin said. "She's different, exquisite. She can't be from our worlds."

A'Ran gazed at her, assessing the battle before him. His blatant disregard for the laws regarding his imprisonment and assumed kidnapping of a *dhjan* guest would see him ordered before the Council, if not hurl him into a war he could ill afford. But he'd won her as Kisolm's younger brother, Romas, had decreed, which *should* alleviate any accusations brought on by their clan, if Kisolm's father talked some sense into the arrogant crown prince.

She agreed to give up her armband, the bond to her sister's family. Romas had made no other conditions, for there were none to be made. Once she gave up her bond and accepted another, she belonged to him. It was no longer kidnapping. Whether or not she wished to accompany him was not his concern. The connection alone might prevent a full-scale war. The two *dhjan* were now bound.

And yet he knew war was not so simple between two clans with a history of blood feud as theirs had. He wouldn't await word from the Council but would warn his counselors and advisors to avoid Kisolm's planet.

The second battle he would leave to his sisters: teaching his lifemate how to behave according to *dhjan* standards. He hadn't met a woman quite as rough around the edges as his was. Even his youngest sister was composed and respectful of her place and a warrior's needs and expectations. His lifemate's expressive eyes prevented her from appearing composed; she had looked either frightened or confused during their short interaction.

From what he'd gleaned from Kisolm and others during his imprisonment, she was new to the planet and their customs. He didn't doubt that once she reached her new home and his sisters reminded her how to act, she would be both exquisite and tame. Perhaps the brief stay on the craft would help her adjust. She'd need more help when she realized the rightful *dhjan* of Anshan and his family were in near-poverty and living in exile. She'd not mated as highly as she might have if she remained with Evelyn and mated with Kisolm, the next ruler of Qatwal. Having been raised as rivals in all areas, A'Ran took a very unwarrior-like satisfaction out of having bested Kisolm finally.

"How do the battle plans come?" he asked without removing his eyes from his lifemate.

"Not well."

He expected the news and turned away from the wall displaying his woman to the wall displaying his battle plans. Ne'Rin didn't have the mind for battle planning, another reason A'Ran hesitated to assume the worst about him. Ne'Rin was the kind of man who took orders, not the kind of man who valued strategy. Someone else would have to do the thinking for him if he were to execute any kind of betrayal.

A'Ran studied Ne'Rin, aware he had more than the potential war with Qatwal to contend with.

FIVE

A'RAN WATCHED her off and on during the several days she spent alone. She was very unlike the women of his society. Where Anshan —and even Qatwal—women would wait for their men to direct them, his woman had disassembled everything in the room she could. The access pad was useless, the clothing unit jammed, the communication monitor too covered with handprints from her searching to work right. Her translator had been lost during restless sleep then crushed in her pacing, and the cell was littered with several dozen pieces of colorful clothing.

It took him a full day to realize she didn't know how to exit her room, that her intent at disassembling the access pad had been to make it work for her. The Anshan ships didn't work like the Qatwali ships did; her access needed to be programmed into the computer, but she'd broken the pad before Ne'Rin could do it. Once she disabled her translator, he couldn't communicate with her. Her tampering successfully sealed her in the room.

Which would've been fine, for an Anshan woman, but appeared to be nothing short of torture to her. She was impatient, anxious, emotional ... nothing like the women he knew, which both interested him and warned him. He waited two more days to see if she would settle. She grew worse. It might take all three sisters to rein her in, if even their hands were firm enough.

He liked watching her despite her odd actions. The craft's computer assured him her health was good; she was just distressed. He'd left her door broken and postponed leaving the ship until she calmed. But as the days continued, he realized that wouldn't happen. On the third day, he decided to land.

A'Ran sent for his sisters to meet them outside the small dwelling they had taken refuge in several years ago. When Ne'Rin signaled all was ready, he strode from the deck into the corridor and straight to her cell. The door jammed at his first attempt to open it. He waited for Ne'Rin to fix it and tried again.

It opened, and the exotic woman within turned to him, surprise on her face. He beckoned her forward and stepped back for her to move into the hall. His woman hurried forward to the hall but stopped in front of him, her intelligent eyes flashing with anger. Without a word, she slapped him.

Women never slapped warriors. In fact, *no one* slapped a warrior full grown, not even his father.

A'Ran stared at her hard, surprised. He conveyed his displeasure with his body rather than his voice. He tensed and straightened, then backed her into the wall. She didn't back down, a trait he was not certain he liked for his woman. She gazed up at him with angry eyes, and he stepped forward until her lush little body was pinned by his to the wall. He felt her racing heart and heard her breathing become uneven. His eyes scoured her face, lingered on the plump lips he had tasted, and glanced lower at the healthy bosom pressed to his chest.

Suns, but she was *perfect*.

Her face deepened to crimson, and her dilating eyes dropped to his lips before flying up again. She tore her gaze away and twisted her head, yielding yet defying him as well. She was tense and waiting while his eyes took in every detail of her face. She smelled of woman, a husky, sweet, faint scent.

He stepped away. She understood him and obviously felt the same energy he did when they touched. It was enough to satisfy him. Warriors were known for their patience and control, but he sensed this woman would test both. He nodded his head to the side in a silent order for her to proceed. She marched away from him. If he channeled that fire, he might find he liked her defiant passion.

A'Ran trailed several steps, watching the way her hips sashayed as she walked. Her walk was unguarded like her mannerisms, a sweet lack of refinement he wasn't sure he liked. Her pace slowed as she caught sight of Ne'Rin. He nodded to his advisor, who waved his wrist before the access pad.

The door cracked open, and his woman shielded her eyes against the sudden sunlight. It was midday. The brilliant suns were overhead, their heat heavy in the still day. He moved around her and stepped onto thick green grasses.

Two of his sisters were waiting, composed and serene in their dark clothing with hands clasped in front of them. The third, the youngest, hurried toward the door, translator in hand as he had ordered.

Both older sisters nodded in deference as he approached, and he glanced over them to assure himself of their health. There was a time before they were exiled where he would've been ashamed to see them in such plain clothing. He'd long since accepted that their health was far more important than where they lived or what they wore. The heavy, masculine features that made him fierce had rendered his sisters too heavy of face to be pretty. They were all unmated despite their *dhjan* blood. The eldest, D'Ryn, bowed and greeted him.

"May the sun shine long on you, brother."

"D'Ryn, Gage," he said in response. "You look well."

A commotion sounded behind him, and he turned. *Nishani* took the hands of his youngest sister, Talal, and began to speak, animated compared to the serene women of his world. For a long moment, he watched. She was meant to be his, this he didn't doubt, though he couldn't stop the trickle of unease that warned him she may not be able to adjust to their world as easily as he wished.

Her tones rose and fell, her hands and arms animated. She appeared to be telling a story, and not a very good one based on the angry shade to her features. His sister appeared calm but glanced at him several times. Something his woman said took her interest; her gaze grew sharper, and she moved closer to *nishani*. Curious, A'Ran neared, hanging back as his other two sisters approached.

His woman was speaking too quickly for the translator to keep up. Her varying tones would have thrown it off as well; it was programmed to the monotonous speech pattern of Anshan. He crossed his arms. *Nishani* fell silent and unsure at their approach, but was prodded by something soft his youngest sister said that threw her into another animated story.

Ne'Rin approached, his eye caught by Gage, who gave a bow of her head but whose face turned pink. A'Ran had long suspected the two favored each other, but neither had addressed him about it.

"You will hold a battle committee despite your mating?" Ne'Rin asked, joining him. A'Ran, assuming his sisters could handle the newest member of their family, turned and started toward the white dwelling before him.

"Yes. We must warn our battle commanders about the possibility of war with Qatwal. I will announce my lifemate at the committee. I believe the Council will be visiting us as well once they receive word of what I have done."

Ne'Rin nodded. A'Ran took in the home he had left several moon cycles before. It was nowhere near as large as their true home but was comfortable and well-maintained, an adequate place for him, his sisters, and now his lifemate. The women would remain until the war was over and he could take them to their rightful home.

That day was near. Now that he was no longer in the slavery of the Council, he would take the last few steps needed to rebuild his alliances and bring his might to full force. With his lifemate discovered, he had everything he needed to reclaim his throne.

"Brother!" The startled cry made him turn. His three sisters knelt over his lifemate's still form. He trotted to them, trailed by Ne'Rin.

"What happened?"

"Brother, she does not understand ..." Gage appeared confused. She drifted off, reddening. He knelt and brushed his woman's hair from her face. She was pale but breathing steadily, her enigmatic eyes closed.

"What was said?" he asked as he scooped her into his arms.

"A'Ran, she believes herself to be your prisoner," D'Ryn said. "She doesn't understand you are mated. When I explained, she became unwell."

"She speaks the truth," he replied as he strode into the house.

"You are not mated?"

"I am," he said.

"She doesn't know."

"No." He heard the troubled note in D'Ryn's voice but ignored it. Instead he strode through the bright hallways into the women's wing and into the first room. His sisters followed, D'Ryn relaying the information to her sisters. He set his lifemate on the bed and sat on the edge of the bed.

"Gage, water," he ordered.

"She's so little," Talal murmured.

"Brother, she is your intended? You felt the signs, as father said?" D'Ryn asked again. There was anxiety in her quiet voice.

"Yes," he said. D'Ryn sighed, and Talal whispered to the eldest sister. It was news they—and the rest of his people!—had been awaiting for many sun-cycles. He was relieved to give it at last.

"Where does she come from?" Talal asked. His youngest sister paused beside him, leaning against his thigh while she studied his lifemate with brown eyes a shade lighter than his.

"Far away, outside the Five Galaxies," he said.

"What is she called?" D'Ryn asked.

"Kiera," Talal responded. "Like one of Anshan's moons. It was a sign, brother."

Kiera. He hadn't asked or cared. He knew what she was, and he was content to call her *nishani*, the title given to a warrior's lifemate. Her eyelids began to flutter.

"Leave us," he directed his sisters.

They obeyed. His woman awoke but was instantly stricken with a look of bewilderment. She sat up. They gazed at each other, and he felt a familiar tremor. At last, she reached for his arm. He let her take it and saw her attention shift to the bracelet.

"You can take it back," she said, at once frustrated when the bracelet gave no sign of loosening. She held out her arm instead. "I didn't understand what it meant."

"You agreed," he reminded her.

"I did no such thing!"

"We made an agreement based on three conditions," he said.

"The first was this, which I didn't understand, the second ... you remember the second, and the third ..." She trailed off, pensive. "You didn't name a third."

"The third was for you to agree to be my lifemate."

"I don't remember that!" she exclaimed.

"You never asked for the third condition."

Realization crossed her features and with it another flash of anger.

"This won't hold up in—" Her last word didn't translate.

"*Nishani*, welcome to your new home," he said, and rose. "My sisters will instruct you in the behavior I expect of you."

And he left her sitting on the bed, aware of how much more work his lifemate would create for him.

THE BEHAVIOR *I expect of you.*

Refreshed the next morning, she still couldn't fathom the statement. Rather, she couldn't fathom how something so medieval could have been directed at *her*.

The behavior I expect of you.

It bounced around her head, first in disbelief, then in shock, and finally, in anger. As for the remainder of their conversation ...

It was unreal. It made no sense. Yes, he had named three conditions, and yes, she remembered agreeing after that fantastic kiss. But damned if she didn't recall the third condition. Had she been that smitten or so desperate to leave?

Other thoughts were skittering through her brain, those that reminded her she was no longer on her own territory and he hadn't told her something she hadn't heard before. Their last conversation sounded eerily like something Evelyn had tried to tell her.

You're a guest of Romas right now, but if he decides to put you on the market, so to speak, pretty much anyone can ... um ... claim you as a ... you know, a bride.

What else had Evelyn neglected to tell her? The idea of being stuck on some strange planet made her want to panic and run screaming for the first spaceship she found. She tried to push the thought away and distract herself by wandering the mansion. It wasn't anywhere near the size of Romas's, and the dwelling showed signs of wear and use. It was well-kept, if aging.

She wandered until she found an exit and stepped into a beautiful midmorning. A set of boy-warriors were practicing with grey swords in the grassy courtyard. They couldn't have been past thirteen but rivaled her in height. They appeared to be playing rather than training; there were five, two standing and mock battling while the three younger ones watched and cheered.

It was unfortunate the cheerful youths would turn into unsmiling, frozen warriors one day. She drew as near as she dared without disturbing them. They battled with great vigor and exaggeration to the cheering of the three younger boys until one turned and noticed her. All five rose and straightened, offering her deep bows. They straightened again and stared at her. She stared back.

"Are you enjoying the day?" she asked awkwardly.

"Yes, *nishani*," the eldest replied. The word did not translate at all.

"You don't have to stop," she said. "You were doing well." The boy seemed unsure how to respond and gazed at her, as did the others. "Or you can teach me a few things." His eyes widened, and the two smallest boys looked at each other.

"No, *nishani*," the eldest almost whispered.

"Why not?" she asked.

"*Nishani*, women do not fight," he answered. Three of the boys nodded vigorously in agreement.

"On my planet, women do fight," she said. There was no contradiction offered. If anything, she thought she was distressing the eldest boy.

"Please show me. You were doing so well," she said.

The boy blushed, appeared conflicted, and at last gave a stiff nod. The youngest skittered away in excitement, crowding each other and whispering a short distance away. The opponent of the eldest hesitated before handing her the weapon. It was light, a curved grey sword made of the same material as the beds and spaceships. Kiera hefted it and relaxed, cheered to be doing something other than thinking or pacing.

The youth showed her how to stand and hold the weapon while the eldest watched with a sharp eye. When set, the eldest demonstrated a simple strike and block, then corrected her form as she followed his example. After several attempts, the two older boys were satisfied and moved onto another strike and then another block.

She concentrated hard, intent on distracting herself as well as learning something new. She needed a workout; maybe she could learn to use a sword instead of kickboxing, which she'd been doing regularly for years. She stayed until she broke a healthy sweat. When the midmorning sun grew too hot, she lowered her weapon and handed it to the boy beside her.

"Thank you. You all are really good," she said. The boys all bowed and watched her walk back into the house, curious and excited. The exercise helped clear her head. She set about wandering the halls once more, pausing to look out of large windows onto expanses of grass.

"*Nishani!*" a female voice cried.

She turned. It was the first girl she met, the tall woman with a long face named Talal. Talal strode toward her, and Kiera waited.

"*Nishani*, we have—"

"My name is Kiera," she corrected.

"Yes, *nishani*. Kiera, we have—"

"Is there anywhere to get some water around here?"

"Yes, *nishani*." Talal motioned to a nearby door. Kiera waved her armband. A door to someone's private quarters slid open. She hesitated, but Talal entered and reappeared several moments later with a small bowl of water.

"We've searched for you throughout the house," she said as Kiera drank.

"I was out back," Kiera responded. At the blank look, she assumed the translator didn't pick up her slang and rephrased. "I was practicing swords with the boys in the yard."

"Practicing swords? *Nishani*, here women are forbidden to fight," Talal said with a shake of her head.

"I needed something to do," Kiera replied. "And where I'm from, women *do* fight."

"There are many things to do," Talal said with a nervous giggle. "My sisters and I are to show you your new home."

"And teach me how to behave?"

"Yes, *nishani*," Talal said. "My brother says your home is very different, that we need to teach you everything."

"Does he?" Kiera felt her cheeks grow red. "Your brother is ..."

Talal appeared apprehensive, and Kiera curbed her tongue.

"Maybe I will teach you how women behave where I'm from," Kiera said, and fell into step beside her.

"My brother doesn't believe your influence would complement us," Talal said.

"Maybe I ought to have a word with your brother," she grumbled, surprised the man could insult her without being present.

"It would not be wise. He wasn't pleased with you for missing his farewell this morn. Maybe when he returns, your behavior will please him."

Kiera didn't know where to start. There was too much wrong with the woman's words, but she dumped her confusion and wounded feelings to ask, "Where has he gone?"

"To the Council and to the Anshan battle commanders."

"Battle commanders?"

"How far is your home?" she asked, giving her a long look.

"Very, *very* far," Kiera responded.

"I will take you to Ne'Rin first. He may choose what to tell you about the war."

"Thank you."

At that moment, it was the only safe thing for her to say. The woman beside her was far too subservient for her comfort; if their brother expected her behavior to conform, he was in for a surprise. Maybe when he realized that, he'd send her home. The chipper thought was fleeting. There was something about the warrior that warned her he didn't lose his battles.

Talal paused in an open doorway leading to a large, green field behind the dwelling occupied by hundreds, perhaps thousands, of warriors organized into sparring groups of four and five. Talal's gaze sought out Ne'Rin before she stepped out of the house. Kiera trailed. Lines had been drawn on the grass, large squares like those used for wrestling, with a circle in the center. Two men populated each circle, sparring with each other, while the other two or three watched. The battles were silent, the swords clashing without the clang of steel she expected to hear. At her entrance, those in the nearest circle with Ne'Rin ceased their activity and bowed, then stood in a line and waited.

She tried hard not to stare at the men. They were magnificent, wearing nothing but snug, dark pants. Their upper bodies were tanned from exposure to the sun, their dark hair and eyes pinned on her. It was not the polite, curious glances of Romas's people but direct looks that made her skin crawl with awareness.

Talal appeared oblivious and approached Ne'Rin, whose body glowed with sweat. He'd been fighting, but tucked the sword behind his body, as if to protect Talal from it. She spoke to him for several moments before his eyes rose and lingered on Kiera. A brisk nod, and Talal stepped away, waiting. Ne'Rin returned his sword to a rack containing half a dozen similar swords in plain grey and approached Kiera.

Talal followed. Kiera stood aside, not as much out of deference but out of sudden realization that if she didn't, the man was likely to run her over. She didn't know why, but Ne'Rin hadn't seemed to like her. A'Ran's behavior was just as distant, but there was something bordering on resentment in the way Ne'Rin looked at her that made her uncomfortable.

They walked a short distance to an open atrium in the center of the house, complete with a small oasis rising up from white stone and curved benches. Trickling water circled the oasis, its source a small spring in the center. Talal handed a translator to Ne'Rin, who accepted it and motioned for them to sit. Kiera sat beside Talal.

"*Nishani*, your lifemate was called away suddenly. Talal says you have no knowledge of our war."

She nodded.

"We have been in war for fifteen sun-cycles, since the death of the previous *dhjan* of Anshan. He was overthrown and killed when A'Ran was off-planet. On his death, one of his advisors, who betrayed him and allied with the Yirkin invaders, seized the title of *dhjan*. He struck when *dhjan* A'Ran was away at battle along with most of the Anshan men, thus leaving the throne of Anshan unguarded. *Dhjan* A'Ran's family was forced to flee with his few trusted advisors. We have hidden on this moon in an unoccupied galaxy since."

"How is *dhjan* A'Ran going to retake his throne?" she asked, surprised at the information.

"Until now, the Council has obstructed his efforts, but that is no longer true. He has gone to them with word of his breaking allegiance to pursue his title without their mediation or interference."

It then dawned that the tale's hero was one of the men she was angry at: the man who claimed to be her *lifemate*.

"So ..." She trailed off, not sure where to start. Images from their first touch replayed themselves in her thoughts.

"Our people have suffered for fifteen sun-cycles," Talal added. "The mines have gone empty, and the women barren since the rightful *dhjan* bloodline has been cast from the land."

"You're cursed," Kiera said with a frown, thoughts on the dead planet from her vision.

"Is it not so in your home? A *dhjan* is bound to his planet. Should his blood and those who carry it be exiled, the planet dies."

"My world is nothing like that," she assured them. "How long do wars last here?"

"As long as they must, *nishani*," Ne'Rin said almost gently. She eyed him, not sure his patronizing tone wasn't meant to rile her. She took the high road and ignored him.

"The men here are training for battle?" she asked.

"When *dhjan* A'Ran calls for battles, we leave the moon and go to Anshan, where we have a small base."

"Does *dhjan* A'Ran fight?"

"My brother is the best warrior," Talal said proudly.

"*Dhjan* A'Ran endangers himself," Ne'Rin countered. He looked at the younger woman hard, and Talal apologized quietly. Uncomfortable, Kiera cleared her throat.

"Maybe you can convince him not to fight, and then convince him he's made a poor choice of a mate," she said. "Or maybe I can learn to fight and go with him, if there's no time limit to the war."

Talal gasped, and Ne'Rin studied her. When neither responded, she returned to a safe subject.

"What does Anshan mine?"

Ne'Rin's response was garbled.

"That didn't translate," she said, pointing to her translator.

"This material." Ne'Rin pulled a dark grey knife from his boot. "It is rare and native to Anshan. Every ship and weapon in the Five Galaxies is made from it."

"Wow. We just stay here until the war is over?" she asked.

A brisk nod.

"Do you have sketch pads here? Or pens?"

Both gave her blank looks, and she sighed, wondering how she'd be an artist in a world without even pencils.

"Do women have a part in the war effort?" she asked.

"To honor their men," Ne'Rin replied.

"That's what I thought."

"We had hoped Ne'Rin's sister would be made *nishani*," Talal said. "But my brother did not choose her."

"He did not feel the signs," Ne'Rin said with another sharp look. Kiera sensed his anger on the topic and said nothing. "When the suns fall into night, I'll speak to *dhjan* A'Ran over the communicator. You may come."

She hesitated. She had nothing to say to the man, unless it was to condemn him for kidnapping her, wedding her against her will, and dropping her like a sack of potatoes for his sisters to retrain.

"No, thank you," she decided.

"We expect visitors to arrive soon. As the *nishani*, your duty is to welcome them on behalf of the *dhjan*," Ne'Rin said with a glance at Talal. "However, I do not feel you are prepared for such a duty. You may accompany me, without your translator, so you do not embarrass the *dhjan* by speaking."

Offended once again, she said nothing as he rose and returned the translator to Talal. He walked down the hall from whence they'd come.

"He's angry about his sister," Talal said. "He feels it was an affront to him because the betrayer who murdered our father came from his family. He is condemned by many people and hoped his sister would restore his family's honor."

"He seems like a dangerous man," Kiera murmured.

"He is, but he's loyal. Just very angry."

"I think I need to rest," Kiera said, beginning to like A'Ran's trusted commander even less. "Can you take me back to my room?"

"*Nishani*, you have duties you must learn before my brother returns," Talal said timidly.

"Does he beat women?"

"No, *nishani*."

"Then take me to my room."

Talal obeyed. Kiera was hungry and overwhelmed once again. All she wanted was the coziness of her studio, where she could block out everything and paint. Her room on this planet contained none of her comforts. She didn't stay long in the boring room. Her mind was too busy, and she felt as if she hovered on the verge of a mental breakdown. Instead, she forced herself to leave and find something to do.

After exploring the halls and grounds for an hour or two, she returned to the main atrium, where she heard one of the sisters call her name.

"*Nishani*."

She turned to face Talal.

"*Nishani*, if you are rested, we must start your behavior training."

Kiera frowned and rose, walking away.

"*Nishani*, please! My brother requests it!"

"No!" she said over her shoulder. "That's so ridiculous! I'm not going to anything of the sort, and if you think you'll make me ..." She stopped, unable to help the tears welling in her eyes. Talal gasped, as if she'd never seen anyone cry, and took a step back.

"Forgive me, *nishani*. Another day," Talal said. "Are you well?"

"Fine. But I'm not going to training," Kiera answered. Talal gave one of her small bows and stayed where she was as Kiera walked away again.

The scene would repeat itself several days in a row, whenever one of the sisters tracked her down. They were quick to backtrack when they saw she was upset, but their persistence annoyed her. She could think of only one thing that would turn her into one of the cookie-cutter women of this world, and she refused to be brainwashed. Kiera liked her mind the way it was, liked roaming through the hallways and spending the mornings in training with the little boys out back.

It was toward the end of her first week in the sprawling mansion that was her new home that she wandered down a hall previously unexplored. She opened the only door in the dead-end hallway with a wave of her armband.

The conference room behind it was large and open, its ceiling cathedral and one wall twice the height of the others. Unlike the cheerful white walls of the house, the tall wall was the unwelcome shade of dark grey that she'd begun to despise after days in the spaceships surrounded by it. There were rows of grey chairs and several white benches in the rear, a handful of tables next to yawning windows, and a wall of what looked like constellation maps.

From the layout, she expected it was A'Ran's conference room for meeting with his advisors. She wandered through the room, trailing her fingers across the tables. A round table in the center had an access pad attached to the top, so she passed her armband over it.

To her surprise, what appeared to be a video game popped into 3D life in the center of the table. The table top lit up with a blank grey screen and four dozen multi-hued buttons, with geometric symbols she assumed was writing. The video game showed two holograms at once, a space battle and a land battle.

Excited to see that even this world had video games, she sat in the chair behind the buttons and screen, studying all three in an attempt to figure out how the game worked. The tiny specs indicating crafts or personnel in the 3D image moved and changed; the image itself spun slowly, as if to present her with all sides of the battle at once.

Until that moment, she hadn't realized how much she missed passing away her nights playing her games! She sat and began playing with the buttons to see how they affected the holograms. As the afternoon wore on, she puzzled through what buttons controlled what, which were oriented toward the space battle and which toward the ground. The displays on the table ran through dozens of scenarios based on what she told it, most of them disastrous as she learned what the buttons did. The game consisted almost entirely of strategy, and it was dark outside before she realized how long she'd been at it.

Mentally exhausted from the intricate game, she rose to return to her room for bed. The next morning, she went to the game room after her sparring session and sat the entire day, learning more and more about the game and experimenting with how the symbols on the keyboard interacted with the images before her. Certain symbols pulled up certain features of the ships or angles of battle, similar to how picture-symbols in her video games on earth brought up different functions, allowing her to maneuver characters in the game or review the armament and skills of her opponents. The game room was the only place the sisters didn't bug her, and for the first time since being kidnapped by Evelyn and A'Ran, she found herself having fun.

She spent the next day in the game room, and the next. Two days turned into a week. Ne'Rin only came for her once during the third day, to bring her to stand by him while he received visitors. He removed her translator from her ear as promised after a stern warning about not speaking to anyone.

She liked him even less after that occurrence and chose to hide in the conference room every day after that, unwilling to deal with him again.

SIX

"YOU ENDANGER YOURSELF, *DHJAN* A'RAN."

A'Ran tested his injured shoulder. It would heal once he reached the main craft with the help of the medical unit but was useless in the meantime.

"A leader is a warrior first," he replied. "We have taken the land advantage, which is all that matters."

He stood in the confined main deck of the transport craft after his own craft had been disabled in an ambush. He preferred land wars to the space wars and had been returning to the main craft when the ambush occurred. He sat in the only seat in the tiny craft, studying Ne'Rin, who transmitted from A'Ran's battle command center on the moon that was his interim home. He'd chosen to leave Ne'Rin on the moon this trip. If what Jetr suspected were true, Ne'Rin would do less damage if he didn't know what A'Ran did while away.

"The Council contacted me," A'Ran said.

"They weren't pleased with your message about Qatwal," Ne'Rin assessed.

"They have no means to control me, which makes them less lazy than they have been for a millennium."

"How have they decided to react to your freedom?"

"How do you think? By threatening me, by condemning me, and finally, by seeking a discreet audience with me." A'Ran let a rare, mirthless smile cross his features.

"Their support can be won," Ne'Rin said in satisfaction.

"We will meet them soon at our temporary home. I have warned them I no longer play their games."

"They may find a way to temper Anshan's defiance."

"For their support against our enemy? I will owe them my life," A'Ran said.

"We may not need the Council's support if you maintain as you have," Ne'Rin replied. "They need our ore more than we need them. We can risk their anger. Do you need me to write any new battle plans?"

A'Ran was silent, studying Ne'Rin. For over a week, he'd hoped his instincts to be wrong. He'd hoped Ne'Rin to be the one sending him daily updates to the battle strategies and plans. His trusted advisor had never done so before, but A'Ran hadn't thought any member of his household capable of the complexities of battle planning. In the past three days, he hadn't made a single change before releasing the plans to his battle commanders.

Somehow, he had known the plans weren't Ne'Rin's. They were too ... different, too unlike the tactics and war planning taught by Anshan or anyone in the Five Galaxies. Over a period of a week, the tactics had gone from infantile to novice to advanced, as if someone were learning the intricacies of battle planning. Some plans he couldn't use for lack of manpower, timing constraints, or other battle-related reasons, but some were brilliant. Given his experience and lauding as one of the most capable strategic battle planners in the Five Galaxies—the only reason he hadn't been driven out by the Yirkin despite his tiny army—he found himself learning a tidbit here and there. And he was impressed. He wondered if all women from his lifemate's planet had such a skill.

"No," he said at last. "You've not mentioned *nishani*."

"She is well," Ne'Rin said with shortness. A'Ran waited. If that were the best Ne'Rin could say of the difficult woman ...

She should have settled by this point, adopted her role and been properly behaved. She apparently wasn't, and it made him uneasy. He didn't need his people to see someone quite so ... unusual. Their confidence in him would fall further.

"She's been ... training with the boys," Ne'Rin said at the long silence.

"Training?" he echoed.

"Swords."

"Women are forbidden to fight." Even as he said it, he knew he was contradicting himself. He hadn't stopped her yet from creating battle plans. Swords, however, were different. The chance for physical harm was too great.

"Your sisters do not possess the temperament needed to deal with her," Ne'Rin said frankly.

A'Ran listened. He intended for the problem to right itself in his absence, once she adjusted. If his sisters could not handle *nishani*, he must.

"You have direction?" Ne'Rin asked.

"I will handle her upon my return," he said.

"Yes, *dhjan*. When will you return to meet the Council here?"

"In two days' time. I have matters to settle first."

"We will make preparations," Ne'Rin said.

A'Ran reached forward to sever the connection. Ne'Rin's face disappeared from the screen. He relaxed and tested the muscles of his arm again, dissatisfied with being injured.

Nishani. Kiera. He could think of one solution to his problem, and his jaw clenched. He altered the course of his tiny craft for Qatwal.

He traveled for a day and slid beneath the radars of Qatwal easily, having stolen the codes needed to jam their tracking systems during one of his scuffles with Kisolm. He landed outside the main city, in the center of which sat the royal family's residence. Waiting until nightfall, he changed into clothing more suited for the Qatwali society and covered his face with a hood to creep into the city.

EVELYN SAT at the window seat, gazing at the dark sky as she had every night since Kiera disappeared. One hand rested on her expanding stomach. She tugged gently on the moon dangling from the necklace Kiera gave her for her wedding. She relaxed after a nice, long soak in the bathtub, her thoughts wandering among the stars.

Suns, she corrected herself with a small smile. They didn't call the distant suns stars in Qatwal. One of those distant suns was hers, and maybe, one of those distant suns might be Kiera's.

Evelyn's smile faded. She had already declared her intention of naming the babe Kiera whether it was a boy or girl. Her days were long but peaceful, wrought with duty and rest. It was a good, perfect little life, so much more than she ever expected, with the exception that her best friend in the universe—Kiera—might as well have been dead to her as far as Romas and his clan were concerned.

Evelyn had little regret for her actions in life, even those she probably should have. Bringing Kiera here was her one mistake. Even after a month she couldn't go a night without thinking of her friend. She sighed, ready for bed, and twisted to swing her legs from the bench. A shape in the corner drew her attention, and she gasped.

The man was as huge as any warrior but not fair like Romas's clan members. He was tall and fierce, standing so still she thought herself dreaming up a hero worthy of a nightmare. Dressed in dark clothes with dark hair and olive skin with a dark stare, he was both riveting and frightening.

"You!" she exclaimed as she recognized him.

He strode forward, and she moved to place a table between them. She interacted daily with the warrior members of her husband's family, but she'd never seen one quite like this, with soulful, ancient intelligence in his black gaze and a predatory walk. Her first thought was that he had kidnapped Kiera and was now returning to take her.

"What are you doing here?" she demanded, reaching for the communications access pad on the table.

"No." His single word was sharp enough to make her jerk. Her hand wavered. He stopped at the opposite side of the table, within reach if he chose, which she suspected he would if she so much as flinched toward the access pad. Her hand dropped to her side, fingernails digging into the meat of her palms.

"What have you done with Kiera?"

The intruder remained silent for a moment then said slowly, "Your sister is well."

The simple assertion was a waterfall after a month without a drop of information about her. Evelyn searched his face. "Oh, God ! You've seen her! If you've hurt her, you sick son—"

"She is well," he repeated. "*Nishani* is well."

"*Nishani?*" The word made her do a double-take. "*Nishani?*" Kiera would never agree to marry someone in so short of a time, but to agree in any amount of time to a man as lethal in appearance as this? "You haven't hurt her?" she pressed. "Where is she? Is she here? What have you done with her? Why did—"

He held up a hand to silence her, and she waited, circling the table to face him.

"Where is my sister?"

"Are all women of your world unusual?" he asked with impatience.

"We are not unusual on our world," she retorted. "Where is she?"

"She is safe and well."

"Why are you here, then, if not to tell me something's wrong?" she asked, perplexed.

"*Nishani* is unusual."

"You come to tell me she is unusual?" She shook her head. "I don't understand. I know she is unusual. She's a brilliant artist, independent, a complete sweetheart, a little too emotional, but she's an artist ... I don't understand."

Evelyn gazed at him, waiting for more. His jaw clenched. By the look of this man, Kiera hadn't wed him by choice. Romas had decreed that the man Kiera chose would have to have her agreement to be mated. Evelyn just didn't see it happening. Kiera could be the most stubborn and frustrating woman Evelyn had ever met, and she'd sworn off any man, let alone an alien. She'd never fit into Romas's society. Realization played across her mind, echoed in a puzzled smile dancing across her face.

"You can't figure her out," she said. "That's it, isn't it?" And she laughed. Kiera was well indeed if she were able to send a man like this to Evelyn's door looking for advice. Kiera's mate hadn't counted on an obstinate bride.

The man before her crossed his arms, not amused.

Hormones and emotions kicked in at the same time, and Evelyn's laughter turned to weeping. She sat on the table and buried her face in her hands, grateful and relieved to be reconnected with Kiera, even if indirectly. She cried until she could control herself, wiped her face, and drew several shuddering breaths.

"My ... my sister is sweet but stubborn," she managed. "I don't have an easy answer to your problem, if that's what you want. Is she speaking to you?"

She imagined the conversation was nothing short of torture for a warrior. She knew without a doubt that Romas's arrogance would never allow him to admit his inability to deal with her to anyone. That Kiera's warrior was at least willing to do something so painful gave her some hope for her friend.

"I have not seen her in a few days," he replied after a pause.

"So you dumped her off and left," Evelyn summarized, and wiped her face again. "Kiera will never be the woman you warriors want. Get used to that now. I'm sure a woman with intelligence will shock you."

"I know of her intellect," he said. "She's bested my best battle planners with her mind. But she is a poor *nishani*."

"She is a perfect *nishani*," she returned. "Brilliant and beautiful? Can you find fault with that?"

"Her behavior."

"You've not spent even a moment with her, and you complain of her behavior?" Evelyn shook her head and rose. She crossed to the boxes she had stacked in the corner and covered with a square of cloth. Romas had discarded most of Kiera's things after her disappearance, but Evelyn managed to salvage two boxes and keep them hidden. She dug through one and withdrew a thick pad of paper and pack of pencils.

"If you take the time to know her, you won't find fault in her behavior," she said to him, and held out the items in her hand. "Give these to her."

He took them, eyeing them as if they'd bite him.

"And ... someday ..." She trailed off. Even if this man agreed to bring Kiera back for a visit, Romas and his clan would deny permission. "Tell her she'll be an aunt soon. When will you see her again?"

"Tomorrow."

"Good. Tell her I miss her, too."

He gave a curt nod. Her Kiera was well and raising hell. There was nothing else she could want. Evelyn knew she didn't deserve to feel at peace after the mess she dragged Kiera into, but she did feel it, and it made her genuinely content for the first time since she'd kidnapped her best friend.

KIERA TUGGED at the moon on her necklace as she walked down the hall toward the video game room. She'd dreamt of Evelyn last night and awoke missing her friend. And then both Gage and Talal had cornered her that morning with news that made her wish she was more like Evelyn. She wasn't good at handling drama; Evelyn had always been like a perfect older sister, capable of patience and listening. Kiera just freaked out with bad news. She wished hard she could talk to Evelyn as she had in her dream last night and ask her what to do.

Voices came from the conference room, whose door was open. She stopped a few feet from the entrance, debating whether she should just leave, until she heard A'Ran's name. She didn't recognize the first man's voice, but the second she did.

"A'Ran hasn't returned?"

"He took a detour and is on his return trip, Father," Ne'Rin said. "Have you been successful?"

"Somewhat. It's been hard to break, but I think I found the weak point," the first man replied. "It'll take me a few days to position myself to take advantage of it. It involves Qatwal. I won't say more, lest this communication is compromised. I'm having some problems with messages being intercepted after they leave the planet."

"I understand. Our other plan is coming along. I believe Gage is in love with me, a simple emotion for a woman," Ne'Rin said. "And she's with child, Father."

There was a short silence. Kiera crept closer.

"So he did find the correct *nishani*, if an Anshan woman is able to bear a child again," the first man said quietly. "We'd all begun to doubt him. I had hoped he'd choose your sister."

"His chosen is the *nishani*, but your doubt may be well-placed. She is not from here, doesn't understand her role. She cannot do what the *nishani* must to help Anshan, and once our people see her, they'll lose their faith in him. My sister would've been a much wiser choice, and far more beautiful."

Kiera frowned, offended Ne'Rin thought so little of her, but not surprised. At least he was ragging on her to his family and not complete strangers. She could almost forgive him expressing his blunt opinion to his father.

"If I fail, mating into his family is the next logical step," the first man said. "And it sounds like you have this taken care of."

"Yes, Father, I do."

"*Nishani!*" Talal's voice jarred her. Kiera spun and darted down the hall, snatching Talal's arm and pulling her around the corner before Ne'Rin saw them.

"You picked a bad time!" Kiera whispered, trotting down the hall.

"I only meant to tell you—"

"Do you know when A'Ran normally calls?" she asked.

"Soon, *nishani*. Do you wish to talk to him?" Talal brightened. "You should, *nishani*! It will shock and honor him."

"Shock and honor?" Kiera repeated. "Those don't sound like good things. Yes, I do."

"You should wear his most preferred color, yellow," Talal advised.

"That sounds nice," Kiera said, distracted. She heard footsteps from the direction of the conference room and offered a smile as Ne'Rin rounded the corner. He eyed them.

"Ne'Rin, my sister Gage is looking for you."

"Take me to her."

Talal struck off without hesitation. Ne'Rin lingered, his hard gaze on Kiera. Kiera bowed her head as she'd seen the sisters do, trying hard not to look guilty like she'd overheard his conversation. He left at last, and she waited for him to disappear from sight before jogging to the conference room. She'd learned how to lock and unlock the doors and entered the conference room, locking it.

She debated what to do about the conversation she overheard. She didn't understand the rules of this world well enough to know if she were jumping the gun, but what she heard made her very uncomfortable.

Maybe it was Gage's involvement. The women of A'Ran's family were sheltered. They couldn't recognize a predator if it sat at their feet, and she was surprised to find her senses much more honed to such a ploy despite their social statuses rivaling those of royalty's on earth. They should have been taught better, she mused with a frown.

She went to the battle game to play until A'Ran called,

wondering what he'd say when she told him her news about his sisters and wondering just how safe it would be to talk about Ne'Rin's conversation with his father. His father hadn't wanted to talk over the viewer; she doubted she should either.

Less than an hour after she'd started playing the game, the communicator lit up and beeped. Excited and nervous, Kiera crossed to it and waved her armband over the access pad. She straightened her hair and took a deep breath.

IT WASN'T Ne'Rin that greeted him for his daily briefing but the woman herself. She was dressed in faded teal that drew out her other-worldly eyes. She perched on the edge of one table, fidgeting hands in her lap and bright features alert as she focused on some point on the screen. A'Ran studied her for a long moment before turning on the reciprocal viewer, curious yet wary as to what his *nishani* had to say in place of Ne'Rin.

"*Nishani*," he greeted her.

"Hello, A'Ran." Her voice was soft and as feminine as her shape. Her pronunciation of his name was pleasantly accented. "How are you?"

"Well, as you see."

"Ne'Rin said you were hurt."

"The medical unit has healed me." He leaned forward, curiosity growing. That she took enough interest in him to ask after his injury pleased him. "Where is Ne'Rin this day?"

"Indisposed." A flicker of amusement crossed her face.

"My most trusted advisor chose not to attend his mandated meeting?" A'Ran raised an eyebrow.

"It wasn't a choice," she assured him. "I wanted to speak to you, but I didn't want him around. I locked him out."

The blatant defiance was so sweetly uttered, he didn't know how to respond.

"He won't even let me wear my translator when we have visitors," she complained.

A'Ran knew he should chide her as he would his sisters and remind her of her place, but the words died before reaching his lips. His conversation with Evelyn lingered in his thoughts. Having spent most of his years in battle, he understood when a traditional approach would not work with an unusual opponent. He needed to adapt his strategies when dealing with her.

"What would you say to them?" he asked instead of lecturing her.

"I would just talk to them. I'm curious, and it's absurd I'm not allowed to talk to anyone! I'm not sure what you or he is afraid of. I'd like to know who is visiting and why, where they're from."

"You're seeking my permission to speak to the visitors," he summarized, gauging her reaction. *Nishani*'s eyes narrowed, and she clenched her jaw. She was independent, an odd contrast given that she was far too delicate to defend herself if left to face the planet's dangers on her own.

"Yes," she grated, displeased.

"You have it, *nishani*."

"Thanks, I think. How far away are you?"

"Half a day," he answered.

"You're returning?"

"Yes."

"Did you win your battles?"

"I did." He was puzzled by the question given that she had written most of the plans. She should already know he won.

"That's good. Will you stay long, or do you go to fight again?" she asked.

"I will meet with members of the Council. They should arrive there before the suns set, and I shortly after. I'm not certain how long I'll stay," he replied.

"When you go again, I'd like to go with you." The odd request made him pause. At his lack of response, she continued, "Ne'Rin disagrees. Your sisters don't like the idea either, but I would really like to go with you. I wouldn't get in the way. I can take care of myself for the most part, and wouldn't mind rough conditions."

"No, *nishani*," he replied. The thought of her in rough conditions or battle met instant instinctual resistance. "You will stay where it is safe."

She hesitated, then ignored the warning edge in his voice. "You don't stay where it is safe, and you're the only remaining *dhjan*."

A'Ran gazed at her silently, making his disapproval clear.

"We'll have to agree to disagree," she relented. "But I don't consider this matter to be closed."

Her directness and pure *courage*—there was no other word for her insubordinate address!—amazed him. He understood why Ne'Rin had refused to allow her to wear the translator with visitors.

"*Nishani*," he said with a shake of his head. "You are too bold."

"How else would I speak to you?" she asked. "And if I'm not allowed to speak my mind to *you*, who do I speak it to?"

"You may speak any mind you wish to *me*. But you must understand my people are not like you, are not as accepting of your loose tongue."

"I know," she said, growing red. There was a long pause where the two assessed each other. "A'Ran, I have to tell you something about Gage."

"What has my sister done?" he asked, making himself comfortable in his chair.

"She's with child."

He stiffened, surprised.

"She's afraid to tell you."

No woman had given birth in many sun-cycles, because the planet's spirit was severed without the *dhjan* and the *nishani*. He was torn between wanting to confront Ne'Rin and demand he make his sister an honorable woman and laughing out loud to know that he had chosen a *nishani* capable of healing his planet, his people.

"It will be taken care of," he said calmly.

"You should let them work it out."

"Ne'Rin will honor my sister."

"I'm sure he will, but you shouldn't force someone into such a relationship," she said, and crossed her arms. "It's not accepted everywhere, you know."

"It is accepted here," he replied. He raised an eyebrow in challenge, and she glared at him.

"And Talal," she continued.

"What of her?"

"She's with child as well. She told me this morning and asked me not to tell anyone, but you probably need to know."

A'Ran said nothing, though he clenched the arms of his chair hard enough for his knuckles to turn white. He sifted through memories to find who might be connected to his youngest sister. No warrior came to mind. In fact, he had never seen any warrior speak to her save Ne'Rin. As much as he wanted to welcome the information of his healing planet, he also wanted to strangle the men impregnating *his* family members.

"Talal," he repeated at last, and leaned forward again.

"There's a man named Ketnan. She's been involved with him for some time now."

The name was unfamiliar, which meant he was not well connected and not among the families of his advisors.

"It will be taken care of," he said once more.

"Please don't interfere," she said with a frown. "They need to deal with things themselves, don't you think?"

"It's my duty as their brother. I must protect them and ensure their honor and mine remains intact."

"That seems to be a very harsh way of regarding your sisters' future happiness."

"Happiness can be restored. Honor cannot," he said firmly. "What other surprises have you for me?"

"No more surprises," she replied. The sudden change in her expression from open to shuttered drew his attention. "I think there are some matters we should discuss when you return."

"What matters?" he pursued.

"This isn't the place, A'Ran."

"Woman," he growled, "you do not tell me my place."

She assessed him again and shifted under his scrutiny before looking away.

"I don't trust these machines and who might overhear," she said. "If it please you, I'd rather wait to discuss this later."

"It does not please me."

"Then you'll have to wait anyway."

She stood, as if to tell him their conversation was over. A'Ran almost echoed her movement. His size might have an impression on her in person, but over the viewer, it meant nothing. She could just as easily flick off the viewer as he could. He didn't doubt the unpredictable woman would do such an incredible thing. At the moment he wanted nothing more than to reach out to her, and he was uncertain whether he wanted more to kiss those perfect lips or shake some sense into her.

He leaned back and drew a calming breath. She was distraught about something, though he couldn't fathom what might distress her if the news of his sisters' impending babes and complete loss of honor did not. That news certainly distressed *him*.

"You're angry?" She studied him.

"I'm not angry."

"You look angry."

"You're trying my patience, woman," he said. He raised his chin to indicate the table to her left. "Have you been using that machine?"

Nishani glanced in the direction he indicated and returned a wary gaze to him.

"Did Ne'Rin tell you that?"

"So you have been."

"Yes, I have," she said. "Ne'Rin *suggested* that I not use it."

"What do you think of it?" he asked, avoiding the direct challenge in her gaze.

"It's a very interesting game, though I don't understand how it works exactly. I think I've got most of it down," she said, relaxing when he didn't lecture her.

"Game," he repeated.

"That's what you're talking about, isn't it? The battle game on that console?"

He was silent in surprise once more, unable to understand how she might consider his battle plans nothing more than a complex *game*. If she were unfamiliar with the accepted societal behaviors of a woman on his planet, he couldn't expect her to be any more familiar with the machine. Yet her naiveté was almost too much for him to bear. How did a woman like this find her way to *him* of all men?

"How do you like it?" he forced himself to ask.

"I like it a lot. I've been spending a lot of time here working with it." She brightened. "I think I've gotten quite good at it."

"I'll inform Ne'Rin you've approval to continue."

"Approval? My world is very different," she said, brow furrowing.

"I've assessed that your men can't control their women," he said.

She gave a startled laugh. "No, and the women wouldn't let them anyway," she said. "It's closer to the opposite."

"If you've nothing more to tell me, send in Ne'Rin," he directed.

"It was nice talking to you," she said. "Have a safe trip."

She walked toward the door. The woman was more peculiar than any ten-legged creature he'd met on any other planet. Her mannerisms, her features, her obliviousness to the world around her, her soft voice. Oddly enough, he was beginning to like the challenging package that was his *nishani*.

He'd see her in less than a day, if the Council didn't absorb all his time.

THE NEXT MORNING, she started her normal daily routine and made her way to the courtyard where she trained with the boys.

Sunlight blinded her as she walked onto the field. When she could focus again, she stopped short.

A'Ran was with the boys.

His naked back was to her. The man was built like a god! Thick, bronze skin coated layers of roped, rippling muscles. His tucked waist and hips were clad in dark brown, his feet bare. Dark hair was tucked into a tight knot at the base of his neck. In the short time since he left, she had forgotten how buff he was. He appeared much smaller on the communications viewer. She watched him move, intimidated by his size.

She *had* been pretty mouthy with him from a distance. She felt the urge to retreat to her room and stay there until he left again. One of the boys noticed her. Instead of the welcoming smile, a frantic look crossed his face.

If the giant of a man before her decided to be angry at her for breaking the rules, she'd panic as well. She was about to sneak away when A'Ran's sword lowered, and he turned, alerted by the boy's reaction. Kiera stared at him, struggling to focus on his face when all she wanted to do was study every inch of his perfect body. His chest was wide and sprinkled with dark hairs that trailed his ridged belly and disappeared into the dark pants.

Her body flushed, her blood pounding. Whatever otherworldly bond connected them prevented her from moving away. She couldn't begin to imagine what a man like that would feel like in bed! To run her hands over the washboard abs or twirl her fingertips through the tight hairs dusting his chest ...Or better yet, to feel his large hands and muscular body against hers ...

"*Nishani*," he greeted her with his normal curtness.

She cleared her throat, forcing herself to focus on his dark eyes. His face was more handsome than she remembered, more rugged with a two days' growth covering his neck and jaw. It made him all the more untamed, unlike Romas's sculpted beauty. Piercing eyes leveled on her, but she could read nothing in them, especially not what he thought of her.

She wondered why she had the sudden urge to know what he thought.

"Welcome home," she managed, and clasped her trembling hands behind her back. A'Ran turned to the boys and tossed his head. It took nothing else to send all five of them scurrying away. She couldn't remember when the outdoors had felt so small or when it'd become so humid she was sweating in place.

A'Ran retrieved one sword from its stand, flipped it in the air, and caught the blade. To her surprise, he offered it to her.

"I know you train with them," he stated.

"I suppose you'll forbid it," she said, eyeing him.

"Come."

Wondering what he was trying to prove, she took the sword and balanced it. He said nothing but dropped into a fighting stance. The sight made her uneasy.

"I'm not good enough to face you," she said, remembering how he'd beaten men bigger than him into a pulp to free her from Romas's clan.

He motioned her forward with one hand. Her heart thudded, her palms damp. He could smash her into a million pieces if he wanted. Given her blatant ignorance of his rules, he had every probable cause to do so. At least he gave her the chance to go down fighting,

She began as she had been taught, focusing on her form. A'Ran met her blows gently, redirecting them without affecting her balance. He said nothing but let her strike several times before shifting to the offensive. She blocked clumsily at first but ordered herself not to look weak in front of such a man and focused hard.

She waited for him to flex his strength and drive her into the ground, surprised when he never did. If anything, he was gentle and patient, traits she hadn't expected from a warrior. They sparred until she grew tired and lowered her weapon. Kiera wiped her forehead, unable but to admire the sheen of sweat on A'Ran's wide upper body. He straightened as she stopped and gave an approving nod.

"They have taught you well."

He replaced his sword and strode toward her. She held out her hand for him to take the sword. Instead, he gripped her sword wrist and moved behind her. His touch sent heated energy through her, and the nearness of his body made her tense. He was heated and *huge* at her back. One massive hand circled her to rest on her abdomen. He drew her into his body.

"Widen your stance," he instructed, and nudged her left leg out farther with his own. "I'll teach you the first weapons form we teach our warriors."

Kiera was dumbstruck both by his willingness to teach her and his touch. Her face felt hot. A'Ran's warm chest was at her back, his intimate touch on her stomach making her feel far more delicate than she ever had. He said something that her spinning mind couldn't catch. Her body was too aware of his. It distracted her until he shifted her body forward to demonstrate and correct her stance. Kiera blinked and forced herself to pay attention. She was too stiff for him to move. He nudged her right foot forward. She complied.

" ... your balance lower."

She couldn't register his words and tried hard to focus. A'Ran locked their bodies together with his large hand on her stomach. He used his body to guide hers. His legs and hands applied gentle pressure while his body balanced her in some of the awkward positions.

They went through an entire range of movements, from attacking to defending in motions that resembled a dance. He said little else, and her breathing soon fell into rhythm with his. She eased against him, awed by his pure strength yet determined not to appear as stupid as she felt. Their movements were slow and methodical, controlled, deliberate. Her body strained under muscle fatigue as the form became increasingly complex and slower. A'Ran supported her. By the time she returned to the starting position, she was sweating and breathing hard. Her sword arm shook, and her legs were rubbery. He pried the sword from her clamped hand.

"Yes, you are forbidden from training with them," he said.

Surprised, she pulled away from the comfortable position resting against him and twisted to face him.

"After this, you'll forbid me from learning?" she demanded. She took in his beautiful body as he crossed to place her sword in the sword stand.

"I said *they*'ll not train you."

"*You*'ll train me?" she asked, unable to keep the disbelief out of her voice.

"Yes." He gazed at her, as if awaiting a refusal. She couldn't determine if she'd won this round or not.

"You seem too busy," she said.

"I will make time for you."

"No, no. I'm not ... I know you're waging a war. Don't overextend yourself for me," she said, her face warm once again.

"I was unaware you wished to see me."

Once again, there was too much behind his simple statement for her to address. Worse, she could think of nothing to say in response that wouldn't get her in more trouble.

"You are not so bold in person," he said, raising an eyebrow in challenge.

She looked at him hard. Anger flared at the tone of his voice. *How* could he say such a thing after all he had put her through?

"You kidnap me, trick me into marrying you, dump me here alone without Evelyn or even a pad of paper, with instructions for your sisters to give me *behavioral training*, and run off to fight some battle somewhere else. I'm not allowed to talk to anyone or do anything! You have some nerve to do all that and make fun of me for trying to fit in or ignore me when you do return! I am so angry at you, and if you were half an inch smaller, I'd whip your hide, *dhjan* or not!"

The flurry of words left before she could temper them. She neared him as she spoke until she was toe-to-toe with the massive man and glaring up at him.

"I will make amends," he said, his gaze taking in her features.

It was better than an apology. Being so close rattled her senses, and she thought again of the kiss they had shared over a month before. She focused on his eyes as much as she wished to focus on his warm lips. He smelled of pure, primal man, his own scent mixed with sweat.

"I am pleased to learn I was wrong," he said in a quiet voice. He made no move to close the distance between them. Instead, he stepped away and strode toward the door.

She watched him go, his touch branded on her skin and her emotions muddled. She cursed herself, aware she had accomplished little as far as advancing her rights but managed to draw the guaranteed attention of a man she was not certain she wanted to notice her. The short time together had been enough to remind her just how strong the bond was between them.

It scared her.

As she retreated to the safety of her quarters, her gaze was caught by the objects sitting on her bed: a fat sketchbook and pack of drawing pencils. She reached out and took them, surprised to find them there and even more surprised at how strongly she'd missed them. They were like old friends who came to visit after a long absence. She flipped open the notebook and buried her nose between the pages, breathing the fresh paper smell. She felt tears in her eyes at the small reminder of her past life and hugged the gifts to her chest.

A'Ran.

It couldn't be coincidence that he returned and they appeared! She forgot her shaky body and the whirling of her emotions and strode toward the door, intent on discovering if he had done this and if so, if he had more. Such a notebook would last her a week or two. Kiera stopped in the hallway, considering where the enigmatic *dhjan* might have gone.

She trotted down the hall, toward the practice fields, not surprised to see all the warriors sparring on the field. A'Ran was several hundred meters out, surrounded by a group of over a dozen. Ne'Rin was closer to the door, and Kiera remained in the shadows inside the house, watching.

He was sparring with another warrior, his fluid, destructive movements far from the gentle ones he used with her. She admired the way his body shifted and moved. The muscles of his upper body bulged as he sparred, their changing shapes amplified by a play of shade and sunlight.

She debated returning to her quarters until she could find a more private moment to approach him. She doubted he'd appreciate her embarrassing one of them. For once, she wished she'd listened to Gage or Talal.

Ne'Rin caught sight of her just as she decided to leave. The cool toss of his head—a blatant dismissal—changed her mind again. She shot him a look and stepped from the house, moving toward the field with the gifts at her side. She ignored him as she passed. Though he made no move to stop her once she was visible, he did trail her. Those who noticed her stopped to bow as she passed them.

She reached the circle where A'Ran fought and joined the observers. Some of the men were exotic even by Anshan standards. One towered just as tall as the other men but was thinner than any waif-like model she had seen on earth. Another was hunch-backed and dressed in heavy robes despite the heat of the day, and a third man barely taller than her had white irises and silvering hair.

The men watched the silent battle in equal silence, their assessing looks warning her they were looking for something. The man A'Ran fought was more than a foot taller, with light skin and black hair resembling one of the observers. They fought with the grey swords, combining the sword dance with hand-to-hand combat moves for a ferocious battle that surprised her. It was more intense than sparring, and she wondered what was at stake with the simple fight.

She considered retreating but suspected that would draw the attention of the men focused on the battle. She gripped her notebook.

The battle continued, and the men around her grew tenser when the first fleck of blood appeared on A'Ran's opponent. His opponent faltered, and A'Ran smashed him to the ground hard. Kiera was more than a little surprised when he raised his sword for what would have been a death blow. The sword implanted next to the downed man's ear, and her small gasp drew the attention of the observers.

The feel of several sets of eyes assessing her made her heart beat harder and her mouth dry. She resisted the urge to leave, instead riveting her gaze to A'Ran.

A'Ran pulled his opponent to his feet, offered several quiet words, and turned his gaze to her. It was the intense, fierce look of a leader and a warrior, and she was surprised to note a difference in the way he regarded her not more than an hour ago.

She felt silly seeking him out for something as simple as a note-book. He was, after all, equivalent of a king on this world! How ridiculous would she seem? She awaited some sort of reprimand, already wounded by the thought of being publicly embarrassed. A'Ran's intense gaze swept over her before turning to the observers.

"Council members, *dhjan nishani*," he announced.

The men around her offered stiff bows. Kiera looked around uncertainly before returning her gaze to A'Ran.

"We will meet in two. Opal, meet me in the command center," A'Ran directed.

Opal, the tall, thin man, nodded and stepped toward the house. The men around her broke away, the two with dark hair joining A'Ran's opponent while the alabaster giant joined Ne'Rin. She wasn't surprised to see the man in the thick robes move to the cooler shade of the house. The small man with white irises drew near her, his eerie, unblinking gaze making her uncomfortable.

"It is not often I find another smaller than I, *nishani*," he said in a thin voice. "The *dhjan* has granted us permission to address you. Be not alarmed."

"I am not alarmed," she murmured.

"I am Jetr. I come from the planet of Dolsom. My people are Anshan's greatest allies."

"Is your planet far?" she asked.

"Unfortunately far, in the farthest of the Five Galaxies. I haven't seen my home in many sun-cycles."

"You must miss your home as I do mine."

He tilted his head to the side, observing her with a faint smile.

"Jetr, you are welcome to join us." A'Ran's deep voice saved her from filling the awkward quiet. "Please accompany Opal."

Jetr took the dismissal with a bow of his head and moved away. A'Ran waited. He kept the distance between them, and she felt it like a rejection. Even so, he was too stunning for her to look away. She cleared her throat then said,

"I'm sorry. I don't want to keep you from your meeting."

"You received them." His gaze fell to her chest, where she clenched the sketchbook.

"Yes. I just wanted to thank you," she said. "I won't keep you."

She intended to walk away but found herself stuck, gazing up at him. She was curious about the softer side of him and captivated by his steady gaze. There were many things she suddenly wanted to know about the man she was stuck with. His every look was penetrating, as if he sought to capture her thoughts whenever she crossed his path. She had the impression of extreme intelligence and extreme determination, a combination that awed and intimidated her. Uneasy with the stirrings within her, she forced herself to step away.

"Thank you."

Only when she turned did she break eye contact, but she felt him watch her. Kiera squeezed the gifts to her chest and walked back to the house, lost in thought. There was something about A'Ran that flipped her world on end. She blinked as she entered the darker house and forced her attention on her surroundings. She returned to her room, eager to spend the day drawing.

She started with a sketch of A'Ran and found she couldn't focus on anything else. She drew him as she'd seen him in the morning, bare-chested and carrying a sword. She drew him as she'd seen him during their conversation the day before, the quietly fierce leader seated in his ship. She found herself sketching him as she'd seen him in the vision from what felt like years ago when they walked hand-in-hand on the dead planet.

It was past dark fall when she finished, and she gazed at her last sketch, intrigued by it. It was what would happen if for some reason she didn't go back to her own planet. A'Ran wasn't as controlling as Romas, from what she knew of him, and she couldn't help feeling as drawn to the picture in front of her as she was to the man himself.

She wondered what life would be like with someone like him, or if he was so bound to duty, there was no room for real affection. She sketched the planet next and fell asleep at her desk.

SEVEN

TALAL SHOOK her awake far too early. She lifted her head from her desk and blinked, the first fingers of dawn rendering the light of the room grainy and grey.

"My brother awaits you," Talal said. She was glowing and refreshed, her clothes neat and her scent that of one who had recently bathed. Kiera groaned softly as she shifted. She ached as much from her workout the day before as falling asleep sitting with her sketchbook.

"Why?"

"He is to train you," Talal said as she crossed to the clothing unit. "You shouldn't keep him waiting."

"So early?" Kiera asked.

"He will be occupied today," Talal chided. "He favors you with his time."

She was cheerful as usual and brought Kiera a set of clean clothing. Kiera grimaced and rose, changing slowly before leaving her room for the training area. The morning was cool, the sky lightening. A'Ran awaited her with two swords looking alert, as if he'd been up long enough for his first cup of coffee to kick in. She felt sluggish in comparison. A'Ran's eyes didn't leave her as she tied her hair in a knot at the base of her neck. She dropped her arms and gave a long sigh, meeting his gaze.

As if he sensed her irritation at the early hour, a look of amusement crossed his face, visible in the shift of his eyebrows. He wore light colors this day of tan, a shade that brought out the depth of honey in his skin. He handed her one sword. She accepted it. It felt heavier than usual already. She stretched again before settling into an awkward stance across from him.

They sparred lightly until her body grew warm and her mind engaged. Kiera concentrated on her movements rather than the silent form across from her, intent on not looking like a fool in front of a master warrior. When concentrating on the weapons, it was also easier to keep from concentrating on *him*.

Sparring lasted until the sky was clear of night's blue, at which point he took the sword from her. Kiera watched him lean both weapons against the side of the dwelling before he returned.

"Fighting stance," he instructed.

She shifted herself in compliance. He moved behind her, keeping within arm's distance. He tested her balance and adjusted her stance before taking both wrists and moving her hands over her head.

"This is the starting position for this form," he told her.

He released her and moved before her, back toward her. Kiera watched as he assumed the same position and shifted his stance into a new position. He waited, head twisted over her shoulder to see her. She echoed the movement. A'Ran turned to adjust her stance before returning to the same pose.

The slow movements continued for an hour, with A'Ran pausing between each new one to adjust her stance as needed. She recognized the same routine from the previous day, only this time they moved through it without swords. When she returned to the starting position, her arms were shaking and her legs burning. A'Ran adjusted her one last time before stepping back and nodding.

"This is the first weapons form warriors are taught," he said.

Kiera lowered her hands and wiped sweat from her forehead. A'Ran appeared none the worse for the session, but she was ready for a hot bath and a nap. He studied her, dark depths taking her in with quiet intensity she was not yet accustomed to. The training had been nothing but politely professional, as if she were another student. The ensuing silence, however, reminded her once more of their awkward status.

"You may use the command center this afternoon," he said.

"You and the Council will be somewhere else?"

A curt nod.

"I assume it's not a woman's place at the Council."

"It is not," he agreed. Before she could be irritated by his words, he continued, "We will discuss matters later."

"What matters?" Kiera asked. "Good matters? Bad matters?"

"Are there bad matters to be discussed?" he asked, an edge to his voice. He raised an eyebrow, his chin lifting in what she recognized as a look very close to commanding.

"I have nothing to discuss," she said. "But if there *are* issues, I'd like to discuss them now."

"We will discuss matters later," he said once again. "I find nothing alarming in what we will discuss. And I thought you had a matter you wished to tell me as well."

She frowned. She doubted anything would alarm this man if tricking a woman into wedding him and discovering the news of his sisters' impending children did not. There were a *great* many things she could think of that would be dramatic issues to *her*. She wasn't about to tell him what she'd overheard Ne'Rin say. No, telling him that she didn't like his most trusted friend seemed ... petty.

"I go now to the Council," he said, and strode to the swords. "I will send for you when I am ready."

Kiera grimaced at the distasteful wording. She said nothing as he disappeared into the house, wondering what surprises he had in store for her.

A'RAN LISTENED to the Council members, uneasy. The Council had been excessively cooperative the past two days, a sign he didn't like. Ne'Rin sat to his right at the largest table within the command center with the Council members arranged by rank to his left.

He didn't like the politicking that accompanied any Council meeting, but he had to be patient with men who might be willing to help him. Today his gaze fell to the white-eyed, small man that had addressed *nishani* the prior day. While he had given them permission to speak to her, he found opportunists distasteful, however loyal they were. Jetr met his gaze with a small smile and deferential bow of his head. A'Ran responded by tipping his chin, and Jetr's attention returned to Opal, who had been speaking too long already.

Jetr was one of the only champions A'Ran had on the Council. A'Ran forced his attention away, certain that this ally was as true as any despite his haste in addressing *nishani*.

Anyone addressing *nishani* irritated him. It was abnormal in Anshan, even if her society held no such apparent boundaries. He'd spoken to his sisters in depth and learned quickly just how different she was, their tales ranging from those that ought to anger him to those that amused him. He understood better the tension between Ne'Rin and *nishani* after several hesitant stories from Talal of their *discussions. Nishani* had a tongue and habits that shocked all three sisters and did nothing short of aggravate Ne'Rin.

He suspected Ne'Rin didn't care for *nishani*. Having been raised to serve his *dhjan* within the boundaries imposed on him, Ne'Rin would have little patience with one who trounced the boundaries that should have been emplaced upon her.

A'Ran hadn't yet addressed Ne'Rin's own failing, that of impregnating his sister without making her a *nishani* first. It was very unlike his friend and second-in-command to allow his control to slip in such a drastic way. He hadn't yet discovered who Talal's mysterious man was. It was part of the reason he wished to speak to *nishani* later that day.

If he had it his way, the woman would rarely leave his side. Despite her oddities, she drew him with her large eyes and quick wit. Even though he'd just met her, the bond between them was as strong as his father told him it would be. He wanted to gauge her ability with the strategic battle planning and measure just how intelligent his *nishani* was. If she proved to be as he suspected she was, she might find herself the first woman in his society given the official position of strategy battle planner, a position traditionally held by the *dhjan* alone.

Opal, the head of the Council, rose gracefully, pulling A'Ran from his thoughts. He and the others followed his lead.

"We will meet after we dine this evening," Opal said.

The men withdrew. Ne'Rin caught A'Ran's eye and nodded toward the door. A'Ran gave a curt nod. His second had training for the day.

"A'Ran, a word," Jetr said as he prepared to leave. He waited for the others to file out of the command center. Jetr crossed to the door and closed it before asking, "Have you given any thought to what I warned you of a few weeks ago?"

A'Ran wiped his mouth, already uneasy with the topic. He trusted Jetr as much as he dared trust anyone.

"I only ask because my own personal guards—who, with your permission, keep an eye on the moon—have had transmissions from Anshan that did not come from your commanders," Jetr said very carefully.

A'Ran crossed his arms, more hesitant to consider his second in command—and closest friend—being a traitor now that his sister was involved with Ne'Rin.

"We traced the communications to be from the personal communications device of the man who claims to be *dhjan* of Anshan," Jetr continued when he did not speak. "Ne'Rin has been talking to his father, A'Ran."

A'Ran pushed himself away from the table he leaned against and paced, thoughts turning to Gage, who would bear Ne'Rin's child. He remembered the look on Ne'Rin's face fifteen sun-cycles ago, when they'd learned what happened. No, Ne'Rin hadn't been a traitor then. Something had changed him.

He'd lost faith in A'Ran. Maybe he missed his home, or maybe he was convinced that what the Council often said—that the Yirkin and remaining Anshans could live in peace together—was true.

"I cannot act until I am certain," he said at last, his mood darkening.

"If you hesitate too long, you risk your life and those of your sisters."

"Ne'Rin wouldn't ..." *kill innocents as his father did.* He couldn't speak the words. His father's most trusted advisor had done the unthinkable, and yet, Ne'Rin had borne all the sacrifices that A'Ran had by coming with him.

"You were no real threat to them without your *nishani*, but now, you can rally your people behind you with the promise of healing the planet. And the Council will help you build allies," Jetr said.

"My forefathers rigged the mines on the planet to explode. I've thought more than once I'd like to set them off." A'Ran bit off the words.

"Your forefathers were barbarians. Their threat is taught to us diplomats as an extreme negotiating tactic. They wouldn't destroy their world any more than you would."

A'Ran said nothing, aware his forefathers had never made a threat they didn't intend to execute. The mines were rigged, and he'd never wanted to think he'd need to destroy his home in order to rid it of the blight affecting it. But to know even his most trusted advisor had lost faith in him enough to consort with the man who slaughtered his parents ...

"We'll talk later," he said, disturbed. Jetr said nothing but offered a small bow of his head.

Leaving the command center for his quarters, he glanced out the windows as he strode through the compound. It was mid-afternoon already, another day wasted with the Council rather than concentrating on preparing for battle. Part of him knew the Council was stalling him for that reason, though whether they did so to hinder his efforts or to maintain the appearance of their power over him, he wasn't sure.

He reached his quarters and opened the link to the command center, pausing before it to see *nishani* had already entered. She had her odd gifts with her and sat at the battle planner. He sat at the table opposite his bed and touched several glowing buttons on the table before him. The land and space battle sprung up before him and began to spin. He took in everything, noting the enemies had begun to encroach upon the neutral territory agreed upon in the cease-fire. He disabled the real-time mechanism, engaged the training program, and returned to the point where battle had been when *nishani* last adjusted the strategy.

He was curious to see how she would react. With there being no current battle, there was nothing to test her. He programmed the computer to respond in training cycle mode and glanced at the communication link again.

Nishani put her gifts aside and crossed her legs in her seat before flicking on the battle planner. Ne'Rin might possess the ability to plan, but it would take him days to do what A'Ran and *nishani* could do within moments.

Nishani studied the scene before her. Both hands rested in her lap as she studied it for two full rotations. He took in her perfect features once more, impressed again with his choice. Beauty hadn't been a requirement for a *nishani*, and his own mother had been far from beautiful. He had waited for the signs his father warned him against, intending to take on whatever woman that brought him. That *nishani* was beautiful was no great disappointment to him!

She was strong for a woman as well, which she'd revealed during their two training sessions. She possessed promising coordination and ability to learn at least the basics of the warrior's trade, skills no other *nishani* had ever needed. Initially fearing her to be brittle by her reaction to the world around her, A'Ran was more assured of her ability to withstand the changes in her life. She was tough but expressive, a combination he found odd but promising.

She shouldn't have to be tough, and if he hadn't failed his people several sun-cycles before, he'd never think twice about training her for battle. But she might need to know how to defend herself. His mother never needed to learn. No *nishani* in his bloodline had learned to defend herself or been exiled from her planet. And no *nishani* in his bloodline had failed to produce an heir the first year.

She had to learn to fight, and he wasn't sure when he'd be able to touch her as a man did his mate. If she were any woman from his planet, he would never have hesitated to take her to his bed, as he should. She hadn't protested to his touch during training. Neither had she sought him in any way since his return. She was scared of him still, and he knew it was their bond as *dhjan* and *nishani* that frightened her.

He watched her over the viewer. *Nishani* started with small adjustments to the battle before her, as if testing for the results of her decisions. She grew bolder quickly. He watched as her decisions turned from thoughtful to instant as she reacted to the battle. Her position at the table shifted as the program grew more complex; she dropped her feet to the ground and leaned forward, taking in the rapidly changing situation.

He leaned closer as well, watching. *Nishani* was not only brilliant, but she was fast in her work. As quickly as the computer tossed a challenge before her, she countered and matched it. He watched for quite a while, until the model reached a level that had taken him years of apprenticeship under his father to achieve.

It didn't seem possible that anyone could learn so fast. In the end, the computer might win, but he suspected *nishani* would not lose the second round. He took a long breath and relaxed, satisfied with his choice once more. As hard as it would be to push her closer to the mold of what a *nishani* would be, it would be well worth it.

He turned both machines off and left his quarters for the command center. *Nishani* was concentrating too hard to notice him when he entered. He approached and stood a short distance behind her, watching once more.

She was murmuring in a frustrated tone. Her small, shapely form grew tenser and closer to the computer as the levels increased. A'Ran shifted forward as well to see. In the end, she made a drastic over-calculation and lost the ground battle. *Nishani* pounded a fist on the table and made a loud sound that was most likely a curse on her planet. It did not translate, and neither did it sound like it could be anything else. He chose to overlook the idea of his *nishani* cursing like a man at battle.

"You did well," he said. *Nishani* jerked and twisted to face him. Her features were flushed, her eyes large.

"Have you been here long?" she asked.

"Long enough."

Nishani at once looked uncertain again, her frame tense. She shifted her body to face him, but he moved to her side and sat on the bench a safe distance from her. She continued to watch him.

"You're taking a break from the Council?"

"How long have you been using this device?" He ignored her question, focused on her for the moment.

"I have your permission," she reminded him, eyes narrowing.

"I know."

"Since you left," she responded. "Against Ne'Rin's wishes."

"You must defer to him in my absence as you do me," he reminded her. One eyebrow rose in challenge, and her jaw clenched. "Rather, more so than you do me, given your usual behavior."

She feigned ignoring him, though he saw the flush of her face grow deeper. He recalled her outburst at him the previous day.

"I'm not comfortable around Ne'Rin," she admitted.

"You're not comfortable around me."

"This is different," she insisted. She paused, as if searching for the right words, then continued. "It's just an instinct I have about him."

"Instinct?" A'Ran prodded. "This guides your judgment on him?"

"Yes, of course, on everything," she said. "Like this game. I don't think when I'm using it. I feel what should happen next."

"What is this instinct about Ne'Rin?" he continued, alerted by her words.

"I don't want to talk about it," she said.

"*Nishani*, you don't determine what we discuss," he growled. Her eyes flew to his once more.

"I don't want to talk about it," she said, but with a tremor of uncertainty. He waited. She looked away before he did but refused to crack. He shifted tactics.

"This ... game, you do very well at it."

"I like it," she said. "Today was difficult, but normally I do much better."

"Today it was on training mode," he said, and reached forward, activating it. He touched a few buttons to take it off training mode. The quiet, uneventful scene on the frontier appeared. He stood and moved to take her place, nudging her aside. *Nishani* rose as he slid into the seat before the console.

"Training mode?" she repeated.

"You understand ground and space battles?"

"Yes." She drew closer until he could feel her presence at his back.

"This is the current battle situation. It's been quiet due to the cease-fire called by the Council," he explained. He flicked buttons, zooming and expanding the scenes and adjusting it until it was as he preferred it: spinning faster than normal with alternating close-ups of each major battle.

"I've been winning up until today," she said. "I don't always understand all the parts. These are large ships, these smaller fighter ships."

"There are three levels of fighter ships."

"I figured that out by the size and speed."

"You know the parts of each ship and can configure the ships' systems?"

"Yes."

"It's not an easy task to learn. Each one has its own specific codes and specifications. I am impressed you learned it."

She was quiet as he flipped through the individual configurations of each kind of ship, from transport to logistic to the hulking carrier ships. He switched to the ground battle and hastened through the size, position, and make-up of each of the major ground armies.

"Why do I have the feeling this isn't a game?" she asked in a hushed voice.

"It is not."

"Then what is it?"

"Strategic battle planning. You've been sending me updates daily," he said. Disbelief spread across her face.

"It's real? But I annihilated the planet when I first started!"

"I approve the plans before they are released," he said. "I've not had to alter the last several you've sent. Judging by the training program, you've reached my level already."

"So I'm helping?" she asked skeptically.

"Yes."

"You'll take me with you to battle?"

"No," he said firmly.

"But if I'm helping you here, couldn't I be more helpful up there?"

He gave her a warning look.

"I'm really as good as you are?" she asked.

"You'll soon be better."

"I can't wait to tell Ne'Rin!" she exclaimed. "You've been bested by a mere *woman*!"

"You've not bested me yet, woman," he growled. "I will announce to the Council that you are being appointed the battle planner for

Anshan. I will be here only another few moon-cycles and will work with you to teach you the different units and their capabilities. If I am satisfied, I'll turn over the planning completely to you."

"No approvals needed?"

"No approvals needed."

To his surprise, she was grinning, her multi-hued eyes glowing. He hadn't thought she would be so eager, given her skill at avoiding all her regular *nishani* duties.

"Thank you!" She looked younger than Talal, and he wondered what her age might have been. He restrained the urge to reach out to her. She wasn't yet at the level where she would feel comfortable with his touch. He returned to the console and turned it off.

"I saw your sister," he said.

"Sister? You saw Evey?" *nishani* demanded. "When? Is she here?"

"She is well, in her home."

Nishani waited. When he did not continue, she sat down impatiently, facing him.

"When did you see her?"

"A day ago." He was purposely vague, enjoying the fact that her full attention was on him. He rose and turned to go. *Nishani* followed and gripped his forearm with both of her small, soft hands.

"A'Ran, wait!" she commanded. "You can't start a conversation like that and leave! How is Evelyn?"

She released him when he turned, and he gazed down at her, eyebrow raised. A familiar look of determination was on her upturned face.

"She is well, *nishani*," he stated. "She sent your gifts and said to convey her news of a child."

"Evey's having a baby? How wonderful! Does she seem happy? What about Romas? Will he let her visit soon?"

"Romas is not likely to allow that, *nishani*," he responded. "Our clans are still on the verge of war."

"Because of what I did?"

"Because of what I did. I knew the risk."

She frowned. He turned and approached the door again, interested when she followed.

"A'Ran, if helping me drew you into another war, why did you do it?"

"It was meant to be," he answered. He slowed his brisk stride for her to draw and keep abreast.

"What was? Stealing me and making me a *nishani*?"

"Yes."

"So you feel *we* were meant to be," she clarified.

"I feel nothing, *nishani*. I know it to be true. I believe you feel it, too. 'Tis the bond between an Anshan *dhjan* and his mate. We are bound together and to the planet, which will only come back to life when we return."

LIKE FROM MY VISION. His weren't the words she expected to hear. She walked beside him, pensive. He didn't regret what he had done, even if it plunged his war-beleaguered people into another war.

"Why are we bound together?" she pushed.

"Perhaps because you are so small," he said with a trace of amusement.

"I'm perfectly average on my planet," she said. "Seriously, why did you feel the need to drag *me* across the galaxy? Aren't there other women you could take as *nishani*?"

He ceased walking and gripped her by both arms, maneuvering her to stand before him. She looked up at him, awed once again by his size. She could feel his body heat and felt pinned beneath the intensity of his gaze.

"You are too bold, *nishani*," he chided once more.

His grip was warm and firm, as it had been the day he prevented her from falling on her face in front of Romas's relations. She felt the familiar, core-deep connection, the one intimate enough for her body to respond, as he held her gaze. Her breathing quickened, and she sought to break the entrancing spell before she began mewling like a cat at his feet.

"I think I deserve an explanation," she breathed. A'Ran's grip tightened before falling from her. He made no move to walk away.

"The babes my sisters carry will be the first birthed to Anshan in over seven sun-cycles," he said. "A *dhjan's* mate is bound to his people, to his birthright as he is. From the *dhjan* comes strength, prosperity, stability. From the *dhjan nishani* comes growth, birth, restoration. If a *dhjan* chooses incorrectly, his world suffers. If a *dhjan* chooses well, his world flourishes."

"Wow," she murmured. "I guess that means ..." ... *you'll never let me go home.* She frowned without finishing the sentence. He waited. "You aren't upset with your sisters?"

"They disobeyed me," he said firmly. "Despite the assurance that you will return health and life to my people."

"Glad to do my duty," she said.

"There will come a day when you must choose between duty to Anshan—and your people—and duty to yourself," he said. "It is the same choice I made."

She didn't want that burden. She wanted to go home, though a part of her had told her upon meeting this fierce warrior her that she'd never go home again. She met his gaze, wondering if any part of him was capable of affection or if she'd wither like a dried-out flower. She couldn't imagine spending her life with a man who viewed her as nothing more than a duty. Evelyn was right: she was too emotional for such an existence.

Yet she knew, even if this were her fate, the man before her would always treat her as he had: respectfully, honorably, dutifully.

"What is it?" he asked as she gazed at him.

"I'm not like you, A'Ran," she found herself saying. "Or your women."

"I know this."

"No, I mean, I'm nothing like you! Your duty is all you really seem focused on."

"You will learn."

"I don't know that I want to learn," she said, troubled. "If I must learn to be dutiful from you, what will you learn from me, or am I expected to be the only one to compromise?"

He faced her fully, studying her for a long moment.

"What would you have me learn?" he asked in the same wary tone.

Affection. Love. Things a man battling for his planet neither had time for nor needed. They seemed like silly emotions when compared to the enormity of his task, and yet, she didn't think she could survive without them.

"I don't know," she said. "I won't keep you any longer."

And she walked away without another word, confused as to why she had wanted him to say there was more to why he chose her than because it was his duty. She wanted him to say he felt the same thing when he looked at her as she did when she looked at him.

A'Ran's penetrating gaze nearly burnt a hole through her shoulder blades.

She didn't have much time alone to mull their conversation or her troubled thoughts. Ne'Rin sent for her less than an hour later with vague explanations of meeting a visitor. Kiera hid a second translator in her pocket and exited the sprawling house to join him. He turned on his heel as soon as she appeared and strode toward the small area beneath a tree where spacecraft traditionally hovered to release their occupants.

Unwilling to appease the man she didn't like, she made no effort to match his pace. She trailed instead, eyes on the much smaller craft hovering near the tree. It was a single occupant transport ship whose passenger stood several feet from it and looked familiar from a distance.

She heard the runner before she saw him and watched as one of the warriors breezed past her toward Ne'Rin. He caught Ne'Rin before he met the visitor, and the two stopped. She approached, but Ne'Rin headed back to her with the messenger.

"Wait here. Do not greet him," Ne'Rin commanded her.

She rolled her eyes. He started past her, then paused, returning to her side to remove the translator from her ear. She said nothing and turned to watch them jog back to the house. Satisfied they were gone, she withdrew the spare in her pocket, placed it at her earlobe, and moved forward to greet the visitor.

The guest watched her as she approached, and she recognized the distinct features of A'Ran's family. He was much older with a full head of silver hair, a similar shade of dark eyes, and a lean build. His gaze was just as intense, his brow low, but his features not as heavy as A'Ran's.

She didn't doubt he was a relative. She paused before him, resisting the instinct to stick out her hand for a handshake. The guest was relaxed, his penetrating gaze calm and weary.

"May the suns long grace you, gentle lady," he said in a quiet, gravelly voice.

"And you," she responded. "May I escort you inside?"

He inclined his head. They started toward the house.

"I'm Kiera," she said.

"I am Mansr. Normally I am greeted by a member of my clan." There was weariness in his voice that disarmed any offense he felt.

"Where are you coming from?" she asked.

"From Anshan central."

"Where there's a war?" She looked at him more closely. "Is this what tires you?"

"Yes to both, gentle lady," he said. "I bring news to the *dhjan* of his people."

"The cease-fire must make it easier to travel," she observed, recalling the enemy positions around the spacecraft launch sites. "I believe your regular launch sites have been well covered by the enemy. You may not have made it out otherwise."

Surprised, he looked at her more fully.

"How are ... the people?" she asked. "Aside from the battles."

"War-torn and weary."

"I would like to travel there."

"It is not a place for one such as you."

She looked up at him, unable to determine his tone. His face was unreadable, but the skin around his eyes had softened with warmth.

"I think I could help," she said. "And I can take care of myself."

Sort of, she added. If what A'Ran said was true, her presence would stop the suffering of his people. Maybe, just maybe, after that happened, he would let her go home.

"Is the Council still in residence?" he asked.

"Yes. A'Ran is with them most of the day," she said absently. "How far is Anshan?"

"Two turns of the sun."

"Will you stay long?"

"I cannot," he stated, his gaze growing distant. "I have a duty to the people. I will address the *dhjan* and leave."

Her intent gaze lingered on him as they reached the house. The etchings of age, pain, and sorrow were upon his brow and cheeks. She sensed the unseen scars of war and strife, the price of Anshan's struggle, buried deep beneath the surface of the hardened man before her.

"Worry not, gentle lady," he said, aware of her scrutiny.

Kiera flushed and looked away. They stepped into the cooler house, and her attention was caught by Talal, who froze in mid-stride along her path toward the northern wing.

"Uncle," Talal managed, and gave a formal bow. Her eyes went to Kiera in surprise.

"Niece." He returned the bow.

"I will guide you immediately to the *dhjan*," Talal said with apprehension and another bow.

Her unusually swift stride outdistanced both of them. A'Ran's uncle remained at Kiera's pace. He was quiet, and her thoughts wandered to Anshan and her alleged, vague duty to the people. How did one save a planet, and how long would it take?

"You may enter, uncle," Talal said, and stopped in front of the war quarters. "*Nishani*, come with me."

Before she could move, Kiera's arm was caught by the man beside her. She gazed up at him questioningly.

"*Nishani?*" he echoed, his eyes on Talal. Kiera watched Talal smile and bob another bow. His dark eyes dropped to Kiera's features.

"I am honored," he said, and bowed his head.

"Come, *nishani*." Talal took her arm before she could reply. Kiera went, looking back once to see Mansr staring hard after her.

"*Nishani*, you are not to greet alone!" Talal chided her as they marched down the hall.

"It wasn't right to leave him standing in the sun all day!" Kiera replied. "What does your uncle do on the planet?"

"He controls the ground armies. If he is here, he has no good news."

Kiera debated how he could have worse news, curious about the man and the war. They nearly reached the women's wing when the strange little Council member with white eyes called out to her.

"*Nishani!*"

She and Talal both turned as he approached. He gave Talal a short bow she took as dismissal, then waited for her to pad out of sight. Kiera waited for him to speak, wanting to hide somewhere until she could think straight.

"How are you, *nishani?*" Jetr asked.

"Fine, thanks."

"I apologize if I am being too direct. I have a concern to discuss with you."

"Okay."

"My warriors have intercepted a message that may reference you as an intended victim. It seems there are people in this house who do not favor you as a *nishani* and who may seek to harm you."

Her thoughts went to Ne'Rin. He didn't like her, but she wondered how far he'd go, especially since A'Ran trusted him so much.

"I will warn the *dhjan* as well, but I wanted you to be aware. Your people are very unlike those on Anshan. Considering this, I felt it right to tell you," he said.

"Thank you," she managed, uncertain how to respond to a vague threat from a stranger. "I'll be careful."

He appeared satisfied, bowed, and walked away. Suddenly feeling alone and vulnerable in the wide hallway, she returned to her room and locked the door, her mind going to the visitor as she tried not to think about Ne'Rin wanting to hurt her.

———

"YOU DID NOT TELL me about her."

A'Ran didn't have to guess which *her* his uncle spoke of. He remained seated before a viewer listing the losses from the most current battle.

"If you're here, the crops failed," he said.

"And the mines give us nothing we can use to barter for more food and water," his uncle added.

A'Ran dropped his feet from the table and rose to face his uncle. Mansr appeared more haggard every time they met. His uncle bowed.

"The people are already starving. They cannot await the results of another planting," A'Ran mused.

"They cannot, nephew." Mansr's scratchy voice was soft. A'Ran's gaze rested on him for a long moment. Mansr awaited a response.

"You met *nishani*."

"I did. Did you await the signs?" Mansr's voice was too casual, too even.

"I did," A'Ran said. "Unfortunately, my lifemate knows nothing of Anshan or even the Five Galaxies. She understands nothing of our traditions."

"Surely women have mates where she is from."

"Her world is very different, uncle."

"She belongs on Anshan. Maybe then she'll see what she must do," Mansr said.

"It's too dangerous for her on Anshan," A'Ran replied. "She couldn't survive if anything happened, and every Yirkin warrior on the planet would be looking for her, once they hear she exists."

"She is yours, and it's your decision, though I think she is stronger than you think," Mansr said. "If it were her decision, she would come."

"It is *not* her decision," he said darkly.

Mansr's presence could not have come at a worse time. With repairs for his armies commandeering the last of the Anshan ore he had to trade or sell, he wouldn't be able to afford to feed his people and fight a war. Yet both must be done. There was always the Council, and the only ally A'Ran still had. Assistance might come from their direction, but any favor from the Council would cost him dearly in another way. Restless, A'Ran rose and paced.

"She fears me, Uncle," he said with difficulty. "She's not ready to take her place."

"*Nishani* was brave with me."

"It was not her choice to come here."

"What choice does a woman have?"

"She is not like ours." He glanced at his uncle, bemused. "Her thoughts and actions are hers alone. I have not the time to spend with her."

"The fate of your people relies on you bonding her to Anshan."

"The fate of my people will not matter if they do not live through the war!" A'Ran snapped.

"You are *dhjan*, but you are also a man, nephew," Mansr said. "Your responsibility cannot always be to your people. Is there no part of you that desires this woman as a man does, as more than a key to save your people?"

"First you ask me to send her to the center of the battle and now you wish me to take my time with her?" A'Ran shook his head. "You cannot have both, uncle. There is not time for both."

"You avoid my question," Mansr insisted. "You can be a man, a ruler, and a battle commander, A'Ran."

"Battle commander first." A'Ran sat once more, calming. Mansr grew grave and leaned forward.

"Son, you are not complete without her. Anshan is not complete and will never heal without her. You may battle all you wish, but you will never win until the balance is struck, until Anshan has its *nishani*, and its *nishani* is on the planet. You have forgotten how to be anyone but a battle commander."

"There has been only war as long as I can remember. Anshan needs her, but she can't stay where it's so unsafe, and she isn't adapting the way she should be," A'Ran said.

"Maybe you must change just as she must. You must grow beyond your role as a battle commander, if you want her to accept her place."

A'Ran frowned at the truth in his uncle's words.

"And there must be a solution to the Yirkin," Mansr said. "Qatwal has supported you before."

"Her sister is wed to the son of a Qatwal *dhjan*," A'Ran said. "The Qatwal disowns her, yet seeks to battle me as well for the affront."

"Qatwal has always been full of itself, but they may still aid you," Mansr said. "She does not look like one of theirs."

"She is not," A'Ran affirmed. "She is from even further."

"She's beautiful, like your sister's dolls."

"Talal has not had dolls in sun-cycles, Uncle," A'Ran replied. "But yes, she is."

"I forget you are all grown sometimes. Do you not ever wish to have a family, to be as happy as your father was so long ago?"

His words struck A'Ran hard. His chest clenched, and he found himself holding his breath. He closed his eyes, recalling how happy he and his sisters were before the war. He recalled his mother, her heavy features nonetheless made beautiful by her radiant smile as she swung a waist-high Talal around.

It was his favorite memory, that which preceded his abrupt knowledge of war and the world at large. He sat with his sisters and mother beneath a brilliant sky atop the small rise overlooking Anshan Palace with its white columns and myriad of windows. Cats wrestled and played around them while D'Ryn's strict oversight of his and Gage's actions could not be shaken.

The memory was achingly beautiful, and he remembered seeing his war-weary father approach from the house. His whole face had changed upon seeing his *nishani* and children, had gone from tired to hopeful.

A'Ran hissed as he released his breath and opened his eyes. A distant light was in Mansr's eyes, a faded glow about his face.

"I remember, before Anshan fell," Mansr whispered.

A'Ran made no response, unable to quell the tremor deep within him. At the age of fourteen sun-cycles, before he reached manhood, he had lost all but his sisters, been proclaimed *dhjan* of a planet he couldn't even visit, and made battle commander of a war he knew nothing of.

Since then, he'd known nothing but war, been driven by nothing but revenge, fury, and the elusive glimmer of hope that he might one day feel as he had sitting with his mother and sisters on that hill above his rightful home.

It would never be the same, could never be the same. As he mulled his uncle's words, the scene in his mind altered and shifted. What if it were his *nishani* on the hill with his sisters? What if she looked upon him as his mother had his father, with adoration and love?

He rejected the thought. It was too fanciful to look so far ahead when he needed to determine how to prevent his people from starving. Nonetheless, he was disturbed far more than he recalled being in many sun-cycles. He'd tried to block all memories of a happier time for fear he'd never see such times again.

"I will find the payment for food," he said.

His uncle looked deflated and even more haggard. "I cannot stay long."

"I know, Uncle." He shook himself mentally to refocus on the dire circumstances before him but was unable to force the thought of Kiera from his mind. "Go and rest, Uncle. I know you get little enough as it is."

"A final warning, A'Ran. The *dhjan nishani* must willingly accept her place at your side and her role in helping the planet. If she does not, the planet will die."

A'Ran despised the words the moment he heard them. She was beyond his control, and so was her choice of whether or not to accept her place.

"You must look beyond yourself to find a way to win her, A'Ran, or the planet is lost."

Mansr offered no other advice but rose and bowed once more before striding to the door. A'Ran returned to his battle loss assessments. Mansr's words had all been true. The more he considered them, the more he realized that he didn't know how to be anyone but a battle commander. He'd never considered it a fault before. *Nishani* wasn't the only problem; he was, too.

THOUGH HE WAS PHYSICALLY ENGAGED in swordplay, Kiera sensed A'Ran's distraction the next morning as they sparred. He spoke even less than normal. His touch was mechanical and instructional, his attention elsewhere. She wasn't eager to draw his undivided attention, but his distance struck her as unusual, if not yet another rejection. She lowered her sword long before the sky lightened. His attention shifted to her.

"We don't have to do this today," she said.

A'Ran straightened, his piercing gaze on her. His thick form was tense, his features implacable. Talal's assessment of there being something wrong returned to her.

"You seem to have other matters on your mind," Kiera prodded. "I don't want to keep you from anything."

"What is it you fear of me?" he demanded, lowering his sword and pacing closer to her.

Surprised, she said nothing. He took a step closer. She retreated a step, regretting drawing his intensity. A'Ran compelled the sword into the ground deep enough for it to remain upright when he released it. He leaned forward and took her sword, driving it into the ground as well.

"Are we doing training forms?" she asked as he returned his dark stare to her.

"No."

"We're done?" she asked.

"No."

The odd tension was between them again, and she wondered what it was about her abductor that made her blood burn, especially when he was so unapproachable.

"So," she murmured, "we're just going to stand out here and stare at each other all morning? If so, I can think of better things to do."

A'Ran's gaze swept over her, making her skin tingle with awareness.

"Well, I'm off then," she said, and turned to leave.

"Stay." The command was sharp. Kiera grimaced.

"I'm not a dog, and I want to accomplish something today," she muttered. "If you aren't going to train me and are just going to stare at me, I'm doing something else with my time."

"I leave soon." His words made her pause in the doorway, and she faced him, frowning.

"I expected you to go soon."

A'Ran moved toward her again, stopping outside of arms' reach.

"You and your duties," she added. *I'm just another one of them.* She stiffened at the reality and couldn't decide if it were good to keep the distance between them or if she really wanted more. If there were something more between them, would he ever entertain letting her go home?

"Travel well," she said, and turned away again.

She walked towards her quarters, uncertain why his departure bothered her. She expected to be left behind many more times. He joined her, and she glanced up at him.

"There is a feast tonight," he told her.

"Very well. What's the occasion?"

"War and our mating. The heads of the clans also in exile will come to meet you."

"Really?" She stopped to face him. He was tense again.

"I will also announce you as the supreme battle strategist. I would be honored if you chose to attend."

She searched his fierce features. She suspected both meeting the clan heads and the announcement to be big deals for a people with such rigid traditions, but A'Ran looked as if he were discussing the whereabouts of her translator.

"I'll be happy to be there," she said at last.

He nodded curtly, as if expecting the response. He turned and walked down another corridor. Kiera watched him, troubled by their morning interaction. The feast must be important, and his attempt to request her attendance—rather than demand it—impressed her.

"A'Ran," she called hesitantly. "I know you're busy, but ..."

He stopped and turned, his gaze on her again, distracting her. She shook her head to focus her thoughts.

"I made something I want to show you. If you have time."

He didn't exactly leap to follow her. When he didn't object either, she started toward her room. He trailed, as if uncertain he wanted to follow at all. She waved her band in front of the access pad to her room and entered, crossing to grab her sketch book. She sat down on the edge of the bed and patted the spot beside her, nervous about showing him her art.

"You may not like it," she said. "And I'll admit, a lot of these are you. You can just ignore them, if you want."

A shiver ran through her as he sat close enough for their bodies to brush. He took the sketch pad she handed him and awkwardly pushed the pages around, unaccustomed to a book. She opened the cover for him to show the first drawing she'd done of him. Stone-faced, he stared at it, and her face grew warm at his lack of response.

"I have a better one," she said, and turned to the second drawing. He didn't respond. She turned a few more pages, until he rested a hand on hers to keep her from turning. Her face flamed hot as she saw the image from her vision: the two of them holding hands while gazing at each other adoringly and walking on the cracked planet. She tugged her hand free to turn the page quickly. He left his hand in place, preventing her.

"You did this?" he asked at last in a hushed tone.

"I did all of them. It's what I do on my planet. I draw and paint," she said, flustered as his gaze stayed on the drawing of them holding hands. "That's not a good one. I can show you more."

"No."

She searched his face, unable to read him or his response.

"This ..." He trailed off, a small frown on his face. "I want this."

Her heart fluttered at his words, and she grew excited about him wanting the type of relationship like she'd drawn, until she saw him fumbling with the page as if to pull it free.

"Here, let me," she said. She took the book from him and carefully pulled the page free. "It's not my best. You don't want another one?"

"No."

He folded it in fourths, rose, and strode away, leaving her alone. She stared after him, uncertain what to think.

EIGHT

A'RAN WENT TO HIS QUARTERS, the thin sheet of what felt like a leaf in his hand. He unfolded it only when in the safety of his locked room and sat it down on the desk to stare at it.

He'd never seen art of this kind, only the statues of his father's court and the multi-hued strands used to decorate homes. The depiction was of him, and her, and Anshan, though how she knew Anshan, he didn't know. He was more interested in them holding hands and the look on her face, one of admiration.

His face, however, was blank. She either hadn't completed the art form, or she didn't know what he looked like when he was content.

Neither did he. Mansr's words returned to him, those that wanted him to be something other than a warrior. He cared for his sisters; they were his blood relations. He'd never cared for another woman in the way his father had loved his mother. He'd granted favors to women as a way of releasing his frustration, but never with any real affection—just physical need. The concept of something more was as foreign to him as peace, and yet he *wanted* the image on the leaf to be real. He found himself wanting his *nishani* to gaze at him as she did in the image. He wanted them to be on Anshan together and bring peace and life to the dying planet.

He wanted there to be something more than war. It was what *nishani* asked him the day prior: if she learned duty, what would he learn? She knew what the answer was, but hadn't spoken it. If she learned duty, then he must learn *this*.

He raised the leaf again, unable to take his eyes off it.

"A'Ran?" Jetr's voice came over the communicator.

"Yes."

"The Council awaits you."

"I will be there soon," he said, and lowered the leaf.

She must choose Anshan. Mansr's words returned to him. She wouldn't, not if he couldn't become the man on the leaf. He'd hoped she would adjust to his world on her own, never suspecting he'd need to change himself. In the past few days, he'd learned just how unready he was to be the lifemate of his own *nishani*. Disturbed, he folded the leaf and placed it in his pocket.

He carried it with him to the long, pointless Council meeting, to his afternoon sparring session with Jetr, to the banquet and introduction of his *nishani* to the clan leaders. He began to think his own actions had cost him the choice he'd yet to give her: to stay forever or return to her planet.

He watched her throughout the night's activities, seeking to judge whether Mansr's parting words were true. He wanted to believe the woman he—and Anshan—chose would in turn choose *them*, but he began to see what Ne'Rin and Mansr had warned him of: she was not one of theirs and would not accept the duties she knew nothing about. Mansr's parting warning, that she must voluntarily accept her role and Anshan as her home, had struck him as odd, for why would she not when he honored her with the greatest honor ever bestowed upon a non-ruling Anshan?

Only now was he beginning to understand that her staying depended less on duty and honor and more on *him*.

Emotions of all kinds played across her face as the night

progressed. She greeted the room full of people with apprehension, her interaction with his sisters with pleasure, her introduction to the clan leaders and her position of master battle planner with both excitement and awe. In between her interactions with people and the spotlight, she watched the world with worry and thoughtfulness. Her frown deepened when she looked at Ne'Rin, and her gaze grew intense and considering when she regarded him.

With a sense of deep dread, he felt for the first time that the role he expected of her may not be a role she chose to fulfill.

She doesn't know her place. She's too different, A'Ran, Ne'Rin had said.

She must choose Anshan of her own will, Mansr had reminded him.

That he might lose her was not a thought he had entertained before. It was not possible that any man could take her or that there was any place she could go that he could not find her. The only possibility—that *she* might choose to leave—hadn't crossed his mind. It'd never happened in the history of Anshan that a *nishani* turned down her position. And yet, this evening, the possibility was as obvious as it had not been that morning.

Another tension was in the air of the banquet. The Council members were restless, with messengers discreetly pacing in and out of the room throughout the evening. HiHiHis own messengers brought him vague news of unrest from the battlefront and news of there being new opponents at the battle. He suspected the Council members knew more and that this night of relative peace was the last he would know for a very long time.

When the evening moved into night, *nishani* appeared too sleepy to stand and took a seat beside D'Ryn. A'Ran approached her then, knowing his journey in the morning would delay the conversation they needed to have.

Nishani followed him from the bustling, warm banquet room to the cool courtyard in front of the house beneath a full sky of suns. He motioned for her to sit but remained standing. She looked at him curiously, and he rolled his shoulders back, prepping himself physically for the verbal discussion to come.

"*Nishani*, have you enjoyed the evening?"

"Yes, thank you. I met all your Council members. I didn't like Ulri but the others were good."

"I travel tomorrow morning with my counselors. It will be some time before I return."

"And you still won't take me with you?" she asked again.

"No, *nishani*," he said quietly. "I go to Anshan."

"I thought I was supposed to go to Anshan."

"Someday," he said. "Do you know why?"

"To save your people and your planet. Then you could send me home, and Ne'Rin could pick you a new *nishani* that he likes."

A'Ran absorbed her words, which fell hard upon his ears. He met her gaze, and she shifted at his intensity.

"What is it?" she asked with a sigh. "What have I said wrong this time?"

"*Nishani*, you must make a choice."

"What choice?"

"You must choose to remain with me or to return to your home."

"You would send me home?" she asked, puzzled. "But I thought I was supposed to save the planet."

"You must choose to stay or return," he repeated.

"Won't Anshan die without me?"

"You cannot remain here at my will," he said with some difficulty. "You must remain here at your will. Or you must go home."

Realization made her blanch. Disbelief and sorrow crossed her face as she began to understand her options. If she chose to stay, she would never see her home again. If she chose to leave, *his* home would be destroyed. It was not a decision he envied; he alone knew what a burden it was to know the fate of a planet and its inhabitants rested upon his shoulders.

"I thought ... I thought ..." Her voice cracked. She drew a deep breath, cleared her throat, and asked, "I can't do both?"

"No."

Her gaze slid to the stone floor. She stood and paced, and emotions flew across her face. A'Ran was uncertain what to expect but found himself disappointed she didn't instantly volunteer to stay.

"I need ... I need to think... about this," she managed. Her eyes welled with tears, and she ducked her head, turning white, then red. "You want me ... to walk away from everything I know, my family ... I knew it was possible, but I didn't think I'd have a chance to go home at all ... but still, I couldn't leave a whole planet to die!"

Her look of soul-deep sorrow touched him, and he recalled what he felt as a youth to find his father and mother dead and his family hunted and forced out of their own home. She turned to leave, and he caught her arm. *Nishani* didn't resist when he wrapped his arms around her but began to cry the soul-deep sobs he remembered from his youth. Her trembling body was warm and small tucked against him. He rested his chin atop her head, knowing there were no words to comfort someone who hurt so deeply and regretful that he caused this pain.

He held her for a long moment, surprised to find her sorrow echoed in his breast at knowing she might choose to leave. He hadn't thought himself attached to the unique woman he chose as a *nishani*. They were bound by fate, and he knew she felt the profound connection between them from the moment they met. Was it possible for such a connection to be stronger than her bond to her own world?

She calmed in his arms, and he focused on comforting her and not his awareness of her soft body pressed against him.

"A'Ran?" she whispered.

"Yes, *nishani*."

She hesitated, then propped her chin on his chest, gazing up at him with stormy, reddened eyes. He smoothed the remaining tears from her face.

"Will you do something for me?" she asked uncertainly. "You can say no."

"What would you have me do?"

"Will you kiss me? Like you did when we met? I just want to know if ... it's important," she asked, face flushing. "You can say no."

"*Nishani*, no man would ever turn down such a request," he said, amused.

Her words floored and excited him for more reasons than one. He'd begun to think he'd lost any chance he had at keeping her. He complied and kissed her deeply, enjoying the taste and feel of her despite the mix of salty tears. Their kiss grew more passionate, the feel of her body against him not enough to sate his growing need. The connection between them flowed with hot energy, the planet's life form itself bonding the two of them together at their touch. She clutched at him, and he tightened his grip around her, dragging their bodies together.

Their kissing grew frantic, their petting setting them both afire. He lifted her at last and carried her to his quarters, senses full of her quickened breath, heady female scent, sweet taste. He'd always intended to bed her when she was ready for him, but he'd never thought that moment would be now, if at all. His body responded with a surge of heat and desire at the idea of feeling her naked body beneath his.

He knew more weighed on her wish than a simple kiss. Deep down, he suspected it was her farewell to him. If she'd chosen to leave, he wouldn't send her away without a night she'd remember for all time.

———

SHE AWOKE ALONE. The bed smelled of him, and her body ached from the active night. She stared at the ceiling, enjoying the breeze skating through the windows.

Wow. There was no other way for her to imagine the night, aside from as otherworldly as her new world. Her blood boiled at the thought of another night with him, and she sat, disturbed.

She hadn't expected to be forced into such a decision. She definitely didn't expect the decision to be so hard. She'd wanted to return home since she arrived, yet when presented with the enormity of her importance in her new world ... when she realized how incredible it really would be to have a man like A'Ran in her bed every night ... when she saw he was capable of passion ... when she found out an entire planet full of people would die if she left ...

She couldn't help the tears at such a thought. It was too large of a concept for her to wrap her head around. That *she,* a starving artist who'd been dragged across the universe because her best friend felt sorry for her, was the key to saving an entire race of people was unimaginable.

He'd certainly made her feel like the queen of the universe.

Pensive and troubled, she dressed for a difficult day. A'Ran was gone indefinitely for a surge operation in his war, leaving her alone with her thoughts. There really wasn't a decision to make. As much as she wanted to return home, she could never leave an entire planet to die just because she wanted to go back to the depressing part-time job and the row house where she and the cat would live alone!

She'd wanted to see if he was capable of being anything more than the cold, distant warrior obsessed with war. She didn't expect him to be as passionate, warm, and gentle as he'd been with her. There *was* a man behind the fierce face, and she'd only confused herself more by spending the night with him!

She gazed around A'Ran's bedroom, conflicted with the idea that her choice would mean she never saw her home, her family again.

She rubbed her face, dressed in grey to reflect her mood, and tucked her spare earpiece into her pocket as she did every day. The house was quiet. The Council would have left at dawn with A'Ran. At the least, she could help him battle plan while she thought hard about what to do with her life. She'd gotten to the conference room when she heard soft footfalls behind her. She started to turn, expecting to see Talal.

A hood made of rough material was thrown over her head and her hands bound before she could scream. Someone threw her over his shoulder and she let out a shout that earned her a blow to the head. Caught between consciousness and darkness, she hung limply for a long time, until the man holding her flung her onto a hard floor. The sound of a door closing and muffled voices outside the door were followed by silence. She tore off the hood, aware she was on a space-ship by the dark grey landscape. The cell where she sat measured six by six with a grey bench.

She sat, confused. She didn't have much time to think before the door slid open, and Ne'Rin squatted in the doorway. The look on his face made her shrink back from him. He reached out to her, placing the translator on her ear.

"Since meeting you, I've felt you were nothing but a curse." His words were hard, his eyes even harder. "If A'Ran had mated with a proper *nishani*, we'd not be losing this war."

"Ne'Rin, what are you talking about?" she whispered.

"I don't know what you did to him, but I intend to repair the damage you've done to our people." He rose and hauled her to her feet, all but dragging her into the hall. Another warrior trailed as he pulled her down the hall.

"Ne'Rin, A'Ran chose me. I do his battle planning. I'm going— "

"He's gone weak after all these years at battle and lost sight of winning back our planet! Do you know how many of my people have starved this moon-cycle alone? All he had to do was choose a *nishani*—my sister!—and the planet would be healed!" His words were accompanied by a squeeze on her arm painful enough to make her gasp. She said nothing and trotted to keep up with his long stride. He led her through the ship to a cargo area filled with pods on the wall. He paused before one and pressed his hand to a keypad. "Instead, he waited for you, and you've made him weak."

The grey wall slid away to display an escape pod, large enough for one person standing. She stared at it, then at him.

"Farewell, *nishani*."

His words were accompanied by a shove. She landed in the pod, and the door slid closed before she could react.

"Ne'Rin!" she shouted, pounding on the door. "Don't do this!"

The pod jolted and dropped, the sickening sense making her nauseous. For a long moment, it was dark and silent, until the interior of the pod lit up with two screens, one displaying the empty space outside and the other displaying a control panel with writing similar to that of the battle planning station.

The pod rotated slowly, revealing the shape of the hulking grey ship as it grew farther away.

Kiera stared, unable to fathom she'd been ejected into the middle of *space* to die. There was enough room for her to raise her arms but not sit, and she leaned against the uncomfortable wall, gazing at the world spinning outside her pod.

The ship grew distant. She looked around her, wondering what the hell to do now. Tears rose, and her chest clenched.

He wanted her *dead*. He'd not considered sending her home—no, he'd decided to kill her! Panic seized her at the thought of floating through space until her air ran out. She looked at the control panel, trying to decipher any of the symbols. There were several she recognized.

Just as the grey ship disappeared from sight, another shape came into view. It was a planet, dusty red, as if it were nothing but dry desert. Her speed was consistent, her destination clear. No, Ne'Rin wasn't stupid enough to send her floating around space. He was sending her straight into a planet!

She rubbed her face and looked at the control panel again. She pressed one button, then another, struggling to understand the symbols that popped up on the screen in response. She'd learned the parts of a warship inside and out while learning the battle planning and looked for the configuration button among her options popping up on the screen. She found it and punched it, looking at the pod from the inside and out.

Its exterior shields were disarmed and he'd disabled the communications capability. Once the plant's gravity sucked her in, its atmosphere would fry her. She swallowed a sob as she realized just how badly someone wanted her dead.

Her hands shook as she manipulated the configuration to arm the shields around it. Ne'Rin underestimated her if he thought she wouldn't be able to figure this much out! Swearing at him, she stared hard at the configuration panels. The air was another issue; he hadn't included an additional air pod on this one. She didn't have much air left, and she couldn't enable the control panel so she could direct the pod elsewhere.

She was headed to the planet no matter what. She hesitated, then looked at what capability the pod did have to keep her from smashing into the planet, even if she made it through the atmosphere. There were thrusters but no way to steer.

The pod jolted. There was a flash of light and what sounded like frying eggs that brought her gaze to the other screen. The red planet beneath her was drawing closer. The pod was well-insulated; she didn't feel the three-thousand-degree temperatures a foot from her. She held her breath, staring at the configuration as she flew through the atmosphere.

Unwilling to see her death, she closed her eyes, never imagining she'd ever be hurtling towards some distant planet in an escape pod booby-trapped to kill her! The strange sound continued for several minutes, and she trembled, trying hard not to think of what happened if she made it unscathed to the planet's surface.

Where the hell was she?

Tears streamed down her face. The frying stopped, and she felt another jolt. Her eyes flew open and she braced herself against the side. The pod dropped fast toward the surface, the sight of the spinning world beneath her sickening. She was pressed against the ceiling despite the gravity controller in the pod.

There was nothing on the red planet, no signs of buildings, no life. At least, nothing she could make out as she spun faster and faster. She closed her eyes, dizzy and stared at the computer screen, watching her speed increase as her altitude decreased. She'd not yet figured out how to convert their measures of distance to miles. She looked again at the spinning ground, waiting until she was able to make out a rock formation clearly before engaging the thrusters.

The effect slammed her downwards, and the pod spun out of control, head over tail, shaking as it fought gravity.

"C'mon, c'mon," she whispered desperately, her throat burning with acid as she struggled to hold down her stomach.

Of all the things she could be thinking about, she thought only of A'Ran. His face was in her thoughts, and the idea of never seeing him again crushed her as surely as colliding with the planet would. She didn't know what she felt for him, but he was her destiny. She belonged with him. Everything else would work itself out.

The pod stabilized upside down, and she was crammed into half of the pod, unable to move with her hands tied. The ground approach slowed drastically as the pod's thrusters roared but was still too fast for her comfort. She braced herself.

The pod bounced once and slammed into the ground. The computer blinked off, and the pod slid, stopping finally.

Bruised, she blinked as brilliant sunlight pierced the cracked door. Almost unable to believe she'd survived, she stared for a long moment, pushed the door open, and tumbled onto the ground.

She vomited, her head spinning from her trip. The air was dry and *hot*, as if she were in a sauna. She struggled to draw deep breaths. Sweat broke out on her skin, and she shielded her eyes against the sun before crawling back to the shade of the pod.

The landscape was open and flat, the heat making the ground shimmer.

She was going to die here, wherever here was. Stricken, she wrapped her arms around her knees and began to cry. If only she'd worked up the nerve to tell A'Ran about her suspicions about Ne'Rin! She wouldn't be stranded on some foreign, deserted planet!

She cried until too tired to cry more, then leaned against the pod, feeling as if her skin was frying despite the shade. She closed her eyes and rested her head against the pod.

She didn't think it was possible to sleep in such discomfort, but a stiff, hot breeze tossed hair into her face awhile later, tickling her awake. She swiped it away, soaked with sweat, and opened her eyes.

She shifted with a grimace and looked down at the brush of grass against her hands. She'd thought the planet completely dead, but there was a bright patch of green grass beneath her and the pod. If there was grass, there was bound to be water somewhere.

The suns were setting. She rose to see how far away they were from the horizon, miserable in the heat. She rustled through the pod to see if there was any water or food.

Ne'Rin didn't plan on giving her any chance to live. She was too hot to cry, and she curled up on the grass. It felt cooler than the air against her fevered skin.

Dusk took away much of the intolerable heat, and a stiff breeze dried her sweat. She remained on the ground, at a loss as to what to do. If she left the pod, she might fry in the morning. If she stayed, she'd never find help!

More tears rose, and she tugged at her hands, furious he'd even thought to cuff her! As if she wasn't completely vulnerable as it was! He wasn't taking chances she'd survive.

A'Ran.

She couldn't think of him, not now. The thought of him made her heart leap and her body ache for him. She wanted to curl up in the pod and sob until he rescued her, even knowing he'd never know where to find her.

A light shined in her face, and she twisted, fear piercing her misery. She pushed herself up and shielded her face with her bound hands. Someone grabbed her and lifted her to her feet. He pushed her sleeve up to see her band.

There was a quiet exchange between two of the four dark shapes around her. She couldn't help but be grateful they at least resembled humans. She was expecting some sort of alien monster to inhabit the brutal planet. One took her hands while another shined the glowing orb on her bindings. He released them with a touch of his thumb.

Furious, she threw them and turned to find two of the beings kneeling by the grass, touching them.

She crossed her arms, exhausted. They rose and shone the light on her again. One took her arm, gesturing at the armband. He faced her, his features dark, and addressed her. She pushed the light away and shrugged, pulling her arm free. One handed her a water canteen, and she drank long and deep, not stopping even when another took her arm and pulled her forward. The light went out.

They walked into the night. Two moons rose, and the four warriors around her kept to a path only they understood. The desert was flat, the rock formations and canyons plentiful.

Beyond a nearby mountain range, lights and explosions lit up both the sky and the air between earth and sky. She watched, unnerved at how close the battles were. They shook the ground, and battleships raced overhead. The men ignored the signs of war, instead keeping to a quick pace along their path. Wherever she was, the battle was intense. Instead of stars overhead, there were ships.

They reached a small encampment at the bottom of a mountain and passed around it, one calling out a greeting as someone trotted out to meet them. They continued up a winding path toward the top of the lowest of the mountains. She lagged, fatigued. Two slowed to keep pace with her while the other three went on ahead.

Night brought a chill as uncomfortable as the heat of the day. Hot, hungry, exhausted, she stopped twice on the trek up the hill to catch her breath. They reached the top, where another set of low buildings were carved from the rock, their doors and windows glowing.

The mountains overlooked an expansive plain lined with encampments, an airfield, small ships, and other war arsenal. The battle waged just past the next range. She watched the flares of color against the night sky with tired fascination.

The men led her into a large meeting hall with warriors clumped in small groups throughout the hall. The air was filled with quiet, serious discussions and with the faint scents of war: sweat and weapons. It was lit with warm yellow light. She paused inside the door, not wanting to deal with anything else. Her body hurt, her head pulsed, and she wanted nothing more than to curl up on a warm rock outside and go to sleep.

The warriors before her looked as if they'd just been released from some sort of meeting. Some left, ignoring her, while others shifted between small groups. She looked around for somewhere to sit or hide, aware the two men who'd followed her up the mountain were still there.

Her gaze stumbled on a familiar face at the other end of the hall, and she gasped. She took in the familiar dress and coloring of the men around her, startled to realize she *did* know where she was.

"Mansr!" she cried, tears filling her eyes again.

A look of astonishment crossed his face as he turned. She raced forward through the men, not caring what they thought, and flung herself into Mansr's arms with enough force to drive him back a step.

He grunted and started to take her arms to pry her away. She shoved his hands away, clinging to him. He relented and spoke, his words garbled. She squeezed her eyes closed, not caring what he said and suspecting he was lecturing her on how not to behave in public. He wrapped one arm around her and touched her ear with his other hand, depositing a translator there.

"*Nishani,*" he chided.

"No!" she almost shouted, pulling away to glare at him with tear-filled eyes. "Don't tell me what to do! I just had the most horrifying day of my life! I almost died a million times over, and if I didn't know how to enable the shields on the escape pod, I would have burned up in the atmosphere, and if that didn't kill me, then hitting the planet—"

He held up a hand, planting it across her mouth when she refused to stop.

"I cannot understand you when you speak so quickly, *nishani,*" he said, warmth crossing his dark eyes. "Calm down."

She hugged him, and he grunted.

"You want to meet the man who rescued you?"

She wiped her eyes and turned without releasing him.

"This is my son and the cousin of the *dhjan*, Leyon."

Leyon was wiry and tall, his whip-like body unlike A'Ran's, who was far thicker. His features, however, were similar, his eyes identical.

"It is my duty, *nishani*," he replied. He looked hard at Mansr, who chuckled.

"*Nishani*, if you'll let me go," Mansr said, "I'll take you somewhere to rest."

She released him reluctantly. He took her arm and led her through the crowd into the night. Leyon followed, and Mansr took her into a small dwelling on the mountain. He led her to a bench in the middle of the house and glanced at an awaiting servant, who darted away. She crossed her arms.

"Can you call A'Ran and tell him where I am?" she asked.

"I will," Mansr said, sitting down across from her.

Grass tickled her feet, and she glanced down at the swath of green beneath her. Irritated, she pulled her feet up and crossed her legs beneath her. Mansr and Leyon both stared at her, and she rubbed her face.

"Mansr, I really need some food," she said, deflated. "I've had a bad day."

"I would say so," he replied. "Do you know where you are?"

"Anshan?"

"I'm not sure how you made it through the enemy's defenses. We can't get any ship off planet."

"I don't know," she said, eyes watering.

"You are the battle planner?" Leyon asked.

"Yes."

"Tomorrow, son," Mansr said.

"A'Ran can't come get me?" she asked, distressed.

"Not right now. He's got a bad space battle on his hands. Your sister's family joined our enemy."

"This is where you want me to be anyway," she observed glumly. "I'm supposed to be here, aren't I?"

"You are," Mansr said with another frown. "I didn't expect you to arrive this way. Leyon said you arrived in an escape pod?"

"Yes," she said. "The communications and control panels were disabled, but I figured out how to engage the shields. I did what I could. You know he even put bindings on me to make sure I didn't survive?"

"Who?" he asked.

"Ne'Rin," she said in a tight voice. "I don't think he wanted me to survive at all."

The two men shared a look.

"Mansr, I want A'Ran and I want to go home," she said, at an end with her endurance. She started to cry again, too exhausted to stop. He rose and took her arm, leading her into one of the small bedrooms, where a grey bed awaited her.

"Sleep, *nishani*. We'll talk tomorrow."

NINE

GOD, her body hurt! Crashing into the planet left the left side of her torso black and bruised. If not for the painkillers Mansr gave her as soon as she awoke and her newest discovery to distract her from the lingering pain, she'd be too miserable to move.

She made grass grow. The realization made her want to laugh and cringe at the same time.

Who the hell could make grass grow?

She planted her hand on the red ground and counted to ten, until she felt the tickle of blades of grass beneath her hand. Astonished, she leaned back and watched it rise, thick and plush, to a height of several inches.

"Leyon?" She turned to find him staring at her from across the dwelling. She motioned to the small patch of grass. "Can you do this, too?"

"Only the *nishani*," he said. He looked at her the way she looked at the six-legged cat that awoke her that morning.

"Only I can ..." She trailed off, recalling her last conversation with A'Ran. She'd never thought he meant she'd *literally* help the planet re-grow. She'd thought her role more spiritual or symbolic. "This is good, right?"

"Yes, *nishani*."

He thought her crazy. She rolled her eyes and finished her breakfast. The dwelling was warm already in the midmorning, and she wondered how she'd survive another day of heat like yesterday's. Drained despite her long night of rest, she didn't look forward to anything this day.

"Do you want to talk to the *dhjan*?"

She rose quickly in response from her place kneeling at the small table. He led her into the hot morning. The battle still raged in the distance, the colors duller against the morning sky. Several fighter ships lifted off from the valley as they neared another of the buildings beside the meeting hall.

It was packed with warriors facing a screen with A'Ran's calm, hard image displayed. Her heart quickened at the sight of him. She couldn't hear the quiet discussions but saw Mansr at the front, speaking to A'Ran. Leyon waited with her at the doorway as the war discussions continued. Kiera pulled her hair into a ponytail, the back of her neck already damp with sweat. Grass tickled her feet as she stayed in place too long.

Agitated, she glanced down, then back—kneeling to pull a handful of it free. She placed it in her pocket, ignoring Leyon's look. The warriors moved and shifted as one, and she backpedaled quickly out of their paths as they exited the dwelling. Mansr and another older man remained. He motioned her in, and she approached somewhat anxiously.

A'Ran was unreadable. He was seated, his fingers steepled and his gaze penetrating. He wasn't happy, and part of her wondered if she'd done something already to piss him off. Mansr glanced at her.

"Hello, A'Ran," she said quietly.

"Hello, Kiera." He'd never used her name before. "Are you well?"

"Yes, I am," she said. She could feel his angry energy even over the viewer. She withdrew the grass from her pocket and held it out as a peace offering, uncertain how to take his mood. "I can make grass grow! Doesn't that make you happy?"

"You may be useful yet, *nishani*," he allowed. A faint smile escaped despite his dark mood.

She rolled her eyes at him.

"You're hurt," he said, his mood darkening. She touched her bruised cheekbone and realized doing so exposed her black and blue arm.

"I crashed into the planet," she said. "It could've been worse. I was able to re-engage the shields and the thrusters."

"She's fortunate. We saw the pod as it fell," Mansr seconded. "It's good you knew a thing or two about configuring a ship, *nishani*."

A'Ran lifted his chin to his uncle, who bowed in response to the dismissal and left. She glanced over her shoulder as the others left.

"Are you angry?" she asked, returning her gaze to the *dhjan*. His position didn't change even when they were alone, his gaze direct and hard.

"Not at you," he replied. "What did Ne'Rin say to you before he ejected you from the ship?"

She looked away and cleared her throat, embarrassed to feel tears in her eyes again.

"I'm sorry," she murmured. "I've never had anyone hate me so much. He seemed to think you'd gone weak and I was the source of your weakness. He said without me, you might win your war." She traced the bruises around her wrists from the bindings. "Are you disappointed with me?"

"I chose you. Anshan chose you."

"Would you choose differently?"

"No, Kiera," he said, voice softening. She crossed her arms, hugging herself.

"I'm so sorry, A'Ran."

"Why are *you* sorry?"

"You have enough to worry about with all your duties," she replied.

"My family should come before my duties. I'll evac you as soon as it's safe."

"I can help you from here," she said. "I can help Mansr battle plan."

"*Nishani*—"

"I want to! I'm supposed to be here!"

He gazed at her, shifting to lean forward, the only sign of his unease. She braced herself for a refusal and a fight. He took her in for a long moment before caving.

"Mansr needs the help."

"You'll let me stay?" Surprised, she met his dark gaze.

"Not too long, and only until the space war is calm enough for me to evac you," he said firmly.

"I don't want to disappoint you," she said slowly. "It's my fault Ne'Rin lost his faith in you."

"That has nothing to do with you, *nishani*. Do not apologize for another's betrayal."

She wondered if he felt hurt at his best friend's betrayal but didn't have the nerve to ask. He appeared hard and strong as usual. There was no sign Ne'Rin's betrayal affected him at all.

"I must go, *nishani*. Are you well enough to battle plan?"

She nodded.

"Have Mansr show you to the command center. The ground battle is yours."

Her breath caught at his words. Thrilled, she realized he'd just granted her something he'd never given anyone else: the position as his equal.

"Thank you," she said in a hushed voice. "Will I see you soon?"

"As soon as I can arrange it. You'll see how difficult our position," he replied. "Send in Mansr."

"Be careful, A'Ran."

"And you, *nishani*. Mansr and Leyon will take care of you."

"I don't—"

"Hush, woman," he said. "Go."

She rolled her eyes at him again, and he offered another faint smile before she left. She joined Leyon outside in the hot morning and waited for Mansr.

"Is everyone from your planet like you?" Leyon asked, his gaze intent.

"For the most part," she replied.

"You have no men on your planet."

"We do!"

He shook his head. Mansr returned and motioned for her to follow him. He led her through the small encampment toward the mountain and up a smooth walkway to the flattened peak of one ridge. In the center was a massive console surrounded by a circular bench beneath the shade of a ledge. Several warriors loitered near the console. Mansr activated the audio communications.

"You'll be able to communicate with me as required." A'Ran's low voice came to her through the unseen speaker.

She approached the console, circling it once as she took in the different symbols. She touched her palm to the activation key, and the ground battle hologram sprung up before her. It whirled slowly.

"A lot changed fast," she murmured.

"It did."

"And not for the best."

"We have reinforcements inbound. The Council split on sanctioning me, and those whose support Jetr swayed for me are sending their armies to battle."

She reviewed the last several days, taking in the swelling number of enemies in the skies and on the ground.

"How many ground forces do you expect?" she asked.

"One and a half times what we have now."

"Where did you learn?" Leyon asked, standing beside her.

"In A'Ran's battle room."

"Check grid 77," A'Ran instructed.

She manipulated the scene before her and saw his concern: the only food repository in the area was under attack. She nudged Leyon aside to punch another set of buttons and issued an order to reinforce the failing efforts there.

"There aren't many good water sources," she murmured. "The next nearest is on the moon and a logistical nightmare."

"I'm sending a list of trouble areas. I've got to go. I trust you to handle these."

"Thank you, thank you," she whispered. "You don't know how much this means to me. You're not treating me like some enslaved woman with no brain."

"I've not given up on righting your behavior," he assured her.

"Good luck!" she retorted. She shook her head as he closed the communication line with a click and concentrated on the scene before her. The grids with issues popped up as a layer over the holo-gram of the existing battles. She couldn't read the writing, but she knew the numbers well enough to find the grids.

She sat down, growing oblivious to those around her as she manipulated and modified the battlefield. A'Ran submitted changes, and she reviewed the images. The day grew hot fast, though the surrounding peaks shaded her from the sun itself. Mansr sat beside her and remained, watching the scene before her. Only when the pain in her body returned did she lean back for a break with a grimace.

"You must rest," Mansr said quietly. "You've done more this day than I could in seven."

"My body hurts."

"Leyon will take you to the medical facility," he said. "Forgive me, *nishani*, I should have taken you yesterday. I wanted my nephew to see what kind of enemy he had."

She wasn't sure what to say and offered a smile instead. She didn't doubt the impact of her battered visage on any man, especially A'Ran. Leyon motioned for her to follow him and guided her through the rocky trails to another of the low stone buildings at the base of the hills.

An hour later, she left the medical facility, completely healed though still exhausted. Leyon took her into one of the mountains, and she sighed at the blast of chilled air that greeted her. The dining hall was vacant and massive, a cave converted into a cafeteria. He motioned for her to sit and brought her food and water.

"How did you learn to battle plan?" he asked, sitting across from her.

"In A'Ran's battle room. I was bored after he kidnapped me and left me with his sisters," she replied. She was getting used to the hard stares the warriors gave her, the only indication of their surprise at her candidness.

"I pity my cousin," he said at last. At her surprised look, he added, "I know him well enough to know you will change him. I do not know if he realizes how much."

"I'm not sure if you're insulting me or complimenting me," she said with a puzzled smile.

"He chose well, *nishani*."

"Thank you, I think."

"Are there many women on your planet?"

"Yes, there are about three billion. You want one?"

"I may." He was serious enough that she laughed.

"At least I haven't scared you away from them!"

"I want to see what kind of planet produces women like you."

She laughed harder, glancing up as Mansr joined them. He tossed his head to Leyon, who left quietly.

"How do you fare, *nishani*?" he asked.

"Good."

"You've mastered battle planning."

"Not yet. A'Ran is better than me."

"As he should be. He's been doing it for many years."

She ate her dinner, beat. He made no move to leave her in the cafeteria.

"I hoped you would come," he said softly.

"I don't know how long I can stay," she replied. "I don't think grass will benefit the war effort, though."

"It's a start. The world and its people will take time to heal."

She paused and stared at him, unable to comprehend an entire planet that depended on *her*. He seemed to assume she was staying for good, and she didn't know how to tell him A'Ran had given her a choice she hadn't yet made.

"A'Ran chose well," Mansr added. "Even if you are unusual."

"He has a lot on his shoulders."

"He has since his parents were killed. He's been the *dhjan* fighting this battle since he reached my shoulder. He's known nothing else in all these years. I am happy he found you, not only for Anshan but for him. He needs someone to remind him that there is more to his life than war."

"I don't want to disappoint any of you," she murmured. "Especially not him. Mansr, I can't help but think it's my fault that Ne'Rin betrayed him."

"It's not your fault," he said with A'Ran's firmness. "Ne'Rin's father betrayed A'Ran's father. Each man followed in his father's shadow. You were an excuse for him to do what he did."

"Ne'Rin's father?" she echoed, surprised to learn she'd overheard them plotting without knowing what they were doing. "That's awful."

"It is. He's asked Leyon to step into Ne'Rin's role."

"Mansr, what about Gage?" she asked more quietly.

"A'Ran told me," he said grimly. "He's taken on the responsibility of raising her child, if she chooses not to mate with another."

"She'll be heartbroken."

"Likely, but Ne'Rin would have killed you all without a second thought, as his father did the rest of their family. At least she and her babe will live."

"There's no saving Ne'Rin from whatever his issue is?" she asked, upset.

"A'Ran's already acted."

"What do you mean?"

"I mean, Ne'Rin is no longer a threat."

She shivered. She didn't doubt A'Ran could be ruthless if he felt his family was threatened. She didn't like to think of how violent the man in control of a world always at war could be. She glanced down absently at the tickle of grass against her feet.

"Can I do anything more useful than this?" she asked.

"It will come," he said. "I know you are tired, but there is a place I'd like to show you."

She hesitated, ashamed to feel a sense of suspicion after Ne'Rin's betrayal. She looked at Mansr, whose sharp gaze took in her features.

"It can wait," he offered.

"No, I'm sorry," she said. "Just a little ..." She didn't finished but sensed he understood.

He rose and started toward the entrance. She trailed, stepping into the chilled desert night. Mansr strode down one of the many paths lining the rocky hills, away from the encampment and into a part of the hills untouched by any but the moons' light. Kiera went, resisting the urge to call A'Ran. She had nothing to fear from these people, especially not Mansr, a blood relative of A'Ran and his sisters.

He walked farther than she preferred before disappearing into a dark crevice. She waited at the top of the sloping walkway until she saw the outline of a door as he cracked it open. The outline turned to a bright square of light, and she followed him again.

Two warriors stood hidden in the dark on either side of the doorway. She jumped when one moved, her heart flipping. The warrior opened the door wider and motioned her in. She entered a narrow, well-lit hall and followed it through smoothly hewn walls. Several more warriors stood at intersections like gargoyles, moving only to point in the direction she needed to go.

She caught up to Mansr at long last. He stood outside a closed door down a short hallway lined with warriors. Her heart quickened as she paced through the silent warriors and joined him. He motioned to a glowing access pad.

"I cannot enter. Only the *dhjan* and *dhjan nishani*."

She hesitated again, not sure she was ready for another trial.

"Inside is one of three temples on Anshan where the heart of the planet and its people is. While I've never seen what lies within, legend says it's the key to the planet's survival."

She wanted to tell him she wasn't ready for this, that she hadn't even decided to stay yet. Her words died on her lips as she took in the deep worry lines and gaunt features of the man before her. After all he'd been through fighting for his home, how could she refuse?

With a nod, she prepared herself for the worst. He stepped aside and she waved her band in front of the access door. She couldn't help but feel surprised when it opened. Inside was another small chamber. She looked at Mansr, who nodded in encouragement, then stepped into the chamber.

The thick stone door behind her slid closed, and there was a pause before another door opened in front of her. She expected another similar chamber with a low ceiling and plain walls and was stunned at the massive cave before her.

The walls were covered with colorful pictographs of couples and Anshan's geometric writing, telling her a story she couldn't read. The tiled floor depicted Anshan and its moons, with the planet at the chamber's center. Two thrones of stone sat opposite her, awaiting their masters. In the center of the chamber was a small fountain whose waters had long gone dry. She walked into the chamber, awed by the drawings and writings on the walls. They were in different hands from different times, the top of the chamber rimmed with drawings of couples holding hands and standing on a ball she took to be Anshan.

She didn't understand the significance of the pictures or writing and frowned, wondering how such a simple place was considered sacred. She crossed the stone tiles to the center of the chamber and circled the plain fountain. More pictographs were carved in the rim, and she circled the fountain twice before finding what she thought was the beginning, marked by pictures larger than the rest.

She trailed her fingers over the first image chiseled into the stone: that of a man. The next depicted the planet, the next a woman holding a knife, then the fountain, a plant, a river. She struggled to understand what the images were trying to tell her. She reached the beginning again and looked around the chamber, perplexed.

The thrones caught her attention, and she crossed to them. One bore the same image of a man, the second of the woman. In the middle of the queen's throne was a low stone box she mistook at first glance to be the world's most uncomfortable lumbar support. When she saw the king's throne had no such stone structure, she returned to the woman's and touched the box.

It clicked, and she jerked back. The top opened of its own volition, revealing an aged stone dagger with dulled edges and a chipped stone hilt. She withdrew it and hefted it. It was as heavy as it looked, as long as her forearm. She held it with two hands and retreated to the fountain, unable to shake the instinct that said the dagger on the fountain was the same.

She set the knife down on the edge and circled the fountain again until she'd reviewed all three of the pictographs where the female figure held a dagger. She almost slapped herself when she realized how simple it was.

The fountain contained instructions for making it work.

"*Dhjan, dhjan nishani,* dagger. Nishani's blood." She looked at the stone dagger and then at the fountain uneasily. There was no way she could fill it with blood!

She looked at the instructions again and saw the queen depicted with one drop of what she assumed was blood.

Kiera stepped back and spun around, feeling overwhelmed. She felt like panicking and running to her room and never leaving! Instead, she drew a deep breath and approached the fountain. Her hands shook as she gripped the heavy stone dagger, and she leaned against the fountain. With another deep breath, she ran her thumb down the jagged edge of the dagger. Stinging made her curse, and she grimaced as she held her thumb over the fountain. She watched the crimson drop form, stretch, then fall into the fountain.

She leaned over the edge to see the stone tile at the bottom of the fountain absorb her blood. She sucked her thumb and stepped back, waiting for something to happen. According to the pictures, there would be plants. Yet there was no earth or place for them to grow around her.

A long, silent moment passed. She began to think she'd misunderstood the pictures when a green sprout appeared at the center of the fountain. It grew to her height as she watched and then bloomed into an orange-pink flower the size of her head, shriveled and died, and returned. A second flower blossomed and remained.

Kiera waited. When nothing else happened, she retrieved the dagger and replaced it. She looked again at the flower, puzzled.

Suddenly, the ground jolted and shook, throwing her onto her stomach. Rumbling alarmed her as the stone lurched and moved beneath her. The sound of a roaring ocean filled the chamber. The flower moved as if caught in a breeze, not an earthquake.

The pictographs said nothing of an earthquake! Kiera climbed to her feet, barely caught herself from hitting the fountain with the next great tremor of the ground, and bolted for the door. She smashed into it as another quake rumbled beneath her, then rose and waved her band before the door. It opened, and she flung herself against the second door. It opened only when the other had closed, and she toppled into Mansr's arms.

"We must go!" he said, steadying himself against the wall. The warriors grabbed her and passed her up the hall before he took one arm and another warrior her other.

They raced through the quaking halls toward the entrance, all while the strange roar of an ocean grew louder. Mansr took her a different route than the one she'd used to enter, one that sloped down and then up. Within moments, they burst into the chilly desert night.

Mansr tripped, taking all three of them down. Kiera grunted as she hit the ground, and he wrapped an arm around her.

"Oh, god, Mansr! I'm so sorry!" she exclaimed. "I did it wrong!"

To her surprise, he barked a laugh of half-pain from their fall and half-triumph. She sprawled on top of him, unable to push herself up with the earth's violent shaking. More warriors tumbled out after them until the last closed the stone door.

Two hauled her up and one helped Mansr. She bounced between them, unable to catch her balance.

"Come!" Mansr ordered, waving them toward another small trail up a hill.

The warriors gave her no choice but pulled her up the hill. She didn't understand why until they reached the top, overlooking a deep canyon. Water shot from the bottom of the canyon, forming hundreds of tall columns whose mist cast rainbows in the bright moonlight. Mansr dropped to his knees as the earth continued to tremble. She pulled away from the warriors and dropped beside him, more comfortable on the ground than trying to navigate the shaking earth on her feet.

Mansr's shoulders shook, and she took his arm, alarmed.

"Mansr, what's wrong?"

He was laughing again. She stared at him, then at the water. A burst of wind sent water from the closest column raining over them. Grass tickled her knees, and she shifted, agitated by water and grass.

"Mansr!" she demanded. "What have I done?"

"Water!" he replied, throwing his arm toward the canyon. "We had none before!"

She frowned. As suddenly as it started, the earth stopped shaking. The warriors regained themselves first and crossed to the edge of the canyon, unaffected by the water spraying on them. They were silent, staring.

Mansr regained himself and rose. She watched as he too crossed to the edge of the canyon before she rose. Her knees hurt from her landing. The distant roar of water pouring into the canyon caught her attention.

"Mansr, I don't understand," she said at last.

"Anshan has had no water since the last *dhjan nishani*," he said. "The plants died, the lakes dried up. We had nothing."

Her gaze went to the columns with newfound interest.

"You mean, I didn't do something wrong?" she asked.

"No, *nishani*, you saved us. As long as you are here, there will be life on Anshan."

As long as you are here.

The words made him smile but weighed on her. She looked at each of the warriors, who watched the water as if they'd never seen it before. She'd wondered why A'Ran's water supplies were located on the nearest moon, a logistical obstacle. The thought that they had no water on the planet itself had never occurred to her.

She did this. She didn't know how, but she did it. The men around her were happy despite their stony visages. She didn't know what to feel, except she wanted to cry.

"Mansr, I'm tired," she whispered. "Can we go back now?"

He looked at her, his smile fading. "Of course. You must be exhausted."

She nodded, not trusting herself to say anything else. Her throat was tight, and she didn't think her legs would carry her. They did. Mansr led her back to the small dwelling she shared with him and his son. The encampment was a flurry of activity, and she wondered how much was normal and how much was related to the water.

She said nothing to him but returned to her small room and closed the door. Kiera lay down in the dark and stared at the ceiling. Despite feeling tired, she couldn't sleep.

"*Nishani.*" His voice made her jump, and she looked around wildly before she realized A'Ran's voice came from the communicator. She rose grudgingly and crossed to the communications viewer. Unwilling to face him, she turned on the audio portion.

"I'm here," she said, and cleared her throat. She knew he heard the restrained emotion by his pause.

"Are you well?"

"Just tired."

"I'm transmitting a message to Mansr. Our enemy figured out you're alive and on the planet. My reinforcements aren't here yet; you'll need to keep moving until I can neutralize the newest threat."

"No problem."

"What disturbs you?" His voice was softer.

"Just tired," she whispered. Tears gathered in her eyes.

"It is not like you to keep the truth from me."

"I, uh, I went to the fountain and figured out how to make it work. There's water now, A'Ran," she managed, struggling not to cry. "Mansr says there will be water as long as I'm on Anshan."

"Water," he said, an odd note in his voice. "He speaks the truth. As long as you are *nishani*, the planet will heal."

"And if I leave, everyone dies."

"It is the way of things, *nishani*." His voice was even, as if he tried to ease some of the weight of her decision.

"I couldn't live with myself if I left everyone to die," she said.

"We share the same burden," he said in a hushed voice. "My failure to protect my people should not be something another should bear."

She wiped her eyes.

"I will accept your decision, no matter which choice you make," he said.

"I don't know how you can say that," she returned, "when one means your people will be destroyed!"

"You must accept your place willingly. It is the natural way of things here."

"So you're obligated to give me the choice."

"Yes."

She closed her eyes, remembering how she'd felt in his arms: like she wasn't just another duty to him.

"I couldn't walk away from your planet any more than I could my own, if me staying means everyone lives," she whispered. "I must stay and do my ... duty." She waited, expecting her words to please him.

"Very well." His tone didn't change, as if she'd just told him she was going shopping instead of sacrificing the rest of her life for his people. "Prepare yourself to move before the suns rise."

She turned off the communicator, not caring if he said anything else. Instead, she cried, feeling more alone than she had since leaving earth. She fell into a restless sleep that was disturbed long before dawn. Leyon's shake rattled her to her bones, and she pushed at him. He shone a light in her face before hauling her to her feet. She stumbled after him into the central area of the dwelling.

"We must go," Mansr said, tossing a small pack to her. "The Qatwali have landed their army nearby. We can't evac you, but we can hide in the hills."

She went to the window at his words. The attackers were down the road. Startled, she froze, watching the giant warriors fight until Leyon wrenched her forward. Their pace out of the dwelling and toward the hills was brutal, too fast for her to keep up, and Leyon ended up swinging her into his arms like a child to keep the fast pace into the rocky hills. The moons hung well above the horizon, and the desert air was chilly enough for her to see her breath.

Mansr led the column of warriors into the hills, not stopping until they reached the canyon she'd last seen several hours before. To her surprise, moonlight glinted off the water of the newly formed lake that filled the canyon. Leyon set her down after they passed it. They were forced to slow their pace when the trail became covered with slippery shale and the path grew steeper. They stopped in the shadow of a hill, and Mansr barked quiet orders at the dozen warriors with them. She replaced her translator as he approached.

"Listen carefully," he said, gripping her arms. "Is your translator working?"

She nodded.

"We're being followed. You will follow this path that leads around the hill back toward the encampment. You remember the chamber where you were earlier?"

She nodded again.

"Hide there. No one will enter. They're tracking us, and I don't know how. We're going to scatter to see who's followed, and if it's you, we'll kill anyone who follows your path."

"You're sending me alone?" she asked, surprised.

"I must know who among us has a tracking beacon. Leyon will be near you at all times. You'll be in no danger."

She was about to object when he released her to signal one of his other men forward.

"Around the hill," Leyon repeated. "Stick to the path. You'll see the trail to the cave."

He gave her a small push toward the path, and she looked down, squinting in the moonlight to see the darkened trail. The men around her moved silently into every direction, and Mansr lifted his chin in a silent command for her to go. Leyon drew his sword and waited, giving her a head start.

Heart pounding, she trotted down the sloping trail, glancing nervously at the hill to make sure she didn't suddenly fall off her path. The night was quiet aside from her foot falls and the sliding shale. The hill was wide and her blood thrummed as she moved as fast as she could.

Suddenly, a dark form launched itself from behind a group of boulders onto her path. She gasped and halted, staring at the sword and the giant holding it. She took a few steps back and then whirled to run. He snatched her, jerking her back. His sword flew over her head and his grip fell away too fast for her to catch her balance. She fell hard on her backside and saw her attacker's headless body land beside her.

"Go. There are more!" Leyon ordered, pulling her up.

She stumbled in the direction he pushed her, horrified. This time, she paid no attention to the shale or placing her feet right. Instead, she ran as fast as she could on the trail. She reached a point that seemed familiar and looked for the dark shadow of the crevice. It was in the near distance, no more than two hundred meters away, down the hill through a boulder-strewn route. She broke from the trail and darted toward it, her heartbeat loud in her ears.

Three figures emerged to block her path. She skidded to a halt, chest heaving.

C'mon, Leyon! she ordered silently.

One headed for her, and she turned to run, only to collide with a large figure at her back.

A'Ran!

Her body jolted in recognition as their bodies met, even though his face was shadowed. He pushed her behind him, sword in one hand. She took a few steps back and flinched at the first silent contact of his sword with another's. Her eyes pinned to the scene, she couldn't help the emotions spinning through her. Happiness, fear, awe ...

The gloves were off this night. A'Ran wasn't sparring; he fought for blood. She watched him systematically behead or run through the three men, her stomach churning at the sight of so much death. He snatched her hand when none of his opponents remained standing and ran with her toward the crevice.

The path to the bottom was unguarded. He pushed her down it and stayed near the top, looking for other attackers. She trotted to the bottom and waved her band before the access pad, waiting as the stone door opened.

He joined her and took her hand again, pulling her into the hall. The door closed behind them as he strode through the lighted, vacant halls, following a familiar path on the way to the chamber. They entered, and she looked up at him, afraid to address the fierce warrior. Only when they were sealed inside the massive cave did he release her.

He said nothing but withdrew a communications device and began issuing calm commands to his men. Shaken, she leaned against the nearest wall and sank into a sit, disgusted to see there was blood on her clothing.

"*Nishani*, I must leave you here," he said without turning.

She said nothing, scared yet unsure what else she felt. He turned when she didn't respond, and his gaze softened. He crossed to her and knelt. His dark eyes took in her face, and she felt her heart quicken for a different reason. She found herself breathing him in, aching for him to touch her as he had not so long ago.

"Are you well?" he asked.

"I'm fine," she replied.

He studied her.

"Go. I'll be safe here," she heard herself say.

"This is not my *nishani*," he said quietly. He cupped her cheek with one of his large hands, and she was embarrassed to feel tears gather.

She wasn't expecting his kiss or the passion behind it. He kissed her hard and deep, his intensity making her hunger for him flare even as she tried to suppress it. Her senses filled with his taste, scent, the heat of his body, enveloping her yet never enough. He withdrew and kissed her cheeks and forehead, then drew her into a hug. She savored the feel of his body against hers, unable to deny what she felt toward him and terrified he'd never feel the same.

"I must go. I will return soon," he said, releasing her. She nodded. His dark gaze lingered on her before he stalked to the door. She had the unsettling feeling that he was about to disappear from her life forever.

She rose after a few minutes and stretched. The single flower still stood in the fountain, and she crossed to it. It grew straight from the stone; there was no dirt or planter. She sat on the edge of the fountain and looked up at the glyphs on the wall.

The sound of a muffled explosion from beyond the door made her rise. Silence followed, and she wondered if her paranoia had caused her to imagine it. She'd just sat down again when the inner door exploded into rocks that flew across the room. She ducked behind the fountain and saw someone shoving the broken stone door open, shocked to recognize the man leading the charge into the sacred chamber.

A'RAN FOUGHT his way through the Qatwali invaders to the secret battle planner hidden within one of the hills. He broke free of attackers before reaching the camouflaged door and waved his band in front of what would look like just another boulder to someone unfamiliar with the path.

His legs trembled, but he forced himself on. The small chamber holding the battle planner was silent, and he waved the computer on, unable to hold himself up any longer. He dropped to his knees, his body shuddering at the energy—Anshan's life force. It surged up through his feet to his head, making his whole body tingle as the planet welcomed back its king.

He hadn't set foot on the planet since being made the *dhjan* upon his father's death. The feel of the planet's life force through his body was staggering, the sensation similar to what he felt the first time he'd met his *nishani*. He'd dreaded his first steps on his planet, fearing it, too, would've lost faith in him.

The planet welcomed him home, reminded him that his own life —and those of his people—was tied to it. The initial sensations passed, and he breathed deeply, finally able to focus as his body adjusted to the feel of the energy flowing through him.

He'd wondered what his initial greeting as *dhjan* would feel like. It stunned him to feel the planet breathing, struggling back to life after hovering so long on the edge of death. The sensations humbled him, and he thought again of Mansr's words, that he needed to be more than an exiled war planner. His planet needed him. His people needed him. He'd waited too long for the Council to support him instead of returning to the planet that needed him.

A'Ran sat at the battle planner and watched the scenes before him. Qatwali was as ruthless in battle as he was. That they'd ally with the dishonorable Yirkin was his fault; his affront at taking Kiera from them was enough for them to overcome their distaste at dealing with the Yirkin, whom they viewed as even less civilized than the Anshan. His reinforcements would come too late; he had one choice to save his planet.

He touched the communications device to activate it.

"Mansr."

There was a pause, then his uncle's familiar, strained voice.

"Here, A'Ran."

"I'm at the battle planner. My communications capability is limited. I want you to issue the evacuation order for the planet."

"Evacuate?" Mansr asked. "The space battle won't allow anyone off-planet."

"Qatwali is distracted with the land battle and the Yirkin won't be looking where we launch."

"I'll issue the warning. We'll need half a day to evacuate the planet."

"You'll have it," A'Ran said. "I'll activate the emergency facilities on the moon."

"Very well. Is *nishani* well?"

"Yes, uncle, she's safe."

There was a click as Mansr closed the connection. A'Ran returned his attention to the battles twirling before him on the planner. He watched, confirming the far side of the planet wasn't the focus of either Yirkin or Qatwali forces.

He sat back for a moment, heart pounding at the prospect of what he was about to do. *Nishani* had proven she could bring the planet back to life. She had looked less than happy about staying, but she would do her duty, as would he. He would decimate all life on the planet using the very ore that had brought his family wealth and power. The dust emitted from mining the ore was poisonous in its raw state. Long ago, his ancestors had rigged the planet to blow the mines and turn the atmosphere into a toxic mix no one would survive.

Long ago, it had been a negotiating point with the Council: allow Anshan to control its own mines without Council peacekeepers' presence, or the planet would be too polluted for anyone to mine at all. What the Council didn't know was that Anshan would heal with its *nishani*, even if it took many sun-cycles for the mining industry to repair itself. The Council had only thought the Anshan rulers barbaric enough to threaten to blow up the only source of ore.

A'Ran's fingers flew over the command panel as he thought of how wise his forefathers had turned out to be. They'd been right to use force over reason with the Council, a lesson he'd learned almost too late.

He spent a few hours setting up the explosive mechanisms and issuing new battle plans for the space war and ordered his ground troops to evacuate the planet. The Qatwali would think themselves winning as his men withdrew. He watched as Mansr expertly organized the evacuations and aligned the space battle to keep the Yirkins' attention off the ships fleeing the planet's surface for the nearest moon, Kiera. Talal had been right; Kiera was a fateful name for his *nishani*!

He opened the communications device and touched two buttons on the flat control panel.

"A'Ran?" Jetr sounded curious.

"I apologize for disturbing you," A'Ran said.

"I am pleased to hear from you. Where are you?"

"Anshan. I need your help, my friend," A'Ran said. "I'm evacuating the planet. The moon can hold us, but we'll need food and supplies until the space battle is over."

"Evacuating?"

"You're my only true ally of any influence with the Council. Keep them out of the galaxy."

"I'll dispatch my own cargo ships to your moon. The Council will want to be involved, even if this becomes an intra-galaxy war."

"It's been an intra-galaxy war for generations!" he said with some impatience. "Let us end it once and for all, not with the Council manipulating each of us for its benefit!"

"You are forbidden from destroying another's planet," Jetr reminded him. "The force of the Council will be at your door if you touch Qatwal."

"I'm destroying all Qatwali and Yirkin on the surface of Anshan. I don't care about Qatwal or destroying its people. I want my planet back, Jetr, and the Council has done nothing in all these sun-cycles but impede me. Keep them out of the galaxy!"

"Suns," Jetr breathed. "I thought the stories of your barbaric forefathers threatening to destroy Anshan were bluffs."

"They weren't," A'Ran confirmed. "And soon, you'll see just how serious they were."

"I'll do what you ask, A'Ran, but isn't there another way?"

"No," A'Ran said. "There's not."

Jetr was quiet for a long moment before he said, "Very well."

"Thank you, friend."

"You're welcome, A'Ran. I have some work to do to keep the Council out of your way. Contact me when you're safe," Jetr said.

"I will."

A'Ran closed the connection and checked the evacuation progress. He was pleased to see it was nearly complete. The civilians were off the planet while his armies remained. He set the timer for the explosions to start on the opposite side of the planet, startled when the first went off as soon as he gave the order. Just as fast, Mansr called him.

"The warriors aren't off the planet yet!" came his uncle's surprised voice.

"It started too soon. I just issued the evac order for those remaining. The mines will chain-detonate. Get everyone off now!" A'Ran ordered. He watched the visual before him as one mine, then the next and the next, exploded and spewed toxic dust into the atmosphere. They were going fast, much faster than he expected.

"I'm on my way to get you and *nishani*," Mansr said.

A'Ran stood, furious the timing was early. He shut down the battle planner and locked it. As he emerged into the early morning sun, he was again surprised to see clouds already forming over the eastern horizon.

He ran toward the sacred temple, suddenly thrown off his feet as a mine in the valley where his men were based exploded. Fountains shot up from the newly formed lake nearby, and the ground rumbled again. The explosions were coming faster, and he launched to his feet, ignoring the bruises and scrapes along his side.

Mansr's small spacecraft dropped from the sky and hovered above him, following as he darted toward the sacred cave. Another nearby explosion knocked him off balance. He caught himself against a boulder in time to see the ground ahead of him ripple, tear, and fold.

The craft above him opened its door and lowered itself as close as it dared to the ground. A'Ran launched himself upwards, catching the door as the ground beneath him crumbled and gave. The door pulled him in, and he sat in the doorway, coughing at the ore dust cloud and staring.

His destination, the cave hidden at the end of the draw where he'd left *nishani*, had been swallowed.

"Mansr, take us lower!" he ordered.

"A'Ran."

Mansr's calm voice sent a tremor through him.

"Lower, Mansr!" he said again.

"There's no life anywhere down there. The temple is gone."

A'Ran heard Mansr's words as if in a dream. Mansr closed the door as another mine exploded and guided the spacecraft farther off the ground. A'Ran crossed to the cockpit and gazed at the viewer.

There was nothing but a gaping chasm where the temple had been. Mansr still scanned for signs of life, and A'Ran watched as they grew farther from the temple.

He'd left her there to die, assuming she'd be safer in the temple than anywhere else. He watched explosions wrack his planet until they rose high enough that the toxic dust storm he'd started marred the surface of the planet from view.

The space battle stopped completely as Qatwali, Anshan, and Yirkin alike watched the devastation of his planet. A'Ran could only stare. He heard Mansr issue orders to others to rally on the moon and Jetr's voice come over the speakers. None of their words registered, nothing but the sick feeling at the pit of his stomach. His people were safe. His planet was destroyed, yet all he could think about was *her*.

"A'Ran!" Mansr shouted. "Suns, man, I need your help here!"

The words jarred him out of his daze, and he blinked, turning to look at Mansr. The momentary pause of the space battle quickly turned to chaos, and Mansr was struggling to outmaneuver the ships darting away from the planet. A'Ran took control of the ship, forcing himself to focus.

Forgive me, Kiera.

He hadn't just destroyed any hope his planet had of recovering, he'd destroyed the woman he needed, too.

TEN

"ROMAS, NO!" Her latest protest was lost on the warriors, who dragged her aboard yet another ship. "I want to stay!"

"Not with these people," he said, once again the egotistical protector who knew better than her. His quick pace forced her to trot to keep up, and the two warriors behind her let her go to pursue their leader. "I promised Evey I'd rescue you when we went to war."

"I don't need rescuing!" she argued. "I want to stay there with A'Ran!"

Romas whirled at the name, and she ran into him before taking a quick step back. His gaze was cold, his jaw ticking.

"That barbarian has dishonored you and my family! If it were up to me, I'd take you back to Qatwal and mate you to one of my brothers, but Evey forbade it," he snapped. "You should be grateful I rescued you before he could sully you."

Her face felt hot as her fear turned to anger. He spun and strode away before she could formulate a response. She continued after him.

"Romas, he's my mate. I can't just leave him!" she tried again. "And I have to stay and help the planet."

"The decision is made. You're going back to your planet. Evey was right—it was a mistake to bring you with us."

His words stung, and any further argument died on her lips as she realized how serious he was. She stopped in the hall. He motioned for the guards to take her down another corridor, and she went.

SHE AWOKE from the nightmare she'd had every night since being dragged off Anshan. It was past sunrise, so she rose and flung off her bed covers. Her things and most of the furniture had been returned with her to the row house. She'd refused to unpack everything, instead digging out only what she needed as the days passed.

She didn't expect her sense of loss to be so deep. It'd hit her on the spaceship ride home and had only grown deeper. Romas hadn't even accompanied her to the row house but sent her on a small shuttle to the local park and left her there. No farewell, no apology, nothing. She'd cried for two days before finally realizing on day three that no one was coming for her.

She looked around her room. Her feet were cold on the wooden floor, and she'd caught herself looking down many times to see if she made grass grow here, too. She didn't, and the disappointment brought tears to her eyes once again. Wiping them away, she padded into the hall, down the stairs, and to her studio, which overflowed with paintings she'd done in the eight days since returning. She stood before her favorite, an image of A'Ran the way she remembered him from the day they'd first met.

Even the sight of him immortalized in paints made her chest tight and her knees weak. She hadn't realized what she felt for him until it was too late to tell him. She may have been a duty for him, but he'd been so much more ... and Anshan...

Her gaze went to her cold feet again. Anshan's energy had kept her feet warm, even on the rocky terrain. Grass had sprung up from boulders she touched, and she'd felt truly a part of her world for once in her life.

And now she had ... nothing. She shivered and twisted to see the rest of her paintings. Talal, their home in exile, the canyon filled with hulking grey ships in the moonlight near Romas's home, the flower in the fountain of the sacred temple.

She missed them. She sat down at her desk and grabbed the waiting sketchpad. Food had become an overlooked stranger, and she'd found herself leaving her studio only for the bathroom and the bedroom. Otherwise, she drew and painted. Today, she returned to the drawing she started long ago on the portrait she had intended to give Evelyn for her wedding.

Her eyes watered as she recalled when she'd last worked on it, the night she was kidnapped. She'd thought that the worst night of her life until now. Wiping her tears, she concentrated on sketching.

The sun brightened up the studio a short time later, her reminder it was time for her midmorning walk. She'd forced herself to walk daily, if for no other reason than to keep her mind off the paintings and memories.

The Monterey mists were in full effect, filtering the sunlight. Moisture clung to her skin as she started down the familiar path to Lover's Lane. The ocean was hidden beneath the fog and the air chilled, so she walked fast until she warmed up. She was happy for the mist; it kept the seaside lovers off the Lane and made her feel more invisible. She'd been ignoring Kevin's calls for two days without caring he was the only person who could help her put food on the table.

She returned to the row house just as the sun began to burn off the mist and the blue sky appeared in the distance. Rather than feel energized by the activity, she felt more drained. She stood for a long moment in the cramped, silent foyer. An odd scratching sound came from the kitchen, like Evelyn's cat scratching at the door after it returned from its morning prowl.

Frowning, she went to the kitchen, worried Evelyn's cat found its way home from its adoptive parents up the street. Not that she wouldn't mind some company; the house was too quiet this morning, and her memories refused to leave her in peace.

She walked into the kitchen and stopped.

A tarantula cat.

Both surprised and horrified, she snatched the broom she'd left leaning against the counter. It ignored her, focusing instead on scratching at a spot of dirt, one of its main food sources. She stared at it, as irritated by its unwitting acknowledgment of her housekeeping prowess as she was about having this of all creatures in her house. The kitchen table, like much of the rest of the house's furniture, had been disassembled in anticipation of moving before Evelyn's wedding. She tugged the top of the kitchen table to block the doorway, hoping it would keep the creature in the kitchen.

Suspecting it was a stowaway from one of the boxes, she took the broom upstairs, where most of the boxes were. She rifled gingerly through the boxes, afraid of uncovering a stash of tarantula cats. When she found none, she returned to the living room, where the rest of the boxes has been deposited, and searched them.

She found no more and returned to the kitchen. The tarantula cat was sucking up dirt and dust from the kitchen corners. She leaned the broom against the wall, unhappy to see the creature but feeling bad for it. It, too, was alone now, somewhere it didn't belong. At least she'd never have to worry about feeding it; the house was a mess.

She left the door blocked, took a quick shower, and opened the door to her studio.

Evelyn stood in the middle of the room.

Kiera gasped, drawing Evelyn's attention from the paintings to the door. Kiera stood dumbly, staring at her friend.

"Happy to see me?" Evelyn asked with a hesitant smile. She wore the alien clothing, though her stomach was starting to protrude.

Kiera closed the door to the studio slowly, uncertain what she felt. She couldn't let her sense of hope seize her for fear of being devastated. She didn't know why Evelyn was there. She wouldn't assume anything.

"I guess not," Evelyn said at her silence. "You don't look too well."

"I'm okay," she replied with effort. "I am happy to see you."

Evelyn frowned. Kiera felt the awkward silence but didn't know what to say. She'd lost the ability to feel anger—or feel at all—and just wondered what her friend wanted. To date, nothing Evelyn had done was for anyone else's benefit but Evelyn's, a realization she'd come to when she'd stopped crying a few days ago. She loved her friend but understood if Evelyn was there, it wasn't necessarily for *her*.

Evelyn turned to the paintings she'd been perusing. "These are beautiful, Kiera. This might be some of your best work."

Kiera's eyes went over all her paintings, settling again on the one of A'Ran. Evelyn caught her look as she turned.

"I didn't think ..." her friend said, looking from Kiera to the painting.

"I know you didn't," Kiera said with no heat. She didn't have the energy for a fight. She crossed to sit where she couldn't see any of her paintings and instead gazed at Evelyn.

"I had that coming," Evelyn replied. "I haven't really taken your feelings into account lately, have I?"

"Not really. A little late to matter," Kiera said with a shrug.

"I didn't come to argue, though I am sorry if I hurt your feelings, Kiera," Evelyn said with a small sigh, as if irritated by the apology. Kiera said nothing, trying to think the best of her friend while anger stirred. "I know I haven't been the best of friends, so if you don't want to talk to me anymore, I'll understand."

"It's fine, Evey. You made the effort to come. I just hope you're not raising my rent. Haven't felt like working lately."

"Rent? Kiera, please. The least I could do is stop charging you at all," Evelyn said, chuckling. "I came for ... a favor."

Kiera wasn't surprised and felt bad for admitting it to herself. She looked at the ground instead of Evelyn, feeling bereft once again.

"The Five Galaxies have just exploded with war. Anshan went crazy and just started wiping out everyone. Qatwal has been under attack directly since Anshan was decimated by that lunatic A'Ran.

Kisolm was killed on the planet surface, and Romas will now inherit the planet from his father, if there's anything left to inherit."

Kiera listened, interested despite trying not to be. She'd seen how brilliant A'Ran's battles were. He'd fought forces five times the size of his and won. He didn't lose. He never would. If he wanted Qatwal destroyed, he would find a way to do it.

"I'm four and a half months pregnant and wondering if I'm better off here," Evelyn said, a troubled look crossing her features. "The Council can't talk any sense into A'Ran, and they're amassing this ginormous army to destroy him. But it'll take awhile, and in the meantime, Qatwal is on its own."

"Like Anshan was for all those years," Kiera couldn't help but add.

"No, this is different," Evelyn continued. "Qatwal is under attack. The Anshan *dhjan* was usurped, maybe because this craziness ran in the family."

Kiera looked at Evelyn, astonished by her callous words. She'd known her friend to be a little arrogant, but this was something different. This was the type of attitude A'Ran had been forced to deal with since his parents were murdered. While she could never fully understand what it was to have the weight of a planet on her shoulders for fifteen years, her resentment toward A'Ran's rigid sense of duty began to thaw as Evelyn went on.

"We've left the capital city for the other side of the planet. Can you imagine? Romas is off fighting all the time. It's just ... god, it's so awful, Kiera."

"Is that why you're here?" Kiera asked, trying hard to control the anger building within her. "To escape the war?"

"Not exactly," Evelyn said. Her gaze returned to the painting of A'Ran. "It's for a favor."

"What kind of favor?"

"Well, I think A'Ran went crazy partially because we took you. I've got a shuttle waiting for me. But, I thought, if you would come out and talk to him, see if you can dissuade him, it might help. Romas said I was crazy with hormones, but I spoke to someone on the Council who thought it was a good idea. I guess they told A'Ran you were killed, not taken. Was the nail in the coffin, no pun intended," Evelyn joked weakly.

Kiera's heart leapt at the information. She'd never allowed herself to ask why A'Ran didn't come for her. She hadn't been able to face the possibility he might not want her or worse—he was dead. She was making it day to day telling herself neither of those things was true.

"I know it's a lot to ask after your ... ordeal."

"You want me to go to the shuttle and talk to him over the communicator?" she asked.

"Yes. You don't have to do anything else."

Kiera rose and turned away, wondering how her friend was so clueless while standing in front of her painting of A'Ran.

"You'll have to take me to him," she said. "He can't be reasoned with over the viewer."

"I wouldn't do that to you."

"Do *what?*" Kiera asked, at the end of her patience. "I told Romas not to bring me back here! You dragged me to space, Evelyn, and you told him to drag me back here. For once, I want to make a decision about my own life. If you want my help, you'll take me to him!"

"Are you sure?" Evelyn asked after a startled pause. "You're kind of upset about it."

"I'm not upset for the reason you assume I am!" Kiera snapped. "Just take me and the damn tarantula in the kitchen home!"

"You *are* home."

"No, Evey, I'm not."

Evelyn's gaze fell to the painting again. "So that is why he's destroying everything," she said softly.

"I don't know why, but I really don't blame him!" Kiera replied. "I'm ready. You can get the tarantula."

It took a full minute for Evelyn to realize just how serious she was. Evelyn moved after a long, considering look, leaving the studio for the kitchen. Kiera released a deep breath and trailed her. Evelyn removed the obstacle from the door and snagged the tarantula cat as it darted past her.

Silently, the two left the row house for the park across the street, where the spacecraft was hidden in the Monterey mist. Kiera's heart still did somersaults, and she felt both doubtful Evelyn would follow through and ecstatic at the prospect. She didn't doubt Jetr had reached out to Evelyn, or her friend would never have come. The odd little man was the loyal ally A'Ran considered him! The spacecraft's door opened, and her excitement grew. She followed Evelyn into the craft, seeing only one Qatwali warrior to pilot the craft.

She sat across from Evelyn, who continued to give her the odd look, and clasped her hands together hard to keep them from shaking as they took off. After a thick moment of silence, Evelyn rose to place the tarantula cat near the pilot and sealed off the door between the tiny cabin and pilot. She reached into a drawer at the back of the craft.

"I've got snacks," Evelyn said. "Oh, and you may need one of these."

She produced an armband. Kiera raised the arm of her sweatshirt to reveal the band she already wore. Evelyn looked at her hard again but said nothing.

Kiera lowered the shirt, glad she'd never convinced herself to remove the band. It was her last connection to Anshan and its *dhjan*. Her stomach churned as the day grew on. There were no windows on the tiny craft, only the two of them and two benches long enough for them to stretch out on. She didn't want to talk to Evelyn and lay down soon after the feeling of the craft ascending—similar to the pressure felt in a plane—stopped.

Her mind went crazy with thoughts and emotions, and she wondered if A'Ran would be happy to see her. She didn't know if the choice she made was the right one, but she knew staying alone in the row house had been the wrong one. She wondered how he'd destroyed his own planet, whether his sisters were still safe. If he wanted to see her.

She returned to this thought often as they traveled for two days. Of all the things she felt, she feared he'd reject her once and for all. She'd never given him an answer about staying with him on Anshan. But he if thought her dead, and he was taking revenge on Qatwal, then some part of him must've cared! She recalled their last kiss, as hot and passionate as she'd ever hoped, despite his aloof sense of duty.

Evelyn tried to get her to eat twice, but she couldn't stomach it. She couldn't remember when she'd last eaten, hadn't had a reason to care. Now, she was too uneasy to eat. The two days were longer than any other two days had been in her life, and she grew more and more nervous, afraid the connection she had to A'Ran wouldn't be enough to make him want her again. She wasn't sure Qatwal deserved a peaceful existence after refusing to help Anshan, but for Evelyn's sake, she wanted the wars to end, even if A'Ran didn't want her anymore.

She agonized over what it would be like to meet him again. By nature, he didn't smile, but would he turn away from her or tolerate her? Would he go so far as to welcome her? Or would the fact that she never gave him an answer to stay or go make him unwilling to give her a second chance?

She slept fitfully between her busy thoughts, sheer exhaustion claiming her in spurts. By the end of the space journey, she was convinced he'd want nothing to do with her and desperate to see him. Near the end of her patience trapped in the tiny box of a spacecraft, she shot up when she felt the familiar pressure of them descending. Evelyn rose, looking as tired as Kiera felt. Kiera had bathed in the bathroom in the back of the craft, but it was too small to have a clothing unit. She stripped off her sweatshirt to be certain people could see her armband in her T-shirt.

The descent felt as long as their two day trip. She pulled her hair back in a scrunchie at the base of her neck, growing nervous once again. There was a gentle bump as they landed. She waited for

Evelyn to go to the door first, uncertain what to expect from wherever they'd gone.

The door slid open. It was dark, the dual moons high in the sky. Several figures awaited them, and she saw a low building with glowing lights in the distance. One female figure moved forward, wrapping a shawl around Evelyn's shoulders and placing a translator on her ear. She handed Evelyn a small bowl of water and then moved to Kiera, handing her a translator.

Kiera took it and put it on her earlobe. She heard no signs of war but saw the distant night sky light up with orange and red flashes.

"They're getting closer," Evelyn said in a tight voice.

Kiera said nothing, her mind racing. The night was chilly and quiet. She looked to Evelyn only to find the group had already moved away toward the distant dwelling. She trotted to catch up to them, trailing. The group was silent and tense, the warriors flanking Evelyn eyeing Kiera as much as the distant flashes of light. She shivered.

Evelyn's entourage shepherded her into the dwelling. Kiera looked around, speechless at the soaring ceilings, the atrium with a waterfall in the foyer, and pristine white walls covered with the multi-colored roping. She hadn't noticed how rundown A'Ran's home in exile was until she saw the house of the Qatwali refugees. It made her angrier at Evelyn and Romas, knowing A'Ran and his sweet sisters had been forced out of their home into a life of poverty.

The group continued without her. She couldn't remember feeling such rejection. The Qatwali warriors had looked her over in full light, as if to ensure she was no threat, then dismissed her with a look that said she ranked lower than the tarantula cat clinging to one wall. Even Evelyn walked away without so much as a glance.

Any resentment she had at A'Ran melted further. She wasn't sure how he'd lived with this type of treatment since he was a boy. She couldn't handle it!

She followed the group down several corridors into a massive conference room filled with people in tight groups talking. There was barely room to maneuver, and she found herself standing on her tiptoes to keep track of Evelyn, who had no trouble with the people around her parting the seas for her. Kiera made her way through the crowd to an area with far fewer people. She was surprised to recognize the Council members, from tall, thin Opal to the Council members whose names she'd never learned. Her eyes sought out a familiar form and found him.

Evelyn waited at the edge of another group, in the middle of which was Romas. Kiera maneuvered through the crowd, out of place in her jeans, T-shirt, and armband marking her as Anshan. Only a few people looked long enough to take in her armband, and she shied away from one who stared at her in alarm. Nervous, uneasy, she made her way down the wall toward the Council members, who held court with themselves.

She stopped within full view of Jetr and waited, not wanting to draw the attention of the entire Council to her. Jetr listened and spoke, glancing over after a few minutes. He looked again, this time meeting her gaze. She gave a nervous wave, watching for his reaction and relieved when he offered a warm smile. He excused himself and crossed to her, motioning for her to follow him out a nearby door into a corridor.

"I knew you'd come, if given the means to return," he said. "You look worn."

"I'm fine, Jetr," she replied. "What's going on?"

"The Council is gathering an army to retake this galaxy," he said. "It's slow to form. Many of it requires negotiations with headstrong warriors like A'Ran. Qatwal will be destroyed or taken over in mere days."

"Did he really destroy Anshan?"

"He destroyed the mines. The atmosphere is contaminated beyond repair but the planet lives, a distinction I've kept from many others."

"I can heal it," she said hesitantly.

"Maybe. No one really knows but A'Ran."

"If you knew he'd go crazy, why didn't *you* come for me?"

"I'm a diplomat. I influence others without choosing sides," he said vaguely. "What's important is that you're here, and here—in the Five Galaxies—is where you'll stay?"

"Yes."

"Good. Mansr won't try to talk sense into A'Ran. I'm afraid you're all that stands between the Council and him. I've been a friend of his family for generations. I don't want to see him assassinated."

"Assassinated!" she breathed. "The Council would do that?"

"The Council believes he's destroyed one planet and is about to destroy a second."

"But if he doesn't destroy Qatwal and the war stops, will they leave him alone?"

"After this display? I don't think anyone will want to cross him for a long time," Jetr said, amused. "That I can influence. When he's running around destroying planets, I cannot help him."

She shivered, wondering just how cunning the small man with the warm smile was.

"Are you ready?" he asked.

"Ready for what?"

"You'll see. Wait here. I'm bringing others with me. Follow us to the battle quarters." He squeezed her arm and returned to the room.

She hugged herself, scared and uneasy. It was hard to trust Jetr when he seemed so ... squirrelly. She leaned against the wall and drew a deep breath, praying A'Ran trusted this Council member for a reason.

A few minutes later, a group of Qatwali left the room. She recognized Romas and his father, two other Council members with Jetr, and a few more strangers. She trailed them as directed down the corridor to a battle quarters that put A'Ran's tiny room to shame. There wasn't just one battle planner but dozens, with every wall featuring viewers. Jetr motioned her to the side, and the men gathered in the center of the room, facing the largest viewer. The lights dimmed as Jetr brought the viewer online.

"A'Ran, I want to try one more time to discuss a peace deal.

This one will make reparations for the loss of your planet," Jetr said. "I ask for your attention one last time, as a personal favor to me."

His words were followed by a long silence. The men around him shifted with Romas shaking his head. No image appeared on the screen, and she began to wonder if A'Ran would respond, even to her. Jetr's confident gaze remained on the viewer.

"The Council and Qatwal has nothing I want," A'Ran's low voice said at last. Her heart soared at the sound despite his sharp tone. She fidgeted, waiting to see him on the viewer.

"First, the Council offers to fund the relocation of your people from the Anshan moon to a suitable planet. The Council will fund everything."

"There is nothing new in your offer, Jetr."

"Second," Jetr continued, unruffled. "Mison has an offer for you." He turned to Romas's father.

"I require peace with the Anshan," Mison boomed. "An end to the blood feud that has existed between my family and yours."

A'Ran said nothing. Jetr glanced at Mison, who glanced at her.

"I will offer one last compromise before the Council sends in its armies to destroy you," Mison continued. "A prisoner exchange."

"You can have your men. You'll need them after I destroy the rest of them," A'Ran replied.

Romas motioned her forward. Surprised, she hesitated before crossing to him. Jetr stepped beside her, and Mison looked hard at her.

"You have not asked what I offer you," Mison said.

"You've captured none of my men, and Jetr is no more a prisoner than anyone else in your house," A'Ran growled. "If this is all you—"

"Your *nishani*."

"My *nishani* is dead!"

"For which you blame me, even though you destroyed her!"

"My greatest mistake was not destroying you sooner," A'Ran said with chilling calmness. "Jetr, ask no more favors of me."

Romas motioned for her to speak. She felt panicked and sick at her stomach, uncertain what to say. In the end, she spoke his name.

"A'Ran."

Silence. Jetr nudged her.

"Romas rescued me from the cave before you blew up the mines. He took me to the planet I came from. Evelyn returned for me a few days ago." As she spoke, the words became easier. "I don't know what happened, but I want to come home. I shouldn't have left. I shouldn't have been so stupid as to not be able to see that what I wanted was right in front of me. I want to come home."

She could almost see him thinking. When the quiet stretched uncomfortably long, she spoke again. "A'Ran?"

"I'm here, *nishani*," he said in a hushed tone. The edge of cold rage was gone from his voice. "Jetr, I will accept the Council's offer. Mison, I accept your prisoner exchange and will release your men on the moon nearest to Qatwal. I am coming to your location. I can track *nishani*. If you try to harm her or me, everyone in your compound will be destroyed."

"I understand," Mison said with a frown.

"It will be an honor to see you again," Jetr said.

The click of A'Ran hanging up was audible. It broke the men around her from their frozen apprehension, and several of them moved away. Mison and Romas spoke quietly while Jetr turned to her.

Her thoughts were flying again in anticipation of seeing A'Ran. Even her breathing was quick as she waited.

"Come. We'll await him outside," Jetr said, and took her arm. He led her through the men, who stared at her warily, and down several halls.

She'd never thought she'd ever hear A'Ran's voice again, let alone see him! Tears rose, and she wiped them away, scared something would go wrong at the last minute. Mison might try to blow A'Ran up, or the Council change its mind, or A'Ran would destroy everything to win his war, even if it meant losing her.

The emotions she'd buried when she'd thought no one was coming for her bubbled. Her body shook from the inside out before they stepped into the chilly night to await her fate.

Fate.

She thought of the image she'd seen so long ago when she met A'Ran, the vision of them walking together on the dead planet. She'd been destined for him—and Anshan—since before she ever met him! She tossed her head back to stare at the stars. They'd escaped Qatwal on a night such as this. All she could think about was seeing, touching, kissing A'Ran and experiencing the odd energy that ran between them.

Her emotions tumbling, her body shaking, she stepped away quickly from the doorway when Romas and his father stepped from the dwelling into the night. Neither spoke to her, only stood quietly while their warriors remained in the hallway behind them. One of the warriors emerged, spoke to Romas, and retreated.

"The attacks have stopped," Romas reported.

She looked in the direction where orange and red lights had bloomed earlier. The sky was dark and peaceful. The hum of a space-craft made her pulse leap again, and her eyes found the small craft descending from the sky to a landing point a hundred meters away. The craft door opened, and a figure strode out. She felt the energy even from the distance and started forward. Jetr caught her arm, shaking his head.

Agitated, she waited. Mison drew abreast of Jetr, and Jetr stepped forward as A'Ran stopped a safe distance away. She gazed at him in the moons' light, tears building again. Everything from his unshaven jaw to his crooked nose drew her hungry gaze, and she took him in, feeling as if she'd never truly seen him before. His fierceness took her breath away, and the dark circles beneath his eyes drew her sympathy.

"You both know how agreements are recorded," Jetr said, holding out his arm with the armband. Mison did so as well. "You both must agree to the terms you made, and I will agree on behalf of the Council."

A'Ran held out his arm as well, saying, "I agree." Mison echoed his words, as did Jetr. The three bands lit up and faded, and all three men dropped their arms. Jetr stood aside. A'Ran's gaze turned to her. Despite the piercing gaze she'd never quite gotten used to, she stepped past Jetr and looked up at her mate, taking him in breathlessly once again. She doubted she'd ever get used to his towering size or strength. He was beautiful in the moonlight, with the gentle light of the moons clashing with his ferocious warrior body. His large frame radiated heat. She couldn't quell the deep ache within her that longed for his touch.

They gazed at each other for a long moment, each taking the other in.

"I made my choice," she whispered. "Thought you might want to know."

"I do," he replied in a tone just as quiet.

"Anshan is mine. You can come with me, if you want," she joked.

He touched her face gently, the slightest smile crossing his features. The hot energy of Anshan branded her from the inside out, and she shuddered. She needed him too much to wait and closed the distance between them, wrapping her arms around him. His heat and the charged Anshan life force washed over her, through her.

She was home.

"Did you really blow up Anshan?" she asked.

"Yes."

"Wasn't that a little brash?"

"It was a high-risk, strategic choice, like kidnapping my lifemate from the Qatwali," he replied, wrapping his arms securely around her. A laugh bubbled from within her, along with tears. Her gaze blurred, and hot moisture burned down her cheeks.

"*Nishani* ... Kiera ... " he said softly. She pulled away enough to look at him. He wiped the tears from her cheeks with a large thumb. "Forgive me. I've been a warrior for too long to understand how to be the lifemate you deserve. It should not have taken this to make me appreciate what I have."

"I've been a fool, too, A'Ran." They stood in silence, comfortable and whole in each other's arms. She wanted to curl up in a ball and sob until she fell asleep, relieved and ecstatic to be with him again. "We better go. I have to clean up the mess you made of Anshan."

"No, *nishani*. First, we will go to the other moon of Anshan, where we can be alone for several days. I will make amends for my behavior." His voice was husky and low, his grip around her tightening. Desire fed into her swirling emotions. "Then we go to Anshan."

"Together?"

"Yes, Kiera. We will create a new beginning for our people and heal our planet together."

She managed a smile, too overwhelmed by her emotions to speak. He pulled away to take her hand, and they walked hand-in-hand toward the small spacecraft. Her gaze went once more to A'Ran's face as they walked.

Fate, she thought. *I owe you one.*

KIERA'S SUN

PROLOGUE: ONE

A FEW WEEKS later

KIERA WATCHED another of her lifemate's men succumb to the strange shield they claimed would protect them from the toxic air of their home planet of Anshan. The transparent goo exoskeleton resembled gelatin that made the warriors look out-of-focus, as if she was looking at them through the murky water of a pond.

Or like they're stuck in Jell-O. It was hard not to smile when she pictured the manly, over-confident warriors floating like fruit in a Jell-O salad, the kind her mother used to make.

When the fourth warrior was fully covered, the man holding the goo-gun turned to her. She glanced at her lifemate doubtfully. A'Ran's arms were crossed, and the look on his face warned her he was an eyelash away from changing his mind about letting her go to the planet. Towering above her, he was every bit the protective guardian and leader of his people.

At her hesitation, though, he stepped closer, sensing she was about to unleash an opinion that would probably not reflect well upon him in the male-dominated Anshan society. A'Ran was close enough for her to touch, and she craned her neck back to gaze up at him. His savage features were too heavy for traditional male beauty, his olive complexion and dark hair reflective of the Anshan people he governed. He gazed down at her, dark eyes unreadable.

At six and a half feet tall, he was considered average in height among the Anshan warriors but he was a full head and shoulders taller than her. As always, when he was close enough for her to pick up the faintest scent of his musk, or to marvel at the contradiction of how tough he was with his warriors and how gentle he acted towards her, she was momentarily lost, gazing at him in admiration.

A'Ran cleared his throat.

Kiera blinked, aware everyone in the room was staring at her. "Does that stuff get in my lungs?" she asked somewhat nervously.

"You fought hard to come today, *nishani*," he reminded her. "I warned you it might not be pleasant, did I not?"

She'd won their argument earlier, not because he wanted her to go, but because he knew she was the only one who could fix the mess he created. He'd blown up the surface of the planet to free it from alien invaders weeks before, leaving a wasteland with a poisonous atmosphere.

As the *nishani* – ruler's mate – Kiera's job was to heal the planet. And its people. And its atmosphere. The *entire* Anshan society. She'd considered many times pointing out how crazy it sounded but was stopped by the hopeful looks of her lifemate and his family. No part of her wanted to disappoint someone as noble and good as A'Ran.

"How are you so sure I can fix everything?" she whispered, doubting herself.

"Because that's what *nishani*s do."

It was so simple to a man accustomed to duty. Kiera snorted, not at all certain how an entire race of people could believe she'd heal their world overnight. Maybe they'd temper their expectations once this trip was over.

"The planet chose you. You are part of its life force," he added.

"We are connected. I know." Yet she struggled with the foreign concepts of a planet being truly *alive* and part of *her* life force. No one could explain what exactly that meant or why she was chosen.

He nudged her, breaking the plane between them. It was his way of showing encouragement without softening his fierce expression or authoritative stance in front of his men. One touch was all she'd get, but was more than he would've done a month before.

"All right," she said. Turning to the man holding the goo-gun, she held out her hand the way the others had. "Goo me."

The warrior frowned, not understanding her slang. The translator pinned to her earlobe wasn't able to translate most of the more creative English words and phrases she sometimes used. Curses and idioms came out gibberish, confusing those around her. The warrior looked towards her lifemate, who nodded.

The gel started at her fingertips and spread up her arm. It tickled. It wasn't sticky or heavy or wet, as she expected, but cool and malleable, like the skin of a balloon. Kiera watched it spread, uncomfortable with the strange technology of her new home. The spaceships that resembled huge whales were gray inside and out, made from the special metal that only Anshan produced. The spacecraft around her was drab, dark, lit by unnatural yellow light she still didn't know the source of. Their medical labs were able to heal anything, and yet they fought with swords rather than some sort of advanced technology.

After a month with the Anshan people, she still found herself trying to figure their world out.

The strange shield was soon in place, and she tested her body. There was no discomfort or difficulty in moving. She felt normal, though the world around her appeared out-of-focus. Kiera experimented with the goo-shield to ensure she was able to breathe and move normally without her feet sticking to the floor like she thought they might.

A'Ran was next. When her lifemate was finished, he motioned her over to the small group gathered by the door.

"You will stay with me," he ordered.

"I know," she replied. She felt his tension and displeasure, even if his eyes were too blurry to read behind the shield.

The door slid open, revealing what looked like a dust storm. The air blew into the room. Instinctively holding her breath, Kiera closed her eyes to the dust and pebbles, the remnants of the planet's outer layer. It pelted the walls of the chamber where they prepared to visit the surface of the planet. Nothing reached her face through the shield, and she slowly released her breath and opened her eyes.

One by one, the four warriors stepped from the ship into the dust storm. They disappeared with their second step out the door, a sign of the poor visibility on the planet. A'Ran waited for her. Feeling somewhat safe in the protective goo, she stepped past him and carefully planted her foot on the solid ground of Anshan.

Above, the two suns were blurry, bright spots. Anshan had been a barren desert before A'Ran blew up the surface, and there was reddish dust everywhere. Kiera stopped after a couple steps, taking in the world with even more distress.

Nothing could live here. No one could fix this place, let alone grow food to feed the Anshan civilization that had been evacuated to the moons around the planet and neutral planets within the Five Galaxies. The idea that so many people believed *she* could make a difference was more than overwhelming; it was ridiculous!

"One step at a time." A'Ran had to shout to be heard over the howling storm. He'd taken up the saying a couple of weeks before, whenever she began to stress out about what it was they wanted her to do. "Our son will be born here!"

Right. She grounded her teeth. She didn't have any miracles in her pocket, which the whole planet – and the rest of the Five Galaxies – would soon be very well aware of. The mention of a son reminded her she had an appointment with the Anshan version of a doctor later that day. She was late for her monthly cycle, yet another reason she'd begun to stress before the trip to the planet. A'Ran wanted an heir, and she wanted more time to adjust before considering a family, especially considering they had no permanent home.

A'Ran passed her, at ease in his goo-suit on the poisonous planet. Kiera took a few more steps after him, searching for something she could twist into an optimistic sign for the future. A bird. A plant. Even one of the dreadful spider-cats that ate dust and mold to keep their house clean.

There was nothing.

Distraught, she turned to face the spacecraft they'd traveled in. At least it was visible, an unmovable gray blob in the shifting sands. When she faced the direction A'Ran was headed, she saw nothing. Kiera squinted and hurried forward. After half a dozen quick steps, she still didn't see him.

She turned to retreat to the spacecraft only to find the sand had blocked it from her vision as well. Panic stirred at the thought of being lost or left behind on the planet, before she recalled the real reason she'd insisted on coming: to find evidence the Anshan people shouldn't put their hope in someone like her. It wasn't possible for one person to make this huge of a difference!

Her gaze went to her feet. The last time she'd been on the desert planet, grass had grown anywhere her bare skin touched.

Kiera knelt on the ground and placed her hand on it. The Jell-O shield seemed to block the *nishani* magic. She tried to fling away the thin layer of gelatin from one palm. It didn't budge.

Scraping her hand along the roughened ground, she managed to free a couple of fingers and then pressed them to the ground. She waited for the familiar tickle of grass.

Moment of truth. Her heart raced, and she wasn't certain what she wanted: to disappoint an entire planet full of people or to confirm the weight of this world was on her shoulders.

To her surprise, she experienced profound relief when she felt it. Whatever magic she'd had before was still there, which meant the man she respected most in the universe, A'Ran, wouldn't lose his faith in her.

Her gaze roved the area around her in disbelief. It'd take several lifetimes to rebuild the planet, if she had to touch every single inch of rock during dust storms!

She scraped more of the shield away, until her hand was completely free then planted it on the ground. Grass sprang up around it more quickly this time, and she smiled, awed by the strange gift. She almost believed she could help the planet and people, if the task wasn't so monumental.

"*Nishani?*" A'Ran's voice made her look up. He seemed to materialize out of the storm and crouched beside her. "Are you hurt?"

"No," she replied, touched by the concern in his voice. He wasn't the best at expressing emotions; whenever something sweet made it through his thick exterior, she thought herself the luckiest girl ever. "Look. It still works."

He knelt beside her and reached out, taking her hand.

"*Nishani,*" he chided. "The air is poisonous to you, too."

He pressed his hand against hers. The gooey exoskeleton resealed, and his attention turned to the grass. He brushed his fingers through it with such reverence and hope, that Kiera grinned proudly.

"How am I supposed to do this for the whole planet?" she asked, smile fading.

"I don't know yet."

The answer surprised her. A'Ran always had a plan.

"We have to clean up the air, first," he added. "Mansr and I have a few ideas, but we need more gray metal."

"Which is why you wanted to check the mines this trip. You can't melt down all the spaceships?"

A'Ran rose and pulled her up with him. "As the strategic battle planner for Anshan, you know that is not a safe option. There are too many people waiting for our guards to drop."

"But it's an option," she insisted.

"A poor one."

"This coming from the man who blew up his own planet?" Kiera rolled her eyes.

He gave her the look, the one that said the hardened warrior she'd fallen in love with hadn't yet learned how to take her challenges.

She knew very well what kind of danger Anshan was in. The rest of the Five Galaxies considered A'Ran a loose cannon after he exploded the surface of his planet to get rid of invaders. He had then declared war on the only possible ally he might have in their solar system, further alienating potential allies. The Five Galaxies as a whole were watching what he did with Anshan, valued for being the source of the malleable gray metal that made up everything from their swords to their spaceships to their furniture. If the planet remained uninhabitable and A'Ran unable to regain his position as its leader, every one of the members of the Council would declare war on Anshan to wrest the mines from their rightful king.

The very idea of being homeless and at war in space scared her. A'Ran handled it all with calmness that amazed her.

"Come," he said. "We should have the readings we need."

"And we know I can still help the planet."

"I never doubted."

"Oh, but I did!" She sighed.

They returned to the ship. Two of the four warriors were back. The door closed behind them, and the man with the goo-gun approached with another small device the size of a pencil. A'Ran held out his arms. The device sparked and sent a visible electric charge through the gelatin exoskeleton. Kiera watched as it hardened, cracked and dropped from his body.

She held out her arms as the warrior approached her and braced herself. First a light, tickling current went through her, then the shards of hardened goo fell.

Despite confirming she still had the ability to help the planet, she wasn't confident about succeeding the way others wanted her to. She had the urge to fold herself into A'Ran's arms and talk more with him about how she was supposed to help. The Anshan protocol was strict about public signs of affection. Instead, she watched him with warmth and longing as he studied mine readings from a small device a warrior handed him.

Feeling her gaze, A'Ran glanced up. His dark eyes lingered on hers, the skin around them softening ever so slightly in a way she knew was entirely for her. She grinned in return, and his look turned to one of disapproval.

The Anshan also did not believe it proper to express emotion of any kind in public.

"*Nishani*, would you join me?" someone asked from behind her.

Kiera turned at the low, quiet voice of Mansr, A'Ran's uncle and closest advisor. The middle-aged man had gray hair and a smaller stature than most warriors, though he was far from what she'd call normal. He stood in the doorway that led to the rest of the small craft.

"I have something to show you," he added. There was energy in his step as he turned and walked quickly away.

She followed him into the hallway. The door closed behind her. He went one door down, to a small conference bay filled with benches around a round table. A three dimensional projection of the planet swirled lazily on top of the table.

Kiera's eyes took in the familiar sight. The console was used for battle planning, too, a duty she'd been officially handed by A'Ran after she mastered their system. Instead of displaying the positions of warships and spacecraft, the model showed the red-orange planet – and a speck of green Mansr had magnified to many times its original size.

He pointed to it.

"What is it?" she asked.

"That is grass."

"My grass? That I made grow?"

"I presume so. We picked it up a few moments before you returned to the ship."

She drew closer, a smile tugging up the corners of her mouth.

"It's growing."

"No way!" she exclaimed.

At his pause, she guessed the translator had tripped over her slang again.

"That's great," she added. "How fast?"

"Not fast enough. And without direct sunlight, it'll be dead by tomorrow."

Kiera frowned. "A'Ran said you had to clean up the air first."

"We do. Our remaining friend on the Planetary Council is offering to help."

"I like Jetr," she murmured. "He's been good to us."

"He is able to see beyond today. He knows the return of Anshan will mean the return of the gray metal, and he'll be first in line to receive it."

"You think he's shady?" she asked, turning.

Mansr raised an eyebrow.

Darn translator. "I mean, not trustworthy?"

"I am old and jaded, *nishani.*"

"But you're wise," she pointed out.

Mansr dipped his head in a polite way of saying he wasn't about to answer.

"He'll have a long time to wait. Cleaning up the planet isn't going to happen fast."

"It will not. But it will happen." His eyes glowed with the same hope she'd seen lately from everyone.

Kiera hugged herself, uncertain why their faith in her made her so uncomfortable. She felt like she was the only one in a room full of kids that knew there was no Santa Clause. She wondered how disappointed they'd be if the planet didn't return to what it was fast enough to satisfy everyone waiting for it.

The door opened, and she glanced up as her lifemate entered. The sight of him made her pulse race, her desire to touch him increasing with her agitation.

PROLOGUE: TWO

HIS BEAUTIFUL *NISHANI* was frowning when A'Ran entered the conference room. Mansr looked away from the visual of the planet, his expression inquisitive.

A'Ran nodded once. Their sensors indicated that the mines were producing the gray metal.

His nonverbal confirmation made Mansr sigh in the only sign of the relief they both felt. With gray metal, they could buy allies, trade for food, and protect their people, who were scattered throughout the Five Galaxies. It was something A'Ran had struggled to do for many sun-cycles, until Kiera.

She was staring at the magnified grass on the planet. A'Ran's fingers still tingled with the sensation of the blades against his skin. It couldn't last without the sun and water. Yet these were minor issues compared to what he'd faced since assuming the role of *dhjan* – king – at the age of fifteen. The planet had begun to die the day he was exiled from his home, and it would stay dead, if not for Kiera.

She was the key to regrowth on the planet, and the gray metal would pay for what it'd likely take to clean up their world and care of his people until everyone was able to return.

What is sunlight when we have hope after so long? Rarely did he let himself feel pride or hope, preferring to keep his focus on his duty and executing his next mission. Today, however, he'd seen how much of a miracle she was. One touch, and his planet had begun to return to life.

He couldn't imagine her frown was for anything other than the fact he wouldn't let her stay longer. She'd been adamant about going that morning. It was too dangerous for anyone to linger with the atmosphere full of toxins.

"We must plan to pull as much metal out of the ground as possible," he said to Mansr.

"So no melting spaceships?" Kiera asked. Her green-blue eyes were bright, her curly hair captured at her neck. Shapely and small compared to the women of Anshan, she was as exotic in looks as she was in her ideas. His gaze lingered on her, the way it always did whenever he saw her.

"No need," he said. "We can trade for atmospheric filtering devices then put everything we have into pulling metal out of the ground."

"I'm guessing these things are not cheap."

"There is only one planet that makes them," Mansr said. "The devices are likely to be more expensive for us."

"Did you pick a fight with them, too?" Kiera asked.

A'Ran allowed a small smile to slip free. "We both did, *nishani*."

"Qatwal?" Surprise crossed her face. She said a few words that didn't translate but which sounded like the ones she'd directed at him earlier that day during their argument. He decided he was probably happier not knowing these words.

"Gray metal is in demand throughout the Five Galaxies," he said. "We have that in our favor. The mines haven't produced it in many sun-cycles."

"And we are allegedly at peace," Mansr agreed.

"I thought they weren't speaking to us at all," Kiera said.

"They are not," A'Ran said.

"You almost destroyed their planet, too. Not sure I blame them." She was smiling.

A'Ran eyed her, recalling just what he'd felt when he saw her on Qatwal after believing her dead. The longstanding blood feud between him and the Qatwali rulers was over, according to their peace agreement, but he harbored no warm feelings towards them. There was some sadness in *nishani's* gaze, which he knew came from missing her sister, who was the lifemate of the next ruler of Qatwal.

"I will contact them," A'Ran said. After all he'd been through, he wasn't about to let the Qatwalis' cold shoulder deter him.

"And then, come to lunch. I invited a guest," *nishani* tried to fake an innocent smile, but there was a wicked gleam in her gaze.

A'Ran crossed his arms. Mansr looked between them and then excused himself. A'Ran waited until he was gone to ask.

"Who did you invite to *my* table?"

"*Our* table," she corrected him. "Remember?"

With Mansr gone, *nishani* felt no need to keep her distance, even if they were on a ship and not in the privacy of their quarters. She moved to him and pried his arms down so she could wrap her arms around him in a tight hug. A'Ran returned the embrace with a glance towards the door. It would be an awkward display, if his warriors saw him. Kiera didn't have the restraint Anshan women did with showing her affections and didn't seem concerned with learning more than she had to about this particular custom.

It was one of the things he found most appealing and vexing. She sighed and relaxed against him, and he let himself enjoy the moment, loving the way her soft, sweet body fit against his hard warrior frame. He'd found the touch of his woman to be beyond satisfying, another reason he'd stopped chiding her so often about how she touched him.

"I invited Ketnan," she said at last, looking up at him.

A'Ran let a breath hiss between his clenched teeth. "I don't want that man at my ... our table. I thought I made that clear."

"You know how sweet and warm and charming and wonderful you are to me?"

He snorted and kissed her forehead. He loved how freely she cared for him and his family.

"That's how he feels for your sister," she finished. "Talal deserves to be –"

"She needs a warrior to care for her, not a *miner*."

"Mining is a respectable profession!"

"Respectable, yes. Able to protect Talal, no," he said firmly.

"You haven't even met him."

"I don't need to. I've seen him at the mines." A'Ran moved away from her. They'd fought once already today. He didn't like it one bit when Kiera was upset and hoped to avoid a confrontation.

"He's strong and loves her. So what if he's not a warrior or from a noble family?" *nishani* argued. "I'm not a typical Anshan woman, and you mated with me!"

"That's different. I can protect you. He can't protect Talal." A'Ran went to one of the benches in front of the whirling planet projection. He sat down and began tapping the symbols on the control panel in front of him.

The man who had gotten his youngest sister pregnant was barely older than her and far too ... different. He wasn't a warrior or from a warrior bloodline. He was tall and thin, his frame just filling out as he transitioned from youth to manhood. He'd been afraid to look at A'Ran the one time they'd met. As the man who'd helped raise his little sister after their parents were killed, A'Ran wasn't ready to see his youngest sister fully grown yet. He also wanted more for his sister than a mere *miner*.

His hands paused as he considered the idea he was behaving more like their father than her brother.

"You can teach him to fight," Kiera suggested and sat beside him, her thigh pressed to his.

"He's too old to become a warrior."

"I can teach him."

He gave her a look.

"I already invited him to the midday meal," she said. "You can tell him not to come. It'll only crush Talal not to have a father for her child."

A'Ran stared at her. *Nishani* didn't back down. She'd gotten brave enough to counter him when she felt something was important. She'd changed him in the short time they'd been together. The man he was several weeks ago would've banished the boy who impregnated Talal and forbidden his *nishani* from going to a toxic planet, even if it was theirs.

"I like him," Kiera added. "You should give him a chance."

"No one tells a *dhjan* what he should do."

"His *nishani* does."

A'Ran returned his attention to the control panel. Kiera wrapped her arms around him as she was wont to do and kissed his temple. The tender act always reminded him he'd almost lost this. She knew it, too, and had done this a couple of times before, usually when she wanted him to agree.

It was difficult for him to deny her anything when he recalled the despair he'd experienced when he thought her dead.

"I will consider it," he allowed.

"Thank you." She beamed and dropped her arms. "I'll leave you alone for now." Her smile had a way of making his world right, of reminding him what was important.

It also made him think of how she looked up at him after they made love. With her cheeks flushed, hair wild and eyes glowing, she had the uncanny ability to make him forget everything in the universe, except for them.

She was gazing at him like that right now, with a spark of what he knew was desire, mixed with affection. It stirred the warm, aching need he experienced deep inside him, whenever their eyes met.

A'Ran wanted anything but alone time at the light in her eyes. He started to reach for her when the door opened. If not for the warrior that entered, he would've put his duty aside to make love to his beautiful lifemate, conference room be damned.

As if sensing his thought, Kiera's features were pink. She ducked her gaze and rose.

"I'll go see Mansr," she said.

He instantly felt the loss of her warmth and presence. "Very well." He rose and watched her leave, attention on the sway of her hips and rounded shape of her bottom. His hands clenched then released at the thought of not being able to touch her right now.

When Kiera's small form disappeared behind the closing door, he turned his attention to the awaiting warrior.

The warrior bowed his head in respect before he spoke. "We examined the readings in more depth. The mines are producing at an accelerated rate."

"How fast?" A'Ran asked.

"Fast enough that the miners recommend we start operations even before the atmosphere is cleared."

"That places them at risk."

"They know this. The alternative is that the metal from the mines overtakes the underground water sources and poisons them."

"What's causing this?" A'Ran frowned.

The warrior hesitated. "We don't know. The planet could be healing itself and trying to replenish fifteen sun-cycles worth of metal at once."

"Or there could be something else wrong."

"Yes, *dhjan.* That is a possibility. We were unable to see beyond the surface mines to determine that."

A'Ran considered the information. He'd never heard of anything like this happening in the history of Anshan. In its raw form, the metal was toxic. It was the reason the atmosphere was poisonous after the explosions rigged to the planet surface took out the mines, too. The idea it might destroy their water sources before he was able to bring his people back left him frustrated. The alternative – that they killed a generation of miners to save the water and ore – was equally as weighty.

His decision to destroy the mines and surface of the planet to get rid of its invaders had been risky, and he began to think that the damage went deeper than the planet's surface. They'd never know for certain, however, until they were able to enter the mines and assess the layers beyond Anshan's outer crust.

"What is their assessment of the potential loss of life, if we start mining now?" he asked.

"There are too many unknown factors," the warrior reported. "We will have to drill new mines without knowing if the ground itself has become contaminated like the air."

A'Ran considered the words. His attention went once more to the planet projection spinning on the conference room table. While pleased with the mines' activity, he had hoped not to place more of his soul-weary people in danger. It was not an easy choice, but it was for the greater good, like every decision he'd made the past fifteen sun-cycles.

"Start drilling immediately," he said with some reluctance. "Convert any of our battleships needed to support the mining. I will contact Qatwal about the atmospheric filters." He would have to tell Kiera she was right about melting a ship or two.

The warrior bowed and strode from the conference room into the hallway. A'Ran was still for a moment, thoughtful. He didn't like the idea of contacting his former ally-turned-enemy, but there was no real choice. They needed the filters to save what miners they could during the dangerous process of trying to extract ore in a toxic environment.

He touched the panel on the planning table. A projection of Mansr's face replaced the planet on the communications viewer.

"We will need Jetr," A'Ran said, referring to his only remaining ally on the Planetary Council governing the Five Galaxies. "I need the filters immediately, and Qatwal will not be likely to respond to me."

"I will contact him upon our return," Mansr said. "We are leaving Anshan now. I am headed back to discuss a matter with you, if you are available?"

A'Ran nodded and tapped the viewer channel closed. The planet returned, and he paced around it. After years of leading battles, he didn't know as much about the planet's mining operations as he thought he should. Mansr had always stayed behind to govern, while A'Ran negotiated with the Council and fought off the Yirkin invaders that took over Anshan.

His thoughts turned to what *nishani* had told him about the man who impregnated one of his sisters. A miner by trade, Ketnan should know more than the basics about the potential for operations in a toxic dust storm.

Maybe there is a reason to meet Ketnan after all.

The door slid open, and his uncle stepped into the conference room. A'Ran braced himself for the news he was about to receive. There was only one matter they did not trust to be carried over the communications system.

"We have confirmed Ne'Rin did not act alone," Mansr began, referring to A'Ran's former second in command, who turned traitor and almost killed Kiera. Now dead, Ne'Rin was no longer a threat, though A'Ran had ordered Mansr to investigate the matter to determine who might've helped him. "It is as we suspected. Gage had a hand in it, whether by her choice or his coercion."

A'Ran did not let himself feel pain at the news. After his brief talk with Mansr that morning, the possibility his sister helped her lover betray their entire family had been heavy in his thoughts since.

"She had to have been coerced. My sisters are good people," he said after a heavy silence.

"They are. I do not pretend to know her reasons."

"Probably to protect her child." It was the only excuse he'd allow for treason, and only because she was his sister. "There is no way to know what occurred between them."

"No," Mansr agreed. "Or if his sister and other family members were involved. All reports indicate Ne'Rin wanted Kiera out of the way so his sister could become your *nishani*, thus further cementing his family's place in the governing of Anshan and its gray metal. Your recommendation is the safest one. Remove Gage from the picture to protect her and the baby from any influence or threat his family might still cause."

"Banishing my sister." No part of it sat well with him. It was dishonorable, nearly as terrible of a betrayal as Ne'Rin's had been.

"If she's in danger, then we have no real choice."

A'Ran pursed his lips, hearing the unspoken words, too. Mansr was not ruling out that Gage had helped the father of her child willingly and still posed a threat to Kiera, if not the others. Ne'Rin's family was on a nearby planet, too far to reach Kiera, if they still had any intention of trying to remove her from his life. If they were threatening Gage and her baby, A'Ran wasn't certain what his sister would do to protect her child. A single tip about Kiera's activities or when she was alone was all it took to render his lifemate vulnerable.

While doubtful his sister knowingly tried to hurt Kiera, A'Ran understood the importance of putting distance between Gage and Kiera, until he was certain the family of Ne'Rin was not still manipulating his delicate sister. Her life might be in danger, not to mention Kiera's.

"Very well. I want your son to accompany her," he said. "When we are certain we have removed all threats from Ne'Rin's family, we'll bring her back."

"I will arrange it," Mansr said with a grim nod. "This will not be an easy transition for any of you."

"I know." A'Ran's mind went to Kiera and his sisters. When he knew more, he would be at liberty to share it with his family. But for now, only he and Mansr understood what was about to happen and why it must be kept quiet.

A'Ran wasn't going to allow danger near his lifemate, sisters or the children two of his sisters carried. He'd learned the price of ignoring warning signs the fist time around and nearly lost Kiera in the process. Ne'Rin's family had already produced two traitors too many, and there would be no more.

Resolved yet regretful, A'Ran drew a deep breath. "Arrange it quickly, Mansr. The sooner we know, the sooner she returns."

Mansr nodded. "I understand. You are doing what is best."

This is one time where it doesn't feel like it.

PROLOGUE: THREE

Kiera's three sisters-in-law were waiting as customary when the craft landed on one of the two moons circling Anshan. While the other was uninhabitable, this one had become the home of A'Ran's family and many others, especially after Anshan's air became poisonous. Square dwellings with flat roofs lined what had been open fields just weeks before.

Kiera grinned when the door opened to reveal his sisters. Where A'Ran's heavy, rugged features made him beyond handsome, the same characteristics did a total disservice to his tall sisters, rendering them awkward in appearance. The youngest, Talal, waved, earning herself a stern look from the oldest, who was most like their brother in her sense of duty and decorum. The middle sister, Gage, appeared distracted and pale, her eyes haunted.

Kiera took in the woman's face, pitying her. Pregnant and widowed, Gage had the extra burden of carrying the child of the man who betrayed A'Ran and their entire planet. That family secret was not likely ever to be revealed, though, not if A'Ran had it his way. It didn't seem to help Gage any, even knowing this.

"Hey, guys!" Kiera greeted them as she reached them.

"May the sun shine long on you, *nishani*," D'Ryn, the eldest, said formally. "I hope your travels went well."

"They did. Mansr said he and A'Ran have some things to do on the craft. We can go ahead inside."

The three hesitated, and Kiera almost rolled her eyes. Talal was the first to break rank, as usual, and Kiera saw the question in her eyes before she spoke. Terrified of offending or disappointing her brother, Talal had relied on Kiera to ask about her fiancé coming to the midday meal.

"I don't know," Kiera replied to the unasked question. "He didn't say no."

"Did he say yes?" Talal asked.

"No."

"You should not place our brother in such a position, *nishani*," D'Ryn, the eldest, chided. "If he chooses not to accept someone into our family, we must respect that."

Talal's face fell.

"If that's his choice, I want it to be because he met Ketnan and didn't like him, not because he doesn't want to be related to a non-warrior," Kiera shot back.

D'Ryn pursed her lips.

"I will do as my brother wishes, *nishani*," Talal whispered.

Kiera had a long way to go in teaching the women of A'Ran's family to be more independent and stop their subservient waiting on the men. She wanted to tell them so but held her tongue, aware she'd made some process with Talal already. The women of Anshan needed baby steps when it came to bucking tradition.

"Shall we go in?" Kiera asked instead.

The three followed her lead as she started towards the sprawling white house that was theirs. Once the only dwelling on this part of the planet, it had been joined by a town of Anshan refugees that sprang up over the course of a month. They passed several other homes much smaller in size, where women were outside cooking or wrangling children. The day was warm and bright. Tarantula cats were everywhere, and Kiera shuddered at the sight of the harmless, six-legged creatures that survived off dirt and mold.

The four of them entered the house. The two oldest sisters broke off and went towards the atrium at its center, while Talal followed Kiera down the hallway lined with private quarters belonging to the family.

"I tried your art," Talal said and withdrew a piece of paper from her pocket.

Kiera took it, grimacing. An artist, she often missed the paintings and drawings that surrounded her in her home on Earth. Talal's attempt would've made her smile, even if rather rudimentary, if she hadn't chosen to draw a tarantula cat.

"I know you don't like them," the younger girl said with a giggle. "I thought it was good."

"It is good," Kiera agreed. "You'll get better with more practice."

Talal appeared pleased with the lukewarm praise. Kiera stopped at the wall outside the bedroom she shared with A'Ran. Her mural was growing daily. She'd carefully sketched then painted A'Ran, followed by Talal. Her current project was trying to imagine D'Ryn with something other than her usual scowl. D'Ryn's body was finished but her face blank.

Kiera wasn't certain what it'd take to make the eldest sister smile, and she didn't want to paint her with a frown.

"You need more of these," Talal said, stooping to retrieve a pencil from the ground. She held it out.

Kiera accepted it slowly. She'd spent a lot of time drawing the past few weeks, since returning from Earth to the Anshan moon. Part of it was how giddy it made her feel when A'Ran praised her work and watched her paint. He truly loved the colors and pictures she created, because Anshan art consisted of gray metal sculptures. She loved seeing him happy.

Drawing was also an outlet for her emotions, both positive and negative. She'd been working on dealing with the emotions of losing her best friend in the universe, Evelyn, when she started the mural.

It had taken her years to finally understand how selfish Evelyn was, but that did nothing to make it easier to lose her friendship. Evelyn had brought the pencils with her, a small sign of thoughtfulness from an otherwise self-indulgent woman. It hurt too much to dwell on what their friendship had been and what Kiera mistook it for being.

"Yeah, I will eventually," she agreed softly. "You can have that one."

Talal smiled at the gift. She rolled the pencil carefully in the drawing she'd made and pocketed them.

"I must go prepare for the midday meal," Talal said, anxiousness returning in her voice.

Kiera smiled at her, not at all certain A'Ran was going to speak to the teen's love interest let alone let him in the house. She expected their family lunch was going to be a tense event.

Talal left her in the corridor. Kiera's gaze returned to her project and settled on a small circle meant to become Earth she'd drawn in the sky above the finished portrait of A'Ran.

While she hadn't yet completed the planet, she experienced a familiar sense of homesickness. She'd sketched Earth as a warm memory of what she'd left behind to stay with A'Ran and her new family. She picked up a pencil and drew in the continents of North and South America.

"I want to go there."

Kiera turned, not hearing Gage's silent approach until the teen girl spoke.

"It's your home, isn't it?" Gage asked.

"My home is here, but it's where I'm from," Kiera answered.

The troubled woman's gaze was on the planet.

"I don't think you'd like it there as much," Kiera added.

"I could start over. A new life, like yours here."

"True, but life there would be much harder for you."

"Harder than knowing my brother hates me for the child I carry?"

"He doesn't hate you, Gage." Kiera frowned at the amount of anger and sorrow in the girl's voice. "He loves you as he always has. If anything, he doesn't know what to do to help you be happy."

"My brother does not wish for happiness. He wishes to mate me off to the son of some Council member and banish me from my home."

"Where did you hear that?"

"This morning, before you left to Anshan," Gage said. "I overheard him talking to Mansr near the atrium."

After a quick breakfast, Kiera had gone to change and meet him in the grass in front of the shuttle that took them to the planet. He had the time to speak with Mansr, but wouldn't he have told *her*, his *nishani* of something involving their family? Especially something of this magnitude? Exiling his own sister?

"You could take me to your planet," Gage said again. "You could show me the villages and how to find food, and I'd stay there forever with my son."

"Or you could stay here and your sisters will help you raise your son."

"My brother is too stubborn. He cares more for his duty than us. I brought shame upon the whole –"

"Let me talk to him before you do anything crazy," Kiera said with a sigh, cutting off the meltdown she heard coming. "Okay?"

Gage looked at her blankly.

"Is this acceptable?" Kiera rephrased. "Promise me you won't do anything until I've had a chance to find out what's going on."

The woman frowned. By the hesitant nod, Kiera guessed she didn't have much time before the pregnant woman took matters into her own hands.

"Ah, darn," Kiera said suddenly. "I'm supposed to go to the medics. Go get some rest. After the midday meal, I promise I'll talk to A'Ran and let you know what he says."

Another nod, this one distracted. Gage's eyes returned to the rendering of Earth. Concerned yet irritated she hadn't had time to work on her project, Kiera left Gage and hurried through the house and into the backyard. More dwellings were built in the open field where A'Ran's warriors had once sparred. Kiera waved to the few Anshans who stopped to stare at her, aware A'Ran's sisters were usually accompanied by an escort wherever they went.

"Hello, *nishani-mani!*" a little boy called as she passed. She acquired the nickname – *nishani* doll – after Mansr introduced her to a few of the newcomers as a doll from another planet.

The child's mother hushed him quickly.

Kiera waved in response and crossed the grassy areas to the cluster of buildings that marked the alley designated for Anshan artisans and the professional caste. The medics were located beside the Anshan metal-smiths, whose massive equipment was used to mold gray metal into household items and weapons at the touch of a button. Spacecraft designers were housed next to a contingent of miners, and technicians that kept the Anshan technology humming faced the building dedicated to storing Anshan records and history.

She entered the building holding the medics. Light spilled through naked windows and skylights and was absorbed into the cold gray metal of the machines Anshans used for their advanced medicine. Kiera eyed her least favorite – but most useful – of the machines: the cell-regenerator, a device capable of repairing wounds and broken bones in a matter of minutes.

It was shaped like a massive coffin and managed to freak her out every time she saw it, even knowing what it did.

"*Nishani,*" one of the medics emerged from another room with a bow.

"Hi, Zanan," she said. "I'm probably early."

"A *nishani* is neither late nor early," he said solemnly. The tall, middle-aged Anshan was thin almost to the point of gaunt with the characteristic dark eyes and olive skin of his people.

"Do I just tell you everything right here?" she asked, looking around self-consciously. Anshans were strange about privacy. The windows had neither glass nor shutters. They were completely open for anyone passing by to hear what was being discussed. The disciplined, general populace trusted that no one would listen who wasn't supposed to hear. For Gage to dare eavesdrop on her brother was a sign of how upset she was.

"If you prefer, or we can sit and talk." He motioned to a bench along one wall.

Kiera went to it, not yet comfortable with the complete lack of privacy of the otherwise reserved Anshans. Zanan sat at the far end of the bench.

"I'm, um, late for my ... you know, woman's monthly curse," she said in a low voice.

"Where does it hurt?"

"Nothing hurts. I mean, my period."

He was studying her hard.

"You know how a woman bleeds every month?" Her face felt hot. It was one of the many times she wished the translator bud at her ear had some sort of rewind-and-delete button.

"Ah, of course," he said. "Forgive me. I misunderstood. Anshan women did not bleed for many years. They were not fertile until you came." He looked particularly pleased with this information. "This is an honor, *nishani*, to be the first to know of our *dhjan*'s son."

Awkward. "Um, thanks. So, do you need to examine me?" Kiera cleared her throat, not about to take off her clothes in front of all the open windows. "Here?"

"I do. Come." He strode to another of the machines.

This one stretched from floor to ceiling and resembled a tanning booth she'd visited once. It wasn't much friendlier looking than the cell-regenerating coffin. Zanan touched the control panel on the side, and a door slid open.

"This will examine all your processes," he said as she stared at the dark opening.

"Do I take off my clothes in there?"

"What? Of course not, *nishani*."

Her face felt hotter at his startled look. She stepped into the exam box. The door slid closed behind her. It was dark and cool. She stood perfectly still, waiting for the bizarre sounds that the coffin made the few times it had healed her. The exam box was silent. After a few minutes, the door slid open again.

"You may come out," Zanan called to her, out of sight.

Kiera did so and saw him at the control panel on the side opposite the door. Consternation crossed his features as he took in the geometric shapes that made up their writing. The shapes flashed across the viewer while different touchpads around the control panel lit up in silent communication.

"It is not a son," he said, puzzled. "Your readings are different than an Anshan's." He continued to stare at the writing and flashes in silence.

She waited a few minutes before prodding him. "What does it say?"

"It cannot be possible."

"Oh, god. It's not twins, is it?"

"No, *nishani*. I am not certain what this means."

"Tell me!" Growing concerned, she inched closer, peering at a screen covered with symbols she wasn't able to read.

Zanan hesitated before speaking. "I will need you to return tomorrow. Your genetic makeup is different enough that I will need to research this."

"You're scaring me, doc," she said, trying to read his features. "Can you give me a hint? Anything?"

"I would rather discuss this with the *dhjan* tomorrow after I–"

"I'm not leaving until you tell me, and you certainly aren't telling him anything you won't tell me!"

He appeared taken aback again as she trampled over Anshan decorum. Still, he said nothing.

"The *dhjan* sent me here alone today to talk to you. If I have to interfere with his plans to bring him tomorrow, because you wouldn't tell me something ..." She shrugged.

"Very well, *nishani*," he relented. "You are not with child, because you cannot carry a child."

It was Kiera's turn to be startled into silence.

"I must confirm what the exam tells me," he added. "It does not seem possible. No *nishani* in the history of our people has been barren. The *dhjan* bloodline has never been broken."

Barren. Like Anshan. Kiera struggled with the words, uncertain how to take them. Part of her felt relieved that she wouldn't be pressured into having kids before she was ready. And then she realized what he was saying. Anshan needed an heir. Her chest tightened so quickly, she could barely breathe.

No nishani in the history of our people has been barren.

"I see," she managed.

"But ..." His frown grew deeper, almost haggard. "This is not the worst. Your cell regeneration is slowing too quickly."

"I don't understand that."

"It means ... I think ... that you're dying."

Kiera didn't move or speak, not sure she heard him right.

"I hope to have different news, but I think it likely I will not," Zanan said. "Return tomorrow. I will research these readings to be certain."

She stood in silence, willing him to tell her it was a horrible joke or that the machine made a mistake. When his features grew grimmer, she backed away.

"Thank you. I can return tomorrow." She left quickly without another word, unable to digest what he'd just told her. Stepping into the sunlight, she stood frozen for a moment.

You're dying.

Had she really heard those words? It didn't seem possible. How much valuable medical information could a tanning booth give him, anyway?

What would A'Ran do when he found out he'd have no son? That the bloodline ended with him?

He'll send me back. She shook her head to clear the thought away. It was the least of her concerns, but it lingered. Death was probably preferable to being barren in a society like this one. A'Ran's sense of duty to his people trumped everything. Would it trump his love for her, too?

"No," she said under her breath. She took a deep breath and started towards her home.

Then again, A'Ran was contemplating sending one sister away and denying the other the chance to marry the man she loved, because the teen boy was a miner.

Her step almost faltered. He'd made a promise to her. What did it mean that only she could heal Anshan – and she was dying? How would he take learning that the force in his blood, the one that kept the planet alive, would not survive his reign?

Maybe the doc will have different news tomorrow, she reminded herself. Yet the resolution in the doctor's face warned her he'd already settled on his initial determination.

Struggling to digest what she'd just learned, Kiera reached her home and moved through the house in a trance, not aware of where she was until she stood before the painting of A'Ran in the corridor. Kiera stared up at his noble features. Her throat tightened.

You're dying.

There has to be some mistake. If her life was connected to Anshan, then what exactly did that mean? Was there something wrong with the plane, too, or had it decided to reject her? Not for the first time, she found herself wishing to understand the relationships she was supposed to have with a chunk of rock floating in space. Because there was a relationship; she'd seen on more than one occasion that she could bring the planet surface to life.

Was Anshan suffering from some other kind of disease, reflected in her medical exam? Or was this truly *her* disease and issue, separate from what the planet was going through?

In a daze of suppressed emotion, she picked up a pencil and began sketching herself on the wall opposite A'Ran and his family. It seemed fitting that she wasn't on their wall, not if she was not going to be a part of their lives for long. She worked furiously, oblivious to the passage of time, concentrating instead on channeling her confusion and fear into something she could handle.

You're dying.

"That can't be true. I feel fine," she whispered to the wall. She'd felt happy and healthy since returning to the Anshan moon. Was it something else, then? A disease that didn't bother the Anshans but did her? How could she feel the best she'd ever been and be *dying?*

"Did you mean to leave me alone with the miner?" A'Ran's deep, low voice jarred her.

The begrudging way he said *miner* made her smile despite the turmoil in her thoughts. She turned and looked up at her lifemate. He wore the loose clothing of his people: trousers and V-neck tunic accessorized by a belt thicker than her thigh. A'Ran's dark eyes were assessing, as if he suspected she'd set him up and wasn't too happy about it. The sight of him always made her body warm from the inside out and her heart quicken.

Until she thought of what the doctor told her. Despair and disbelief trickled through her.

How can I be dying?

"No, I meant to greet him. I just got a bit ... involved with my work," she said, tossing the pencil.

"My *nishani*, who has no sense of duty at all," he said, his words softer. His gaze warmed, and he held out a hand to her.

Kiera took it and hugged him, comforted by his familiar scent and warmth. She rested her head against his warm chest. His heartbeat was slow and steady, its rhythm calming her.

"That doesn't bother you, does it?" she asked.

"You are my *nishani*. I have already claimed you."

It was his way of saying no. She hugged him more tightly. How did she tell him what the doctor told her? What did she say? That she was barren but not to worry – she'd be dead soon anyway and out of his life?

He loves me. I'd crush him. Yet there was a small voice in her mind that also pointed out how likely he to choose his duty and people over her, that he'd send her on the first ship back to Earth.

Not that she blamed him. He had a responsibility to an entire planet!

"You are upset?" A'Ran asked, stroking her hair.

She debated how to tell him news she didn't quite feel ready to admit was true yet. "Just ... homesick a little," she lied. "Do you think you'd ever like to visit where I'm from?"

"One day, after Anshan is well."

"We have a duty to the people."

"We do, *nishani*." He pushed her away enough to see her eyes. "A very important one that only you can do. I felt the grass." For a moment, a different glow was in his eyes, one she knew stemmed from hope. "You can do what I failed to do."

"You never failed at anything," she said, touched by the words. "It's not possible for a *dhjan* to fail."

"You are mocking me."

"Only a little." She smiled. "You are the most incredible man in the world. Your people are fortunate to have someone like you to lead them."

"And someone like you to heal them," he added, warmth in his features. "You are the reason for everything, *nishani*. Because of you, the planet will live and so will the people. It is my honor to be the one who found you."

She forced a smile and rested her ear on his chest once more, feeling as if her world was starting to implode. What would he do when he realized she wasn't going to save anyone? When his planet died, and so did his bloodline?

Anshan chose the *nishani* for its king. Why, then, had the planet selected *her* out of everyone in the universe and given her such a gift to heal it, if she was never meant to live long enough to help? The more she thought about it, the more she believed that the planet itself had to be having its own issues. The doctor hadn't been able to explain what was happening. Was it desperation that made her want there to be a problem with the planet and not her or was it really how her bond to Anshan might work?

The idea of letting down someone like A'Ran after all he'd been through made her feel ill. She'd left everything behind to be with him. Was she really about to lose it all?

"What is it, Kiera?" When A'Ran used her name instead of *nishani*, he was worried.

She forced her attention out of her thoughts and sought something to say. "Are you really considering sending Gage away?" she replied at last.

A'Ran was quiet too long.

Fear trickled into her. "Please tell me you'd never do that to someone you love, even if the circumstances were ... less than perfect." She held her breath, praying for him to clarify what Gage overheard.

"There are some parts to my society that you do not yet understand," he began softly. "Some duties and trusts cannot be broken."

Kiera's heart tumbled to her feet. "But she's your family."

"Even for family."

Oh, god. She'd been with him for a few weeks and already wasn't able to imagine a life without him. How much would it hurt when he found out she wasn't going to live long enough to carry out any of the duties that were hers?

How long would it take him to send her back to Earth, once he discovered there would be no more rulers in his line?

"It is for an honorable reason, one that is a sacred duty to me," A'Ran said.

"I love you," she whispered. "No matter what."

"You are my *nishani*," he squeezed her more tightly against him. "I would not do this if it weren't necessary. Trust me, Kiera. I do this for us."

Famous last words, she thought. Listening to his heartbeat, she didn't want to imagine what life would be like without her new family.

What if that didn't matter? What if her *cell regeneration*, as the doctor called it, was slowing enough that she wouldn't last too much longer anyway? She'd ask him the next time she went to the medics. She already knew that, no matter what timeframe he gave her, she wanted to spend what she had left with the man holding her.

Her thoughts drifted back to Anshan and the mysterious bond she had to the planet. If the doctor wasn't able to shed light on what was happening, her only choice appeared to be returning to the planet to figure out if it, too, was suffering what she was going through. If so, maybe she could fix it before things got worse, the same way she woke up the planet a few weeks before.

If not ...

The pain of possibly losing A'Ran made it difficult for her to breathe.

I need to go back, she vowed. *I need to know for sure.*

ONE

ON KIERA'S first visit to Qatwal, she'd been kidnapped into space by her best friend. On her second, she'd been brought back from Earth by the same friend to save Qatwal from destruction.

But her third visit was ranking as the most awkward yet. She stood in the hallway outside the banquet hall in the traditional, formal robe of the Anshan *nishani* – peach, silk-like material interwoven with threads of gray Anshan metal and a wide, red leathery waistband. A ceremonial knife made of the metal was at her hip, and her jewelry was made of the same subdued metal worked into the shapes of animals and random doodles she'd designed with the help of the metalworkers. A filigreed tiara was snugly attached to her hair and the rose-gold band marking her as A'ran's lifemate around one arm.

A'Ran was stiff beside her, dressed similarly in the understated uniform of the Anshan royalty. The small crowd across the entrance from them was decked out in clothing far more colorful and lavish with gems that glowed every color under the sun. After her time with A'Ran, she understood all their gems were worth far less than the metal she wore, and they openly admired her tiara with envy.

At the moment, the two parties were waiting for Romas, the king of Qatwal, before anyone moved.

Kiera strained to recall her latest dream. She'd been dreaming of Anshan for a week straight, but the images were too quick and liquid for her to make out many of the forms she saw before they had changed into something else. She didn't think the Anshan palace looked like this one, though. At least, she hadn't seen it in her dreams, though she'd seen other places: the storm, a field of green grass, an underground river ...

"Why did Gol-dee-locks go into a house if predatory creatures lived there?" A'Ran whispered without breaking his I'm-in-charge façade.

She blinked out of her thoughts and glanced up at him.

"Was this the same village where the seven little men lived?" Leyon, her lifemate's cousin, piped up from behind her.

They spoke quietly enough for the party across the hall not to hear.

Kiera sighed. She'd been trying unsuccessfully to explain the concept of fairy tales to men from a culture that didn't understand the difference between history and fables.

"No," she replied. "All the stories I told you happen in different places."

"Like the Five Galaxies. They're on different planets," A'Ran said.

"Did they have spacecraft?" Leyon asked.

"You said each tale has a lesson. What is this lesson?" asked Mansr. "Should she not know better than to go into the house of beasts and eat their food?"

"Maybe she meant to go into the house with the seven little men and make them breakfast," Leyon suggested.

"No," she snapped. "You can't mix the stories!"

The party across the hall from them shifted as Romas appeared, and they fell silent.

Sounds of cheerful talking and laughter tumbled out of the banquet hall, along with the scent of food, into the silent hallway. But for once, Kiera couldn't find any reason to smile.

Evelyn, her pregnant, former best friend was radiant as always at the side of the Qatwali ruler, Romas, who was A'Ran's on-again, off-again enemy. Kiera had spent much time trying to figure out what she felt towards Evey, whose selfishness had nonetheless brought Kiera to A'Ran and a world that needed her.

But this evening, it wasn't her internal conflict over all Evey had done troubling her. It was the bump of her friend's belly, the reminder of Kiera's visit to the Anshan medics when she'd learned the awful truth.

She'd considered herself the luckiest woman in the universe to have found A'Ran, only to discover she was going to devastate both of them when she broke the news to him.

The tension between the two kings was palpable. A'Ran hadn't wanted to come at all let alone bring Kiera, but the ruler of Qatwal had insisted they both be present before they began negotiations about trading Anshan metal for the atmospheric cleaners A'ran needed from Qatwal.

Kiera wanted to take A'Ran's hand and experience his strength, a reassurance against an unfriendly reception. Newly arrived to the planet, she held no love for the spaceships ferrying them around and felt little less apprehensive about being here than A'Ran. He had, after all, destroyed half the planet. She'd learned a lot about politics, but even she was surprised they hadn't been blasted out of the sky upon arrival into orbit.

"It's a pleasure to see you again." Ever the socialite, Evey was the first to speak. Kiera was almost relieved someone had broken the awful silence.

A'Ran didn't make any move to respond, but Kiera felt it necessary. "Thank you."

"Would you ... uh ..." Evey glanced at her husband before decisively breaking ranks with the Qatwali royals to enter the space between the two parties. "... care to walk in with me? The Queen always goes first." Her eyes twinkled at the words.

Kiera didn't want to leave A'Ran's side after their last interaction with the Qatwali. She glanced up at him. He was impossible to read when he was in king-mode, but he didn't indicate she should stay. He was leaving the decision up to her.

"Sure," Kiera said. She stepped forward and was accompanied by three of the personal guard A'Ran had brought to ensure her safety. The huge warriors made it hard to be inconspicuous and even harder to have a moment of privacy with anyone.

She joined Evey, and the two of them entered the banquet hall lined with low tables, close to a hundred strangers and heaps of food.

All talk silenced the moment Kiera walked in. Her step slowed, and she took in the looks ranging from disbelief to anger to sorrow, unable to help feeling guilty knowing A'Ran had destroyed so much of this planet. She'd always been self-conscious around the people of Qatwal, all of whom resembled tall, lithe models from Earth with flawless features and clear-colored eyes. She was on the small side, hence her nickname *nishani-mani* among the Anshan, who were themselves darker skinned yet still tall and willowy.

"Keep walking. Never let them see weakness," Evey said and took her arm. A large smile was on her face, and she walked on as if nothing was wrong. If there was one thing Evey knew, it was how to fake a smile.

Kiera went with her, squeezing her friend's arm to her side hard. They reached the table on a dais at the center of the hall and slid into their seats beside each other. Kiera clenched her hands in her lap, uncertain what troubled her more this night: being unwelcome by an entire planet or the secret she kept from A'Ran.

Talk trickled through the onlookers and slowly, they returned to their food and discussions.

"Are you well?" Evey asked when the attention of everyone had shifted away from them.

Are we really going to pretend we're still friends? Kiera gave the blonde beside her a long look before answering. "Yeah. You?"

"Lots of challenges but overall amazing," Evey said. "We've managed to start rebuilding."

"Already?"

"I know, right? Their technology is incredible. Any luck with returning to Anshan?"

"Some," Kiera replied, uncertain how much she was supposed to say about A'Ran's plans. "I went to visit last week."

"Isn't it toxic?"

"Yeah. They have these weird Jell-O suits that let you walk around in the middle of all the poisonous storms and stuff."

"Jell-o suits." Evey giggled. "We're the only two here who would get that."

Despite not wanting to fall into the trap she always did with Evey, Kiera found the charismatic woman's smile and cheerful voice hard to block. "Yeah."

"Is something wrong?"

Kiera raised her eyebrows.

"I mean, more wrong than usual," Evey added. "Aside from the war, politics, and whatever else."

"Like you said. Lots of challenges." It wasn't like Kiera to be guarded around anyone, and she hated how it made her feel. But there wasn't anyone she could really trust with the secret eating her up inside, though being with Evey again left her wishing she could. Her gaze went to the entrance, and she waited anxiously for A'Ran to join her.

"I think they wanted to talk first," Evey said.

"Oh." Disappointed, Kiera glanced over her shoulder at the three Anshan warriors that stood at the base of the dais. The sight of her husband's men comforted her in the hall full of strangers.

"Here. Try this one. It's my fave."

Kiera waited for her friend to spoon one of the many strange casseroles lining the table onto her plate. Instead of utensils, the Qatwalis used flatbread to eat. She tried the sweet potato colored casserole. "It tastes like cookies," she said, intrigued by the texture.

"That's what I thought!" Evey spooned another onto her plate. "This one is like red velvet."

Within moments of swearing she'd never open up to Evey again, Kiera was laughing and talking to her old friend. It was hard not to. Evey was outgoing and cheerful, and she'd always been good at drawing Kiera out of her shell, even if Kiera had many reasons not to trust her friend. If she'd learned anything, it was that she could have fun while knowing better than to confide in Evey. Gradually, she stopped glancing towards the entrance and waiting for A'Ran to appear.

The dinner was long, and the two of them ate alone on the dais at the center of the hall. When she was full, she sat back and glanced around the hall. The people of Qatwal seemed generally happy considering the disaster that had hit them so recently, and Kiera began to relax. She couldn't help envying them having a planet to live on, and knowing the people weren't going to starve if they were eating this well.

The Anshan people still struggled. She understood how much was on A'Ran's shoulders. He needed the rare gray metal to trade for food for his people, to clean up the air on the planet where they should have been living, and to bring back everyone who had been scattered across the Five Galaxies until they had a home once more.

With everything he was already juggling, A'Ran didn't need to know she, and his planet, were dying. At least, not until she was able to figure out how to fix it.

At least Qatwalis had a place to live, even if half of it was destroyed.

"You're not usually like this," Evey said, pulling her out of her thoughts.

Kiera focused on her surroundings once more. Evey's gaze was concerned. "I'm fine," Kiera said. "Just a lot going on."

"You want to go for a walk and talk about it?"

Kiera hesitated too long, and Evey rose. "Come on. I can show you my favorite place."

"Um, okay." Kiera glanced towards the door then the warriors. "Is it far?"

"No. This is our central palace, for lack of a better description. It used to be the vacation spot for royals, but the real palace was destroyed. Basically, it's a backup."

"This is a backup?" Kiera stood and gazed around. Everything about the palace was opulent, luxurious, from the precious gray metal statues adorning the hallways to the gems and metals acting as floorboards to the dress of those who lived here.

It was the opposite of the Anshan moon where she lived far more simply.

"My husband says the Anshan are savages." Evey winked.

"They're good people," Kiera replied.

"Come on." Evey took her arm again and walked through the banquet and into the hallway.

No one stopped to glare at Kiera, for which she was relieved, and she breathed a sigh when she reached the quiet, wide corridors, away from public view. Evey had no guard detail, and Kiera's bodyguards kept their distance, rendering the walk down the hallway almost peaceful.

Evey led them through several hallways into a private courtyard guarded by two Qatwali warriors. Low, stone benches made of ruby colored stone were placed among blooming night flowers and a trickling stream that wove through the garden. Qatwal's two moons were close together overhead, their light bright enough to bath the area in silver.

The Anshan moon was getting crowded, with even the smallest patches of available terrain used for gardening smaller vegetables.

The atriums of the home where she lived had been converted this past week into fragrant herb gardens.

Evey sat on one of the benches, and Kiera sank onto it beside her. She had forgotten what it was like to have a few moments of quiet.

"I love it here," Evey said. "It's a little oasis from the rest of the world."

"It's beautiful," Kiera agreed.

"I know you, K-K. Something's bothering you."

Kiera was quiet.

"I know things between us got weird." Evey paused and cleared her throat. "I don't want that. I want my friend back."

"I don't think that can happen, Evey," was Kiera's quiet response. "Some things are hard to move past."

The silence was awkward. Kiera breathed in the scents of water and plants.

"How about acquaintances or ... I think they call them allies around here. The good kind of allies, not like our frenemy husbands who alternately blow up each other's planets."

Kiera laughed, unable to help it at the too-accurate description.

"I don't want to be frenemies. If we can't be friends, how about allies?"

"I'll think about it," Kiera said uncertainly. "I don't want to be enemies. I just don't know what we are now."

"I can respect that." Evey sounded a little sad. "I've learned a thing or two about navigating these male-dominated societies. Sometimes it helps to have powerful female allies who can influence their husbands." She grinned.

"Is that why you're being so nice to me? You want something from Anshan?"

"What? No." Evey appeared genuinely surprised. "Do you really think that?"

Kiera's cheeks grew warm. She shrugged.

"Wow. I didn't realize you were that mad at me."

"I'm not anymore," Kiera replied.

"I'm sorry. I'm not sure what to say. I can't undo anything."

Kiera focused on the stream running near her feet rather than Evey's concerned features. It was hard to explain to Evey no one event had caused Kiera to think this way but a combination of things that shed light on how little Evey thought of someone outside of herself.

"Can I do something for you to prove I mean well?" Evey asked. "You can move here while you wait for Anshan to be ready or something."

"No, no, thanks," Kiera said and then made a weak joke to break up the tension. "Not unless you can get me to the Anshan surface so I can figure out what's wrong with the planet."

"I can try."

Kiera laughed uncomfortably. "No, I'm just ... joking. Sorta. Frustrated I guess. A'Ran has a lot on his plate and I'm not sure how to help him."

"I get that. Romas is the same," Evey said. "We've emptied his treasuries to rebuild." She gasped. "Which I wasn't supposed to tell anyone."

Kiera glanced at her, surprised. "You all act like you've got tons of money."

"It's part of the culture here. The royals have to always look and act royal, even if we're broke. But you have to promise not to tell anyone, even A'Ran!"

"I don't think he'll care. We're broke, too."

"But everyone knows that already. Qatwal being broke would mess up our new trade agreements."

Kiera rolled her eyes. "I won't tell. Besides, I imagine you'll soon have a few spaceships filled with that gray stuff to sell."

"Hopefully our significant others can come to an agreement that doesn't involve blowing up another planet."

There's no guarantee, Kiera thought.

"You sure there's nothing bothering you?"

"I just want to help rebuild Anshan but don't know how," Kiera replied truthfully. "That's it." *Except for the part about dying.* She wasn't ready to tell anyone that secret, especially not Evey.

"*Nishani.*" A'ran's low, husky voice made her temperature rise a few degrees. She twisted to see him in the entrance, his wide shoulders taking up most of the empty space of the doorway.

She rose a little faster than she meant to, excited to see him after the awkward exchange with Evey.

"Thank you for dinner and bringing me here," she said to her hostess.

"Of course." Evey stood. "Not a problem. Think about what I said, okay?"

Kiera nodded and stepped away briskly, anxious for some alone time with A'Ran after the stress of space travel and dealing with Evey. A'ran retreated into the hallway to await her, and she joined him, flanked by the three warriors. She searched is face. He was tense but didn't seem entirely displeased, which gave her some hope his meeting went well. He was an extremely private person, though, so she didn't ask him about the details in front of his men.

One of the Qatwali servants led them through the single story structure to the hallway for high-ranking guests and left them in a spacious apartment three times the size of the master bedroom they shared.

"Finally!" Kiera closed the distance between them and wrapped her arms around her lifemate, breathing in his scent. His muscular frame relaxed beneath her embrace, and he hugged her in return. A stir of dread, if not outright pain, went through her, and she debated how long she had until she either died or broke down and told A'Ran and was then exiled. "How did it go?"

She rested her chin at the center of his chest, studying his heavy features.

"Well," he said with his normal punctuality.

"So we'll get the air cleaners?"

"They've requested a deposit of ore first. They have only two purifiers ready, and we need ten. I was assured we would have the remainder before the next star cycle."

"Hmmm. That's quite a ways away," she said, disappointed. A star cycle was equivalent to about a year. "What can we do in the meantime to rush things along?"

"Not much. The two cleaners can be placed over the mines where the men will start working. It'll alleviate some of the danger to their health."

She reached up to touch the planes of his face. To mine Anshan metal, the workers would be in danger with a prediction of half of them dying before the end of the cycle. She understood the importance of the ore he needed to trade to feed and protect his people but felt sad whenever she considered how many people might die in the process.

"You're doing awesome," she told him, gazing at him in tenderness. "These are tough decisions."

"I'm doing what a *dhjan* does," he replied in a chiding tone. "It is my duty to make such decisions."

"I know." She smiled. "I don't know that I could make them."

"We are different."

"Very."

"How did your talk with your sister go?"

Kiera sighed and ducked her gaze, resting her ear against his warm chest. The Anshan and Qatwali didn't understand what *a best friend* was and had originally translated her relationship to Evelyn as *sister*. There was a time when Kiera loved the designation, because Evey had been like a sister for years. "Not bad," she said, unable to express the complicated emotions she felt towards Evey. "I don't like visiting here."

"We do so only out of necessity."

She didn't reply, unable to fully enjoy his company the way she usually did, not when the secrets she kept seemed to stay between them.

"What troubles you, Kiera?" he asked gently.

She loved the sound of her name on his lips, the affection in his tone.

I'm going to miss this. She didn't know how to answer. Lying had never been her forte and she loved A'Ran too much to want to try. So she gave him the same, rehearsed version of the truth she told Evey. "I feel like I need to be on Anshan to fix it. I'm not helping you enough."

"You cannot go, *nishani*. No one can."

"I know. But there must be some way, right? Is there anything in Anshan history like this?"

"Not to my knowledge." He gazed at her too long.

Her stomach was filled with butterflies, her lower belly burning for him as it did every time they touched, but her mind was as far away as could be. On her fate. On his disappointment. On the people of Anshan who would never return to their home again.

"It distresses you so much?" he asked and lifted her chin.

"Of course it does. I want it to be my home, too. Our home," she replied. "It feels like we're moving farther and farther away from every seeing that become reality."

"I understand this fear," he said, gaze warm. "I lived with it for many cycles, until I found you. You know you can help the planet. You must only wait until it's safe to be there."

"What if the planet dies in the meantime?"

A flicker of awareness went through his gaze, one she knew to be dangerous to her secret, if she didn't find a way to explain her question away.

"I mean, I had a dream it died. If I'm tied to it, and its life force is tied to mine, then what if it's trying to warn me?" she asked, hoping he didn't challenge her notion of dreams. She was only partially telling the truth. She'd dreamt of Anshan but not of it dying. "I had dreams of Anshan before."

He was quiet long enough for her risk a peek at his face.

His was pensive – but not surprised.

"What's wrong?" she asked instantly.

"It surprises me how strong the bond between you and Anshan

is," he replied. "There is a problem. The Anshan mines are over producing ore at a rate we won't be able to keep up with, even when we get the miners to the surface. It's why we're going to mine before the atmosphere is clear of toxins."

She listened, intrigued by the insight into his daily life as a ruler. He didn't tell her everything; this much she knew. She didn't expect him to. But to realize there was something wrong with the planet, that it wasn't just her burden anymore, filled her with as much worry as it did relief.

A'Ran was more than worried, though. He was disturbed. His dark eyes were distant, and she could almost see his mind working through the challenges of saving his planet. He moved away from her and poured them bowls of water.

"Mansr and I are concerned the planet is going to poison itself," he continued. "The miners will be focused first on the ore too close to water sources. Initially, we considered the idea Anshan was trying to make up for fifteen cycles of not producing ore."

"But now you think something is really wrong," she guessed, accepting one of the bowls.

He nodded.

"What?"

"We can't remain on the planet long enough to know for certain," he replied. "The readings we take are off the charts in every way. Too much toxin in the air, too much ore being produced. The soil is too acidic to sustain plants." His frown deepened.

He was too confident to look at his past and regret any choice he made, but she suspected he was wondering what would've happened had he not blown up the surface of the planet to rid it of the invaders trying to take it from him.

They were quiet, each dwelling on the puzzle of Anshan, before she asked the question she'd been dying to ask for several days. "Are you certain I can't handle the toxins and poisons and whatever else is wrong? Are you sure the planet won't let me be there?"

"The risk is too great. You are different from the Anshan people, but you are similar enough for an environment lethal to us to be toxic to you."

"But I'm connected to the planet."

"Connected does not mean immune to its poisons."

She considered the response. "Can we try?"

"No, *nishani*," he said firmly.

"What if there's no other way to save the planet?"

"Then we will stay on the moon."

"And the rest of the people?"

"We will extract what ore we can and trade it for their safe relocation."

She shook her head, frustrated. "There must be another way, A'Ran."

"If you think of one, tell me immediately and I will act."

She was unable to stop her smile. He had come a long way since they met, from viewing women as incapable of rational decision to appointing her as the supreme battle strategist of his forces to now, asking her to help him discover opportunities to save their planet. "You're a good man, A'Ran," she murmured. "The best in the universe."

"And you are my beautiful, irreverent *nishani*."

She rolled her eyes at him. "Speaking of which, it's time for some hugs and cuddles and other stuff the *dhjan* of Anshan doesn't do," she said, mocking the stern tone he often used with her when she broke their customs to touch him or argue with him in public.

A'Ran's worry melted away into a smile, and he opened his arms to her. "I want more than hugs, woman."

Kiera crossed to him with a laugh. "I know. My sweet, passionate *dhjan*."

He kissed her, and she melted into him, loving his heat and strength.

Tomorrow I'll to tell him. She'd told herself this every night since the first visit to the medic. She hated bearing the secret alone but hated the idea of hurting him even more. With the heat of desire in her blood, she wasn't about to spoil what could've been one of their last nights together with the truth.

───────

AFTER HE EXHAUSTED her with lovemaking, she fell into a deep sleep. The most vibrant of the dreams about Anshan reappeared, the one she'd had several times before. A faceless person with six arms stood in the middle of a green expanse surrounded by a storm. The green grass was receding, being eaten by the storm, and the faceless person reached out to her.

It didn't speak. It didn't move. It simply watched her, if a creature with no face could do such a thing. In her dream, Kiera tried to approach the strange figure without ever being able to reach it. It stayed the same distance from her no matter how fast she walked or ran. In the end, she ended up bent over and panting, frustrated, and stuck.

The vibrant dream faded into fleeting, less tangible images as she drifted deeper into sleep.

TWO

THE NEXT MORNING, Kiera was pacing. A'Ran had sensed his lifemate was upset by something for several days. What he didn't know: if it was more than the planet's situation causing Kiera's eyes to become so shadowed with worry.

"Can we talk about Gage?" she asked.

A'Ran looked up from pulling on his boots, hearing Kiera's concern. They'd discussed his sister twice and each time, neither ended up happy.

"What is there to discuss?" he asked.

"The fact you're exiling a member of your family."

He leaned back and studied her. "I do not expect you to understand my decision but I would ask you to respect it."

"I can't respect a decision that sends a pregnant woman away from her family because of a bad choice she made. She had no idea she was seeing a traitor!"

A'Ran hadn't slept well after making love to Kiera, too leery of being caught unaware in the home of his enemy. He rose and debated what to say. Kiera was brilliant, which was the reason she was the supreme battle commander. But she was also soft hearted sometimes, a trait he found an endearing trait for his *nishani* since he had no room for mercy in his position. However, on some topics, her gentleness and his devotion to duty caused them to disagree.

"The child of an Anshan woman belongs to the father's family," he said slowly. "I know this is not how it is on your world, but here, it is so. If she stays, I risk Ne'Rin's family declaring war on me. If she stays, there's a possibility they can use her the same way Ne'Rin did."

"I know the logic behind your decision. But she's your sister. If anyone can change customs here, it's you."

"I told you I'd consider it. But I cannot right now. My planet – *our* planet – and its people need me to help them first. I cannot put my personal feelings or my family above my duty. I must take the action I deem necessary first and when the time comes, I will review the decision."

At his firm explanation, Kiera appeared more devastated than he thought the situation warranted. His instinct warned him once more he was missing something.

"I know how much your duty means. I understand why," she said at last. "But sometimes I think you should let your heart decide."

"I do not have that luxury."

"You blew up Anshan." A small smile tugged up the corners of her bow-shaped lips. "Tell me that was logic."

"It was not my finest decision," he admitted. "But I would rather destroy my home than see my enemies take it from me."

"And you'd rather destroy Gage emotionally than take the time to evaluate her situation."

"You seem to think I feel nothing about the decision," he replied. "She is my sister. She is my blood. I love her and I would do anything to protect her. I'm sending her away as much for her own good as anyone's."

Kiera shook her head, frustrated, and crossed her arms. His lifemate was beautiful, even when she grew angry with him.

Her explanation about wanting to help the planet and concern about Gage made sense, but there was still more he sensed to her moods of late. He hadn't yet had the time to focus on unraveling why.

As it was, he risked being late to the critical meeting with Romas to hammer out the final details of their deal or he'd talk to her longer.

"I do not like to see you unhappy, *nishani*," he said and stood. He crossed to her and cupped her soft cheek with one hand. "I promise I will review the situation when I am confident we can save our planet."

"What if that never happens?" she asked, a haunted expression on her features.

He gazed into her blue-green eyes, admiring the unusual hue as he did every time he looked at her. He loved her warmth and softness and how little she tried to rein in her emotions. She was so unlike the women of Anshan. Rather than be repelled by how different she was, every new idea and feeling he encountered in his lifemate increased his affection. Her uniqueness saved his home planet on the battle-field, and he knew he was just scratching the surface of how special she truly was.

Even if, at times, that uniqueness caused some friction between his duty and his love for her.

"It will," he assured her. "The universe did not bring you to me only for us to fail to save Anshan."

Her features softened into a smile. She took his hand in both of his. "I want to believe that, too."

"Then believe it. We will heal our planet together."

"I want that so much." She hugged him.

"So do I." He embraced her briefly. "We can talk more later."

Kiera released him, and he left the room guarded by no less than five warriors. Two trailed him, and he paused when he reached the first curve of the corridor.

The instincts he trusted in battle and negotiations were agitated, and he didn't think it had anything to do with the meeting he was about to attend. Whatever was bothering Kiera, he hadn't been able to figure it out, and it surprised him to consider she was keeping a secret from him. He didn't want to think such a thing of his lifemate, but he wasn't able to shake the feeling, either. He had done his best not to let his duty interfere with the time he wanted to spend with her. He returned home most nights and involved her when it came to issues she needed to know about as the battle commander.

Duty came before everything, except for Kiera. She was the Anshan to his moon, and he had begun making his schedule revolve around his ability to see her every day.

When the meeting was over, he'd take her somewhere private for a day or so and talk to her in depth. Perhaps he hadn't spent enough time with her, or perhaps, the issues with Gage warranted his attention now rather than later.

"*Dhjan,*" one of the warriors said. "Have you forgotten something?"

"No." A'Ran shook off the thoughts. Even with such a mental compromise, he wasn't certain why his instincts weren't settled. He struck off down the hallway, hoping the meeting with Romas and the Councilmember, Jetr, was finished quickly.

He entered a room resembling his command center, except much larger. Everything on Qatwal was so much larger than anywhere he had been. He wasn't able to recall if the palaces on Anshan were this luxurious or large, but he didn't remember them being so. It had been too long since he and his people were driven from the planet. But as he observed the displays of wealth, he found himself uncomfortable with them. He had no intentions of mirroring this style of royal wealth when Anshan was habitable again. If anything, he had grown fond of the rather cozy setting where his family lived on the moon. He enjoyed seeing his sisters and Kiera when he passed through their home and knowing they were close enough he didn't need to worry about them.

His uncle and chief advisor, Mansr, stood from his position at the table where Romas and one of his surviving brothers sat. Jetr, A'Ran's remaining ally on the Planetary Council governing the trade and relationships among the Five Galaxies, stood waiting for him. The brothers regarded him with wariness, and it was only partially out of resentment after he had blown up half their planet. The Five Galaxies considered him a lethal liability, one no one was willing to oppose for fear of what he did. The shortage of gray metal had made many men desperate, but even desperate men knew better than to turn against a *dhjan* who destroyed his own planet.

The wide berth most found necessary gave A'Ran room to maneuver and time to heal his planet but worked against him when it came to trade agreements. Few people wanted to make an agreement with a madman. Mansr, a widely respected battle leader and senior member of the family, attended to help ease the fears of others.

Jetr was smiling. A shrewd politician, A'Ran had never trusted Jetr as much as Kiera did. Such a man saw much and said little, unless it suited him, although he had at least proved to be dependable and consistent.

And ... Jetr had been right about the betrayal of Ne'Rin – A'Ran's former second-in-command. It wasn't rational for A'Ran to despise the Council member for being smarter than he was about his allies, but the topic of losing his closest friend and advisor, the idea he'd been placing his family in danger for years without knowing it, still bothered him.

"It is good to see you well rested, A'Ran," Jetr said with unblinking black eyes in an unusually white face. The hunchbacked man wore several layers of robes.

They clasped forearms in greeting.

"You as well, Jetr," A'Ran said.

"I am optimistic about today," Jetr said.

The Qatwalis didn't appear anywhere near as cheerful as the wealthy politician.

They all sat at the table, and A'Ran glanced at the holographic, three-dimensional projection of Anshan swirling lazily at the center of the table, above their heads.

"I reached a separate agreement with the Qatwali," Jetr started.

"One of every ten ships filled with ore they receive will be turned over to me as payment for brokering the deal."

"This is between you and them," A'Ran said.

"It is of interest to you as well, A'Ran. I have agreed to front them the ore deposit they requested yesterday, since you have not yet begun mining."

A'Ran didn't like the reminder he was not only poor but couldn't mine his own planet. He wanted to tell Jetr to keep his ore and the Qatwalis not to make any more deals behind his back about *his* ore, but he had learned much about being humble at the negotiation table.

And ... everyone at the table knew he couldn't provide the deposit they required without the atmospheric filtration systems in place.

"This sounds reasonable," he forced himself to say.

Mansr gave a subtle nod of approval.

"I believe this was the sticking point last night," Jetr said, glancing between the two parties.

"It was," Romas, now the leader of his people, agreed. "We agree to turn over two of the devices immediately and to send an additional eight within a quarter cycle. We can expedite, if you're willing to increase the ore payment by ten percent."

"So you want me to repay Jetr," A'Ran said.

Romas gave a cold smile.

A'Ran pretended to consider, aware of how important it was to make it appear he had a choice when he and Mansr alone knew they didn't. This deal was the only way for them to begin working on Anshan and stop the overproduction of ore before it poisoned the rest of the planet.

But to watch his lifelong competitor and enemy gain the upper hand would never sit well with him, especially when Romas knew A'Ran had to have been desperate to approach them at all.

"Agreed," he stated. "And I will offer a bonus ten percent if you can deliver the eight machines in half the time."

"You will not find me turning down such an offer," Romas said.

"A Qatwali ship will accompany you back to Anshan towing the two machines. I assume you will wish to leave immediately."

"I do," A'Ran agreed.

"We will have the ship prepared to leave as quickly as possible."

"I cannot tell you how pleased this makes me and the other members of the Council," Jetr said.

A'Ran half listened as the Councilmember went on for a short time about the Council's position on trade in the Five Galaxies. He was unable to shake the unease in his system stemming from the idea he'd soon be sending his miners to die in Anshan mines to pay someone he had no respect for like Romas. The sacrifice was necessary but didn't sit well with him. If not for the mines over producing, he could wait until all ten atmospheric filters were in place.

Jetr finished speaking, and everyone at the table exchanged formal farewells before standing to leave.

A'Ran waited for Mansr, and the two of them headed towards the direction of the guest quarters.

"You did well, nephew," Mansr said. "I know it is difficult to negotiate with the Qatwali."

"It's necessary," A'Ran said. "Any new ideas on how to stop the mines from over producing?"

"None. We cannot make sense of the readings except to return to the same conclusion our analysts drew initially. The planet is off balance, and we cannot determine the cause."

"The cause is clear. I destroyed the surface."

"This stems from something much deeper, A'Ran." Mansr turned to face him.

A'Ran waved his personal guard back and studied his uncle's concerned features.

"It is believed the ore is part of the planet's life force, just as the water and other natural resources are. It is possible the planet has been dying for some time."

"*Nishani* said something similar," A'Ran replied, disturbed. "She dreamt of it dying."

"We should consider the possibility Anshan will never be habitable, even if we can mine it for ore."

"You of all people should not be saying such a thing."

"I am not giving up, nephew," Mansr replied. "But you might wish to make more permanent plans for the population, in case we cannot rebalance the planet."

The words were painful for A'Ran to hear after all that had happened the past few years. The invasion, exile, the poverty of his people, all of which became shadows in dazzling sunlight when he had found the lifemate capable of healing his planet. "I cannot accept this," he said with a shake of his head. "I cannot believe we will never return to Anshan. It is our home."

"I agree, A'Ran," Mansr said. "But as the *dhjan*, you cannot afford the optimism and hope every Anshan citizen possesses since *nishani* appeared. You must always plan for the worst."

"I'm not ready to let go of my hope, Mansr."

"I'm not suggesting you give it up. I'm suggesting you create alternatives, just in case."

"I will consider your counsel, as always." A'Ran didn't want to feel the heaviness of dread that had weighed him down for so many years. "If you will handle the preparations to return home, I want to discuss Anshan with Kiera."

"Of course." Mansr smiled. "Give my regards to *nishani*."

A'Ran nodded once and struck off down the hallway, grateful to have some time with Kiera before leaving.

Leyon, one of the three warriors stationed in front of the guest quarters, stood at attention when A'Ran approached.

"*Nishani* has gone to the gardens with her sister," he reported.

A'Ran nodded.

"How did the negotiations go?"

"Better than expected," A'Ran said. "Come. We will ready the ship."

Leyon drew abreast of him, and they strode together through the quite halls.

Disappointed not to find Kiera present, A'Ran knew he would have time on the spaceship. Kiera deserved some time with her sister. Aware of his lifemate's inner turmoil concerning all that had passed between the two of them, he suspected she needed some space to repair her friendship.

THREE

DRESSED in normal space clothing once more, Kiera was more comfortable this day than the previous evening. She walked with Evey into the massive garden behind the palace beneath warm, sunny skies. The colors of Qatwal were so much richer than those of Earth or the Anshan moon. The sky was sapphire blue, the grass emerald, and flowers gem-like.

The first time she'd set foot on Qatwal, she'd been astounded by the saturation of color and found herself marveling at it still. As an artist, she appreciated the uniqueness of the world before her. A small part of her ached at the fear Anshan would never have a chance to bloom like this.

"Gorgeous, isn't it?" Evey asked with a sigh.

"It's amazing, Evey."

"What's your moon like?"

"Not like this." Kiera smiled. "It's cozy and comfortable."

They paced through the various flowers and trees. A small, gray spacecraft flew overhead, landing close to the palace. Kiera concentrated on the flowers to keep her thoughts from returning to their dark path towards despair. A'Ran's promise to reconsider Gage's situation helped, until the caveat about waiting for the planet to return to health first.

"This is driving me crazy!" Evey said finally. "Are you that mad at me or is there something really wrong?"

Kiera forced a small laugh. "Just a lot on my mind."

"This is different."

"Nothing I want to talk about, Evey."

Evey sighed noisily. Kiera almost felt bad when she saw the saddened look on her friend's face. It wasn't in her nature to keep the distance between them she thought she should.

"What's going on?" Evey was gazing towards the palace.

Kiera turned to see five of the Qatwali warriors approaching, all heavily armed as if for battle. Their pace was quick, their focus on the two women. Her heart skipped a beat and she prayed something bad hadn't happened during the negotiations.

"Forgive the intrusion." The Qatwali at the head of the procession bowed his head to Evey. "There has been a threat to the life of the Anshan *nishani*. We were instructed to take her to a safe place."

"A threat? What kind of threat?" Evey asked, frowning.

"There is some dissension among the Qatwali." His eyes slid to Kiera then back to Evey.

"This is because of our visit?" Kiera asked.

"It is."

She and Evey exchanged a look.

"Is the *dhjan* safe?" Kiera asked eagerly.

"He is. He's waiting for you."

She looked past them, puzzled not to see her warrior bodyguards present. What exactly was going on? Was this some sort of Qatwali plot for vengeance? If so, why did Evey appear as surprised as she was?

"Okay," she murmured. "I'll go with you."

"I will as well," Evey said.

"We were ordered to evacuate the Anshan dignitary," the warrior responded.

"You want me telling my husband, your king, you disobeyed me?" Evey snapped.

He hesitated once more the stepped aside for them both to pass. Kiera tried to convince herself this was the right choice to make. His explanation made sense. She'd seen the looks directed her way by the people in the banquet hall, and if A'Ran had a bad meeting, she was easily able to imagine they were being punted off the planet.

But she didn't think A'Ran would let anyone but Leyon share such news.

She and Evey stepped into the midst of the five, who began escorting them at a brisk gait towards the side of the palace.

"Where is A'Ran?" Kiera asked.

"He is being evacuated as well," came the disinterested response.

Something's fishy about this. Kiera went along with them. With any luck, she'd see A'Ran soon to ask him what was going on. If not, then ...

Her doubt grew when she saw the small personnel carrier that had landed in the open area beside the part of the palace facing a cliff. As the battle commander, she knew every ship in the Five Galaxies on sight, from its specifications to its functions to its appearance. And something was very wrong with this ship.

Layers of gray metal sheets had been used to patch up scorched areas from where laser fire had hit the craft, and only one of its three engines was purring.

"Wait a minute," she said, slowing. "I don't think –"

The warrior nearest Evey snatched the blonde and settled his sword across her belly. Evey gasped, and Kiera froze.

"Get in. Or the Qatwali will be mourning the loss of two more," said the warrior in a hard tone.

Cold fear streaked through Kiera. Evey appeared too shocked to know how to respond, and Kiera swallowed the lump in her throat.

"I'll go with you," she said. "Will you leave her here?"

"That's not possible now." The warrior pushed her towards the spacecraft. Evey was released, and Kiera took her hand.

They climbed into the war torn craft. More signs of damage and shoddy repairs were inside the craft, down to the absence of seats to sit on. The warriors motioned them to the far wall, and Kiera sat next to Evey.

"Who are these people?" she whispered.

"No idea." Evey was pale.

The craft door closed, and two of the warriors removed the Qatwali helmets and tunics they wore to reveal familiar symbols on their clothing.

"It can't be!" Kiera breathed.

"What?" Evey asked, following her gaze.

"Yirkin."

"The guys who invaded your planet and drove A'Ran into exile?"

Kiera nodded. The spacecraft pitched one way then the other as it lifted off the ground. Kiera gripped Evey to prevent them from being flung across the open floor of the ship. With a howl, the single engine managed to lift them into the sky.

"That doesn't sound good," Evey said.

"I've never heard of a craft this size running on only one engine."

One of the Yirkin glanced over at them before approaching with gray handcuffs. He knelt. One of his eyes was bright blue, the other gold. They stood out in his tanned face, along with the shock of white-blonde hair marking him of neither Qatwali nor Anshan heritage. A knotted scar ran down the side of his face and his hands were discolored as if by burns.

"There is no escape but death, *nishani*," he said and cuffed Kiera's hands and then Evey's.

"The Yirkin motto," Kiera murmured, recognizing the words from her studies of the invader enemies of Anshan.

"What do you want with her?" Evey asked in a hushed tone.

"It will become clear soon enough." He moved away without another word. "Stay quiet."

The howling engine soon grew into an outright scream, making it impossible for them to talk anyway. Kiera plugged her ears with a grimace and watched the warriors do the same. Three were crowded into the cockpit, two hovering and the third at the navigation station. She suspected they were as concerned about the craft making it anywhere as she was.

The trip was longer than she expected the disabled ship capable of traveling, over six hours, long enough to make it to Anshan or out of the solar system completely if they went the opposite direction. The shouts of the warriors were lost over the wailing engine, and they resorted to hand signals she didn't understand to communicate.

Her chest tight with fear they were going to stall out any moment, she could do nothing but wait.

The engine began to wind down, an indication they were descending, only to be replaced by another sound. The craft was battered by winds strong enough to tear off at least one piece of the metal used to patch it. Kiera and Evey braced themselves against the wall to stay in place. What sounded like hail smashed into the sides of the ship.

Just as suddenly as it started, the winds and pelting stopped. The engine was reduced to a purr and the craft bumped gently against the ground. At long last, the nerve wracking descent was over.

The Yirkin with mismatched eyes approached and grabbed Kiera's arm, hauling her to her feet. Two of his men wrestled with the door and managed to open it manually. It fell away and hit the ground with a puff of dust. The area beyond the door was dark, and Kiera's heart began to pound. She dug in her heels, but the Yirkin jerked her forward to the exit and all but dragged her to the ground beyond.

She caught herself in time to keep from falling, her gaze darting around wildly. They appeared to be in a cave. The rocks and gravel at her feet were reddish, and sickly yellow lanterns glowed every twenty feet or so from their positions jammed into crevices along the cave walls. It was about forty feet across and too dark for her to figure out how deep.

She was about to demand to know where they were when a

familiar tingle of electricity fluttered through her. She looked down towards the source of the charge, always intrigued by the way Anshan greeted her. The planet's energy was light – and far weaker than she recalled it being when she'd last been on the surface for an extended period of time.

"Anshan?" she asked, puzzled. "What are we doing here?"

Her captor didn't respond. He marched her forward. She sucked in deep breaths. The air was stale without being toxic that she could tell. She tried to see Evey over her shoulder but was yanked forward once more. Neither at home on the planet whose life force she shared nor afraid to be there, she struggled to understand how anyone was alive after what A'Ran had said about the toxic environment.

She observed what she could of the cave. Most of it appeared to be a natural formation, while swaths of the floor, nearest wall and ceiling held marks of drilling and scraping by manmade tools to reveal thick veins of familiar, pale gray metal trapped in the rock.

We're in a mine, she realized, surprised once more. A'Ran had blown up the mines closest to the surface, which meant they were in a deep mine or perhaps, inside one of the many mountain ranges on Anshan.

"How have you survived here?" she whispered, recalling what A'Ran had said about the ore poisoning the water supply. Anshan hadn't grown food in years either.

"You would not like to know this," the warrior at her side replied.

Her heart skipped a beat and she silently agreed. Survival on Anshan was impossible to consider, and she began to wonder why the Yirkin had bothered to drag her back to a dying planet to begin with.

FOUR

"A'RAN, Romas, just think for a moment about what you're doing!"

Jetr stood between the warriors, each of which was being restrained by his respective guards.

A'Ran had not experienced this level of fury since the moment he discovered Kiera was on the planet when he destroyed it. It blinded him, made him disregard any thought about peace and trade treaties, no matter how much his people needed them.

"Separate them!" Mansr ordered in a tone not even the Qatwalis were going to ignore.

Against his will, A'Ran was all but dragged from the atrium into a small chamber. He yanked free of his men, who moved swiftly to block the door.

The blind rage ebbed enough for him to realize he'd almost killed Romas. His own nose was bloodied, and at least one swipe of a sword had penetrated his guard and cut him deep enough to bleed. Romas had been in little better shape when their scuffle was broken up.

"Everyone out!" Mansr commanded, entering. He was stiff, his face flushed with anger.

The warriors obeyed.

A'Ran growled deep in his chest and touched the warm trickle of blood running down his face.

Mansr waited until the last warrior was gone before he closed the door. "*Dhjan* or not, you're behaving like a child!" he snapped.

Surprised by the outburst from the man who had been among the first to treat him as the *dhjan,* A'Ran paused in his pacing.

"Really, A'Ran! What possessed you to do something so stupid? To risk the armistice or the air purifiers?"

"My lifemate is missing!" A'Ran roared in response.

"If you'd bothered to ask before attacking him, you'd know his lifemate is gone as well!"

A'Ran made a disgusted sound and whirled, pacing once more.

"An unidentified craft entered the air space above the palace and left shortly after landing. They had no clearance and went unchallenged, since the Qatwali are too proud to tell anyone the truth – the planet is vulnerable. They are giving the appearance of rebuilding, but they have no funds. They're cannibalizing existing systems, to include defensive systems now that we're at peace, to rebuild."

A'Ran faced him again. "How do you know this?"

"How do you think, nephew?" Mansr replied.

"Jetr." A'Ran's calm began to return. "So they just let anyone who wishes to enter their air space fly in and kidnap royals without concern about their people!"

"Once the Yirkin were driven out of the Five Galaxies, we were the only threat. I imagine they thought, as we do, that we'd have some space and time to rebuild and heal before we faced another threat."

A'Ran didn't like Mansr's pointed tone, the one subtly telling him he was more like Romas than he ever wanted to admit. He, too, had left his people mostly vulnerable and scattered across too many planets and moons to name.

"This ship. Whose was it?" he demanded, wracking his thoughts for an explanation as to who was bold enough to carry away two *nishanis.*

"There's no imagery available. Witnesses said it had no markings and it appeared to have been badly damaged."

"Damaged?"

"It barely made it off the planet."

"Then it should be easy to find!"

"I already called our command carrier," Mansr said with tried patience. "They dispatched scouting ships in every direction."

"How long ago was it spotted?"

"This morning."

A'Ran calculated how far a damaged ship could go or where it might have come from. There were many planets in the solar system, none of which were hostile to Qatwal that he knew. He didn't doubt he had enemies, but Romas had the sympathy of the system after A'Ran's attack on Qatwal.

"This doesn't make sense," he said finally, unable to explain what had happened or why. "If it came from outside the system, Qatwali allies would know."

"And no one is speaking."

"So the craft either had help leaving or never left the system."

"Correct."

A'Ran could do nothing from the ground and felt helpless knowing the Qatwali didn't have the technology available to spot the spacecraft if it was just outside their orbit. "We need to return to the ship," he said brusquely. He preferred to be in space and battle than trapped on the planet's surface.

"I'm going with you." This terse voice came from the doorway.

A'Ran's eyes narrowed as Romas entered. The blond man's hair was mussed, his gaze fiery and his shoulder bloodied from where A'Ran had stabbed him.

"This is no doubt another of your messes that's just so happened to drag in my lifemate and son," Romas added.

"At least I have the means to find them again. What made you leave your planet defenseless?" A'Ran shot back.

"Enough," Mansr said. "With the *dhjan's* permission, we will all return to the command carrier in orbit and commence searching for them."

A'Ran clenched his jaw and gave a nod.

"Do you have any enemies, any insight into what might've happened?" Mansr asked Romas.

"None. I have no enemies, unlike Anshan," came the arrogant response.

"The Council has been alerted," Jetr said, entering the room as well. "My fleet is at your service."

"At what cost?" A'Ran growled.

Mansr shot him a look, and Jetr politely pretended not to have heard.

"Thank you," A'Ran said loudly. "But I have my own ships and capabilities."

"I would like to accompany you, on behalf of the Council."

Even Romas stiffened at the request. A'Ran understood why. The Planetary Council loved information it could use against others, which was why most planets and rulers tried to keep their private affairs private.

"It would be our honor," Mansr said in the thick silence. "Would you meet us at the space dock as soon as you can be ready?"

"Of course." Jetr flashed a smile and ducked into the hallway.

Mansr waited until certain he was gone before facing the two. "You two need each other for this," he said to A'Ran. "We have ore, but Romas has the good will of the entire Five Galaxies. He can obtain what we can't buy, namely assistance, peace and safe passage, should we need it."

A'Ran said nothing. Romas appeared equally as agitated by the forced alliance. No matter how long he thought, A'Ran could come up with no one who wanted to anger Romas, even if someone was foolish enough to offend A'Ran.

The distinct possibility someone had taken Kiera to ransom for the ore produced solely on Anshan caused A'Ran's blood to boil once more.

A'Ran and Romas stared at one another, the hostility thick in the air between them.

"If you are both prepared to leave?" Mansr prodded.

"I am," A'Ran replied.

"I need to coordinate with my advisors," Romas said. "But it will take little time."

"Meet us at the space port," Mansr said.

Romas left without another word.

"Nephew," Mansr said, facing A'Ran. His features softened into concern. "No one would risk hurting her."

"I'm not as certain of this as you," A'Ran said. "My *nishani* doesn't understand the politics of our world."

"She's done well so far."

"She has. But she doesn't know enough of Anshan history or my long list of enemies to know who to trust."

Mansr didn't respond. They both knew Kiera was still learning about their customs and the Five Galaxies. The more he thought about her, the more he realized she wasn't entirely helpless. She had a commander's knowledge of spacecraft and all their systems – including the communications. She'd be able to contact him, if given the chance.

Hopefully, he found her before she needed to call for help.

"Let's go," he said and strode into the hallway.

———

LESS THAN AN HOUR LATER, the personal spacecraft that conveyed him and Kiera to the Qatwal surface returned to the space carrier orbiting the planet. With the knowledge that Qatwal didn't have defensive systems to detect it, A'Ran had ordered it out from hiding behind one of the Qatwali moons. The bay was even more confined with Romas and his five companions. A'Ran was relieved when they docked with his larger carrier and immediately set out for the command center.

He and Mansr stepped into the circular hub, where displays of everything in the local orbit appeared as holograms, and his battle command desk was actively scanning the area with multiple kinds of radars.

"You brought an armed battleship into my space?" Romas asked, stepping into the command center behind him.

"If you're planet wasn't completely vulnerable to everyone in the Five Galaxies, you wouldn't be surprised," A'Ran replied in the same tone.

Romas said nothing but joined A'Ran at the battleship command station. A'Ran searched the surveillance and radar logs for the space-craft, finding it with some effort among the comings and goings of similar sized ships and space trash in Qatwal orbit.

"It headed towards Anshan," Romas said, anger in his voice again.

A'Ran watched the spacecraft disappear several times, assessing its trajectory with the help of the computer.

"Mansr," he said at last. "We lose it at the bigger of our two moons. There's no way to know where it went from there."

"Long range radar?" Mansr asked, approaching.

"Unable to pick it up again once it entered the distorted magnetic fields around Anshan." A'Ran stared at the small planet of Anshan, at once angry and pitying of the planet that couldn't help being the disaster it was.

Mansr was quiet before he ordered the ship to return to Anshan quickly.

"Do you have a strategy to find the craft?" Romas asked.

"We've been experimenting with our systems," A'Ran replied. "We can track more from the moon than anywhere else. If they passed between the moon and Anshan, we'll have a log of it and be able to track them."

Romas said nothing. With no other choice but to wait, A'Ran sat in front of the command station, watching the replay of the spacecraft disappearing over and over. His thoughts were on Kiera, his frame so tense, he was ready to snap if anyone passed too close to him.

No one did. Even Romas and his team huddled in the far corner of the center, talking for most of the trip.

At full speed, the carrier halved the travel time home, but it was still too long for A'Ran's comfort.

Whoever dared touch my Kiera will die in my hands before the day is over.

FIVE

KIERA WAS FORCED DEEPER into the cave, and she glimpsed tunnels running off in several directions from the main cavern. She'd seen a part of the underground tunnel network when she awoke the planet before A'Ran blew up its surface. Each tunnel was small and lit by weak lighting. They passed several before her captor turned down one.

Unable to imagine what was going on, Kiera concentrated on not tripping over her feet on the rocky terrain. The tunnel ended at a cavern far better lit than the cave they'd landed in.

The Yirkin escorted her to the end of the tunnel to a shallow cliff overlooking the cavern the size of a city below. Thousands – perhaps tens of thousands – of people were located in the cavern, walking along makeshift roads running among shelters built out of anything that could be salvaged: metal, rocks, clothing. The people were gaunt and pale, most with blond or white hair, and dressed in clothing that had seen better days. Clusters of housing were located around personal spacecraft marked sloppily with the sign for medics.

He released her. She didn't move, slowly taking in the scene.

"This is what remains of the Yirkins who lived on Anshan for fifteen cycles. Those we could save," came the bitter words.

"You're refugees," she murmured.

She studied his scarred face, uncertain what to think. The Yirkin had invaded Anshan and stolen it from A'Ran. Most of the people below, however, appeared to be women, children and the elderly. She saw few men among them and even fewer men of warrior age.

She hadn't thought much about those on the ground as the battle commander. She assumed everyone present was a combatant.

"Do you want revenge against me?" she whispered.

"Revenge?" he echoed.

"Against the *dhjan*."

"At one point, I did," he answered deliberately. "But I want now to save what's left of my people."

"You're trapped."

"The Five Galaxies expelled the rest of our people, and the magnetic storms in the Anshan atmosphere prevents us from calling for help, even if we could build long range communications."

"I don't understand." She faced him. "You left to get me."

"We used the scrap metal from dozens of ships to create a single working craft," he replied. "It was too small to evacuate anyone, so we did the next best thing. We came for you."

"You know what A'Ran did to get his planet back. What makes you think he'll let any of you live for taking me? He doesn't really negotiate in hostage situations."

"You are not here to *negotiate*." The man scoffed. "And you are not a hostage. You are on your own planet, the planet you are connected to. You belong here."

He's not wrong. She feared voicing the words and stood in silence, pulse racing.

He spun and started down the slope towards the base of the cavern.

She released the breath she'd been holding and glanced back. Evey wasn't behind her, and Kiera craned her neck to see past the massive Yirkin guard between her and the tunnel. He nodded his head towards the Yirkin leader.

She went reluctantly.

The scarred leader with mismatched eyes wound through the refugees. Kiera trailed, more worried about her reception here than she had been in the Qatwali banquet hall. Instead of glares, the Yirkin watched with guarded curiosity and moved out of her path. Most stopped what they were doing to whisper amongst themselves.

Kiera slowed, uncertain what to do. If there were one thing she hadn't yet adapted to, it was the amount of attention she attracted everywhere she went. It was usually a combination of being the *nishani* and how different she was in appearance. She had no idea what the Yirkin were thinking when they saw her and whether they were malicious or ... not.

She lost track of the Yirkin leader for a split second and quickened her pace. The cavern was rocky and hilly, and it smelled heavily of people living too closely confined.

She hurried after him and reached him just as he disappeared into one of the salvaged spacecraft being used as central gathering points. This one was empty, and she stepped in behind him.

He beckoned for her to join him in a room. She went, and he closed the door behind her.

"Where's my friend?" she asked anxiously the moment she sat.

"Safe for now. Unless you fail to do what I tell you."

"Which is what?" Kiera resisted the urge to fidget. "If not revenge, what do you want from me?"

"You are the Anshan *nishani* are you not?"

"Yes."

"I want you to fix the planet so we can either reclaim what we lost or leave without the rest of us dying."

She gave a startled laugh. "Oh, is that all?"

He wasn't smiling. His direct gaze was intense, his anger simmering.

She swallowed her amused surprise.

"It is what the Anshan *nishani* does, is it not?"

Kiera cleared her throat. "In theory. I have not been a *nishani* for long."

"Your life force is linked to that of the planet. If you are well, so can it be."

Doom crashed down upon her at the reminder. Her face grew hot and she averted her gaze.

"You are not well," he guessed at her silence.

"No," she said in a tight voice. "I'm dying, too. Like Anshan."

"Then you have nothing to lose by trying. Or perhaps, by being here, you can both heal. Either way, you are not leaving until you make it so we can escape." He set a bowl of water before her. "You can think what you will of our leaders and warriors. We are called parasites by many and it is true we steal worlds from others." He shrugged. "But there are innocents in every world. The warriors can be flayed alive but their lifemates and children should be spared."

She sipped the water, listening.

"Our fates are intertwined with Anshan's and through the planet, yours," he finished. "You are already dying. Why not die trying to heal the planet?"

I wanted to be on Anshan. He made more sense than anyone in her life at the moment. Unable to accept A'Ran's rigid duty-first logic at times, she was finding it hard not to empathize with the man who wanted only to save his people.

A'Ran had been in the same position when they first met. He was an exiled prince whose people were scattered across the Five Galaxies. He saw in her what this Yirkin did: the secret to healing Anshan.

"Even if I succeed, A'Ran won't let you stay," she pointed out. "And he'll do whatever it takes to find me."

"We spent six weeks experimenting with the right combination of factors to let us leave Anshan. I lost forty of my warriors to the toxic surface," he replied. "I will deal with what happens after you save my people. It is said he destroyed his planet for you. He will free a few Yirkin for the same reason."

Kiera nibbled on her lip. Was it wrong for her to be just a little relieved at being on Anshan, the place she'd wanted to go for weeks to see how she could help the planet? Was it wrong to want to help the enemies of A'Ran? To get rid of the suffering of those who didn't deserve it?

Her fear and anger melted as she considered what he was asking her to do. The Yirkin wanted her to do what she'd felt she was supposed to since she first crash landed onto Anshan. How was it the only person willing to let her try was an enemy of her adopted people?

"I really don't know how to help Anshan," she said after a long moment of thought. "I'm not from the Five Galaxies. I don't understand how a *nishani* can be bound to an entire planet. It's not like that where I'm from."

"It's not like that anywhere," he replied. "We are not from the Five Galaxies, either. We ventured here when we heard of the plentiful resources and relative peace."

"You can't stay here," she said without thinking. "I mean, assuming we survive. You can't have Anshan back."

"You wish to make terms with me now, before we have healed the planet?" A flicker of amusement was in his eyes.

"Well ... why not? You all leave the Five Galaxies when this is over."

"And you save our lives."

She shifted uncomfortably. "If I can."

"What other terms would you have?"

"Um, I've never negotiated with another um ... people. Planet. Whatever."

"Then I recommend you request immunity to Yirkin war law for you and your friend."

Kiera wanted nothing to do with war crimes in another galaxy.

"Agreed. And for A'Ran. You can't seek revenge against him and his people."

The Yirkin scowled.

"He's my lifemate. If you think I'm going to help you with a guarantee, then –"

"Your terms are acceptable to me so long as you will guarantee the safety of my people as well," he interjected. "Your *dhjan* is not likely to look any more favorably upon us as we are him."

"I can do that," she said. If she healed the planet, she'd do whatever it took to convince A'Ran to spare the people trapped beneath its surface. They were what the Yirkin claimed: innocents. Women, children and vulnerable members of a colony who hadn't been able to escape in time and didn't deserve to pay for the crimes of their leadership.

"We're agreed? You on behalf of Anshan and me on behalf of the Yirkin?"

She nodded, uncertain if she was supposed to make deals in A'Ran's name or not. But she had little choice, if any of them were going to live through this.

"Good. Your friend will be provided a suitable resting space." He stood. "Come with me."

Her stress level was rising with the stakes. Kiera trailed him out of the spacecraft, scared for Evey despite the deal. She at least had something the Yirkin wanted, even if no one knew how to access her connection with the planet. She caught up to him, self-conscious about the stares.

"You brought families with you to war?" she asked.

"We colonized the planet. Families accompany the warriors after the planet has been taken."

"But why colonize it at all? Why not stay on yours?"

"We have no planet of our own. It was destroyed many, many cycles before."

"So you all just roam around. You're like space gypsies."

He gave her a displeased look. She didn't know if it meant he was offended by *gypsies* or the translator hadn't caught the word correctly.

"Why not just buy or conquer your own planet and stay?" she pressed.

"It is not our way."

"But you can change that."

"Do you speak this nonsense to your *dhjan*? About changing his customs and traditions?"

"Every day."

The Yirkin said nothing more but continued walking. They entered the tunnel network once more. This one slanted upwards and was narrow with a ceiling low enough for him to hunch over to walk through it.

"Where are we going?" she asked.

"It will be clear soon."

"Do you have a name?"

"What does it matter?"

She rolled her eyes. He was unfriendly considering he'd asked her to save his people. "If we're going to be working together, I thought it'd be nice to know."

"Turi."

"I'm Kiera."

"Like the moon."

She smiled sadly at the reminder. She'd been gone from A'Ran for half a day and already ached for him. He had always been fascinated by the fact she bore the same name as the larger of the two moons orbiting Anshan. The sight of the Yirkin refugee camp left her confused about whether or not what she was doing was right or wrong. It felt right to help innocent people, but they were so different, from a society that viewed it as acceptable to steal someone else's planet. What if they found Earth one day and uprooted her people as part of their customary gypsy ways?

She wished she could talk to A'Ran about what she was doing or perhaps even Evey, who had more of a political sense than Kiera cared to learn. She enjoyed the battle strategies because it was a challenge, but politics were better left to those who had thicker skin, such as A'Ran, or those who could smile when they were sad, like Evey.

"You know nothing of the connection between you and Anshan?" Turi asked as they walked through the winding tunnels.

"Nothing."

"Even if you have one?"

"That much I know," she replied. "I've seen the proof of it. I'm not sure how to heal the planet, though."

"What proof?" He stopped walking and faced her.

She knelt without hesitation and placed her palms on the ground. Seconds later, grass tickled her fingertips. She lifted her hands. The vibrant green was a cross between the hue of grass she knew and the emerald of Qatwali. "This is pretty much all I know I can do for now," she said, unable to help her smile at the grass. It was spreading rapidly outward from the spot where she'd touched it.

"How did you come about this ability?" Turi crouched beside her, a look of surprise crossing his hardened features. He touched the grass with the back of one hand.

"It's always been that way," she said with a shrug.

"Before the *dhjan* destroyed the surface, there was water. Did you call forth the waters from the depths of the planet?"

"Not on purpose but yes."

"And you do not know how you did this, either?"

"Well." She hesitated. "I awoke the planet in a chamber beneath the surface, where the *dhjan* and *nishani* go to bond with the planet."

"There was a ceremony?" He studied her hard.

"No. A knife and a flower," she replied awkwardly. "I cut myself and dropped blood into the pot where the flower was and stuff happened after that." She shrugged.

Turi appeared pensive, somewhat doubtful.

Kiera waited, hoping he knew something more about Anshan and her connection to the planet than she did. "Does that mean anything to you?" she prodded at his quiet.

"It might." He stood and started walking once more.

She hurried after him. "What?"

"The *nishanis* that came before you. They were alive past becoming mates to the *dhjan*?"

"As far as I know. A'Ran's mother had four children with multiple cycles between them."

"The blood awoke the bond but is not required to sustain it."

"I suppose."

"The planet should be able to stabilize itself."

"I can't imagine A'Ran destroying the surface is helping things."

"But your bond runs deeper, to the life force. The surface mines should not disrupt the planet's life force."

I'm not entirely certain what a life force even is. Kiera was once more frustrated as she ran in the same circles as always about how to help Anshan.

The tunnel grew narrower until they could no longer walk side by side and the space between lamps longer. She stayed behind him, not liking how much darker it was now than when they started out.

"What exactly is a life force?" she asked finally. It seemed easier to ask Turi than A'Ran or his sisters, whose expectations of her ability to help the life force of the planet were so high, she felt like she constantly disappointed them.

"It has a spirit. Do you have these where you are from?"

"Theoretically," she said.

"The Yirkin believe every living person has a spirit. The Anshan believe the planet holds the spirits of all its people, and these form a single spirit that is the planet's life force."

"And that's how the people's lives are connected to the planet," she said, unable to help her surprise at the simple explanation offered by an alien who had no knowledge of Anshan before fifteen years before.

"It did not accept us for this reason," he added. "It would not let us farm it, and the mines, such as this one, were pulled deeper underground to keep us from mining them. The planet did not want us to take any part of it away, because we do not belong."

"How can I belong when I'm from somewhere else, too?"

"I do not know this," he replied, sounding irritated. "But you do belong, and your life force is shared with the planet. This was what the Anshan told us."

"That's kind of cool." *And maybe a little creepy.* Like the Yirkin, she had grown up to believe her soul was in her body. That the planet held those of its people was as magical and enigmatic as the planet being truly alive. A'Ran had claimed the planet chose her.

She looked anew at the walls of the tunnel, unable to imagine how an entire planet was a single living entity but awed by the idea it was the case for Anshan.

The wail of the storms on the surface of Anshan reached her, a distant roar in the otherwise quiet tunnel. The air was growing staler as well, and it was too warm to be comfortable.

"Where exactly are we going?" she asked.

Turi didn't respond.

Unease churned in her stomach. If they didn't need her alive to help the planet, she'd be concerned about his ulterior motive in escorting her away from everyone else after kidnapping her.

A'Ran will find me. He'd do whatever he had to in order to rescue her. Although, there was a tiny part of her that wanted a chance to try to fix the planet before he did arrive to take her back to the moon.

Turi stopped before a dead end consisting of a gray metal door. "The Yirkin must be an adaptable people to survive on so many different planets," he said. He planted his hands on the door and ran them along the smooth metal as he spoke. "Each new home is mysterious when we first reach it, and we must figure out how to survive no matter where we are. You are newer to this world than we are, but I feel this is the same for you. You must connect with the planet before you can survive it."

"Makes sense," she said.

"We found many underground chambers such as you described

when we were exploring the tunnels." He brushed dirt away from a false compartment in the metal door and smashed it open with the hilt of a knife. "But we could not open all the doors." He gripped her wrist and pulled her closer.

Kiera didn't have a chance to react before he'd touched the sharp edge of the knife to the soft padding of her index finger. She winced. Turi squeezed out several drops of her blood onto the blade then released her and tapped the knife against the edge of the compartment until the drops slid into its depths.

The door groaned and shook.

Kiera hopped back as it wrenched one way then the other before freeing itself from years of dirt and cracked open.

Turi gripped the edges and wrenched it the rest of the way open. He stepped into the room that light bright as day the moment Kiera entered.

"Was the chamber you found like this?" he asked.

She gazed around with a frown. Compared to the chamber she'd once visited, the room was plain and bare. No paintings adorned the blank surfaces, no giant flower or thrones against the far wall, and no fountain of any kind was present. A set of tall double doors was across the empty space from them. It appeared to be more of a foyer than anything else.

"No," she said.

"Then we move on. Perhaps we will rediscover it or another like it."

His footsteps echoed in the chamber as he strode to the double doors.

Kiera trailed, wishing she knew more about Anshan history than she did. A'Ran's ancestors had kept underground chambers for some reason. Had they experienced an event similar to this before and moved beneath the surface of the planet? Or had the mining people connected the network of caverns running beneath the surface as they uncovered them?

As she neared, she realized the two doors were ajar with one of them off its frame.

Turi gripped the edges of one door and pulled until there was enough room for him to slide more of his body between them. He braced his back against the fixed door and shoved the other open. Sweat popped out on his forehead.

Lighting from unknown sources flickered on as she crossed the threshold. They walked through to a long corridor with at least six intersections she was able to see.

"You think one of these chambers holds the key to helping Anshan?" she asked, walking with him.

"I have exhausted every other possibility."

She glanced at him, hearing the grim tone. Turi was in his forties, in warrior shape, with tightness around his eyes she guessed came from concern about his people. She hadn't given A'Ran's enemies much thought. It struck her as odd that she was in the company of one of them – and he wasn't the monster she expected to find.

"We'll figure it out," she said softly. "I want to help Anshan, too."

He gave a brisk nod and started down the corridor. "We must explore this place quickly. There is only a five day air supply left for my people."

If there was one thing she knew about the aliens she'd met since leaving Earth, it was they were far tougher than she thought she'd be in their shoes. His calm pronouncement of his people's fate left her speechless and urgent to help him.

SIX

FINALLY. The moment A'Ran set foot into his home on the moon, he knew something was wrong.

The normally calm D'Ryn's eyes and nose were red as if she'd been crying, and his youngest sister, Talal, was openly sobbing.

He assumed the news of Kiera disappearing had reached them and strode past them towards the battle station where Kiera had learned to fight, trailed by Mansr, several Anshan warriors, Romas and his advisors. His instincts tingled, however, and he paused at the door, waving for the others to enter ahead of him. His sisters hung back, as was customary, without leaving. When the last of Romas' warriors had entered the battle command room, A'Ran stepped towards D'Ryn.

"We'll find her," he reassured her. "I do not wish to be disturbed." He turned to join his guests.

"Brother," D'Ryn ventured. "I must speak to you."

"It can wait."

"It cannot!"

A'Ran paused, unable to recall when his oldest sister had spoken out to him. He turned, frowning, unable to imagine what warranted his attention now when his *nishani* was missing. "What is it?"

"Gage. She ... left," D'Ryn said in a tight voice.

"Left," he repeated.

"She said you were planning to exile her, so she left before you could send her away."

"When?"

"This morning."

"Did you alert the local battle commander?"

She nodded. "I took him the news and he told me about *nishani*."

A'Ran cursed silently, hating to know Gage was alone and vulnerable – and so was Kiera. "We will find them both," he told her.

"I know where she went."

Talal appeared terrified while D'Ryn took a moment to recompose herself. He waited, unable to imagine how his life turned from incredible to a nightmare in such a short amount of time.

"She went to Anshan," D'Ryn whispered.

"Gage did what?" he demanded, louder than he intended. "The surface is toxic!"

"She knows. She ... she told Talal she didn't deserve to live after ... Ne'Rin."

A'Ran tensed, horrified to think his sister truly meant to kill herself rather than face exile. "Tell me everything she said prior to fleeing."

With halting words and many breaks, D'Ryn obeyed.

There was no mistaking Gage's intent. His own sister had feared being banished enough to risk dying on Anshan. Without another word, A'Ran spun and went to the command center.

"Mansr," he called and waved his uncle out of the chamber. "Gage has fled to the surface. Ready a rescue mission to leave immediately. You are to bring her back. I'll head the search for *nishani*."

"It won't be necessary." Mansr was frowning. "The spacecraft carrying *nishani* went down on the planet."

For a long moment, A'Ran wasn't able to breathe. He couldn't live with the idea of losing one of the women he loved let alone two, but to know his own planet had a hand in their deaths ...

It was unbearable. All he had done the past fifteen cycles, every battle he'd fought to keep his family safe and his people alive, was all for nothing if he lost Kiera and Gage. Finally, he drew a breath.

"Then we're going to the surface," he said simply. "Get the first two atmospheric cleaners in place and melt down whatever else the Qatwali need to build them here. None of them are going anywhere until *nishani* is returned."

D'Ryn gasped.

For once, Mansr didn't try to remind him it wasn't smart to keep the ruler of another planet hostage. He nodded and hurried away, issuing commands on his communicator as he left.

"Take Talal and rest," A'Ran said to his oldest sister. "She does not help us in such a state."

D'Ryn nodded and moved towards the private wing of their home where the family lived.

"*Dhjan.*"

A'Ran wasn't ready for more bad news and glanced at the slender, tall man approaching him. "What is it?" he asked.

"I wish to go to the surface with you."

A'Ran considered the somewhat skittish miner. They had shared a meal for the first time a week before, when Kiera invited the young man to lunch. Ketnan was smart, a member of the lower class – and the man who had impregnated A'ran's youngest sister. He hadn't forgiven the miner for the slight, but he wasn't about to put someone else Talal cared about at risk, either.

"No," he said and started into the command room.

"*Dhjan,* please!" Ketnan followed him. "I know the mines and surface of Anshan better than anyone. I know the cavern system beneath the surface, too, and I want to help my family."

A'Ran stiffened and clenched his jaw, hating the reminder he was expected to reward the fool who impregnated his sister by giving his blessing for Ketnan to marry into the royal family.

The practical side of him acknowledged Ketnan had a point about going to the surface with a miner.

"It is because you are going to become my family that I refuse my permission," he said through clenched teeth. "My youngest sister cannot handle losing a sister, *nishani*, and you."

"I cannot live with knowing I can help and must stay behind. She would be more proud of me if I died saving her sisters than if I stayed here."

This is the first thing the fool has ever said that's sounded Anshani. A'Ran faced Ketnan, whose features were determined. Bravery was a distinctly Anshani trait.

"Very well," he replied reluctantly. "Report to Mansr."

Ketnan bowed hastily and darted out of the command center.

A'Ran watched him, not at all convinced this was remotely a smart course of action. For Talal's sake, he'd keep the boy close.

"*Dhjan*."

On the day A'Ran wanted no distractions, he was faced with yet another. "What is it now?" This time, he barked at the man at the other end of the hallway. Small for his age, the bald man lowered his gaze quickly and appeared ready to flee. Anshan recognized the patch on his arm indicating he was one of the medics. "You are here for the mission," he said, regaining control over his anger.

"Forgive me, *dhjan*. I did not mean to intrude. I wish to -"

"Come." A'Ran didn't bother waiting for the man to finish but finally joined the others in the command center. The others were gathered around the hologram of Anshan being managed by Mansr.

"*Dhjan*, the spacecraft carrying the *nishanis* went down here." Mansr pointed and replayed what the moon's radars had picked up. The ship disappeared quickly into the storms, but their finely tuned systems were able to track its movement even after it was no longer visible.

A'Ran expertly scanned the images. "We can trace its trajectory after we lose the signal based on speed and angle of descent." He took over from Mansr and deftly manipulated the computer systems, mixing the live feeds with a simulation used to train pilots. The simulation stripped away the storms to reveal the planets topography. Everyone watched with interest as the craft was projected to have a controlled descent into a deep draw rather than crashing.

"It was not an accident. They meant to come here," Romas was the first to speak.

"Who meant to come here?" Mansr asked, puzzled. "We have full accountability on every pilot capable of navigating the storms."

A'Ran studied the area around where the spacecraft appeared to have gone. "The simulation can't give us the current condition of this area. This mountain may not be there anymore."

He didn't say what else was on his mind, that the central palace – home to his family for thousands of cycles – located at the center of the mountain range was possibly gone, too. If so, it was a testament to how badly he'd hurt his own planet and his own family in the name of saving everyone from invaders.

"The mines are," said the soft voice of Ketnan.

The men turned to look at him, and the young man's gaze darted from Romas to A'Ran to the floor.

"What are you saying?" Mansr prodded.

"The mines have levels. When we tested them, before the surface was ... ah ... before the surface ..." His face blazed red and he stopped.

"Before I destroyed it," A'Ran pushed. "It is no secret or shame I destroyed the surface to repel the invaders."

"No, *dhjan,* of course there is not," Ketnan said quickly. "Before the incident, we surveyed the mines."

"I know this," A'Ran said impatiently. "I read the reports."

"What we did not include in the report was the theory that many of the mines had sunk. Over half of them in fact."

"What does this mean *sunk?*" Romas asked with a frown. "How does a hole in the ground grow deeper? The Yirkin?"

"No. It was not done by men."

"Then what did it?"

The planet. A'Ran exchanged a look with Mansr, who appeared pensive. He had been young enough when expelled from Anshan to know the history of the planet without grasping its true nature in the way an adult or true ruler might.

"It's possible," Mansr said, answering the question in A'Ran's head. "We surveyed the mines recently without finding most of them. We assumed they were destroyed. It's possible they simple became deeper than we knew to look."

"This is not logical," Romas said. "How does your planet have a mind of its own?"

"It's a living being," Mansr replied.

"The reason isn't important," A'Ran returned. "What is important is that the mine where our lifemates were taken may be deep enough to have avoided the fate of the shallower mines."

"Then we go there now."

"On this we agree." A'Ran tossed his head towards the door. "You, medic," he turned to face the older man lingering nervously near the entrance, "how many are coming with you?"

"Well, no one, *dhjan*. I did not have any intention of –"

"You'll do. We only need one medical monitor. Go to the ship. All of you. We have exoskeletons on board already."

Romas' party left quickly, as did Ketnan and the confused doctor, until it was just Mansr and A'Ran. Mansr was already adjusting the images before them, aware of what A'Ran was going to ask next.

"Gage," he said. His chest tightened at the word. Whoever had Kiera hadn't wanted her dead, or there would be no effort to put her in a mine deep enough to protect her.

But Gage ...

"She did not fair so well." Mansr zoomed in on an area not too far from where Kiera had disappeared.

A'Ran watched her spacecraft tumble into the atmosphere before beginning an ascent too rapid to have been controlled. He wasn't able to breathe as he watched her craft fall out of the sky into the plains on the other side of the mountains near which Kiera had gone down. The two ships had reached the planet within moments of one another, both from the direction of the moon. It was a blessing during a time when he had few others to count, for it meant they were close to one another and not spread across the planet.

"What do you wish to do?" Mansr asked.

A'Ran blinked, unable to look away from the possible site of Gage's crash. He debated for a long moment, torn between going after his sister and lifemate. "I'm going to Gage first," he said finally. "Find Kiera. Use whatever leverage or bribery you need on Romas. Once I determine ..." *if Gage is dead.* The words stuck in his throat and he cleared it. "Once I determine my sister's fate, I'll come to your location."

"This is wise," Mansr said. "Gage has no one to go for her."

The words stung, though A'Ran knew Mansr didn't plan for them to. In that moment, he realized how right Mansr and Kiera were.

Gage had no one but him right now to protect her, to care for her, to love her, and he had been willing to exile her out of what was nothing more than fear of Ne'Rin's family. He had blown up his planet, defied the Planetary Council at every turn, even almost destroyed one of the most respected planets in the Five Galaxies.

What did he care if Ne'Rin's family went to the Planetary Council and petitioned them to return Gage's child to them, as was customary? How was the opinion of the Planetary Council, and avoiding the family of a traitor, more important than defending his sister?

"You are better equipped to handle the surface than I am," Mansr added, breaking into A'Ran's thoughts. "I cannot use the respirators yet." He patted his chest, a reminder of the injury he sustained during the final battles on Anshan.

"I will go in your place, cousin," Leyon said. "I will find *nishani.*"

A'Ran looked at the member of the family who most closely resembled him. Near the same age, Leyon was as trustworthy as his father, a valiant warrior and someone who knew Kiera well enough for A'Ran to entrust him with her safety. "I would have no one else lead this mission," A'Ran said.

"It is my honor, *dhjan,*" Leyon said and bowed his head.

"I will take my personal battle cruiser," A'Ran said and moved away from the hologram.

"Coordinates have been sent to it already," Mansr said. "*Dhjan,* may I ask something of you?"

"Quickly."

"When were you last on Anshan?"

"Several days ago."

"When were you last on Anshan when the planet might recognize you?" Mansr clarified. "The exoskeletons retain the normal signature our kind gives off. It allows nothing in or out."

A'Ran paused to think and shook his head. "Not for any length of time since I was exiled. I have flown through its airspace, visited you once in the ground command weeks ago and a second brief encounter in an exoskeleton. What are you thinking?"

"In the history of Anshan, there was never a time when the *dhjan* and *nishani* were so long gone from the planet's surface. We know *nishani* is connected to the life force. What if you are, in a way we do not understand, as well? What if it takes more than the *nishani* to heal?"

"You believe both of us must be present."

"I believe the answer was lost with your parents, in the knowledge passed down from *dhjan* to *dhjan,* a chain unbroken for thousands of generations until yours."

"Such secrets, let alone their existence, cannot be discerned in discussion."

"No."

"Then what would you have me do?" A'Ran was unable to prevent the frustration in his tone.

"I do not know. It was a thought only."

"We do not have time for such thoughts." A'Ran touched the buttons on the battle station, and the images disappeared. "Be safe."

"May the suns long grace you, nephew."

"And you both." A'Ran spoke the words over his shoulder. He waited until he was in the hallway to break into a run. Despite the urgency racing through his veins, he found himself going over Mansr's words. He had no doubt a great deal of information was lost when his father was killed before A'Ran came of age. He was not willing to spend time fantasizing over what that might be.

But the idea the planet needed both him and Kiera present struck him hard. What if finding his *nishani* was the first step? What if there had never needed to be a second step in the past, because Anshan had never been conquered and invaded?

What if he could fix the planet better from the surface than he was able to orbiting it on the moon?

A'Ran ignored everyone whose path he crossed as he hurried towards the gaping canyon acting as a space port for the massive gray ships anchored in the open space of the canyon. He flung the plate-sized personal transport device onto the ground and leapt onto it, using his body weight to launch it from the edge of the canyon and steer it towards the tiny spacecraft dwarfed many times over by the hulking ships.

His state of the art, personal ship was worth five of the huge ones, built solely from the highest grade metal Anshan produced. He placed his hand on the hidden pad outside the door and entered, stopping to retrieve his personal transporter before closing the doors behind him.

His thoughts weren't on flying or Gage but on the image in his head, the one first drawn by Kiera soon after they met. She'd used her strange Earth tools to draw a picture of the two of them walking together hand in hand on Anshan's surface. He settled into the cockpit and pulled the drawing free.

It had cored him the first time he saw it, the dream of an exiled prince finally within reach. This time when he unfolded the delicate paper, he had the same strong reaction, except it was laced with fear instead of hope.

There was no way to know what happened to anyone who went to the surface now let alone dare to hope the image on the paper before him was possible. After studying it for a moment, he tucked it away.

"*Dhjan,* you are cleared to proceed," said the local battle commander.

A'Ran sparked the engines and shot off into the atmosphere around the moon. His focus was straight ahead, on Anshan, his mind playing Mansr's comments over and over. He was missing something; he felt it.

His attention soon turned to the rapidly approaching planet, and he shifted the ship towards the coordinates Mansr had loaded into the navigation components. The history of Anshan wasn't going to matter if he was reckless trying to get to the surface of the planet.

A'Ran plunged into the storms and relied upon the navigation system to guide his approach. Gusts of wind tossed the small ship while dust and small rocks pelted its side. He continued, concentrating hard on his destination and not imagining what he was about to find there.

An alarm went off in the navigation system, and he snapped to the right to avoid a massive chunk of ... something headed towards him. It didn't read as metal or a ship on stealth ode, which meant it was likely a chunk of the planet's surface caught in the hurricane winds. With gravity, the winds and debris in the air, more effort was required to steer the craft than navigating an asteroid field in space.

He avoided the incoming rock with relative ease, a second one twice as large, and smashed into the third originating from the opposite direction. A'Ran's craft began to spiral downwards into the storms. Another boulder, followed by three more, pelted the craft, throwing him off course and tumbling out of the sky towards the planet below.

He issued an emergency call before employing every last one of the measures meant to keep him from exploding into thousands of pieces when he hit the surface. One by one, each measure failed, and he was left with a grim choice: eject without an exoskeleton or face the full impact of a crash.

A'Ran's decision was quick. He was going to die both ways, but he had a little better chance of surviving if he remained in one piece.

Stretching back, he engaged the craft's beacon and smashed his elbow into the emergency release. The top half of his ship flew off, and sand pelted him hard. He closed his eyes, drew a breath, and jumped out of the spacecraft.

The gray metal was swallowed by red storms. The emergency escape apparatus around his upper body flared to life, slowing his fall. He righted himself in the air and changed his course to land closer to Gage's crash site.

A shadow loomed out of the storm. A'Ran struggled to redirect the equipment, avoiding the boulder lazily whirling through the air by a hair's width. A down draft snagged him and yanked him towards the ground faster.

He plunged towards the planet's surface at a speed he knew to be dangerous, if not deadly.

SEVEN

"THERE'S NOTHING HERE," Turi said, frustrated. He planted his hands on his hips and stared at a wall.

Kiera nodded, exhausted after the hours they spent exploring the underground network of corridors and chambers. It appeared to have been some kind of dwelling at one point, perhaps a larger version of the lunar home where A'Ran's family lived. However, the chambers were completely empty without any indication of when or who had lived there.

"I need a break," she said and sank down with her back against one wall. The energy of Anshan was fainter here than anywhere else. It had gone from a tingle to an inconsistent spark.

The stale, heavy and still air was worse than in the cavern. It reminded her of a hot, muggy day in her home of Monterey. Sweat trickled down her neck, back and legs, and she'd braided her long hair to keep its weight from annoying her.

"We spotted no other entrance or exit, no windows, nothing," Turi stated.

Kiera was feeling too lightheaded to listen. She was thirsty, hungry and guessed it was past her normal bedtime. Combined with the stress of being kidnapped and trapped underground, she wasn't feeling up to much of anything. No grass grew here in the stone chambers, though the lights went on in whatever room she stepped into. She rested her head back against the wall and closed her eyes for a brief moment of rest. Anshan had appeared to her in dreams recently, but the images were generally blurry and disjointed. She sought to recall something of the dreams as she sat.

Red rocks, a storm and ... the green space with the strange creature beckoning to her ... the images were too fleeting. She always saw the surface of the planet and had no recollection of the dreams ever mentioning the underground world.

Turi nudged her with a foot. Her eyes opened.

"Did you not hear me?" he asked with tried patience. His eyes were bloodshot and face flushed, as if he, too felt the lack of oxygen in the air.

"No, sorry," she replied.

"Tell me what is wrong with the planet."

"Aside from A'Ran blowing it up?" she asked with a forced chuckle. "The mines are overproducing ore and poisoning everything. The storms are toxic and creating electromagnetic fields that mess with any ship within range."

Turi was listening.

"If what's happening to the planet is also what's happening to me, I think ..." she drifted off. "Well, the life force of the planet is where the trouble lies. My cells are degenerating rapidly. I'm dying from the inside out, and Anshan seems to be poisoning itself from the inside out."

"In your world, how would they fix you?"

She snorted. "They wouldn't know how to. Our medicine is many cycles behind the Five Galaxies."

"I am almost grateful Anshan rejected us," he grumbled. "We found another door on our initial exploration of the caverns. Let us try it." He struck off down the hallway back towards the way they'd come.

Kiera got up with a groan, ready for some sleep, and started to follow but stopped short as she considered another possibility. In the chamber where she'd awakened the planet, she'd been alone. Was it possible the planet would communicate with her somehow better if she wasn't with Turi? It was responding to her with light; she knew it was aware of her being there.

Closing her eyes, she listened, uncertain how a planet communicated with anyone. The heavy air was stifling. No daydreams emerged from the depths of her mind. No sounds, no flickering lights, not even the faintest breeze reached her. The only difference between standing here and exploring the rest of the underground building: the sparks of Anshan's energy were more frequent here, as if she were getting warmer on her search for she knew not what.

She sighed and started forward, irritated that she didn't know what she needed to about the planet.

Turi was waiting in the dark, dingy tunnel outside the structure when she reached the doorway. Kiera's eyes went to him and then down.

She laughed, unable to help her startled reaction to what had happened in their absence. As with the surface, when she'd touched Anshan recently, the patch of grass she created had expanded outward from the initial place where she rested her hands.

The floor of the tunnel was carpeted in bright green for about twenty feet, and it had begun to creep up the sides of the tunnel as well. Its fresh scent was light, cool, and she breathed deeply, surprised by how stale the air beyond had really been.

"How is this possible for it to grow so fast?" Turi was crouched in the grass, gazing hard at it.

"I don't know," she replied honestly.

"You have no control over this?"

"None."

"I have been to over thirty worlds and never heard of this." He stood and took an exaggerated breath in. "There's more air to breathe here."

Ah. It wasn't the underground building. Kiera mirrored his movement, and understanding brought a smile to her face. The grass was doing what plants did: creating oxygen.

"Come. I have an idea." Turi started away.

She sucked in several more deep breaths before following him. The farther they walked from the grass, the stuffier the air became once more. Fascinated by the ability to grow grass, Kiera was nonetheless becoming aggravated by the fact she had no idea how much more there was to the link between her and the planet.

Rather than return to the central cavern housing his people, Turi set off down another small tunnel off the main one. This one, too, slanted upward, towards the surface and ended with a similar door to the first. The sound of the storm raging beyond the tunnels was louder here, and she glanced upward, leery of how strong and thick the rock between them and the toxic surface was.

Turi wedged the hilt of his knife between the doorframe and door and pried it open. "We explored this room before," he said with a grunt. He pulled it open, and a puff of red dust burst into the tunnel.

Kiera rested a hand over her mouth and Turi coughed. He stepped back, waving a hand to clear the dust from in front of his face.

"Is it safe?" she asked.

Turi didn't answer. He tugged his shirt up over his nose and went back to opening the door the rest of the way.

It was dark beyond, and the roar of the storm was louder.

"You go. Turn on the lights," he directed.

Kiera hesitated before reassuring herself he wasn't about to toss her out on the planet's surface when he needed her alive to help him save his people. She squeezed past him through the doorway. Dust was heavy in the air, but the staleness was gone. She sneezed and covered her nose.

No lights went on, and the surface beneath her feet was rocky, uneven, unlike the building they just explored. She moved several feet from the entrance, waiting for the lights to flip on. None did.

Wind whipped past her, and she froze.

"Be a Yirkin. Figure this out," Turi called from behind her. "Your friend will be safe with us until you succeed or are confirmed dead."

She whirled.

The door closed with a groan, and Kiera raced to it. No doorknob, keypad or keyed entry was visible, and she pounded against it, panicking at the thought of being stuck on the surface of the planet to die.

"Turi!" she cried. "Don't leave me here!"

No response.

Kiera stared at the door, horrified at her potential fate, and turned to search the area behind her for somewhere to hide. Her eyes adjusted to the darkness, and she was able to make out the shapes of rocky hills rising out of the ground on either side of her, forming natural protection around her. A path led from the depths of the draw back towards the surface.

Wind wailed overhead, and another burst of dust danced through the draw towards her. She coughed, covered her mouth and staggered towards the small area of the rocky terrain around her spared the storm's fury.

Crouching between two boulders, she rubbed her irritated eyes until they were clear of debris and hunkered down with a look at the sky.

No stars or Anshan moons were visible. It was dark, warm and dusty. Kiera wrapped her arms around her knees, thoughts on A'Ran. Her death on Anshan was fitting, even if it filled her with despair to know she'd never feel his strong embrace or breathe in his scent again. She closed her eyes, both numbed to her fate and devastated by it. She wasn't able to purge the image of A'Ran from her mind, and she closed her eyes, grateful his face was the last thing she'd see as she died.

How long did it take for the toxic atmosphere to kill someone? Did it hurt, or was it like falling asleep and never waking up again?

Why was the energy of Anshan stronger out here, warming her feet while she waited to die?

Tears mixed with dust on her face, and she waited for the planet to end her misery.

EIGHT

EXCEPT IT DIDN'T. Kiera cried for some time, waiting anxiously for any symptom she was dying. If she were, it was similar to the degeneration of her cells the medic had claimed was occurring. She felt no different.

When her legs became cramped from her position jammed between boulders, she lifted her head – careful to keep her shirt over her mouth and nose – and stretched them. Kiera tested her body. She was sore from all the walking, starving, and too wired to sleep through her looming death.

She felt ... fine. Itchy, though, and uncomfortably warm.

Kiera shifted and ran her hands along the ground beneath her. Grass was tickling the exposed strip of skin between her shirt and pants as well as her ankles. She shivered as something brushed the back of her neck, and she stretched back to feel thick ribbons of grass three feet tall.

The darkness was lifting around her. The storm blocked the sun, but it was definitely morning on Anshan. Weak daylight turned her world from black to gray. As she sat and debated what to do next, the gray took on an orange-ish hue as full daylight reached the planet's surface through the red dust storms.

She rested her head against the rock behind her, eyes on the storm above her safe alcove above. Small funnel clouds touched down and skipped over her. Bursts of red dust that appeared like smoke plumes often trailed them. The sky on the other side of the storm remained invisible.

The grass was growing quickly enough to agitate her. Kiera shifted out of her spot and knelt on the ground near the boulders. Beautiful green splashed against the charcoal and reddish rocks. As she watched, the patch of grass expanded.

I know Anshan senses me.

She wasn't dead, either. Was this a sign the planet was protecting her, or was she safe away from the storms? A'Ran had said the air was toxic, since the mines used to blow up the planet's surface were filled with toxic ore. None of his men dared venture out into the storms without the goo-suits she'd worn once.

Yet she was in the open, breathing the air of Anshan without a problem, aside from the occasional sneeze. If anything, the air was much easier to breathe than that of the caverns.

Her gaze went to the path leading out of the draw. She took two steps onto it, and the energy of the planet sparked inside her stronger than before. Two steps to the left, and the warmth all but vanished.

Anshan wanted her to leave the draw next to the door to the underground world.

Fear made her heart race and her palms clammy. Dared she leave the relative peace of the protected spot? She knew from her first visit it would be impossible to find her way back, once she had gone more than a few feet from the mouth of the draw.

The universe didn't bring you to me for us to fail to save Anshan. A'Ran's words were louder in her thoughts than her pounding heart.

Kiera tugged the shirt down from her face and took a cautious breath. The air was thick with dust but otherwise seemed normal.

She glanced towards the door through which she'd been shoved once more then rose and crossed to it. It was impossible to budge from this side. She rested her palms against the cool metal for a moment before turning away. The energy was gone from this direction, too.

Either she stayed where she was and prayed someone saved her, or she did what the planet and Yirkin told her – and ventured into the storm to see what was there.

Her gaze lingered on the grass rapidly expanding from its spot in the corner of the draw. When she'd left Anshan last time, the expansion had ceased and was presumed killed off by the toxins in the air. It showed no sign of slowing despite the puffs of dust and full exposure to the Anshan atmosphere.

What if she had to remain on the planet for any terra forming to be successful? Was her distance, as close as the moon was, causing her and the planet pain?

I wish I knew a single thing about this relationship. "If you can hear me, please help me," she said to the planet. "I don't understand what I'm supposed to do. I don't understand how we can help each other survive."

She didn't expect a response and wasn't disappointed. Kiera drew a breath and started walking. Her step slowed as she tackled the uneven terrain leading out of the draw, and she held the shirt across her mouth to keep dust from choking her.

The storms of Anshan howled across the scarred planet, and she closed her eyes as she reached the edge of the trail. One more step, and she'd be fully exposed.

But this opportunity was what she'd wanted for weeks – to see if she really did belong here, if there was any chance in the world she was able to help the planet and people.

I need to know if I can survive here. If the planet's accepted *nishani* wasn't able to live on the surface, its people would never have a shot either. Kiera steadied her breathing and left the safety of the draw. She hunkered down and braced herself, ready to be knocked off her feet or pelted by dirt and dust.

Nothing happened. She cracked one eye open then the other. She had the strange sense of being at an aquarium, watching the underwater world yet protected from it by a clear layer of glass. The winds and dirt went around her, staying a consistent two feet from her at all times, as if she were in a bubble.

Kiera frowned. The grass was growing faster now. Whenever she paused, green shot up around her feet. Already her ankles were itchy from the blades poking at her skin.

She feared losing track of the entrance to the underground world. Turi would have to confirm whether she lived or died, and he'd have to open the door to do it. She ventured farther from the draw with some apprehension. She wasn't able to see more than half a dozen feet ahead of her, though the energy of Anshan remained steady and warm, as if to encourage her to continue.

With a deep breath of clean air inside her strange bubble, she started walking. The uneven terrain was littered with sudden dips and gashes as well as boulders and loose shale. She had little warning before reaching the obstacles, and even less ability to gauge how treacherous her path ahead became.

Kiera walked, praying the planet showed her the path it needed her to take to help them both. No such road formed, and she continued forward at a slow pace.

A shadow passed overhead, and she lifted her eyes from the ground. At first, she prayed a ship had found her. To her surprise, it wasn't a ship but a boulder larger than her caught in the violent winds far above. She watched in disbelief as the boulder tumbled through the sky before it was swallowed by a cloud of red.

"C'mon, now, Anshan. You gotta be able to stop this stuff," she murmured, waiting to see if another rock soared through the sky.

The ground dropped out from under her right foot, and she toppled down a slope littered with shale and small, sharp rocks. Bursts of pain shot through her. Kiera covered her head the best she could, unable to stop her momentum or even release the breath caught in her throat. She slid and rolled down the slope, scraping her arms and legs as she went.

She dared open her eyes. The blurry, spinning, gray form of a boulder was directly in her path. She flailed – and then smacked into the rock.

Kiera's world went dark.

NINE

AS A WARRIOR who had been fighting for fifteen cycles, A'Ran was accustomed to pain in all its levels and intensities. The sharp pain in his shoulder was likely from it being jarred out of socket, the burn radiating down his forearm a break, the warm pain in his chest and one leg indicating shallow stab wounds onto which his clothing clung.

He categorized his injuries and came up with the almost satisfactory conclusion that he'd been through worse on at least one other occasion. It wasn't just pain he felt, either, but a familiar thrum of energy. He had first experienced it when he returned to the planet for the first time in fifteen cycles several weeks ago. The planet had welcomed him with an internal hug similar to the warm energy inside him now.

With a grunt of pain, A'Ran pushed himself into a sit with his good arm. He didn't have to guess how he'd landed; the left side of his body was damaged while his right was fine. He rested his limp left arm on his lap and prodded the most serious of his punctures to ensure they weren't too deep. When he finished, he looked around –

and realized what he'd missed the first few moments of waking after the brutal landing.

He was alive on the toxic surface of Anshan. The air wasn't choking him with poison, and the storms weren't hurling boulders and dust at him. He reached out with one hand and tested the strange bubble around him. It was impossible to pierce, because it moved with him. It wasn't an exoskeleton or at least, not one his people had created.

His hand dropped to his side, and he stood, testing the bubble around him. It continued to go wherever he did. A'Ran limped to a large rock and knelt. Steeling himself for more pain, he gingerly placed his hurt shoulder against the rock, drew a breath and smashed the shoulder back into place. Agony pierced him, left him close to passing out, and he concentrated hard on breathing steadily until the throbbing pain descended into something more manageable.

When it did, he shifted and pulled off his shirt. His left arm was going to need medical attention. He tore a long strip from his clothing and created a sling then went to work binding the tears in his body the best he could. When he was satisfied with his work, he rose and looked around.

One of the reasons he preferred to be in space instead of on the ground: perspective. On the planet, he wasn't able to see what he could from space. In the middle of an Anshan storm, he saw even less - only what was directly in front of him, and he hated the limited perspective of his world that caused.

He returned to where he had landed and surveyed the shattered emergency landing equipment he had used once it was clear his ship was going down. For a long moment, he simply stood and stared at the scene. He hadn't noticed the ground beneath him before. His blood marred the equipment and had soaked into the red desert of the planet. But it wasn't this holding him transfixed.

Grass. A small patch had sprouted beneath where he had lain. He had heard Mansr and Leyon speak of how Kiera brought the planet to life with a single touch, but he had never considered what happened when the *dhjan* touched the planet. His brief visit weeks ago hadn't been of too short duration for him to do more than land, attend a meeting, rescue Kiera and fly off again. He had spent less than half a day on Anshan and another several moments during the trip to assess the mines.

Mansr's question about when he had last visited the planet was back in his thoughts. He had been exiled seconds after officially becoming the *dhjan* and had never spent more than several hours on the planet. He had certainly never sat long or slept or been still enough to see if he had the same power Kiera did.

A'Ran bent on his good knee and ran his palm through the grass. The moon had grass, of course, but this was different. It might as well have grown out of his own spirit. It was *his*. His touch had done this. After spending well over half his life in exile, and destroying the surface, his planet still remembered him, still welcomed him, still loved him.

And this realization stirred emotions as deep as those he felt for Kiera. He had never consciously felt the fear of rejection from Anshan, never been willing to admit he was afraid to return and find the planet wouldn't accept a ruler who had been unable to save his home. The relief at his core left him grateful and shone a light on the secret reason he had both fought for his planet to the death yet never ventured to its surface except to save his lifemate.

"We are one, as we were meant to be," he said in a hoarse voice. "I will not leave you again."

The flickering navigation hologram light drew his gaze. It was on its last leg, and he swiped it off the ground. Two points remained: his location and the approximate location of Gage's ship. He wasn't far, though there was no way to know what stood between him and his sister.

A'Ran oriented himself until the beacon turned blue to indicate he was facing the right direction. With a lingering glance at the grass, he began walking at the fastest pace possible given his injuries, determined to find and help his sister. As he moved, he mentally prepared himself for the worst-case scenario, for the discovery of his sweet sister dead.

Not long after starting off, he made out the intact form of a personal spacecraft. A'Ran's pace quickened until his leg was pulsing with pain. He reached the craft and circled it once to gauge what shape it was in. The landing had been hard enough to destroy the engines in the rear and put a deep dent along one side – but his sister somehow had managed not to smash into the planet.

A'Ran went to the dented side, guessing Gage hadn't left the vehicle since the door was damaged. He tested it and then pounded on it.

"Gage!" he shouted above the harsh winds. "Gage!"

After a brief pause, the door shuddered and screeched as it tried to open. A'Ran gripped the door the best he could and yanked once, twice, three times before the beleaguered motor overcame the damage and helped him open it.

"Gage?"

The interior was well lit. Dust swept into the craft, and he heard his sister cough in response from somewhere in the rear.

Uncertain how she would handle the planet's poisoned air, A'Ran climbed in and forced the door closed to the storms.

Gage sat in the rear of the carrier, her sleeve over her mouth. She stared at him, speechless, before springing up and throwing herself into his arms.

A'Ran didn't chide her like he would have before meeting Kiera. Anshan women were supposed to be more in controlled and embracing another family member was almost scandalous.

But Kiera had changed much about his family, about him, and he wrapped his good arm around his sister instead of reminding her of her place. She shook and was pale, but he saw no sign of blood or other injury.

"You were very fortunate," he said and held her against him. "The storm destroyed my craft."

"You came to find me?"

"Yes."

Gage looked up at him, her dark eyes in turmoil. He saw the unasked question in her gaze but wasn't able to explain his actions to her. As far as they had come since meeting Kiera, it was still awkward to discuss emotions with his family.

"Is there a medical unit here?" he asked instead.

She nodded and released him, moving to the rear of the compartment once again. "How did you survive the storm?"

He sat down and began unraveling his hasty bandages. "The planet did not wish me dead," he said simply.

"Anshan saved you?" She paused from her position sorting the various devices used for mobile injury treatment.

"Yes." A'Ran wasn't entirely certain how else to explain it. The reminder of what he felt seeing the grass left him closer to emotions than he cared to be, so he focused instead on his wounds.

Gage helped him maneuver skin patches into place to stop bleeding and soothe the pain, at least until he was able to spend some time in a tissue rebuilder. He used a bone patch on his shoulder and another on his left forearm meant to stabilize and prevent swelling. The patches didn't fix the wounds but made it easier for him to continue functioning.

She ordered clothing for him from the clothing generator.

A'Ran stood and stretched his injured limbs gently. He wasn't going to do any heavy lifting or fighting, but he was strong enough to help them escape to wherever they could take cover from the storms.

"Why are you here, brother?" Gage whispered, her back to him as she waited for the clothing generator to spit out new clothes. "I bring nothing but shame to you."

"Your actions may at times," he allowed. "But you do not. You are my sister."

"I won't be exiled."

The women of his family had grown brave since learning from Kiera how women on her planet acted.

"No one will be exiled," he said. "Ever. It was a mistake."

She faced him, mouth agape in surprise. It was the first time in his life he'd admitted fault to any of his sisters. They may have blamed him for misfortunes or his actions but warriors did not admit to mistakes. They fixed them. Like her sisters, Gage appeared ready to cry.

At his limit with women, A'Ran indicated for her to hand him the clothing and took it into the front of the spacecraft to change. His body cooperated but not without pain and stiffness.

He went to the cockpit next to check the systems. His attention was immediately snagged by one of Kiera's papers lying crumpled on the floor. He retrieved it. On both sides were crudely drawn symbols and commands for the navigation system.

"This is how you landed the spacecraft?" he asked and left the cockpit to confront his sister.

She nodded. "I asked Kiera to explain it to me and drew it."

A'Ran bit back his immediate response, that it was the most foolish act he had ever heard. Some of the symbols were inexact, as if Gage hadn't known exactly what Kiera was describing or wrote it incorrectly. The process laboriously outlined on the paper was nonetheless dangerously wrong, and he began to think Gage was luckier than he first thought.

Itching to reprimand her, he likewise knew she was already taxed and upset from her experience. His lifemate would also point out it was his fault Gage had fled in the first place. So he turned away silently and returned to the cockpit to check the instruments and computers.

The emergency beacon was working. Not that it'd matter, since the magnetic storms would skew the location before the signal reached the moon. But Mansr knew where he had gone. If any ship were able to get close enough, they'd locate the beacon.

As long as they hurry. He tapped the symbol indicating the craft's atmosphere was lower than he liked. Alone, Gage likely had a day, maybe day and a half, of air left. With him present, the supply was cut in half.

Hoping they were rescued was not the way of a warrior, and his thoughts returned to the deep mines Ketnan claimed existed.

"Sister, I need for you to remain here," he said and left the cockpit. "There are emergency respirators stored with the medical supplies. Should the air run out before I return, use them but do not leave the ship."

"You're leaving?"

"I will find somewhere safe for you and return." He paused at the door when he saw the dismay on her features. "I will return, Gage. Very soon."

She nodded and hugged herself. "Be careful, brother. Forgive me for placing us both in danger."

"This is of my doing," he said firmly. "Regardless of what you may have told Ne'Rin to aid him, I should not have turned my back on you."

She was staring at him again in completely shock. "What I told Ne'Rin?" she repeated. "You think ... you think I betrayed you?"

"He knew things he shouldn't have about our family, about Kiera. She nearly died at his hands."

"Brother, I never told him anything that would put you or *nishani* in danger."

"You may not have known you did," he said.

"And you would banish me for that."

"And because I feared his family would use your child against you to manipulate you."

For a long moment, Gage studied him. The shock from her features was gone, her look one of consternation.

"I love you, A'Ran," she whispered. "But Kiera is right. You give your sisters no credit. You underestimate how strong we are and how dedicated to you and our families we are. I never told Ne'Rin anything, and no one, including you, will use my child as an excuse to determine my fate. His family has no claim on me or my child. I do not care what our traditions are or how you think it should be! I will go to Kiera's world, and I will live among people who will accept me!" Fire was in her eyes. Usually the meekest of his three sisters, Gage was furious with him.

A'Ran suspected his sisters' independence, which began blooming when Kiera arrived, was going to be part of the legacy Kiera left behind for Anshan. She was a *nishani* from a different world, and some of her traditions and customs would become his traditions and customs, just as his would become hers.

The first thing he had to contend with: the returning sense he had never truly seen his sisters as women or treated his family the way they deserved. It left him ill prepared to determine how to handle the insurgency in his own home. But he didn't feel as though Gage was wrong, and he pretty much already knew what Kiera would think. Gage was willing to kill herself, or try to, in order to prove her point to him. She was as dedicated and loyal as any warrior, and it struck him he didn't really know how to rule his people when there was no war. When he needed to wield more than the heavy hand of a ruler whose life had been nothing but war and strife.

"Very well," he said.

Gage waited for more.

"All my sisters will have the ability to choose their fates, their life-mates, and when and how they speak to me."

"You aren't angry?" she asked.

"I am regretful that my actions and decisions left you with no choice but to risk your life here on Anshan," he responded slowly. "My *nishani* is correct – I cannot overlook a second chance to see you alive and honored to be part of my family. If change ... *my* change ... will make you, D'Ryn and Talal happy, then I will change."

She offered a small smile. "I think you already have, brother."

He knew as much, too.

"Thank you," she murmured.

"It is my honor." He bowed his head before turning to the door. "I will return for you."

He jimmied the door open and stepped outside once more. The protective bubble reappeared around him. He oriented the beacon tracker and reviewed what he knew of the terrain before striking out into the storm in the direction opposite of where he had crashed. If the topography of Anshan resembled what it had been before he detonated the surface mines, the mountain range separating him from where Kiera had been taken was in this direction.

A'Ran didn't let himself think too long on how he was going to scale mountains and make it back to his sister within the time she had remaining. Doubt had never been part of his makeup. The same faith that made him fight for a planet the rest of the Five Galaxies assumed he had lost guided him towards the mountains and the caverns that may be deep enough for there to be untainted air.

Except this time, it was more than frail hope. Anshan's energy trickled through him, from his feet to the tip of his head, leading him in the direction of the mountains.

TEN

THE STRANGE FIGURE with six legs was back in her dreams. This time when she ran towards it, she managed to close half the distance between them before she experienced the same level of fatigue and frustration as usual. The grass was retreating even faster, towards the figure, and Kiera could do nothing to stop it.

The dream shifted and changed, morphing into one of the fairy tales she'd been trying to tell A'Ran, Leyon and Mansr about on their trip to Qatwal. In place of Goldilocks, she saw herself walking into a house with three bears. Before she could talk to them, the dream slid away into darkness once more.

When she awoke sometime later, it was nighttime on Anshan. Kiera's head pulsed with pain, and her hair was sticky with blood. She was wrapped uncomfortably around the moss-covered boulder she'd smacked into earlier. She struggled to sit, safe from the storms in the strange bubble. The grass around her was waist high, and she smelled flowers blooming in the Anshan desert.

She touched her head gingerly. The bleeding had stopped and her hair was gummy.

Instead of the pitch black Anshan night she'd experienced in the draw, light glowed from the opposite side of the boulder. Too miserable to dare hope it was the light of a ship, she nonetheless prepared to discover what it was.

Bruises, burns and cuts ached with her movement. Nothing seemed broken, and she climbed to her feet unsteadily. One knee was unusually stiff, and she limped around the boulder to see what lay beyond.

During the day, she'd been unable to see the basin into which she'd fallen. But at night, the entire area had been covered with grass and small, glowing flowers unlike any she'd ever seen on earth. They stretched as far as she could see into the basin, a carpet of darkness that appeared almost to repel the storms sweeping by over the edges of the shallow basin.

Trees had begun to grow as well and were twice her size in height but unlike any she'd seen on Earth or Qatwal. Instead of branches, chains of broad, flat leaves connected one tree to its neighbor to create a single, solid canopy above the basin.

Kiera paused at the first bunch of glowing flowers and knelt to examine them. Her head hurt too much for her to squint. She plucked one free and lifted it to her eyes. The flower continued to glow. It was shaped like a miniature sunflower the size of her thumb.

She started to smile despite her pain. The glowing sunflower emitted soothing, quiet light. As her senses awoke from sluggishness, she heard the trickle of water from somewhere in the basin.

Kiera stood with a grimace and limped towards the sound, pausing to admire the fields of glowing sunflowers and look up at leaves as wide as she was tall. She began to make out other types of flora, some of which were nothing more than dark shapes between patches of sunflowers, and one of which appeared to be a living glow stick that grew at the bases of trees.

She reached the small spring at the center of the basin and dropped beside it, exhausted. After drinking her fill, she leaned over and did her best to rinse the blood out of her hair before sinking back onto her heels. A flicker of movement distracted her, and she waved the sunflower over the surface of the water. Its light reflected off the rainbow scales of fish darting beneath the surface.

Fascinated by what an Anshan fish looked like, she peered into the depths of the water. The fish had five fins, resembling a starfish, and an eye in the middle of its body.

"Not as scary as the cats," she murmured.

And then it hit her. The planet was not just producing flora but had begun to repopulate its critter population as well. She touched her head as she rose, grimacing at the wave of pain, and gazed around. Anshan days were longer than Earth days, and she estimated she'd been out for about ten hours.

Ten hours. And she'd regrown an area the size of a football field. Kiera's hand fell away. Astonishment filled her as she realized exactly what she'd done.

The trees, short for Earth, with their interconnected leaves, appeared impervious to the winds and dust, providing shelter for the plants to grow beneath them. Vines wrapped around the tree trunks, giving the trees a fuzzy appearance in the dim light.

Was this what Anshan once looked like? The lush jungle was very different than Earth's yet beautiful in its own way. Kiera started towards the rim of the basin to venture back out into the storm, stumbled, and stopped, gripping her hurt knee. She lowered herself to the ground at the base of a tree with a deep sigh.

"Looks like we aren't going anywhere," she murmured. Somewhat relieved, she was also worried about finding a way to escape underground or communicate with the moon, and the Anshan energy seemed to be tugging her to leave the basin. No part of her looked forward to leaving the oasis for the storm despite feeling there was somewhere else she needed to be.

She sat back and sighed. Was this patch of green large enough for those on the moon to see with their radars, as Mansr had once shown her? Or would the magnetic distortions prevent anyone not on the planet's surface from seeing it? She looked up at the leaf canopy, saddened once more by the idea she had no idea how to help the planet or alert her lifemate about her location.

Her stomach growled. She rested a hand on it with a grimace and pushed herself up. She wasn't about to try to catch a fish let alone start a fire. She'd never been a camper.

"I can eat flowers," she said and limped back towards the fields of glowing sunflowers. They were small enough, though, that she quickly assessed she'd need to eat all of them to put a dent in her hunger. She knelt in the middle of the field, left leg extended to relieve the pressure from her aching knee, and began plucking up the moon colored flora and gathering them in a pile. "Thanks for not killing me," she murmured to the planet. "I don't know what to do next, if you have any ideas."

She spent an hour gathering flowers before starting to eat them. The handfuls of blooms held a tiny drop of honey flavor, and barely took the edge off her hunger. Tired and beat up from the fall into the basin, she curled up in the grass shortly after for a nap.

THE GRAY MORNING ROUSED HER, but it was the light, tickling touch of something along her neck that made her eyes open. Kiera stared briefly into the tiny eyes and anteater-like nose of a familiar creature until realizing what it was. She yelped and sprang up and away. Pain radiated through her left knee, and she gripped it, cursing under her breath.

The Anshan and Qatwali versions of cats resembled basketball sized tarantulas with outwardly jointed legs, round bodies and tiny heads. The main difference: the creatures were the cleaners of the alien worlds. They survived off dust, mold and mites sucked up through their tiny trunks. At first scared of the creature that awoke her, she soon straightened.

"Wait a minute." She twisted to look at the rapidly changing world around her. The grasses had spread outside the crater and showed no sign of stopping. The trees in the original section were taller today, their leaves connected to new trees that had sprung up while she slept. More flora was visible in the Anshani jungle, and she counted a second stream forming on the opposite side of the oasis.

And then there was *it*, the creature she mistook for a shadow at first glance, at least until it blinked its three eyes.

Kiera rose, peering into the darkness between trees, unable to confirm if the shape she saw was real or her imagination. She limped closer and stopped uneasily. The world was coming to life quickly, and she had no idea what kind of creatures to expect of the alien planet.

The six-legged cat behind her was young and energetic, running in circles and occasionally bumping into her. She shuddered each time it did, unable to shake the image of a huge tarantula. It bound past her into the shadows of the trees surrounding the meadow where she'd slept the night through.

White fangs snapped at it as it neared the shadowy creature beneath the tree, and the spider-cat cart wheeled out of the shade, smacked into her legs and righted itself before darting off in another direction.

"Please don't be something horrifying from *Aliens* or *Predator*," she whispered, stepping back, her thoughts filled with images of the monsters from science fiction movies. Whatever lingered in the shadows stood and slinked out from the shade.

Kiera stared at the creature. It had six legs, like the spider-cats, but the thick, powerful body of a bear. Its three eyes glowed orange-red, the same shade of the Anshan earth, and its body was covered with shaggy red fur lined with jagged golden stripes. Its ears were at the top of its head, its triangular shaped face offset by a scruff around its neck.

It was ugly and threatening but nothing like the monsters from movies. The creature sat on its haunches not far from her, its sinewy legs jointed like a normal animal's and bearing claws on the front and back legs while the middle set were padded.

"Okay. Giant Anshan bear-bug or something," she said. She had never been this close to a bear on her planet – but she knew they only had four legs. This was purely an Anshan creation, no matter how closely it resembled a bear.

The creature was regarding her closely, as uncertain about her as she was about it.

Kiera retreated to the middle of the meadow. She was hungry again, borderline starving, and not at all certain what to do about it.

The bear settled onto its belly in the grass, unconcerned about her. She left it in the meadow, praying it wasn't hungry enough to eat her, and went to the stream. Drinking more water, she gazed longingly at the five-finned fish before realizing she'd never be able to catch one.

She limped through the jungle and plucked up various leaves and plants, collecting them to try to eat.

"Won't have any problem getting my fiber in," she muttered unhappily. "Come on, A'Ran. Look at Anshan." She glanced at the green canopy above and reached a boulder at the edge of the meadow. She sat and sorted through the unappealing collection of plants. "Never was a salad person."

She tested one, found it bitter and went on to another. Most of them were edible, though the flavors left her frowning. When she'd exhausted the supply of food, she was still hungry and dissatisfied.

Kiera stood and tossed the stems and least tasty of the plants. The sounds of the storms were more distant today, as if the upward sprouting trees were pushing back the moody Anshan weather.

I have to do something. Turi's people, along with Evey, were still trapped beneath the surface, their air supply running lower the more time she spent trying to understand her role. The planet's energy wanted her to leave.

The silent padding of the bear didn't reach her, but the creature spitting something out at her feet jarred her out of her thoughts. She leapt away, staring at the Anshan monster that appeared even bigger up close. It had yanked three of the glow-stick shaped plants from the roots of trees and flung them down at her feet.

Kiera stared at the creature, whose mouth was open in a silent pant, before she looked down. The creature followed her gaze and snatched one off the ground, smashing it between its powerful jaws. The stick-plant crunched like celery.

"So it's edible," she said and bent to grab one. She grimaced at the animal's drool still on the surface and went to the spring nearby to wash off the plant. She bit into it cautiously afterwards. It was fleshy and thick, unlike the thin leaves she'd been trying to eat earlier. It had little taste but was filling.

She ate both of them and rose.

The animal appeared to be watching her again.

"Those fangs don't look like something an herbivore has," she murmured, uncertain why a predatory creature like this was showing her how to eat Anshan celery.

It rose and crossed to a nearby tree, rooting around the roots for more of the celery sticks and using its middle legs to paw and capture the vegetation without damaging it with its claws.

She watched it for a long moment, unable to understand the animal's motivations – if it were even capable of thought – before she, too, began looking for the plants. She found several and wrestled them free from their deep roots and piled them nearby. The bear did the same, its pile covered in drool.

When she had ten of the sticks, Kiera piled them all like logs into her arms and went to the stream to wash them.

Kiera ripped off one of her sleeves to wrap them in and stood. Her knee was stiff but not painful this morning, though her bruises and cuts sent random stings through her as she moved.

When she turned, she saw the bear moving across the meadow. She searched the area around her once more, puzzles as to why there was only one large creature to develop from the basin. She had spotted at least six little spider-cats frolicking among the trees of the jungle and only one bear.

Kiera trailed the creature curiously. It paused at the opposite end of the meadow and twisted to look at her. The bear tossed its head towards the direction it was headed, as if telling her to follow, and began walking once more.

How was it possible for the animal to communicate with her? To show her food and even bring her some of the celeries? She had never thought twice about the ability for animals on earth to think like humans, but this creature seemed capable of it.

Then again, she was on a different planet, one that had its own soul. How different would that make any living creature that grew on it?

So she followed the animal. It led her to the edge of the basin and into the newer part of the jungle until it reached the edge. The animal didn't stop, but Kiera did. She watched the jungle grow outward at a pace of about a foot a minute, unable to identify anything as incredible as knowing she'd caused it.

She lifted her eyes to the storm once more and stepped after the bear. Its ambling pace showed no sign of hurry, and the same bubble that formed around her when she entered the storm was around it as well. They walked away from the safety and food of the jungle, and she glanced frequently over her shoulder, until the vibrant green was swallowed by the red dust storm.

The bear plodded away. Kiera stared after it. If every living thing on Anshan was connected, it was possible the animal was more in tune with the planet and taking her somewhere safe.

Or ... it was hunting or wandering or had some other motivation to lead her away from the oasis.

"Hey!" she called to the bear.

It didn't acknowledge her and continued walking.

"I hope you know where we're going," she said and clutched the bundle of Anshan celery to her chest.

The bear stayed just within sight, leading her through the storms at a pace she was able to tolerate despite her achy knee. With it guiding her, she didn't fear falling into another depression but neither was she certain she needed to go wherever it took her.

The terrain turned from generally flat to sloping to steep after several hours. The bear seemed to understand she wasn't able to navigate as fast as it could and often sat on its haunches several feet ahead and watched her climb with some effort up the sides of hills. By the time twilight fell, she had eaten half the glow sticks before reminding herself she needed them to act as her flashlights once it was dark.

Just before night fell, the bear led her into the dark mouth of a cave. Kiera followed slowly, not noticing how loud the storms were until deep enough in the cavern for it to become quiet.

The cave sloped downward, and the bear showed no sign of stopping. The raging storms grew farther and farther away until she wasn't able to hear anything but the padding of the bear's paws against stone.

At long last, the bear stopped. Kiera almost sighed in relief and drew nearer, lifting the light sticks when she saw the round door in front of which the animal stood. She drew nearer, gaze resting on the imprint in the shape of a large hand in the middle of the door. The bear moved to the side, and familiar apprehension drifted through her. She lifted her hand and pressed it to the imprint.

The door depressed several inches, and she jumped back, waiting. After a pause, it rolled to the side to reveal a dark room beyond.

The bear led her into the room. As with the other chambers she'd explored with Turi, the moment she crossed the threshold, lights flickered on from evenly spaced points around the chamber. This room was round with an open entry on the opposite side of where she stood.

Kiera followed the bear through the chamber and down the hallway on the opposite side. Once more, the corridor sloped downwards, and they walked through a tunnel whose corners were old enough to be rounded.

Anshan was an ancient planet with a history far longer than she knew of Earth. It had to have taken thousands of years to wear down the corners carved by far removed ancestors of A'Ran. The deeper they went, the more Kiera considered how incredible such a history truly was. Human history on Earth was relatively shallow with more unknowns than knowns.

But here, on Anshan, traditions had been passed down through A'Ran's forefathers for millennia. That *she* was chosen by the planet left her feeling more humbled than before.

"You're amazing, aren't you?" she whispered to the ancient planet whose soul had chosen her out of everyone else in the universe.

The corridor reached an end beside a wide, quickly moving river running beneath the mountains. Kiera gazed at the waters racing by and moved to the edge of the stone walk running alongside it. The river stretched in each direction, disappearing around a curve downstream and swallowed by darkness upstream.

Glimmers of metallic rainbows came from the massive fish swimming in the river, and she leaned over to get a better look. The aquatic animals were as large as the bear, each with five fins and eyes huge enough to scare her back from the edge. The creatures were cute when they were the size of her hand but a little freakier the size of a Smart car.

"What next, bear-bug?" she asked, turning to the furry creature.

Once more, it was ahead of her. The bear had walked a short distance away to a section of the stone walk protruding into the river. Kiera joined it on the mini-dock and peered uneasily into the waters once more before the tremble of the stone beneath her feet threw her off balance.

She scampered from the edge and dropped to her knees. The stone was moving. Like a chunk of ice carrying penguins in Antarctica, the stone left the bank of the river and drifted towards the middle of the wide river. The bear sat down as well, and Kiera quelled the mild panic racing through her at the idea of being stranded in the river with the huge fish.

She moved to the center of the stone and sat by the bear that had led her this far, uncertain once more how or why the wild animal was capable of guiding her anywhere at all. Its six legs left her leery.

Accompanying a bear somewhere was less weird than considering the creature to be an oversized bug.

"I guess you're more bear than bug," she reasoned, studying the creature.

It settled onto its stomach, as if to tell her they were going on a long ride.

She lay down on her back to gaze at the ceiling and was surprised to see similar paintings on the ceilings as had been in the chamber where she awoke the planet. They were faded, sometimes to the point of flashes of pale colors with no real forms. The river propelled her by them too quickly for her to make out what story the drawings might be telling. But one thing she knew: before the planet's art consisted solely of metal statues, it had been rich with colorful paintings and drawings. A'Ran was always amazed by her artwork, and she was happy to know she had more in common with Anshan than she initially thought.

Over the next several hours, Kiera nibbled her way through two more of the glow plants while the six-legged bear dozed beside her. She gave up looking for meaning in the artwork flying above her head and instead admired the colors and forms created by a civilization far older than her own.

A jolt made her sit up quickly.

The flat stone conveying them down the river was moving from the center of the river to one side, as if the unexplained ride was over. The bear roused itself as they neared the stone walkways lining the opposite side of the river, and their conveyance bumped lightly against the walkway.

Kiera stood, tested her balance, and then stepped off the self-propelled rock. The bear trailed her and padded past her to the opening of a corridor sloping upward. Lights glowed to life the moment she entered the hall.

They walked upward for ten minutes before the bear led her into what felt like a maze of corridors lined with closed, stone doors. The well-worn hallways grew wider as they went, the ceilings taller. Some contained more modern metal statues or markers and at least one the colorful, twisted cords used by Anshan and Qatwali to decorate the ceilings and corners of their homes.

Shuttered windows began to appear shortly after the simple decorations, followed by dim entrance pads marking modern technology at the side of doors.

The massive building they were in was empty of life, though she guessed it had been inhabited not so long ago. Far from luxurious like the back-up palace of the Qatwali, it was nonetheless far more glamorous than the moon home where she'd been living with A'Ran and his family, too.

They entered a new part of the building, this one with soaring ceilings and towering doors lining a hallway wide enough to fit a four-lane highway. Sculptures made of gray metal and outlined by red dust punctuated the middle of the corridor and stood between doors. The shapes were different than the statues she had seen on the moon: these were of exotic animals and people instead of geometric shapes or artistic twists and curls.

Kiera walked along the middle of the hall, studying the fantastical creatures she had yet to meet that she assumed represented the wildlife of Anshan. She identified the shapes of the spider-cats and many other animals she wasn't quite able to imagine in person. The bear, however, was not among those animals present.

As if sensing she thought of it, the bear gave a plaintive roar from its position in front of the two largest doors.

She returned to it, guessing it wanted her to open the doors. She tried lifting her armband to the access pad beside the door first without success before planting her palms against the doors.

They opened at her touch, and she stepped into the room behind the bear.

Light flared to life, one torch at a time, until the massive chamber was brightly lit to display brilliant works of art covering every inch of the floor, walls and high ceiling. Kiera gazed around her, smiling, sensing the

warmth and energy of Anshan more here than anywhere else. The room
– or perhaps the planet – was welcoming her. Her first interest was in the
art, and she explored it ravenously with her gaze, identifying the different
techniques and marks of dozens upon dozens of different artists.

The art displayed on the walls ranged from faded, barely discern-
able, to newer, bolder paintings. Pictures of people and Anshan
battles and monuments were intermixed with letters from Anshan's
symbol-based language. Metal statues lining the floor of the chamber
were the newest additions to the story of Anshan plastered on the
walls, and the floor consisted of mosaics in various hues of sand, red,
orange and faded yellow.

Absorbed in studying the marks of a people she was just starting
to know, Kiera's focus left the walls only when the bear gave another
cry of complaint. She joined it at the center of the chamber, where it
sat next to a raised dais. Two stone chairs, far simpler than the
Qatwali thrones, were at the center of the dais.

Kiera paused before them, innately understanding what they
were. The artsy chamber at the center of the elaborate mazes, as bois-
terous as the people of Anshan were reserved, was the throne room,
the center of Anshan's royalty and people.

The Anshan palace was plain compared to Qatwal. As she stood
in the silent chamber, the energy of the planet tickling her feet, she
experienced a heavy emotion not entirely her own.

Unlike Qatwali, no life existed on Anshan. The throne room, the
palace, even the oasis where she'd rested, were engulfed in a sense of
loneliness. Abandonment. Sadness.

But here, the sorrow so painful, so palpable, it made her breath
catch.

Kiera studied the beauty on the walls, the sign of how well loved
and happy the planet had been filled with so many people who
appreciated it before the events of the past dozen years or so.

The planet was barren, abandoned, yearning for the lives
connected to it to return. Yirkin had claimed the spirits of the people

were contained within the planet itself. If true, then how could it survive without them?

"That's it, isn't it?" she whispered. "That's why we're dying."

Unable to speak to her directly, Anshan wasn't able to tell her if she was right. But Kiera didn't need to hear the affirmation to know she'd hit the truth.

Without its people, Anshan would die. Kiera had struggled with the foreign concept of a living planet, one with its own spirit, as alive as any of the people who lived on its surface. Able to feel Anshan in the air around her, it suddenly seemed far less complicated. She no longer dwelt on *how* or *why* a planet could be alive and instead, focused on the emotions of a being she was connected to yet unable to communicate with. What made a planet living mattered far less than saving the being who was dying before her eyes.

A'Ran couldn't have known how his actions would affect the planet itself when he blew up the surface and made it impossible for the Anshani to return to their beloved home. She knew from her time as a battle commander that a small ground force of Anshani had remained on the planet after the Yirkin invasion to fight for A'Ran's claim.

The planet's fate had been dire with such a small contingent, but without any Anshani at all, it was outright dying, unable to heal itself, unable to repair the damage A'Ran had unknowingly caused by making it uninhabitable.

Anshan didn't just need its *nishani*. It needed all of its people or as many as she could bring back to the planet.

The bear pawed at the air before her.

"I know, I know," she murmured. "I think I know what to do." She cast another worried look at the ceiling, wishing she could see the sky and moon beyond or send word to those off planet somehow. "I don't know how to do it, though."

ELEVEN

A'RAN'S NEWFOUND INSTINCT, the one connected directly to Anshan, led him towards the mountains, but not in the exact direction he preferred to go. He was taking a leap of faith and trusting his planet to guide him. Gage was forefront in his thoughts, and he mentally calculated how much air she had every time he paused to rest the battered left side of his body. The fear of losing her drove him, along with the knowledge Kiera was a prisoner somewhere within these same mountains.

And ... there was another reason nagging him, one he didn't want to acknowledge. This range had been the seat of Anshani royalty for many generations, the location of the only palace his family ever built, the center of Anshani trade, power and mining operations.

The planet was taking him home, and he didn't know exactly what he'd find once he arrived. Was everything he remembered decimated? Had he destroyed millennia of Anshan heritage?

Had he lost more than he saved?

The world around him grew dark as he reached the draws and spurs of the foothills around the mountains. As a child, he had played in the underground caverns and tunnels running beneath the surface.

Anshan had been a mining community long before the true value of the metal became known. The world beneath its surface was as rich as that above the ground, but it had been too long since A'Ran explored the underground. He didn't recall much about the maze of hallways running through the mountains.

He paused to rest his left leg and readjust the sling across his chest. Hunger and pain were distant in his thoughts. He had grown used to physical discomfort in exile, and the physical sensations did nothing to distract him from his goal of finding somewhere safe for Gage. With the emergency respirators, she likely had a full day left. He hadn't yet reached the point where he needed to turn back. After a breather, he continued on, following the invisible, insistent energy trail.

The pulse of the navigator beacon became the only light, further limiting his sight, and he slowed to place his feet carefully as the sloping path became littered with shale and loose rocks. He reached a stone wall and slid into the depths of a shallow draw, stopped to right the bone bandage starting to slide out of place, and continued walking.

Draws hid many of the entrances to the underground world. The energy remained strong within him, and he walked carefully until he reached the metal door. A'Ran waved his armband before the hidden access pad at one side. The door opened, and he stepped into the tunnel system of the mountains.

Quietness descended upon him as he entered the caverns. Warm light sprang up on either side of him, and he observed the condition of the ancient tunnels briefly. They appeared to have been spared the worst of the damage, perhaps protected by the mountains. He touched the nearest wall, the cool stone welcome to his senses.

Gage would be safe here. He turned to leave and waited in front of the door. It didn't budge. A'Ran waved his hand before the access pad. No response.

The energy was prodding him away from the entrance as well, tugging him towards the depths of the tunnel.

He pushed at the door only to find it secure.

Glaring at it, he finally turned away and started into the tunnel. He had trusted Anshan to guide him thus far, but he wasn't certain the planet understood his sister was in danger.

It didn't appear ready to let him leave now that he'd entered the tunnels.

A'Ran calculated Gage's air once more and quickened his step to a jarring jog that sent spirals of pain shooting through him. The faster he got to wherever he needed to be, the sooner he could return for his sister.

He was disappointed to realize how unfamiliar the underground world was. He recalled so little of his life before war and battle, and he didn't know for certain if he'd ever be able to return to the home that had been his growing up.

A'Ran moved through the hallways and corridors. They expanded as the tunnel system merged with the above ground corridors of the palace he vaguely recalled. His childhood home had once teemed with people and light. It was a skeleton of what it had been, an abandoned wasteland. He found himself stopping before a set of familiar doors with the symbol of the *dhjan* carved into them, almost able to remember when he had last stood in this spot.

A sense of loneliness followed him, not fully his own, though he felt the silence of the hallways as a weight on his shoulders, a reminder of everything that was missing from his home. Uneasiness tightened his chest the further he went into the palace. He had no fear of his home, but the condition it was in left him disturbed. He had seen many abandoned buildings on the moons of Anshan and on other planets. None of them *felt* abandoned like his former home did.

He entered the wing of the palace reserved for official use. The priceless statues were numerous here, and at least one chamber along the long hall was filled with enough of the gray metal tokens and statues – intended as gifts for visiting dignitaries – to fund the trade for the Five Galaxies for an entire cycle.

Treasure had long since taken a back seat to concern for the safety of his people and planet. A'Ran began to remember the purpose of each room as he passed. He spotted the open doors of the throne room and slowed his pace, drawing a dagger. No one should have been at the heart of the Anshan civilization, and any Yirkin or Qatwali or other unwelcome visitor wasn't going to leave with his head if he came to steal what remained of Anshan's history and wealth.

He slid into the chamber – and froze.

Kiera. And ... some weird creature. It wasn't Anshani or anything he'd ever seen on any of his visits. The creature was lying on its belly, dozing, clearly not a threat to his Kiera.

His heart somersaulted at the sight of his beautiful, brilliant life-mate, as it did every time he set eyes on her. This time, he felt the same sense he had when they first met – the near painful experience of intense energy shooting through him. It came from the planet and jarred his mind, rendering him breathless and setting his injuries on fire.

A'Ran braced himself against the wall, waiting for the sensations to pass.

"A'Ran!" Kiera's gleeful cry pulled him from the pain of his body.

Before he could react, she'd thrown herself into his arms. A'Ran sighed deeply and hugged her to him hard, swearing never to let her go again. He breathed in her scent and marveled at the feel of her warmth and softness. He hadn't let himself experience the fear of possibly losing her, but it hit him now, cored him, made his insides run cold even with her warm frame in his arms.

"I cannot bear to lose you," he whispered fiercely and held her to him more tightly.

"You're hurt!"

A'Ran closed his eyes, enjoying the attention. "I am well, *nishani*."

"Stupid warrior," she retorted softly. She clung to him and fluttered kisses over his features.

A'Ran opened his eyes. "How did you find this place?" he asked, gazing down into her multi-hued eyes. He cupped her cheek in one hand, needing to touch her more, to reassure himself she was truly alive and in his embrace.

She cleared her throat, her cheeks flushing pink. "I followed the ..." The last word didn't translate correctly.

"The what?" he asked.

She twisted to point at the animal.

"What is it?"

"You don't know?" She peered up at him.

He eyed the beast. "It is not Anshan."

"Whatever it is, it brought me here. How did you find me?"

"Anshan brought me."

She smiled. Kiera lifted on her tiptoes and touched her lips to his in a light kiss.

No small kiss was going to appease the fire and relief in his blood. A'Ran responded by capturing her lips and deepening the kiss, wanting to devour his lifemate in passion right then and there. Kiera melted into him as she always did, and her arms went around his neck. He kissed her long and hard, hoping to convey his worry and love for her with a single kiss, because it was all they had time for now.

He broke away long before he wanted to, aware they had more challenges than time. He listened to her ragged breathing, unable to help the surge of need and heat roiling through him.

"We must go," he said and nuzzled her hair.

"You have a communicator?"

"No," he replied grimly.

"A'Ran, we have to contact Mansr. I know how to save Anshan."

Startled by the calm announcement, he shifted back to search her face. "How?"

"Anshan needs its people back. *All* of them."

"We cannot return them to a toxic planet."

"We can. We have to," she said. "A'Ran, the planet is dying. It's the only way to fix it."

He considered the confirmation of what they'd both suspected. Releasing her reluctantly, he started towards the door. "Mansr is close. He came with the Qatwali to search for you. When we reach him, I'll tell him we need to the atmospheric cleaners online immediately."

"You're not understanding me." Kiera's hushed tone stopped him. "We don't have a cycle or half a cycle to wait for the air to be cleaned. We don't have time at all."

"I can't endanger my people any more than I already have. The air must be clean first," he said firmly.

Kiera's gaze was troubled.

"Trust me, *nishani*. I want what's best for our people and planet," he added. "We cannot know how long the planet has."

"Yes, we can." She stepped away from him. "I didn't have a dream about it dying, A'Ran. I know it's dying."

He tested the energy within him. It felt strong and stable.

"A'Ran, I'm dying, too."

His world seemed to stop at Kiera's sad words. The anguish and sorrow he experienced when he thought he had lost her weeks ago returned, stealing his breath. "What do you mean?" he asked and drew near her once more.

"I went to the medic, and he told me my cells were rapidly degenerating, and there was nothing he could do to fix it," she explained, averting her eyes. "I didn't know how to tell you."

"This is why you have been so worried?"

She nodded. "I thought you would exile me. If I couldn't perform my duty and save the planet, if I couldn't have children, if I couldn't even stay alive long enough to be of any use ..." Her voice broke, and tears were in her eyes.

"You thought this of me?" he asked hoarsely. "You thought I would send you away?"

"Like Gage."

What troubled A'Ran the most: it wasn't outside the realm of possibilities he'd consider exiling her – if he were still the man he was before they met. If he hadn't fallen in love with her. If he hadn't learned love trumped duty. If he didn't openly acknowledge she was the center of his world, the only hope of his people, his anchor in a universe that had never been kind to him.

Kiera was more than his lifemate. She was his life.

He didn't know how to express any of this and clenched his jaw.

"Would you?" she whispered, gazing up at him. "Or ... will you?"

"Never." It was the only word he could utter.

She searched his features before wrapping her arms around him once more.

A'Ran held her to him tightly, feeling as if he'd never properly appreciated his family in his life, if his sister opted for suicide and his lifemate kept such a secret from him. What good was all he did, if he sacrificed those he loved?

"Never, Kiera," he said more vehemently. "I will exile no one, and you will never be farther from me than my eyes can see."

"You will spare Gage?"

"I will. I have told her she can choose her own destiny. I offer the same to D'Ryn and Talal. You have shown me a better way than what I knew, and I will see them safe for my sake and happy for yours."

She gazed up at him, tears glimmering in her eyes, and a smile on her face.

"But you will not keep secrets from me anymore, Kiera. I will not be swayed to change in this regard. We are one with each other and Anshan," he added sternly. "You cannot be dying." He brushed the pad of his thumb across her soft cheek. "I cannot lose you."

"You might not," she said, her smile fading. "I thought ... well, *felt* it had something to do with the planet and when I got here, I kind of knew it to be true. Anshan is dying. I'm dying. There's only one way to save both of us – by saving the planet."

His chest was too tight to breathe, his thoughts at first silent then raging.

"Your people have to return, as many as possible, as soon as possible," she continued in a whisper. "They can go to the caves where the Yirkin are or maybe I can make another jungle like –"

"Yirkin?"

"Oh. I forgot about that part." She offered a weak smile. "There are thousands of them trapped in caves beneath the Anshan surface. They were able to evacuate part of their population before you blew up everything."

"They brought you here?"

She nodded. "Their leader, Turi, heard the *nishani* could heal the planet. So either I succeeded in healing it so they could leave or he was going to use me as a hostage to negotiate for their freedom."

"I will crush every last one of them!"

"That's what got us here," she pointed out. "And I made a vow, in your name, not to hurt any of them."

A'Ran had a few choice words for anyone negotiating a peace treaty with his mortal enemies on his behalf, but he swallowed them, studying her features instead. Of everything going through his mind, only one thought stuck. What if this was one of the last times he looked upon the face of his lifemate? What if he failed her as he had his planet and people?

These questions sucked his anger from him, left him with the sense of despair he'd known as a prince living in exile watching his people and planet perish before his eyes.

"I made a jungle," she said again. "We can put some people there and there's tons of room underground. I think we can fix the planet as we go, but Anshan needs help fighting to live. It needs its people."

"Then we will bring them. For both of you."

"Thank you."

The strange creature grumbled from its position at the foot of the thrones. A'Ran glanced up then back. It struck him where he was, in the place where he'd last been fifteen cycles before. Hastily elevated to the position *dhjan* in this very room, after watching his parents die, he'd shortly after been swept away by Mansr for a brief ceremony in the traditional place and taken by his father's personal guard to a spacecraft before the Yirkin's invading forces reached the city.

The heart of Anshan was before him, the chamber that marked the beginning of his rein far quieter than it had been during the chaotic ceremony cycles ago. It felt like a completely different life, a different world.

It was no coincidence Kiera had been led here by the unfamiliar animal.

"How did you come by this creature?" he asked, moving away from her. He slid his hand into her as he stepped away, not ready to stop touching her. They approached the creature seated on its hunches.

"It found me in the jungle," she said with a shrug. "I thought it was an Anshani animal."

"I do not know what it is."

"It kind of looks like a ..."

The word didn't translate correctly, but it was familiar. "The beast from the Gol-dee-locks tale?"

She nodded.

"Perhaps Anshan saw it in your mind and made it to guide you here."

"It tried to mash something from my world with yours," she said, considering it. "I did ask Anshan to help me in a way I understood. I was thinking of a letter or something, though."

"It is possible it took this from your mind and tried to recreate it, thinking you would understand."

"How incredible is such an idea?" she whispered in awe.

"You are never alone if you are an Anshani. The planet is always with you. When we are in pain, it is in pain." He eyed the beast once more before facing her. "We need to alert Mansr immediately, but I must bring Gage here first."

"Gage?"

"She's on the planet. She ran away when she discovered I wanted to exile her."

Kiera raised her eyebrows, and a familiar spark was in her gaze.

"*Nishani,*" he growled before she could lecture him. "I have learned my mistake."

"I hope so. You don't usually get second chances like this, A'Ran," she said.

"I know."

"I'm proud of you." She squeezed his hand. "Is there a communicator here?"

"Everything was destroyed when we left. It is protocol not to leave anything the enemy can use," he replied. "Mansr is on the surface. I know about where he will be. You must stay here. I will–"

"No."

It was his turn to raise his eyebrows.

"Turi has a communicator. You can send Mansr word about Gage and bringing the people back."

It took every bit of A'Ran's self control not to admit he hated the idea more than anything else she'd said. But the reminder they had little time, either to save Gage or his lifemate, left him with little choice. He had no way to find Mansr or even know if his uncle was still on the planet.

"Very well," he managed.

Kiera flashed him a grin. "I love you. I know that was hard."

He growled in response. She hugged him briefly before waving to the strange creature that was already headed towards the door. "Come on! We have to find Turi! We're going to save Anshan together!"

He watched her hurry to the door. The image of her dying was in his head, rubbing his emotions raw, making his mind work furiously to discover a way to save her and Anshan both without losing the entirety of the Anshan population. He sought some story his parents or Mansr had shared, some tale of the past to guide him.

Evacuating thousands of Yirkin and bringing in his people was going to take time Kiera didn't seem to think they had. The palace was the center of Anshan civilization for a reason, chosen many thousands of cycles before by his ancestors. The throne room was part of an ancient tradition he barely recalled.

The ground beneath his feet quaked suddenly, and he dropped to one knee to keep from falling outright. A crack formed in the stone floor of the chamber. It raced to one wall and up, severing a painting in two. The trembling stopped, but his gaze lingered on the splash of green along the wall. The image depicted was that of the hill over-looking the palace nestled between the foothills and lower mountains of the towering range.

A'Ran crossed to it, his instincts humming, his heart hammering. The planet was suffering. He had less time than either of them knew.

The familiar painting on the wall filled him with familiar yearn-ing. One of his last memories of peace was sitting with his mother and sisters on the hill. He had looked out over the palace and the bustling city at its feet and fantasized about the day when he'd become an honorable, respected *dhjan* like his father. The sacred area where only the ruler and his family visited had always resonated with Anshan's energy. He felt it even as a child and knew one day, he would experience so much more as the ruler of his people.

He had never thought about why the hill was off limits to mining, but it was said only Anshan royalty were permitted to visit the sacred place. His hasty coronation ceremony had been on the hill, like those of his forefathers as far back as he knew.

If he went there now, what would he find? A hill of green grass? A hole where it used to be?

Instincts kept him alive in battle, but he was less certain about the sense he had now, the one urging him to visit a place of memories when he had no time to reminisce. Anshan's energy trail was concen-trated around the image, but no part of him was able to logically explain why or how such a place held any significance beyond the memories of a better time of his life.

Yet his planet, his home, wanted him to go. Whether this was its dying final request or he'd find a way to save Anshan, he wasn't able to refuse.

"Kiera," he said quietly. "We need to go somewhere else first."

He turned to face her. His breath caught in his throat.

Kiera was lying on the floor, the animal standing over her and nudging her with its long snout.

A'Ran rushed to her and knelt, cursing his injured body for making it hard to hold his lifemate.

"Kiera," he breathed the word.

Her eyes fluttered open, and she smiled. "Not sure what happened." She pushed herself up, expression pensive.

"Are you hurt?" He ran his good hand down one side of her face and searched her body visibly for blood or wounds.

"No." She took his hand and nuzzled it. "I think something's really wrong, A'Ran."

Coldness shot through him again.

"Whatever's happening to Anshan is getting worse."

A'Ran sat, frozen in indecision and rare fear, debating what to do. "Can you walk?" he asked at last.

She nodded and rose, wobbled, and caught her balance.

"How do you feel?"

"I ... don't know. I don't feel right," she said, frowning. Tears lined her eyes again. She swiped them away and looked up at him. "A'Ran, I'm scared."

Her whisper hurt worse than every injury he had ever suffered combined.

The ground beneath them trembled once more. Kiera clung to him, and he held her against him tightly, torn between the feeling he needed to see the hill and the urgency of finding Turi to warn Mansr.

He sensed without knowing for certain he didn't have time for both. "I know the underground tunnels better than you do. I'll-"

"A'Ran! I don't want to be left here alone like –"

"Stop, my sweet Kiera," he said gently. "You need to go somewhere else while I'm gone."

Her objection died on her lips, and she waited for him to finish.

He gazed at her tenderly, every cell of his body praying this wasn't the last time he held his lifemate. "Tell the creature to take you to the hill behind the palace," he said. "Something is there. I don't know what, but Anshan wants us there."

"And you'll go to Turi?" Her expression turned skeptical. "You won't kill him?"

A'Ran gave a rare smile. "Not this time."

She rolled her eyes, some of her spark returning. "You have to hurry. So does Mansr. I can feel whatever is happening." She motioned to the stone flooring.

"The hill isn't far," he said.

She gave him a long look before rising up on her tiptoes to kiss him. "Don't be gone long, my A'Ran."

"Never," he breathed again and rested his forehead against hers. "Nothing will keep me from your arms, my brave, beautiful Kiera."

She grinned, though he saw the flash of sadness and fear in her gaze as well. With reluctance, he withdrew from her warmth and calming scent and left.

A'Ran didn't care how much he hurt. He was concerned only with saving the life of his lifemate, even if it meant negotiating with the people who tried to steal his planet and slaughter his people.

TWELVE

KIERA GAZED up at A'Ran's roughly hewn, noble features, admiring his strength. His movement was slower than she was accustomed to, and white lined the skin beneath his eyes. His left arm was limp across his chest. She almost asked if he was all right but stopped herself, knowing the warriors of Anshan regarded concern for their physical conditions as a personal affront. She slid her hand into his and squeezed, happy to have her lifemate with her on the final leg of their journey to save the planet.

"Go. We'll be together soon," she told him with as much cheerfulness as she could muster.

A'Ran hesitated, as if he wanted to say more, before he started away.

Knowing A'Ran had changed since they met didn't fully prepare Kiera to appreciate how much. The mischievous part of her loved to see how far he'd come, but her humor was soon swallowed by the realization the planet was losing its fight to survive. He disappeared around the corner and she resisted the urge to scream for him to return, to stay with her.

The primal quake within her mirrored the trembling planet in the throes of death and left her weakened, terrified and wanting nothing more than A'Ran's arms around her when the worst came.

"Keep it together, Kiera," she murmured and wiped way more tears. "We have to save the world." She almost laughed but found herself starting to cry instead. Jamming distance between her emotions and her new mission, she began walking. "Hey, bear, can you take me to the hill?" she called to the beast.

It plodded along, heading left down the corridor once it left the throne room.

She dwelt on *it*, the bewildering, unsettling awareness of Anshan. She hadn't felt this strongly how connected the planet was before. The deeper they went into the palace, the more intense the presence became, as if Anshan were walking beside her, bringing with it all the despair and urgency of one struggling to live.

The emotions threatened to overwhelm her, and Kiera found herself pausing too often, crippled by fear that wasn't hers. The bear prodded her when she froze up, and she refocused on the world outside her head.

At long last, they left the palace. Her protective bubble formed around her at once, and she was dismayed not to be able to see in front of her once more. The storms continued to rage, the renewal of their howling and dust scaring her even more.

A'Ran was right. How did they bring hundreds of thousands of people back to the surface without killing everyone in the process? If the ships made it to the surface, did A'Ran have enough exoskeletons to protect everyone?

Realizing she'd stopped to stare at the storm raging around her, Kiera hurried forward before the bear disappeared from view. It led her up a rocky hill and through a shallow valley whose exit was blocked by rubble and boulders. The bear turned its attention to the steep hill running to her right. The slope left her gaping.

"You're serious?" she asked the bear paused beside her.

The earth trembled once more. Kiera caught herself against the bear. As before, the quake started beneath her feet before it tore through her. The sensation of being ripped in two left her gasping and aching, and she hugged the bear to keep from falling. Shaking as much as the ground, she waited for the worst to pass and looked anew at the hill.

Anshan was in crisis, and she wasn't going to withstand the tremors much longer if she and A'Ran didn't hurry. Trusting her life-mate and the bear, Kiera focused on scaling the slope.

The presence of Anshan clung to her, and she found herself talking to it without knowing if the planet was able to understand her or not.

"Almost there. Reminds me of the one time I tried rock climbing," she said, grunting with effort. "There's a reason I never ..." She stopped, another shudder running through the ground and her. They were growing in intensity and frequency. This one left her breathless and clinging to the side of the hill, her vision blurred from the shared sense of desperation.

When she had recovered enough to climb once more, Kiera began making her way upwards without seeing the top of the hill. Her frame shook with effort and exhaustion, mixed with the side effects of the quakes ripping Anshan apart from the inside out.

"Hang in there. I'm almost wherever I'm going," she murmured. Her hand slipped, and she gasped. Her own strength was ebbing. She concentrated hard on the area before her, trying not to think of how they were going to save the planet this late in the game.

With some relief, she reached the top of the hill before another tremor hit. Kiera hauled herself to the plateau on the other side and lay still, horrified by the sensations of the quakes working through her body. She knew she was connected to Anshan, but *feeling* it inside her was absolutely terrifying.

The tremor stopped. She lay still for another moment, unable to recover fully from any of the quakes. They were eating away at her strength a little more with each one, to the point she wanted a nap.

Grass tickled her ear, and she sat up instead. The storms soared overhead, as if the entire acre-sized area of grass before her was sheltered by the same bubble protecting her. The top of the hill appeared as if no storm had ever touched it. A small pond was at its center.

The bear wasn't anywhere in sight, but someone else was.

Kiera's heart slowed, and her breath hitched, as she stared at the figure before her.

"You're real," she breathed finally. "Like *really* real."

The form before her nodded. Neither male nor female, with no face and six arms like everything else on its planet, it resembled a human – yet distinctly not. It had initially scared her in her dream, but in person, the form Anshan took was slight and emitted a peaceful calm like sitting beside a lake.

"You're hurting," Kiera added sadly and approached the form the same size as her. "How do we fix this?"

No response.

"Can you talk?"

It shook its head.

"Okay. Are we on the right path? Bringing the people back?"

The figure nodded.

"And you sent the bear to find me?"

Another nod.

Kiera looked around. The sense of peace filled the small part of Anshan that hadn't been destroyed. "What is this place?" She felt the answer without the figure moving. It was the last part of Anshan that hadn't been lost, the place where the planet's spirit was trying to make its last stand.

And it was tiny compared to the planet at least twice the mass of Earth. Even as she watched, the grass was receding slowly, inch by inch from the edges.

Kiera knelt and placed her hands on the ground. A ripple went through the area around her, and the recession stopped. Mushroom-sized trees sprang up near by and grew as she watched them.

The figure knelt beside her and placed all six palms on the

ground. Another ripple spread through the grass, this one smaller, weaker. It didn't make it to the edges of the greenery.

"I'm so sorry," Kiera whispered. "I had no idea you needed me so much. Needed *us*. A'Ran will bring everyone back, but the air is poisonous to everyone else. Can you fix this?"

The creature leaned back on its haunches, its faceless head bowing in what she took to be resignation.

Kiera kept her hands pressed to the ground, aware of how quickly the jungle had sprung up beneath her touch. "You saw or um ... felt or whatever the jungle, right?"

The figure nodded.

"Maybe we can expand this area so there's more room for people to come back."

The figure stood abruptly and strode to the edge of the green space.

"Or not," Kiera murmured and climbed to her feet. She limped, stretched her knee, then joined the figure.

It pointed towards the palace.

"You think it's better there?" Kiera asked. "There's no ground really." She glanced at her feet. "Just ... oh. People can stay inside the palace while the plants take over and push back the storm."

The figure nodded.

"You know where to go?"

It took her hand in two of its, and she flinched at the reminder of how many arms it had. The figure's palms were slightly waxy and cool, like the topside of leaves. It held up her hand and squeezed.

"So don't let go, right?" she asked.

It nodded.

"It's a tricky path down." Kiera peeked over the edge of the hill. "Might be rough." Grass had begun to spread down the side of the hill. She sat on her bottom and swung her legs over, hoping to scoot down.

The figure followed her lead. They began inching down the hill, at least, until she slipped. Kiera tumbled down the hill, clenching the hand of the planet's representative hard. They landed in a tangled heap onto the floor of the valley.

"Oh, god!" Kiera cried when she'd caught her breath. Pain radiated through her body from new and old scratches, bruises and tears. She crawled to her knees and glanced at the figure.

It appeared in the same shape she was. Its skin had torn in a few spots, and it bled the same color green as the grass. But it was alive and it climbed to its feet.

A quake made both of them clutch one another. If having two hands holding her was odd, having six arms wrapped around her was unnerving. Kiera clung to it, feeling the tremors pass from the planet through her and into the faceless figure.

"They're ... they're getting worse," she whispered. The quakes rattled her teeth and left her feeling lightheaded. This time, they didn't completely leave. The earth, and her insides, quivered incessantly. "Way worse. We have to go. Now."

She stumbled away, accompanied by the figure, and ran down the valley as fast as her aching body let her. When they reached the door leading into the palace, she opened it with a touch and then paused.

The figure moved ahead of her, intimately familiar with every part of the planet in a way Kiera doubted she'd ever be, even if she spent her life there. She was pulled through hallways of differing widths and heights, through hidden doors between empty chambers, and up a stairwell that ended on the roof level, which consisted of expansive gardens and courtyards long since dead and formed the landing area for an upper level of the palace carved out of the rock of the lower mountains.

The figure stopped walking in the center of the gardens and knelt, placing five of its palms on the ground. Kiera sat beside it, grimacing at the renewed pain in her knee. She took the hand of the figure and placed it on her ankle instead.

"I don't have enough hands and you have too many," she joked weakly.

The figure was focused on the ground. Already, grass was starting to peek out around its hands. Kiera focused on the earth as well, and grass sprang up and outward even faster than before, covering the ground of the courtyard where they sat and scaling the walls.

"This might work," Kiera said, startled and pleased by the speed. *Hurry, A'Ran,* she added silently.

THIRTEEN

THE LONGER HE stayed in the palace, the more he remembered. A'Ran took only a couple of wrong turns before finding his way back to the entrance to the underground tunnel system running beneath the palace and throughout the mountain range. The walkways became noticeably narrower as he descended beneath the surface, the air staler. He recognized the river from his youth and also knew where Mansr was supposed to have landed. If their navigation had guessed correctly, the distance would take him several hours to cross.

He stopped when he reached the river. He vaguely recalled how to cross it; he had done so as a child. Floating stone beds bumped against the walkways, awaiting their next passenger.

He strode onto one and waited. The stone shifted away from the boardwalk and floated to the center of the river.

"Across," he said quietly.

It continued, crossing the fast, wide river and docking on the other side. He moved at the fastest pace his body was able to handle through the tunnels, following the faint energy of Anshan as it guided him. Quakes hit several times, and each tremble of the earth motivated him to push his body.

The energy from the planet grew weaker with each tremor as well, and he found himself sprinting, holding his hurt arm to his chest and gritting his teeth against the pain in his leg.

The tunnels turned from carefully carved and meticulously maintained over the years into the rudimentary canals created tens of thousands of cycles before by miners seeking to connect the underground caverns and mines. He passed through several caves and was forced to slow to a complete stop and crouch next to the ground to feel the ever-fading energy of Anshan.

At long last, he reached an ill-fitted door overlooked by those who fitted the palatial entryways with access pads several generations before. He pressed his hand to the central door, and it opened with a groan marking its age.

No lights came on beyond the door; this area of the caverns was too old for there to be light.

He stepped through and strained to feel the trickle of Anshan's energy. It was gone, but he heard something else coming from the lit end of the tunnel a distance ahead. People. The air was stagnant here, the distant thrum of people drawing him forward. He had found the underground hiding spot of the Yirkin. As he approached, A'Ran braced himself to deal with his enemies. Out of everything he expected to feel facing the people who had stolen his planet from him, all he could think about was Kiera, Anshan and his sister surviving.

Before he emerged from the tunnel, he removed the sling and straightened his clothing. He could do nothing about the bloodstains – except pretend the wounds beneath them were minor enough not to impede him. Alerting his enemies as to his weakness was not an option.

He emerged into a massive cavern housing the thousands of Yirkin Kiera had told him about. This part of the cavern was sparsely populated. He expected to be recognized on sight and confronted by several hundred warriors.

Not only did no one look his way twice, but the people were

running around frantically, snatching what they could carry of their meager belongings and headed to the far side of the cavern.

A'Ran's guard lowered some as he waded through the throngs. Whatever was happening, the Yirkin were too occupied to pay attention to a stranger in their midst. Kiera's description of the refugee camp was correct. Prepared to fight his way through Yirkin warriors, he would first have to find one. For nearly an hour, he wandered through families consisting of women and children too young to fight, the elderly and wounded men.

He saw no one to fight, no one to confront or negotiate with. He finally veered out of the pathways they had created and climbed on top of a fence corralling a pile of useless debris so he could see the layout of the sloping cavern.

The people were surging en masse towards one of two entrances leading deeper beneath the mountains while a tiny contingency of warriors was at the north side of the cavern, in front of a door they were bracing with pieces of spacecraft.

He caught a flash of blonde hair and recognized the distinctly Qatwali dress of the woman it belonged too.

Leaping down, A'Ran strode through the cavern against the flow of people, arriving to the cluster of Yirkin warriors and the man he knew was a commander by the sash tied around his arm. He stopped beneath the elevated entrance they stood before, assessing quickly what was going on.

The sound of laser fire hitting tough Anshan metal thumped, audible at the close distance where it hadn't been before. Evelyn appeared shaken but unharmed and the warriors ready to die defending the people fleeing towards the tunnels under the cave.

Mansr had found them.

A'Ran scoured the area for a trail leading to the top of the small overhang and hurried up it. He slowed as he drew near, tension coiled in his belly as he considered how unlikely he was to be welcomed by the invaders.

Evelyn was the first to notice him. She gasped, growing pale.

One warrior turned then another. Shocked to see him in their midst, their reactions were slow enough for him to speak first.

"Turi," he commanded sharply.

The warriors sprang into action and drew their weapons, the focus of the group shifting from whatever was trying to come through the door to him. A'Ran stood where he was, unwilling to back down or show any sign of weakness.

"I am Turi." One of them ventured forward, his gaze sweeping quickly over the cavern, as if he sought the warrior force A'Ran would have brought with him.

"I am A'Ran, *dhjan* of Anshan."

Turi focused on him, eyes narrowing. "You did not come alone."

"I did."

"Where's Kiera?" Evelyn exclaimed.

"Safe," he replied.

"She survived the surface," Turi said softly, satisfied.

"I am here to negotiate with the Qatwali and my uncle. To secure your safety and that of my people." A'Ran managed to say the words he'd never dreamt of uttering without scowling.

Turi started to laugh then stopped, his scarred features confused. "You? Negotiate on our behalf?"

"My lifemate swore you an oath in my name," A'Ran growled. "If she were not it danger, if my planet were not dying, if I did not need to save them both now, before it is too late, I would slaughter you where you stand. All of you and your people."

"*That* is the *dhjan* of Anshan," Turi said, anger flaring in his gaze.

"You have no rightful claim here. You should be exterminated like the vermin you are."

"Your lifemate made me a promise."

"And you cast her out into the storm." A'Ran bristled. "I will spare your people but not you."

"You are at a disadvantage, *dhjan*," Turi reminded him, motioning to the men around them.

"You doubt the resolve of the warrior who destroyed his own planet to rid it of your kind?"

"Perhaps we should negotiate first, argue later?" Evelyn called anxiously. "Turi, A'Ran would not be here if the danger weren't real."

The earth quaked beneath them, a reminder of how little time he had. "We must hurry. No one will leave Anshan if we do not act now." A'Ran shoved past the first few rows of men.

No one made a move to stop him, and the remaining warriors stepped aside as he approached Turi. "Do you have a communicator?"

For a long moment, the Yirkin commander stared at him. He shifted finally. "Yes. But we cannot reach anyone off planet because of the storms."

"We don't need to." A'Ran motioned to the two warriors holding Evelyn. "Release her." They obeyed without a word from their commander, and A'Ran turned to the door. "Take this down." He motioned to the obstructions they'd placed to brace the entrance. "And bring me the communicator."

"What is your plan?" Yuri asked warily. "Do you intend to keep the oath your lifemate gave to spare my people?"

A'Ran was quiet for a moment. If Kiera didn't have the soft heart she did, he'd suspect she was forced into the oath. But she didn't see war the way he did. She wasn't going to let anyone, even her lifemate, harm the innocent. He knew this as well as he knew he would destroy every last Yirkin in the Five Galaxies, if he had the chance.

"She guaranteed your safety from *me*," he replied in a hard voice. "But you also kidnapped the Qatwali *nishani*. I advise you to negotiate with her before you face her lifemate."

A warrior handed Turi the portable communicator. A'Ran snatched it and strode to the blockaded door. Its signal was weak, and he waited for the master list of networks to populate. More laser fire drew his glance to the door. He ignored it, aware of how tough Anshan metal was, and waited for the frequency he needed to pop up. The secured network was accessible to three people: Mansr,

Kiera as the supreme battle strategist responsible for commanding his armies, and him.

A'Ran passed the communicator by his armband, which contained a record of his unique genetic code, and waited for the channel to open.

Mansr's face appeared seconds later. "A'Ran! Where are you?"

"Behind the door you wish to knock down," A'Ran said with rare mirth. "We have little time. I need you to listen to my instructions and execute immediately. Do not think twice, Mansr."

"I await them eagerly."

A'Ran slowly rolled out his orders about the Anshani population, Gage and bringing him a personal craft immediately, aware of the expression on his uncle's features changing from grim determination to surprise. His reaction was mirrored by those around A'Ran as well as he instructed Mansr to utilize every available ship – cargo, carrier or personal – to bring back every Anshani within the solar system.

When he finished, he grated his teeth for a moment before reluctantly following through on Kiera's promise to the Yirkin. "Once the people are safe, send the ships to my location. The Yirkin refugees are to be evacuated outside the Five Galaxies. Unharmed. Our war is no longer with them."

Mansr outright stared at him, speechless, before his uncle quickly recovered. "As you command. Romas will not be convinced by me to cease what he is doing."

"I'll handle him," Evelyn said from behind A'Ran with the confidence that came natural to the women of her world.

A'Ran passed the communicator to her and stepped away, unwilling to eavesdrop on the conversation between a *dhjan* and his *nishani,* even if he had little respect for Romas.

His body was aching, but his mind was on Kiera, on the how he'd left her alone, and how little time Gage had left.

"Save my people and you can do what you wish to me." Turi's quiet voice was for his ears only.

"Your fate was never in question."

"Kiera survived the storms?"

A'Ran bit back the snarled response he wanted to give. "She did."

"Done!" Evelyn proclaimed and shut off the communicator. She returned it to A'Ran with a quick, if tight, smile.

The laser bolts ceased smashing into the door.

"He's not happy with you," she told A'Ran.

"I have never been concerned about his opinion of me or his good will," he snapped.

"You're welcome," she said, raising her eyebrows. "He wanted to bury you both."

"It is in his favor to do as I command," A'Ran replied.

She rolled her eyes like Kiera often did when he was being unreasonable in her eyes. "I owed Kiera to try to make things right. You'll tell her, won't you? And ask her to visit when the baby's born?"

Assuming we survive this. It was difficult for A'Ran to imagine tomorrow when the planet was dying at his feet. But he tried, for Kiera's sake. "Yes," he said.

"Good enough." Evelyn shook her head and retreated from the door.

"Is irreverence common on their planet?" Even Yuri appeared uneasy with her level of candidness.

"It appears to be," A'Ran replied. "Have your men get that door open now." He stepped back. It took all his effort not to limp in front of them; he had no strength left to help with the heavy lifting and was sidelined, forced to watch the final hurdle between him and saving Kiera fall away.

FOURTEEN

THE TREMORS CAME MORE FREQUENTLY as the day progressed. Kiera lay on the ground next to the figure of Anshan, clutching its leg. Instead of sending her energy, the planet was soaking up hers. She didn't realize how much time had passed until the coolness of twilight swept through the courtyard, and grass tickled her nose.

Kiera opened her eyes and swiped at her face. Her limbs were heavy as she propped herself up on her elbows to peer around. Glowing celery sticks had sprouted up nearby at the base of trees at least thirty feet tall. They were shaded by the interconnected canopy, rendering the dusky area darker.

She sat up with some effort. Her head was throbbing dully, her bruised body achy and stiff. The thick, lush forest was quiet, aside from the swaying trees and brush, and she peered through the trunks of the jungle to see the nearby corridors of the palace. She wasn't surprised to see the moss covering the walls or that the grass extended down the center of the hallways for as far as she could make out in the dim light of evening.

"Hey. We're doing it," she said in a voice roughened by exhaustion to the figure whose ankle she had been gripping long enough for her hand to cramp in that position.

When she heard no response, she shuffled on her knees closer to the six-legged figure and rested her free hand on the cheek of the form with no face. The form was distinctly not human, even if it had human-like mannerisms. Unable to identify how to check it for a pulse or determine if it was breathing, Kiera finally shook it gently.

"Hello?" she murmured. "Can you hear me? Are you okay?"

The form shifted and then seemed to sigh and collapse in upon itself. The body went limp, and grass began to climb up on its clothing.

Horrified at the idea the planet was swallowing its own representative, Kiera released its ankle with effort and reached out to push the grass away as it began to devour the figure.

The moment both of her hands touched the figure, a shot of lightning originating from the ground tore through her, jarring her from toes to the top of her head and flinging her away. She landed in a heap at the base of a tree. Blinking to clear sunspots, Kiera righted herself and shook her head. She still felt the current of lightning running through her. The unsettling sensation was intense without being painful and seemed to connect her to everything around her. She felt the tree's energy, the earth's, the faint thrum of a current in the air. The planet's life force ran through every part of the planet and through her, too. She felt it like she did her own heartbeat.

A'Ran was right. All of Anshan was connected. All of Anshan was alive and for whatever reason, she belonged to a world she'd never known before two months ago. She marveled at the strange feelings and waved her hands through the air, able to see the trail of faint light each movement left in its wake.

Her gaze fell to where the figure had been, and she scrambled forward. Nothing remained of the form that brought her here, not clothing or a bump in the ground like a fallen tree covered in moss. Ribbons of grass tickled her fingers, each one sending a faint charge of energy into her that pooled in her core.

The figure was gone. She sat for a moment, taking in the magical world around her and concerned the disappearance of the six-armed person meant the worst for Anshan.

She rose. A wave of dizziness hit her. The planet was starting to pull some of the lightning from her, desperate for the energy it needed to grow and repair itself. She caught herself against the nearest tree, shaking from fatigue and fearful of what happened when she, too, ran out of strength. A small quake worked its way through the courtyard.

She made her way through the jungle to a corridor. Light wasn't needed with the layer of glowing sunflowers that lined one wall, and she traced her fingers along them, shivering with the small spark of electricity each gave off.

Uncertain how long she'd been lying in the courtyard, she was shocked by how far the greenery had spread. Trees sprang up in cavernous rooms, courtyards and atriums while grass and moss coated walls, ceilings and floors where the trees were too large to grow.

The world was coming alive. She smiled faintly and paused to rest against a wall, amazed yet exhausted. Yellow lights turned on beneath the moss on the walls, washing the palace's interior in a greenish glow wherever she went.

Kiera paused at an intersection, unable to recognize a familiar path now that everything was covered in moss. A warm thrum of energy came from behind her, and she turned, sensing the planet was taking her a different direction than she wanted to go. Her thoughts were on A'Ran, on finding him and learning whether Gage, Evey and Turi were safe.

But she listened to Anshan and retreated back the way she'd come, past the jungle in the courtyard and down a combination of halls until she exited the back of the palace. The grass and moss had even reached here. She paused to watch it sweep a path through the draw leading to the side of the hill where she'd first met the figure from her dreams.

Kiera took a step to follow and faltered, smashing to the ground on her hurt knee. Dizziness swept through her once more. As if in response, the earth quaked and cracked as tremors raced away from her. She drew a steady breath and stood. She began walking once more, this time slower.

She followed the familiar path. The grass was moving fast now, enveloping everything it touched, climbing the sides of hills and covering the boulders in its path. She reached the massive rock blocking the trail and sighed. The energy of Anshan wanted her to return to the hill. She gritted her teeth and struggled up the slope once more. Another wave of dizziness hit her before she reached the top, and a corresponding quake spread outward from where she was.

Sensing her connection with Anshan was even greater now, Kiera forced herself up to the hill and rested on the small plateau. The grass followed her and raced by until it met the receding greenery on the hill.

Beat after the climb, Kiera gazed up at the dark sky, able to see the storms swirling far overhead. The area above the palace was free of dust and storms, and she imagined the ever growing trees pushing the clouds away as they grew and protecting the smaller plants beneath them.

"Take care of the Anshan people, too," she murmured. She hadn't thought to grab celery to eat and was too tired to retreat to the jungle and retrieve some. Her hands trembled with fatigue. She sank down onto her back and watched the sky above, wondering what it would look like to see the moon where she'd lived with A'Ran and his family.

Darkness fell, and she drifted into a restless sleep filled with images of the jungle, of the figure melting into the grass, of Anshan's palace covered in moss.

When she opened her eyes again, the sky was light enough to be morning, the red storms swirling far above. Kiera tried to move and found herself too weak. Anshan was both tugging at her and tickling her with its energy. She lay still for a long time, too tired to be alarmed by the feel of the planet's life force moving through her. Her thoughts fluttered from topic to topic, but always returned to A'Ran and how she prayed he'd been able to save Gage and Evey before it was too late. Darker thoughts moved through her mind. It was growing harder to breath, and she was starting to feel cold.

Was this how Anshan felt? Scared, alone, paralyzed? Had it wondered how much longer it had to live or wept for those faces it would never see again? Did it experience terror every time it began to think it was too late to save anyone let alone survive?

A'Ran had once told her the *dhjan* brought strength and stability to the planet while the *nishani* healed and sustained life. It had never occurred to her this meant she would become part of the planet and its life force.

She was no longer able to separate what she felt from the life force of the planet, unable to identify if she were dying, or if Anshan was – or both. A'Ran had claimed she was connected to Anshan, but as her life began to fade, she realized how deep that connection truly was. She and Anshan didn't share a life force; she had *become* the life force of the planet. Its hopes, dreams, fears ... her spirit and Anshan's were intertwined – and sliding away.

A hot tear slid from the corner of one eye into her hair and fear spiraled through her. If she'd only come sooner, if she'd known how important it was for her to be in direct contact with the world that so desperately needed her ...

She was getting colder, and tunnel vision began to form. Was she crying, or was it Anshan?

Was there even a difference anymore? She couldn't feel where she stopped and Anshan started.

"Kiera!" the bellow came from the direction of the palace.

I'm here, she screamed mentally, unable to speak the words aloud.

An agonizing moment passed before she heard A'Ran's shout again.

"Kiera!"

He was getting closer. She waited and stared at the sky, praying to see the face of her lifemate one last time.

She heard the sound of him climbing the steep hill and finally glimpsed him from the corner of her eye.

A'Ran dropped on his knees beside him. He didn't so much as flinch when he lifted her into his arms, even though she knew he was hurt from earlier. At his touch, she could breathe deeply again, and the coldness fled from her limbs. She gasped in air and lifted a wooden arm to touch the heavy features of his face. He was a buffer against the planet, a source of strength that seeped into her drained body.

Balance. She understood what A'Ran had tried to tell her from the beginning, how the planet derived strength from him and life from her. Both were necessary for there to be an Anshan.

"You are so pale," A'Ran was scouring her features with his gaze. He hugged her to him closely and settled on the ground.

Kiera closed her eyes and breathed in his scent, grateful to touch him again. "Gage," she breathed the name.

"She is well. Mansr found her. And ... Evey," he added in a tight voice.

The longer he held her, the more her strength and feeling returned. She huddled against him, happy to feel his warmth and solidness. Her gaze drifted towards the sky once more as a shadow passed over. She expected to see another massive rock float by. To her surprise, it was a hulking ship, one of A'Ran's war cruisers.

It was followed by another and another and another, until the gray sky whales dotted the sky.

She gasped, watching them begin to descend to the planet's surface. She didn't need to see the first that touched down; she felt Anshan's burst of warm hope whip through her.

"Four million," A'Ran whispered, following her gaze. "I ordered Mansr to do whatever he had to, promise whatever he needed to. The ships of twelve planets are bringing four million Anshani back now, and we anticipate half the surviving population will have returned to Anshan by tomorrow morning."

As if hearing his words, the planet sent a spike of energized excitement through her. A'Ran jerked, feeling it pass into him as well. A surge of strength rippled through her as hope morphed into joy too powerful to be solely hers.

"You did it," Kiera said, staring at the spaceships in awe. She had never been so happy to see the huge ships! More and more appeared in the sky. She shifted to wrap her arms around A'Ran's neck and hugged him hard, barely able to contain her glee or the planet's. "I knew you could do it!" She fluttered kisses across his face then captured her lips with his.

A'Ran responded hungrily with the emotion they both experienced, and she pressed herself to his strong body. When she felt warm tears on her face, she broke away from the kiss and hugged him hard. Relief swept through her, and this time, it was emotion that left her crippled.

"We did it, Kiera," A'Ran said hoarsely. "Together."

She nodded, unable to speak for fear of sobbing.

A'Ran held her until she began to calm once more. Lifting her face from the nape of his neck, she wiped her features and gazed into his dark eyes. She traced her fingertips over his strong face.

"Can you feel it?" she murmured. "Anshan?"

"I can. I can feel your life force, too." He placed a hand over her heart. "It beats like my own heart."

"I understand now," she said. "The balance. Why you needed your *nishani*."

"You are life, Kiera. Mine, our people's, Anshan's. There is nothing without you. I could fight for a million cycles to save my planet, and we would all perish, had I not found you." He rested his forehead against hers. They breathed each other's air quietly. She shivered each time the planet sent a spike of happiness through her when another ship touched down.

"We both must be here," she said. "Anshan will need time – and us – to heal. I feel like ..." She drifted off, staving off her bafflement to gauge where the planet was at the moment. "... I think the worst is over but there's still danger."

"The people returning will help stabilize." He withdrew, gaze distant, as if he, too, were reading the planet. "I never knew how strong the bond was."

"It's amazing."

His focus returned to her features. "We need to heal as well." He let a rare wince of pain show as he shifted to reach into a pocket. He pulled forth a crumpled, blood-speckled piece of paper and handed it to her.

Kiera took it and carefully unfolded it.

The first image she'd drawn of them was on the paper, his favorite of all her drawings. She had sketched them walking hand in hand on the desert surface of Anshan. She started to smile. This picture had pierced A'Ran's emotions the first time he saw it. She recalled the look on his face clearly, when he'd realized there was hope for his planet, for him. It was the same day she realized he was more than an alien brute who kidnapped her after some bizarre claim about her connection to his planet.

The simple drawing had helped lay the foundation that brought them here, and she gazed at it, tears in her eyes again. They'd be able to walk hand in hand on Anshan soon, as they both dreamt of doing, once they were healthy.

"You will have to draw us like this again," he said. "But with grass and trees."

"Yes." The word was barely audible. She wrapped her arms around him, no longer able to contain the emotions within her.

They watched the ships above bring new hope to their planet. A'Ran held her as she shook, and she clung to him.

EPILOGUE

HIS PEOPLE WERE CROWDED into the palace and under-ground network of tunnels and caverns for two months. A'Ran had assumed his list of allies was blank, but over the course of several weeks, he began to realize just how many he had. The Qatwalis shifted some of their own atmospheric filtration systems to Anshan while Jetr managed to convince the Council to fund the relocation of Anshani back to their planet. Kiera's jungles covered half the planet, and the miners were able to prevent the poisoning of the water supplies with the help from mining colonies on other planets.

Two months, and his planet was his again.

Two months, and he began to see the world in an entirely new light after so many cycles of struggle. He was even hopeful enough to bend to the soft heart of Kiera and spare the Yirkin leader, Turi, who had unknowingly helped save Anshan by throwing *nishani* out into the storms.

A'Ran lowered his sword and tossed his head back to see the larger of Anshan's two moons. It hovered above in the bright blue sky. Every time he saw it, he remembered just how fortunate he truly was to be home. Anshan energy was warm and cheerful within him, and his muscles were loose after an extended session sparring.

The sounds of his warriors practicing around him brought him satisfaction. He had dreamt of the day he would lead his people home and had lost none of the emotion he felt the day the first ships landed.

He was content enough he almost didn't mind the Yirkin refugees were temporarily housed on his moon, awaiting relocation by the Council.

Shifting his focus to his opponent, he offered his hand to Leyon and pulled his cousin up off the ground.

"You fought well," he told Leyon.

"Thank you, *dhjan*. It is an honor to face you, as always."

"You both did awesome," Kiera said from behind him.

A'Ran turned to face her. She was accompanied by the nervous medic who had accompanied Mansr to the planet two months before. Her eyes were sparkling with mischief, and her features glowed.

"*Nishani*." Leyon bowed his head in deference.

A'Ran glanced at the medic. A person's physical condition was a private matter, so he did not ask if his lifemate was ill in public.

"*Dhjan*, may I speak to you in private?" the medic asked.

Kiera shot him an annoyed look.

Leyon slid away, and A'Ran approached the two.

"No," Kiera said as the medic opened his mouth.

"*Nishani*, it is customary for –" the medic stammered, eyes on the ground.

She glared at him, and he fell silent.

"What is this?" A'Ran asked.

"What do you call the *dhjan* if he's a woman?" Kiera asked.

"I do not understand," A'Ran replied. "A *dhjan* cannot be a woman. He can have a *nishani* lifemate."

"So there's no word for a female *dhjan*?"

The medic sighed, and A'Ran raised his eyebrows. "No," he replied. "There has never been a woman *dhjan* in the history of Anshan. The firstborn has always been male for millennia."

Kiera started to smile. "I think that's about to change," she said.

"It is most unfortunate," the medic agreed.

"Unfortunate?" she rounded on him, hands on her hips.

A'Ran sensed the lecture he knew was coming. "*Nishani*," he chided before she could start.

She turned her glare from the medic to him. "Well you better come up with a word for a female *dhjan,* because your first child is going to be a girl."

A'Ran blinked, not expecting the news or the timing. They had been absorbed in helping Anshan heal, in bringing back its people. He had spent every night making love to his *nishani,* but his mind had been as far from producing an heir as could be.

"It is true," the medic said with resignation. "Anshan will have a woman *dhjan.*"

"You're done," Kiera snapped at him. "You delivered the news."

"It is customary, *nishani.*" The medic gave her a quick bow and then fled, as if fearing being caught in the crossfire after relaying the news.

Kiera crossed her arms and waited, gazing up at A'Ran with a combination of apprehension and joy. The emotions were carried across their bond.

A'Ran was silent. He forced his public façade to remain in place and made an effort to figure out what he was feeling. The shock of the awkward announcement wore off, leaving him ... humbled. Grateful. More hopeful for the future of his planet and people with each passing day.

And unable to express any of it.

After all they'd been through, the idea of a woman on the throne of Anshan didn't faze him the way he thought it would. It would take some time for him and his people to grow accustomed to the idea, but he suspected it would be easier for them to accept at this time, after regaining their home and starting their lives anew, than if they had not spent fifteen cycles in exile.

"Anshan clearly likes the idea," Kiera added. "I do, too. It's time for a change." She held her breath and waited, eyes pinned to his features as she tried to read what he was thinking.

"Very well," he said gravely. "If it must be so."

Kiera's jaw dropped. She stared at him, horrified by the response.

A'Ran did something he hadn't done in a very long time.

He began to laugh.

If he was surprised by the sound, Kiera appeared shocked, and those warriors within hearing distance stopped to look towards their *dhjan* in confusion at the uncharacteristic display of emotion of any kind.

In the course of several months, he had gone from desperate and homeless to the *dhjan* of his planet once more with an heiress on the way. Pride and amazement swept through him. Without Kiera, the planet would be dead and his people left to the mercy of the neighboring planets and systems.

"My daughter will be *dhjan*," he said. "I am honored."

Kiera's grin lit up his world, and she covered her face with her hands to keep from crying in public.

A'Ran didn't bother reminding her of royal protocol. If ever there was a time to break with custom it was now. He drew her into his arms and hugged her hard. Not one piece of him cared what the warriors or anyone else thought of the public display of affection.

His brave little Kiera hugged him fiercely.

"Deeply honored," he added in a whisper.

"I love you," she said between tears.

"You are my world, Kiera."

The Anshan Saga
Kiera's Moon
Kiera's Sun

ALSO BY LIZZY FORD

Young Adult Fiction

Non-Series Title

The Door (teen sci-fi)

Esme (teen paranormal)

Part One

Part Two

Part Three (2018)

Lost Vegas Series – young adult post-apocalyptic

Aveline

Tiana

Arthur

Black Wolf

Lost Vegas Series Omnibus

Spell Realm Series – young adult romantic fantasy

Water Spell

Dragon Spell (2018)

Moon Spell (2018)

Sword Spell (2019)

Omega Series – teen dystopia with Greek Gods

Omega

Theta

Alpha (2018)

Omega Beginnings Miniseries – individual episodes

Alessandra

Mismatch

Phoibe

Lantos

Theodosia

Niko

Cleon

Herakles

Omega Beginnings Miniseries Omnibus

Theta Beginnings Miniseries

Silent Queen

Mercenary

Shadow Titan

People's Champion

Theta Beginnings Miniseries Omnibus

Anshan Saga – new adult science fiction romance

Kiera's Moon

Kiera's Sun

Witchlings – young adult paranormal

Dark Summer

Autumn Storm

Winter Fire

Spring Rain

Broken Beauty Novellas – new adult dramatic fiction

Broken Beauty

Broken World

Broken Chains (2017)

Foretold Trilogy – young adult fantasy

Elle's Journey

Shadow Rising (2018)

Journey West (2018)

Voodoo Nights - young adult paranormal

Cursed

Erotic Romance

Non-Series Titles

Star Kissed (erotic sci-fi)

A Night Worth Dying For (short story, contemporary erotic thriller)

Trial Series – erotic paranormal romance

Trial by Moon

Trial by Thrall

Trial by Blood

Trial by Heart

Trial Series Omnibus

Heart of Fire – sexy dragon shifter

Charred Heart

Charred Tears

Charred Hope

Incubatti Duet – Buffy meets 50 Shades

Zoey Rogue

Zoey Avenger

Writing as SE Reign, erotica writer

101 Nights Box Set (featuring all seven serials)

Adult Sweet Romance

(no graphic sex scenes)

Non-Series Titles – 2014 - 2018

White Tree Sound (2018)

Black Moon Draw (fantasy romance)

Highlander Enchanted (historical romance)

History Interrupted – Time Travel Romantic Adventures

West

East

North

South (2018)

Super Villainess Chronicles – twisted superhero romance

It's Not Easy Being Evil

It's Not Easy Being Good

Starwalkers Serials (with Julia Crane) – new adult science fiction serial

Severed

Trapped

Exiled

Revealed

Escaped

Ascended

Starwalkers – Omnibus

Sons of War – contemporary military romance

Semper Mine

Soldier Mine

SEAL Mine (2018)

Rhyn Trilogy – new adult paranormal with demons

Katie's Hellion

Katie's Hope

Rhyn's Redemption

Rhyn Eternal – Death finds love

Gabriel's Hope

Deidre's Death

Darkyn's Mate

The Underworld

Twisted Fate

Twisted Karma

War of Gods – paranormal with gods, guardians and exceptional humans

Damian's Oracle

Damian's Assassin

Damian's Immortal

The Grey God

Damian Eternal

Xander's Chance

The Black God

Hidden Evil – paranormal with angels and four horsemen

Hear No

See No

Speak No (2017)

Unnamed Series

Unnatural (TBD)

Short Stories

Santa's Ninja Elves: Natasha

Santa's Ninja Elves: Hunter

Snow Whisperers (retired)

Non-Series Titles – 2011 - 2013
A Demon's Desire (paranormal romance)
The Warlord's Secret (fantasy romance)
Maddy's Oasis (contemporary romance)
Rebel Heart (sci-fi romance)

ABOUT THE AUTHOR

I breathe stories. I dream them. If it were possible, I'd eat them, too.
(I'm pretty sure they'd taste like cotton candy.) I can't escape them -
they're everywhere! Which is why I write! I was born to bring the
crazy worlds and people in my mind to life, and I love sharing them
with as many people as I can.

I'm also the bestselling, award winning, internationally acclaimed
author of over sixty titles and counting. I write speculative fiction in
multiple subgenres of romance and fantasy, contemporary fiction,
books for both teens and adults, and just about anything else I feel
like writing. If I can imagine it, I can write it!

I live in the desert of southern Arizona with a pack of spoiled dogs
and Tubbs, the Godfather cat who rules them all.

Connect with Lizzy

Website: LizzyFord.com
Facebook: www.Facebook.com/LizzyFordBooks
Twitter @LizzyFord2010
Instagram: @LizzyFordAuthor